Praise f

UNRULY HUMA

"In *Unruly Human Hearts,* Barbara Southard has created a delightful and poignant novel about the Beecher-Tilton scandal in the Reconstruction Era. Focusing on Elizabeth's internal struggle to cope with her husband's public support for women's rights while maintaining the double standard in private, this story will inspire readers to ask themselves how women should confront similar challenges today. Perfect for fans of well-researched and engaging historical fiction!"

—JACQUELINE FRIEDLAND,
author of *The Stockwell Letters* and *Trouble the Water*

"The strength of Elizabeth's character is at the novel's core. There are moments of eroticism in which she exercises power and agency, refuting her husband's claims that she was stupid and naive to fall for Henry's seduction. Elizabeth is also the only one of the three to take responsibility for her actions. . . . She also reminds herself of the good within Henry and Theo, who are both willing to sacrifice Elizabeth to save their own reputations. Her penchant for forgiveness and understanding is conveyed as not a weakness but a strength. . . . The riveting novel *Unruly Human Hearts* is sensitive in following a strong woman as she overcomes adversity."

—FOREWORD CLARION REVIEWS

"In *Unruly Human Hearts,* Barbara Southard uncovers the remarkable voice of Elizabeth in elegant, flowing prose. She paints a strong woman who knows her own heart and fights to defend herself and her loved ones from ruin."

—ELENA LAWTON TORRUELLA, English Department,
Universidad del Sagrado Corazón

"This is not just a story of a woman who tried to be a good Christian wife while passionately in love with her pastor, it's a revelation of her anguish as she struggled to protect herself, her children, and the two men she loved from the toll of escalating public scandal."

—LINDA ULLESEIT,
author of *The River Remembers* and *Innocents at Home*

"'Free love?' Elizabeth Tilton wasn't counting on the two well-known men she loved at the same time to attack each other so vehemently, shattering her life, but neither were they expecting her to finally admit her own truth so openly. In this complex portrait of power, lies, and sexual attraction, Barbara Southard conveys foibles not too removed from the present, yet peppered with the intricacies of nineteenth-century characters and situations that engross readers. I couldn't put this novel down."

—MARÍA SOLEDAD RODRÍGUEZ, English Department,
University of Puerto Rico

Unruly Human Hearts

Unruly Human Hearts

A Novel

BARBARA SOUTHARD

SHE WRITES PRESS

Published 2025
Printed in the United States of America
Print ISBN: 978-1-64742-830-3
E-ISBN: 978-1-64742-831-0
Library of Congress Control Number: 2024917238

For information, address:
She Writes Press
1569 Solano Ave #546
Berkeley, CA 94707

Interior design by Stacey Aaronson

She Writes Press is a division of SparkPoint Studio, LLC.

For Elizabeth—

the woman named in the scandalous Beecher-Tilton adultery trial of the 1870s, whose voice was barely heard in her own time.

I heard a fly buzz when I died;
The stillness round my form
Was like the stillness in the air
Between the heaves of storm.

—EMILY DICKINSON

Contents

PART ONE:

Our Souls Are Made for Love 1

PART TWO:

The Human Heart Is Unruly 49

PART THREE:

Miscarriage and Recovery 111

PART FOUR:

Why Won't People Just Leave Us Alone? 145

PART FIVE:

Things Fall Apart 201

PART SIX:

Is This War Never to End? 245

PART SEVEN:

My Truth, My Very Own Truth 285

APPENDICES

Author's Note 309

Sources of the Poems, Letters, and Testimony 315

Acknowledgments 317

Our Souls Are Made for Love

Brooklyn, April 1897

Elizabeth Tilton lay still, a small figure on a large four-poster bed. The curtains were drawn, and the soft light of late afternoon illumined her deeply lined face and white hair spread out over the pillow. Her daughter Florence opened the door.

"Mother, dear, Aunt Annie's here."

Elizabeth did not respond. Her gaze was fixed on the bedroom window, which framed a great sycamore tree. She could barely see the outline of the branches, but she remembered that Flory had told her that there were already tiny buds heralding the spring.

How strange, she thought. My sight is all hazy after that trouble with my eyes, but God has granted my wish to see the past clearly. Just a moment ago, I saw my little Paul all dressed in white. The blue sky was not marred by a single cloud, and the birds that nested in the tree in front of the house were chirping, while my child lay dead. I could see my husband, Theodore, dry-eyed with a stunned expression, and Reverend Beecher comforting us all.

"Are you awake, Elizabeth?" Annie approached her bed.

Elizabeth smiled at her sister-in-law. Annie was tall and slender, like her older brother, Theodore, but her eyes were not as penetrating.

"Auntie, you sit here in the rocker; I'll get the tea things ready while you chat with Mother." Florence started down the stairs.

"Flory takes good care of me," Elizabeth told Annie.

"She is so competent, running a household, teaching music."

"Yes, the eldest has to grow up quickly."

Elizabeth slumped against the pillow, worn out from the short conversation. Annie took over and gave her sister-in-law the latest news of friends and family. Elizabeth had trouble understanding all the details, but Annie's voice and presence were warm and comforting.

After a pause, Annie opened a small package. "I brought you the new anthology of Theodore's poems."

Elizabeth reached out her hand. "Oh, Annie, I have always loved to read his writings."

Annie got up and gave her the book. A tremor passed over Elizabeth's body and her face twisted in a grimace. The book dropped from her hand with a loud thud.

Annie retrieved it and said, "Sorry, I didn't mean to distress you."

Elizabeth raised her head. The muscles of her throat worked, but no sound came. When she finally spoke, each word was articulated with vehemence. "I loved Theodore deeply and I hurt him; he loved me and he hurt me. There is no escaping the terrible wounds that we inflicted. I am dying, Annie, and I now see things clearly—God is giving me new vision."

Annie stared at her sister-in-law. In all those years since her brother had accused his wife of adultery with the Reverend Henry Ward Beecher, the two women had never spoken of the scandal, the church investigation, or the public trial. The sick woman's breathing was labored. Had she unwittingly brought on a crisis? To her relief, Elizabeth smiled.

"Annie, please read me a poem. Pick out a favorite of yours. A romantic one."

Then, to the rock-bound main,
Along the billow-beaten strand,

Amid the flying spray,
He led her by her tiny hand;—
And, just above the water's reach,
They sat together on the beach,
And piled the shells and sand
Into a palace grand.

Elizabeth listened. What a lovely rendition of the first stirrings of young love. Her eyes closed as the words penetrated deeper into her consciousness. She could no longer distinguish Annie's voice. The bed, the coverlet, the bay window framing the branches of the sycamore all disappeared.

Theodore himself was talking. He had waited for her to finish putting the children to bed so that the two of them could sit together by the fire in the parlor of their home on Livingston Street. It was not poetry, but a political statement he wanted to read to her.

Brooklyn, October 1866

"Dear, I have finally put it into words. I have been smoldering with indignation for a week, unable to reply to that cowardly letter written for the Cleveland Convention by *your* pastor."

Theodore is looking at me. I'm not going to react to the emphasis on *your*.

His voice rises. "*Your* pastor, *my* friend and associate in the antislavery movement now wants to capitulate to the South, leave the Negro to the tender mercies of those who beat and tortured their slaves, raped their wives. I will not be silent even if Henry

Ward Beecher, the greatest preacher in this country, advises that we treat the South with brotherly love."

He's waving a manuscript in my face. We are both sitting in large easy chairs, drawn closer to the fireplace for warmth. Although it is early fall, the weather has turned cold.

"But that cannot be his intention," I exclaim. "Henry has always been a true friend of the Negro. And he is as much *your* pastor," I feel my face flushing, "as *mine*."

"True friend of the Negro, indeed!" he replies, almost shouting. "Henry is more concerned with brotherly love for the slaveholders who dragged us all through four years of horrendous war."

Theo is sitting erect in the easy chair, his body refusing to conform to the contours of the soft cushions. "Here, this is my reply to such sentimental drivel." He drops his eyes, releasing mine from the grip of his gaze, and reads, "Mr. Beecher has united with the party of Andrew Johnson, and if we do not raise our voice in protest to roundly condemn his action, we become accomplices in his guilt."

"Theo, I don't think that Henry supports President Johnson, he would never do that."

"What does it matter if he does not openly support that traitor? He wants the troops to leave the South, let the former rebels run for office so they can once again control this country as though the war never happened."

"But . . ."

"But what? Speak up."

"Our pastor is not a politician. Henry is a man of religion who looks at every situation as a Christian."

"That is just the sort of sentimental mush that is ruining this country." Theodore has risen from his seat and is pacing back and forth as though neither his long limbs nor his excitement can be contained in the chair. "If you treat those Southern planters in a spirit of Christian charity, they will turn around and use force to keep the freedmen down. Can't you see that?"

My body feels very small, perched on the large easy chair. The embers of a dying fire still glow in the brick fireplace, but a chill pervades the parlor. I look past Theodore through the window toward the street and notice that the wind has picked up. Swirls of leaves are being blown hither and thither in the waning light of early evening.

"But, Theo, how can we expect the Southerner to treat the Negro with love if we in the North treat Southerners with hatred and contempt?"

Theodore sighs. "Lib, dear, you are a woman. You are not exposed to the hard realities of politics." He smiles at me, as though to excuse a woman's weakness. "But what of Henry? He knows how the world works. What kind of leadership is he giving us?"

"Theo, Henry is our friend. Just think how he will feel when he wakes up in the morning and reads your reply in the newspaper attacking him."

"Are you suggesting I shouldn't publish it?"

Theo must know that publishing it will endanger the friendship. "I'm not sure, dear. I just thought that perhaps you could put something in to say our friend's heart is in the right place."

Theo resumes his seat and mumbles something about being grateful that Henry was instrumental in getting him the job of editor of the *Independent*. "But if he is a true friend, surely he would not hold it against me that I speak my own mind and follow my conscience."

"He has been a father to us and a spiritual guide."

"Yes, yes, that goes without saying." Theodore brushes aside my comment with a wave. Has he forgotten that it was Henry who united us in marriage and has been looking out for us ever since? Henry has been like a mentor to Theo, guiding his journalistic career at every step. For years they were comrades in arms in the antislavery movement, spending hours and hours at our home discussing strategies to strengthen the cause.

Aloud I say, "My dear, Henry is your best friend."

Theo nods. "True, but I can no longer respect his judgment as I once did. You know people are still talking about him. Rumors are going around about Reverend Beecher."

"If it was something told you in confidence, I will not ask."

Theo gets up and pokes idly at the fire. The embers glow slightly, and then die down. He turns toward me and says in low tones, "You know I believe in honesty between men and women. I don't believe that men should keep women in the dark."

I look hastily toward the dining room and through to the kitchen to see that no one is about. Our ward, Bessie, who is fast becoming a young lady, has gone upstairs to read bedtime stories to the children. "What is it? Tell me."

"There are rumors that our friend seduced Mr. Bowen's wife. She was his parishioner. It's said she confessed on her deathbed."

"I don't believe it! It is a foul lie."

Theodore looks at me, and I realize that I am shouting.

I lower my voice. "Even the best people have enemies. There are always people who are envious and spread vile rumors."

"Why are you so upset?"

I lean back against the chair to keep my body from shaking. "A man should be considered innocent until proven guilty. And even if the rumor were true, and *it is not*, we must hate the sin, not the sinner."

"Ah, but you don't understand, I'm not blaming our friend. It would be perfectly natural under the circumstances. The man must be considered a saint if for nothing else but living with Eunice Beecher."

Theodore has never gotten along with Henry's wife. He considers her narrow-minded, but she's still the wife of a dear friend. "She may not be a pleasant woman, but she has borne his children."

"That's not sufficient reason to stay in a loveless marriage."

"But the welfare of the children . . ." I protest.

Theodore shakes his head. "I don't agree. Marriage is meaningless if people are forced to stay together when they no longer love one another."

He puts the manuscript down and takes up a book. The conversation is over, and I make no attempt to revive it. It must be Theo's dislike for Eunice that is making him talk so strangely.

Theodore lights the lamps. A yell resounds from upstairs, followed by a thud. What is going on? I should be helping Bessie to put the children to bed. Inside the house, it is already dark, though the twilight lingers outside. I take a lighted candle to illuminate the stairway.

Bessie already has everything under control. She is so good with the children. When we accepted responsibility for her as our ward, she was just a child herself. Abandoned by her parents, she had been passed from family to family. She used to be very naughty when she first came to us, but now she helps me encourage good behavior in my little ones.

Little Carroll assures me that he said his prayers. I sing his favorite lullaby, kiss him good night, and softly close the door. Flory and Alice, being older, have permission to stay up with Bessie for a while.

By the time I come back downstairs, Theodore has rekindled the fire. A portrait of the two of us is propped up in the center of the mantelpiece. Although it was painted eleven years ago, not too long after our wedding, it is still a very good likeness of Theo. The wavy sandy locks are a bit thicker in the picture, but the lofty brow, the sharp nose, finely chiseled mouth, and keen blue eyes are the same. The fine long fingers of one hand seem poised for movement, hinting at the restless energy of the subject. The artist made me sit on a high stool while Theo, who ordinarily towers above me, was placed in an ordinary chair.

On both sides of our portrait, there are crayon drawings of the children in natural poses. I did not want the children to sit in a rigid position for hours, and the artist agreed that it would be better to watch the children go about naturally and capture the spirit of each. On the right wall is a lovely painting of a flowering tree that Henry gave us when he returned from England.

I pick up the book I am reading. The clock strikes eight.

Theodore puts his book down and stretches his long limbs, frowning slightly.

"My dear, can I interrupt you for just a moment?"

Why is he talking with such exaggerated politeness? He must be angry because I defended Henry. "Yes, darling?"

"I am terribly worried. Why do we need such expensive curtains and cuts of meat? And is it necessary to serve oysters? I am making more money now that I am editor, but where is it going?"

"I am trying, but furnishing a new house is so . . ."

"It's your *job* to hold down expenses. Don't you understand that I cannot be worried with managing the house? I need your cooperation to concentrate on my writing—otherwise, we are all ruined. We each have to do our part." Theodore's voice rises to an angry shout. "I *hate* it when you make excuses."

My back stiffens. Ever since we moved to our new home he has been critical of my housekeeping.

"That is so unfair! You know perfectly well that I wanted to buy cheaper curtains, but *you* said *no*, it was about time we had decent things like other people. If I buy cheap curtains, you say I have horrible taste like my mother!"

"You are still making excuses. I am talking about a serious matter, the possible financial ruin of this family, and all you can think about is who is to blame."

"That's not true, *you* are the one pinning the blame on *me*. If I don't spend money, I am a woman of no taste, no imagination, no sense of fashion. If I do spend money . . ."

A timid voice breaks in. "Ma'am, excuse me, but Alice won't go to sleep. She says that you promised to tell her a story." It's Bessie. I rise to go upstairs, but Theo's voice stops me.

"Don't go, my dear. She is too old to need a goodnight story. That child is becoming very spoiled."

A loud wail sounds from above. Alice really sounds distraught and soon she will wake up little Carroll.

"Oh, go ahead, Elizabeth. She is already so spoiled one more time will make no difference. Bessie, sit here beside me and I will read you something. A young lady like you must take off a little time from household chores and develop her mind."

Alice calms down when I put my arms around her. I start to tell her a story, but she falls asleep after only a few sentences. Poor little lamb, what a tiring day you have had! I take off my shoes and lie down close beside her on the bed for a long while. Her body is warm and comforting and my thoughts begin to drift.

Theodore calls me to come to bed. I rouse myself and walk slowly toward our bedroom, my bare feet chilled by the cold wooden floor. I shiver as I change into my nightclothes.

"Come, darling, snuggle up with me. I am sorry I was so sharp about the curtains. I am just so worried about all our bills." Theodore holds me tight for a moment, kissing my eyes, my mouth.

He pulls up my nightgown and I can feel the night chill on my bare skin. He covers my breasts and neck with kisses. I am open, moist, pliant to his touch, but I do not feel that quickening in the most secret place of my body. He enters my inmost being easily, shuddering slightly before starting the familiar motion. Theo calls out my name, but I am not with him. I float outside our bodies, hearing his groans of pleasure.

Theo rolls over onto his back. "Elizabeth, you seem far away."

I am silent, trying hard not to cry aloud.

Theodore reaches for my hand. "I keep thinking about our conversation. I know I am right. The Southern planters must not be allowed to re-enslave the Negro, but sometimes I wish that I could see it as you and Henry do."

Still too close to crying to trust myself to speak, I stroke Theo's arm.

He draws me to him and tells me, "Oh, if only I could have your belief in the healing power of love and forgiveness." Theo assures me that tomorrow he will look at the article again to see whether he can work in something about Henry's heart being in the right place.

"Oh, darling Dory, I love you so much. I know you understand more about politics."

I snuggle next to him with my head cradled in his armpit. I long for him to touch me again in all those soft and sensitive places, a longing so strong that it is almost an ache. Theodore is fast asleep.

April 1897

Elizabeth, sensing someone smoothing her hair back from her forehead, opened her eyes. Flory was lifting her head up so that she could drink a glass of water. She drank slowly.

"Mother, I made you chicken soup. Can you try to eat some for me?"

When Flory returned from the kitchen, she fluffed the pillows to give her mother more support. Elizabeth's right arm and leg had been partially paralyzed since the stroke, making it difficult for her to sit up without help. She didn't feel hungry, but she swallowed a spoonful or two of soup.

"I always gave your father chicken soup when he was ill. Whenever he said, 'No more chicken soup,' I knew the worst was over. It was time for beefsteak."

Flory smiled. "Shall I cook something solid for you?"

Elizabeth shook her head. "I can barely swallow the soup, but thank you, dear. I was dreaming about your father. He was reading me a letter he had written for the press defending the rights of the freed slaves."

Flory, who had risen from her chair, sat back down again. "Father was a leading abolitionist, wasn't he? And unlike some others, he remained a powerful voice for the rights of the freedmen."

Elizabeth nodded. She wanted to tell Flory how her father and Reverend Beecher had worked together for the abolition of slavery. As editor of the *Independent*, Theo's scathing revelations about the evils of slavery whipped up public enthusiasm for the abolitionist cause. Henry backed him up from the pulpit at Plymouth Church with eloquent sermons about how the love of God is best expressed by fighting against cruel injustice to our fellow men. And he had been instrumental in making the church a transfer point for the Underground Railroad, helping slaves escape. It was only after the Civil War that their views on Reconstruction parted ways. But it wouldn't be appropriate to talk about all this with her daughter.

She smiled and said softly, "Yes, dear, your father always spoke out against injustice."

Flory leaned forward to catch her mother's words, waiting expectantly to hear more.

The doorbell rang.

"That must be my pupil come for her piano lesson." Flory took the soup bowl. "Are you sure you don't need anything, Mother?"

"No, dearest. But after the class, play a few pieces for me. I love to hear you."

Flory smiled in assent and left the door ajar.

July 1867

Someone is practicing the piano far away, but then the sound comes closer. It is bright daylight, a warm summer day, and little Flory is practicing her lesson in the next room.

"How beautifully she plays for one so young. How do you get her to practice?"

It is Henry Beecher speaking. He sits easily on the larger of two great easy chairs in the parlor, his portly figure solid and substantial, his voice resonant and melodious. Henry has become a regular visitor. At first, he talked mainly with Theodore about their collaboration in the antislavery movement and various journalistic endeavors, but now he is equally at home talking to me. It is always a pleasure for me to abandon my domestic chores when he stops by.

"I don't have to urge Flory. She loves the piano," I reply.

Henry shakes his head. "I remember my stepmother forcing my sisters to practice. How they hated it."

"What a shame. Children should never be forced. I always played and sang to Flory from when she was a baby, and soon she was begging me to learn. I try to pick out songs that are not too hard for her, songs that she knows and loves, to encourage her. My youngest daughter, Alice, on the other hand, usually doesn't want to practice the piano, but she loves to draw. Sometimes, I tell her I will get the crayons and paper out for her if she finishes her lesson."

"What an excellent way of teaching!"

Henry understands the world of children so well. Such a dear man! He is a famous preacher, yet here he sits, listening with such interest to the details of my home life.

"Each child is different," I tell him. "We have to find the key to each one's nature."

"How right you are! I always imagined that my real mother, if she had lived, would have been a woman just like you, gentle with children."

"What were you like as a child, dear friend?"

"I was the sort of child that needed encouragement. Sometimes I was rebellious against discipline, but if someone spoke a kind word and appealed to my better nature, all rebellion would disappear. My stepmother, God bless her soul, was a good woman who always did her duty, but she was completely lacking in imagination. I am happy to see mothers like you who do things differently. God is inspiring you, my friend."

Henry pauses, and at that moment, a robin's melodious song bursts forth. The bird is perched in the poplar tree just outside the window, his head tilted back and his beak wide open.

"Well," says Henry, "all God's creatures are singing today. Your Flory has been challenged by a feathered friend."

Henry smiles at me, the corners of his eyes crinkling. I am seated on the middle cushion of the sofa, but I move over and put my hand on the armrest that is nearest to his chair. "You know what I am remembering at this moment? The sermon you gave a few months ago about the power of the love of God. You talked about how a mother tries to lead her children on the right path through love, not fear of punishment."

Henry nods. "Yes, I remember that sermon well. It is because of you, and people like you, Elizabeth, that I go on with my ministry. Sometimes, I feel discouraged—but when I talk with you, my dear friend, I know that my words have reached some hearts."

"Your sermons reach many hearts, my friend, including mine."

"I have been admiring the portrait of you and Theodore," says Henry, gesturing toward the mantelpiece. "Talking about hearts, those dark beautiful eyes of yours must have reached many hearts indeed. The likeness of you, my dear friend, is quite extraordinary. The sweet seriousness of your expression! If the eyes are the window to the soul, yours tell of depths of feeling and of faith."

A warm flush moves upward from my neck to my forehead. Henry takes my hand and presses it.

"You have the loveliest soul. I feel that your faith is greater than mine, that you are so much closer to God than I can ever be."

"No, I am not. My spiritual progress is slow, but I often feel God helping me."

We fall silent. He releases my hand.

I tell him, "You know what worries me is Theodore's spiritual progress."

"Have you heard from him?"

"Yes, I had a letter. He will be home next week."

"Elizabeth, Theodore talked to me about his religious doubts, but I don't think that I was much help."

"He never goes to church, even if I beg him to give an example to the children. My friend, could you tell him that you miss him at church? He would surely listen to you."

"Well, I am not sure . . ." Henry pauses and looks away. "Theodore is a grown man, with his own ideas, and how would it look for me to ask him to come back to the church where I am pastor? Better you talk to him. He often tells me how he respects your purity, your capacity for faith."

"Oh, I wish I had such influence over Theo, but it is not me he talks to, but all these people in the vanguard of social progress who talk about women's right to vote and a new type of marriage. I am nothing compared to them; I feel stupid among all those people." There is a tremor in my voice.

"Elizabeth, I love you and Theodore dearly; you are my closest friends. The suffragists make a lot of noise about changing the world, but progress is more likely to be achieved by people like you who quietly and with humility raise their children with love. Believe in yourself, my dear friend."

"Oh, Henry, in my darkest hour I can always count on your friendship. You give me strength."

I grasp his large hand in my two small ones. The fingers are thick and blunt, almost like those of a farmer who works the land.

"Elizabeth, what can I say? It is I who am sustained by your spiritual insight. Whenever I feel those dark moods of uncertainty, a visit to you and the children lifts me up."

He lifts my hands to his lips and kisses my fingers lightly, first on one hand, then the other. My eyes close for an instant. His lips are warm.

The piano has stopped playing. I quickly withdraw my hand and

Henry takes up a book from the side table. Flory comes bouncing in.

"Mother, I think I practiced enough. Oh, Mr. Beecher, did you like my playing?"

"Beautiful. You play almost as well as your mother. I wish I were musical, but God has not given me that gift."

Flory smiles shyly, pleased with the compliment. Her sister, Alice, calls to her from the kitchen, and she runs off. Henry puts down the book, and asks me whether I have a few minutes to spare to talk about his novel *Norwood*.

He says that he is suffering from the withdrawal symptoms of an author who has finished his creation and now feels a strange void without the weekly chapter to complete. The writing of *Norwood* has given him great pleasure. He wanted to say something about the God-fearing character of country people and prove that ordinary folk can become heroes when tried by the crisis of war. But he is unsure that his skill as a novelist is sufficient to get his message across.

Now it's my turn to tell Henry to believe in himself. I reassure him that his message is clear and the emotions of the characters are convincing. "Your readers won't be able to put the book down. Last night I reread one of my favorite scenes before going to sleep."

"My dear, you are only talking about what you like about the book. An author about to publish needs encouragement, but he also needs to hear about what is wrong with the book. Was there any scene that did not ring quite true to your ear?"

I hesitate. "Yes, there is one scene that bothers me. When Rose receives the news of her brother's death."

"In what way did it bother you?"

I explain that the reaction of Rose and her father, Dr. Wentworth, to the news of the death of Arthur in the war seems too idealistic to be real. "The doctor and his daughter are spiritually advanced, but even for the most devout Christian, there must be a period of horrible despair after a loved one dies, of questioning the goodness of God, of rejection of what seems like His cruelty. My friend, you and I have both lost a child."

Henry replies gently, "I know what you mean, but I wanted to give my readers the tools to help them overcome despair when tragedy strikes. Did you like the way the mourners dressed in white to celebrate the purity of Arthur rather than the black of mourning?"

"Yes, very much. But Rose wouldn't talk to her father right away about how Arthur's death inspired her to volunteer as a nurse to care for the wounded. She would first talk about her distress, how she passed through several days in which everything felt like a void of despair."

Henry nods. He praises my discernment as a reader and thanks me for my honest advice. "But let's talk of something else, my friend. This conversation is making you sad. Let's rejoice in life. It's a beautiful sunny day and our feathered friend is still singing."

Flory appears and announces, "Mother, Bessie is going to show me and Alice how to make gingerbread cookies. She has a question for you. Come quick."

I rise and turn to Henry. "I think I should go and find them the recipe. The last time Bessie did not get the proportions right, the dough was too soft, and the cookies ran together. Will you excuse me just a moment?"

"I will excuse you both if Flory promises to save a cookie for me. No, make that two cookies."

"I'll just be a minute," I assure him.

"I never feel in a hurry when I visit your home, my friend, because it is like a sanctuary against cares and tribulations, a place that heals the spirit."

I smile at Henry and follow Flory into the kitchen. The sunlight is coming through the latticed window, creating a dappled pattern on the white porcelain sink. The girls are working at a wooden table in the middle of the room. Behind them, the gleam of well-scrubbed copper pots hanging on the wall casts a rosy glow. A summer breeze ruffles Alice's fair hair as she watches Bessie and Flory busily measuring the ingredients. How beautiful everything looks!

If only my little Mattie, the baby of the house, named for my best friend, were here with us making cookies, her chestnut curls bobbing between her sisters' heads, but I cannot let sad thoughts destroy my joy in my living children.

I talk cheerfully with the girls about how to make cookies, thinking all the while about Henry waiting for me.

April 1897

Flory's voice roused her. "Mother, are you sleeping, did you hear? I played 'Moonlight Sonata,' your favorite."

"It was lovely." Elizabeth wanted to tell her daughter that she had been confused, unable to distinguish the present from the past, thinking Flory was still a little girl and remembering how Henry had admired her piano playing. But she must not talk of Henry.

"Your father loved to hear you play," she told Flory. "He is so proud that you and your sister are both artists, you a musician and . . ."

Flory smiled and finished the sentence. "And Alice a well-known painter."

"Yes, your father always wanted his daughters to be women of accomplishment."

The effort of speaking left Elizabeth exhausted and spent.

Florence said she was expecting the doctor to visit tomorrow morning and expressed confidence that he would find her mother much improved. Elizabeth felt no such confidence, but she said nothing, just pressed her daughter's hand. After Flory kissed her and went downstairs, Elizabeth let her eyes close and concentrated on recapturing memories of that summer long ago.

When taking his leave, Henry had said he was sorry to go but looked forward to seeing her and the children on Sunday. How she had loved Plymouth Church! It was a brick building, unpretentious but welcoming to the faithful. There was a plaque commemorating where Abraham Lincoln had attended a sermon that she often pointed out to the children. Elizabeth had liked to get there early and take a seat near the front. The semicircles of pews and the immense gallery above would still be empty, waiting for people to arrive and fill the church so there was standing room only. She would always reserve a pew for Mattie and her family. Mattie said she didn't understand how Elizabeth got her children to church so early, but it was simple. She didn't urge them to wear fancy clothes. Dressing simply didn't take much time.

The preacher's pulpit was on a platform decorated with fresh flowers. When Henry entered, he always greeted the faithful with an earnest, penetrating look that would break into a smile if he should lock eyes with a child. Then he would glance at the gallery above the pulpit where the organist was seated. How Elizabeth had loved the deep tones of the organ. Sometimes little Flory fidgeted during the sermon, but she was always perfectly quiet when the organ played.

Henry's sermons had always been a revelation. He talked of love in all its manifestations as the road to salvation. One human soul, infused with God's love, has the power to influence and uplift another human soul. True love is a power that carries its object upward toward nobility. He emphasized the prodigious power of personal influence, particularly the influence of parents on their children by educating them through love rather than punishment.

Elizabeth remembered kneeling to pray, conscious of being surrounded by friends, people of like mind dedicating themselves to discovering truth and unlocking the goodness in their hearts. Gradually, that warm feeling of community would give way to a profound stillness, a feeling of oneness with God.

And then there was the singing. Surely there was no other congregation with so many rich voices, from mezzo-soprano to bass, melting into one another. And Henry would always join in. Even Theo's deep voice could be heard when he accompanied her and the children. How happy she had been on those rare days when he yielded to her entreaties to go with her to church.

That summer when Henry visited often, she had been in perfect health, except for a bit of morning sickness now and then. Had he noticed that she was expecting? Probably not. Men are not observant. Even Theo was surprised when she broke the news.

After giving birth to Paul in the dead of winter, she had become very ill. The difficult birth had left her almost as weak as she felt now. But she was young then and the desire to live and care for her baby was strong. God had answered her prayers. For over a week she had been confined to bed, but then her strength began to return. The nurse helped her stand and walk slowly around the bedroom.

It was another week before the nurse had allowed Elizabeth to join her husband downstairs in the parlor during the evening. Theodore had placed her rocking chair close to the fire and sat beside her. After the initial talk about the progress of her recovery, he said very little, giving only brief answers to her inquiries about his work. Elizabeth took up some knitting begun weeks before and watched the red glow of the embers in the fireplace, still giving off enough heat to warm her fingers. Theodore suggested she retire to bed early so as not to risk a relapse. She started to protest that she wasn't tired, but thought better of it and rose from her chair.

January 1868

My steps feel light as I climb the stairs after bidding Theo good night. How good it is to feel a renewal of energy, my body once more returning to health. It is very cold upstairs, but I linger for a minute at the window. There is snow on the sill and the pane feels like ice to my fingers. Outside the half-moon has broken through the clouds, illuminating the wintry landscape. The limbs of the dark trees are etched with glimmering white snow clinging to their branches. The neighbor's windows still glow with a soft light, but I leave the candle next to my bed unlit so as to better enjoy the beauty of the night God has created. Mrs. Mitchell, the nurse, enters with my little Paul all bundled up.

"What are you doing up and about in such cold?" she scolds me. "Please put on something warmer and climb under the covers before you have a relapse, my lady." Holding Paul with one arm, she expertly lights the candle on the nightstand with the other hand. "There, that's much better."

Obediently, after draping a heavy robe over my shoulders, I lie down and she hands me Paul to nurse. The baby and I snuggle together, warming up under the thick patchwork quilt. I look down at his small face so intent on eating. Such a healthy little chap! He already seems to be gaining weight. I doze while the baby sucks rhythmically. Mrs. Mitchell, who is leaning over the night table, asks whether she should snuff out the candle. Theodore's tall, lanky figure is silhouetted in the doorway. Now fully awake I say, "No, leave it lit." The nurse straightens up and retrieves the baby from my side. Murmuring good night to us, she quickly retires, taking the baby to her own room to sleep.

"Theo, dear, I feel so much better, and Mrs. Mitchell is such a conscientious nurse, she takes such prodigious good care of me. The baby is so healthy, and it is wonderful that you can stay home for a while. I feel a woman blessed."

Theodore sits down on the bed next to me, caresses my hair, and gives me a peremptory peck of a kiss. "It's good to see you feeling better," he says, but does not look directly at me. After a moment he rises from the bed and begins to pace the room, his head almost touching the beams of the low ceiling. In the dim candlelight, his face can be seen only intermittently, but his stride tells me of his agitation. I sit up in bed. He was so happy when the baby was born, but now he is sinking once again into one of his despairing moods.

"Theo, what is it? Is something wrong?"

Theo stops pacing and walks toward me, his shadow looming larger and larger until it covers the wall and half the ceiling. Abruptly, he crouches before me, reaching for my two hands.

"Everything is wrong. Oh, Lib, I am not the man you think. I strive to be unselfish, to love you and the children with a pure love, to defend what is honest and right." His voice rises to a higher pitch. "My life is a lie. I am living one giant falsehood. I am not true to myself or to you."

"But, darling, we all make mistakes—we are human, we can only try our best." I stroke back the lock of hair that has fallen forward on his forehead.

He recoils from my touch. "Don't give me platitudes about how God loves us in spite of our sins. I hate that sort of talk."

It's hard for me when he talks this way. Theo could be moody even in the early days of our marriage, but now the darkness comes welling up out of nowhere.

"Theo, darling, tell me what is bothering you." My voice sounds high-pitched and far away, the voice of a little girl.

He finally looks me full in the face. "I have been unfaithful. I have not kept my marriage vow."

I say nothing. He stands up, looking down at me, waiting for my reaction. My face is averted, my eyes focused not on him but on his shadow once again looming large against the far wall. My only thought is to get out of the room. I try to swing my feet onto the floor, but my legs are wound up in the quilt. When my legs get untangled, they buckle beneath me and I have to clutch the headboard of the bed to keep from falling. My body sinks back onto the bed.

"Elizabeth, say something," Theodore implores, but I cannot look at him, I am numb, no words come to me.

He resumes pacing. "It happened because there is no longer any real bond between us."

"What?"

"There is no longer any spiritual affinity."

"I don't understand."

"That's just it. You don't understand my work or my beliefs."

How unfair he is! How can I be expected to follow him in all his intellectual wanderings when I have three children, now four with the baby?

"It's your mother that drove us apart," Theo continues. "Always criticizing me and my ideas."

"I know Mother can be difficult."

"Difficult? She is poisonous, trying to destroy our marriage so she can have her daughter all to herself."

Mother did interfere too much when we lived with her to save money, but Theo remembers only the bad times, not the times when she treated him with affection and helped us through the illnesses of the children.

"But, Theo, that's why we moved to our own house, to have privacy."

"She's always coming over."

"To help me with the children."

"I don't want to deprive them of their grandmother, but I hate it when she interferes. Why are my friends her business? She hates everyone in the movement for women's right to vote, wants to keep her precious daughter limited to the Plymouth Church people. That's why we've grown apart."

"Theo, are you saying our marriage is a sham?"

"Not exactly a sham, no. But, Elizabeth, you seem far away and I am very alone. Sometimes I want to find you, but you are not there."

He says that I seem far away, but he's the one who has become a stranger. His mood swings are more violent than ever. I tell him that all marriages have ups and downs. Neither of us should expect that we will always have the same blissful contentment of the early years.

Theodore shakes his head. "Lib, you don't understand. I don't want halfway love."

As the meaning of his words sinks in, the void in the center of my stomach deepens and expands. Theo goes on, telling me how one of the new friends he met on lecture tour became something more. He does not use the words *sex* or *lovemaking*, but a vision of his carnal relations with the woman is clear in my eye. The treasured memory of my own first kiss, in the early days of our courtship, when Theo, with a frightened look on his face, crouched low so that his face came level with mine, and just barely brushed my lips, is obliterated by a mental image of my husband passionately joined in embrace with another woman, hungrily seeking her lips, her tongue.

The picture fades, leaving me drained and trembling, adrift in an alien room with unfamiliar furnishings. The flickering candle looks hazy through the film of my tears. I hear cries, but it is a moment before I realize that the sounds are from my own lips. Convulsive sobbing is shaking my whole body with a force beyond my control.

"Elizabeth, for God's sake, stop! Oh my God, what have I done to you? Darling, control yourself. You are hysterical. I am sorry, please, please, think of the children. Tell me what to do. I will do anything you want." He holds me, caresses me, but I thrust him from me.

There is a knock on the door and Theodore opens it. My sobs continue as though they have a life of their own, my whole body trembling, unresponsive to my will. He talks to the nurse, who assures him that everything will be all right. New mothers are very prone to emotional upsets. He should go and leave me to her capable hands. She tells him to reassure Bessie, who is very worried, and check that the children have not wakened. Theodore protests that he cannot leave me like this, but he goes.

My sobbing gradually lessens under the nurse's gentle ministrations. Now that the gasping for breath has ceased, she encourages me to go ahead and cry, telling me that it is all right, all of us need to weep at times. The sobs become quieter and farther apart, exhaustion overcomes me, and I enter a deep and dreamless sleep.

When I awaken in the morning, for a moment I do not recognize my surroundings, thinking I am back in my childhood home. With a rush the memory of last night's revelations and the ache in the pit of my stomach comes back. The children are up and about, and the nurse brings me the baby to nurse. There is no help for it. I must get up and go about the household routine.

At the breakfast table, Theodore urges me to eat, but when I reply that I don't feel hungry just yet, he says no more, burying himself in the morning newspaper. Shortly after breakfast, he leaves for the office of the *Independent*. I accompany him to the door as always. He steals a glance at me before giving me the customary goodbye kiss, and then says that he will be late because he has a political meeting to attend after he finishes work at the office.

After Theo leaves, I go to my room and try to form the words of prayer. Dear God, help me to understand, to meet this crisis with love rather than hatred. I cannot pray for long. Images of Theo with the other woman cloud my mind.

As the afternoon shadows lengthen and the winter chill in the house deepens, I begin to pace in the parlor. Flory passes by and looks at me curiously. I must not break down. I have to remember to maintain normality for the sake of the children. Theodore does not return for supper. The children, absorbed in their own games occasionally interrupted by little spats, do not notice his absence.

After they are all safely tucked into bed, Mrs. Mitchell brings me the baby to nurse in the parlor. She urges me to get some sleep, but I insist on my wifely duty to wait for my husband's return, telling her to go ahead and retire.

When Theo strides in the door, I meet him and kiss him full on the mouth. He holds me close for a moment and then releases me.

"Elizabeth, I did not expect you to wait for me so late."

"Why would you not expect me to wait for you? Haven't I waited for you every time you were late ever since our marriage?"

"Lib, darling, I thought you needed to be alone, that my presence was unwelcome to you. I was even thinking of not coming back tonight, of moving out of the house. Of course, I will continue to support you and the children."

The casual way he talks of supporting us, as though the issue were money, not betrayal, sticks in my gut. My voice rises to a scream. "You say you didn't come home because you wanted to give me a chance to be alone. I don't believe you. You don't care about my feelings. You were hoping I would already be in bed. Coward! You can't face me."

Theodore flinches. "Lib, I'm sorry. I did not think. I wasn't trying to hurt you."

I notice that he is still in his overcoat and take it from him. We collide as I move past him to hang the coat in the foyer, and the touch of his arm on mine feels electric; my senses are suddenly all alive. We sit and talk. He tells me about the meeting he attended.

Later, in the bedroom, I ask him another question about his work. He answers me and we fall silent. While sitting at the night table, brushing out my hair, I furtively watch him putting on his nightclothes. The hair on his arms is sandy-colored and fine, but the hair on his chest is darker and curlier, setting off the pallor of his skin. His collarbone catches the light of the candle for a moment as he twists to get on his nightshirt. I imagine tracing his collarbone with my finger, touching the curly hair on his chest, but when we lie down in the bed, Theo carefully keeps to his side, our bodies not touching.

"Theo, please hold me."

My voice is unsteady. Theo takes me in his arms, but it is not an intimate embrace. He holds me as though I were a porcelain doll. I hold his head in my hands and trace the aquiline nose with my fingers, kissing his eyes, his lips, his throat, but his body remains rigid.

"Lib, we have to be careful. You've been very ill," he whispers.

I mutter something about the doctor saying I'm fully recovered. The only thing that exists is my need for him. I am a woman possessed. Gradually he responds to my kisses, and his excitement rises in response to mine. He calls out my pet name as I dissolve in shuddering waves. He starts to pull away but I cling to him, pulling him close. The awful void inside me is still there. The waves possess me once again, so intense that I cry out, over and over again, until my body collapses against his, exhausted, and I weep.

In a muffled tone, his voice almost inaudible, Theo asks, "Lib, does this mean you forgive me?"

"I love you."

Theo strokes my hair and we lie together for a long time without speaking. Then he opens his soul to me and we lie half the night talking. He says it was horribly selfish of him to confess to me. In order to assuage the burden of a guilty conscience, he had inflicted needless suffering on me.

Theo reassures me that the love affair is over, that he broke it off earlier this winter, feeling that he was being unfair to me and leading on a young woman who should be looking for a husband to create a family of her own. She deserves better than an editor in his late thirties with a wife and three, no four, children. I cringe inwardly, for his words are beginning to sketch a real person. When he tells me how well-read she is, how understanding about his doubts of the existence of God, I feel all my own doubts and insecurities returning, even as I lie embraced in Theo's arms.

"Do you feel that your soul has a special affinity to hers?" I ask.

"There was a time when I thought so. Last winter, I was in an almost suicidal state, and the conversations with her—nothing else was going on then—saved me. But now I think it was an infatuation, born of loneliness and desperation. Elizabeth, I have never felt so close to anyone as to you. You are the loveliest and most forgiving of women."

April 1897

The voice that spoke those loving words with such fervor faded. With her eyes closed, Elizabeth could still imagine reaching out and touching him, but instead found herself alone on a bed in a darkened room. Theo was far away, across the ocean in Paris, where he had taken up residence many years before.

All their idealistic discussions of friendship and love came back to her. Theo had expounded his views on the importance of keeping mind and heart open for the occasional contact with a truly superior soul that has the power to uplift us and provide us new insight into our own nature. The marital bond should not be a constricting tie that prevents us from forming other deep friendships. Elizabeth had agreed but pointed out that there is a difference between friendship and the sacred love between man and wife.

Other conversations flooded her memory. At one point, in order to convince Theo that she understood his philosophy, she had told him that she never resented his friendship with the suffragist leaders, Elizabeth Cady Stanton and Susan B. Anthony, because they gave him something of value that she could not. Of course, she was not telling the whole truth. When Theo stayed up long hours talking and playing chess with Mrs. Stanton, she felt resentment, even jealousy. Mrs. Stanton was friendly enough. It was the way Theodore ignored his wife in the great lady's presence that wounded her.

Unable to sort out this tangle, she had spoken to Theo of her own friendships, with Mattie Bradshaw, godmother of their little daughter Mattie, and with Henry. Her love for them was not the same as her feelings for her husband. Theo had assured her that he understood, although he said with a slight laugh, "I think Henry loves you better than me."

Elizabeth had protested that Henry loved them both, and the love and esteem that the two men shared had deeper roots. She reminded Theo how often he had given credit to Henry for setting him on the right track in life. And Henry had proclaimed that the younger man was his source of inspiration.

I've only become close to Henry recently, she had told her husband, because you are always on lecturing tours. Henry became accustomed to visiting our house for sympathy and inspiration, and in your absence, he found a poor substitute in me. But you are his true soulmate, Theo.

How well she remembered Henry's almost daily visits to their home to talk with Theo during the war and the way he had embraced Theo so warmly upon leaving. The reverend had spent hours and hours at Theo's side. The visits usually started with a long session of planning editorial strategy for the *Independent*, but as the afternoon wore on, they exchanged opinions about everything that mattered, from raising children to faulting President Lincoln for being indecisive about ending slavery. Then the story-telling began. Elizabeth remembered one afternoon in particular. She was in the kitchen preparing to serve refreshments. Theo was laughing about Henry's reminiscences of toppling off a horse while riding to deliver a sermon in a church in Indiana. He had almost been refused entrance when he arrived at the church looking like a muddy madman. Elizabeth had served tea and apple fritters. Henry looked up and said thank you. But when she came back half an hour later, the teacups were still full, and neither of the men had touched the fritters.

Elizabeth wondered whether Theo had been joking or serious when he said Henry loved her more. Were the two men still soulmates then? By the time Henry had come to occupy a central rather than a peripheral place in her own heart, the men were growing apart.

Her mind jumped to the time when she went walking with Henry in the early fall about a month after little Paul's death. Elizabeth had been lying down upstairs, feeling paralyzed by one of those waves of grief that suddenly overwhelmed her.

September 1868

Bessie knocks and enters my bedroom to tell me that Reverend Beecher is downstairs waiting to see me. Wearily, I explain that I am in no condition to receive him.

"Tell him I'm sorry, but could he come back another day?"

Bessie shakes her head and starts to leave the room, but at the door she turns back and pleads with me to please rouse myself. The reverend has come all the way, knowing I am despondent, to take me for a walk. It will do me good, she says.

After forcing myself to get up, I consider whether it is necessary to change my dress, but decide not. I smooth down my hair with one hand while Bessie fetches my bonnet.

When I approach the landing, there is Henry, waiting at the foot of the stairs, expectant, looking up at me. Our eyes meet and he breaks into that familiar smile that leaves crinkles at the corners of his eyes.

He greets me with two hands outstretched. "Oh, Elizabeth, I am so glad to see you. I was about to come to see you two days ago, but I was not sure, I did not want to intrude, I thought I must give you time."

He urges me to come take a walk in the fine fall weather. As we walk out onto the sidewalk, I feel assaulted by the brightness of the sun. Since Paul's death, I seldom leave the house and my eyes are accustomed to the dim light of indoors.

Henry is giving me the latest church news and requesting my advice on the problems of a widowed parishioner left with small children. I listen and make brief replies, wondering why we talk of another's suffering rather than my own. Doesn't he understand my need to talk about Paul?

I interrupt the talk of church affairs to thank him for presiding over the funeral. "Thank you, dear friend, for making that day a beautiful day, for making Paul's death ceremony as beautiful as his short life." In response, Henry talks of how he had chosen white oleander, the symbol of purity, as the most appropriate flower for the beauty of Paul's soul.

"Yes," I reply. "I can see him clearly all dressed in white with those beautiful flowers, but I could not understand why he was so still. It seemed that at any moment he should wake up, smile up at me. Oh, Henry, he was the healthiest of all my babies. There was no trouble with my milk, we never had to look for a wet nurse, and he had such an appetite. Even after the illness, his little arms were still chubby. How could he die?"

The tears begin to flow. Henry takes my arm and gently guides me. He tells me that it is hard for us to understand and accept God's will. He himself can only guess at God's purpose, but he feels that Paul was a special child and that God called his soul to him early to spare him the suffering that is the lot of all humankind. Henry remembers that Paul was a happy child who brought joy to all around him.

"Yes, he never fretted and almost never cried after he was a month old. Why take him from us? He loved us, he wanted to stay with us, and he brought us all joy. He made us forget all our problems and look upon life anew. Theodore and I have never been as happy as during those months right after his birth. Now I cannot understand why he had to die."

I explain to Henry that I am very worried about Theo. When baby Mattie died, it was I who was completely prostrated by grief. Theo was the stronger one, who comforted me and was patient through all those long months when I could scarcely get out of bed and attend to him and the children. Now, it is the reverse. Theo is in a daze. He goes back and forth from home to work like a man sleepwalking. I cannot talk to him about Paul. Our grief should bring us closer together, but I feel that he is far away. Sometimes he becomes animated when friends drop by and the conversation turns to Grant's campaign for president or the movement for women's suffrage, but once they have gone he is silent and remote.

"Grief cannot be bottled up inside," says Henry.

"You know when I talk to you about Paul, I can see him clearly, that special smile of delight he had for me or for his brother, Carroll, when he approached the crib and twirled his musical toy. How the brothers loved one another, and what wonderful comrades they would have been!" I pause, struggling to regain control.

Henry recalls how he used to toss Paul gently and how the baby's merry laugh lifted every heart within earshot.

I smile briefly. "You know," I tell Henry, "sometimes I feel only despair."

I go on to describe what tortures me most. "Until that last day of his life, my little one, even when crying and in pain, would smile whenever I came near. He was always comforted by my presence. But toward the end, my friend, I am not sure that he even knew that I was there. I am his mother, but I could do nothing for him. In those last hours, God did not grant me the power to comfort my child, to help him face pain, to make his last journey easier."

Henry gently persuades me that Paul knew I was there and felt my love. "The little fellow was too weak to give you any outward sign, Elizabeth, but his inner self was absorbing your love, which fortified his soul in those last hours." Henry earnestly urges me to believe in the goodness of God.

I thank him for the comfort he brings me. "Today was one of those black days when I was so caught up in my own misery that I could not even be a mother to my other children. I am so glad that you persuaded me to come out walking. Suffering can be selfish, and I must strive to overcome it."

Henry nods but says that grief should not be suppressed, for we must let it run its natural course.

I explain that my misery is not constant. "There are times when I feel that I communicate with Paul. I feel a sense of light and peace and my son seems very close to me, trying to guide me. I hear his voice, his gurgling tones, and if I close my eyes, I feel his presence, his baby smell."

"You know, Elizabeth, there are many mysteries of the spirit that we cannot understand." Henry pauses deep in thought. "It would not surprise me if you were granted a vision by God because your soul is pure and loving. I think that Paul was ready to go to God, but even though he has passed on to that better world, he knows that you were not ready to lose him, and he comes back to comfort you."

"Do you really think so? The happiest moments of my life now are when those visions of Paul come to me. They are always unexpected. I know not what triggers them."

Tears are welling in my eyes once more. Henry takes my arm. We enter a small park and he guides me over to a bench. We sit watching a squirrel scurrying about, collecting food to be stored for the long winter.

It is one of those clear and crisp days of early fall that make Brooklyn beautiful. The leaves on the nearest tree are just beginning to turn yellow, and they look lovely against the intense blue of the sky. Paul's funeral was on a brilliant day just like this. The sky was the same deep blue. It was the balmy weather of August, and summer greenery was still lush. I explain to Henry that the bounties of nature on that occasion only made me feel more bereft. He listens intently, without suggesting that I should feel differently or that it is already time to let go of my sorrow.

The tears are coursing down my cheeks as I speak. Henry reaches out, and with one finger he slowly traces the path of each tear. I close my eyes for a moment and all that exists are those soft caresses. Henry kisses my eyelids, over and over again.

"Elizabeth, dearest friend, I love you. If only my kisses could wipe out your sorrows, I would kiss your dear face forever."

As always he calls me dearest friend, but now the words sound different to me. I lean toward him, he cups my chin in his hands, and I kiss him lightly on the mouth.

We quickly move apart, glancing anxiously around the park. The squirrel is sitting upright watching us, but the two girls playing hopscotch on the far sidewalk are completely absorbed in their game. Their nanny looks the other way.

The brightness of the day fades momentarily as a large billowing cumulus cloud floats over the sun. A brisk breeze strips leaves from a nearby oak tree. I watch the leaves float to the ground. The limbs will soon be bare. The sudden coolness makes me shiver, and I wonder what I am doing. My place is not in the park but at home alone in my bedroom with the memory of my baby for company.

"Henry, dear, it was so good of you to take me walking, but the children need me at home."

Henry quickly rises and escorts me. We are shy of each other, and on the walk back to the house I do not meet his eyes.

April 1897

"Mother, the doctor has come," said Flory, opening the curtains to let the light into Elizabeth's room.

A short man of ruddy complexion entered, carrying the black bag of his trade. While performing a brief physical examination, the doctor asked whether Elizabeth was alert during the day. Florence replied that the patient often seemed to be asleep or absorbed in her own thoughts. She then excused herself for a moment to check on something in the kitchen.

Elizabeth turned her head and said, "I spend most of my time remembering my past life. My eyes see the present only dimly, but the past is crystal clear to me."

The doctor, who was already packing his instruments, looked her in the eye for the first time.

"Doctor, don't tell my daughter, but I do not believe that I am destined to recover from this illness."

"Do not lose hope. You are still in your sixties. You should still have many years to enjoy your grandchildren. Give modern medicine a chance."

The doctor looked very young and confident to Elizabeth. She wondered whether he would have known how to save Paul.

"My son died before his first birthday of infant cholera," she said. "No doubt modern medicine could have saved him."

"It is hard to say. It all depends whether it was ordinary infant cholera or the more virulent kind."

The doctor bid Elizabeth good-bye, saying that he would leave the instructions regarding additional medications with her daughter.

Left alone, Elizabeth wondered whether her life would have taken a different course if little Paul had not died. That afternoon long ago in the park, she had entreated Henry to take her home, because she could not bear the confusion of emotions. He left her at the door, pressing her hand with no word spoken, but they both knew a powerful bond had been forged between them.

When Elizabeth closed her eyes, she could remember clearly how she had waited one morning about a month later for Henry to visit. He had promised to come by in the morning to take her to see portraits done by an artist friend. Little Carroll had been spending a few days at her mother's house, and that morning Alice and Flory wanted Elizabeth to take them over to their grandmother's house, too. Since Elizabeth had a prior engagement with Henry, she sent Bessie with the girls, telling them all to have lunch with Grandma.

October 1868

The clock chimes eleven times and still Henry has not come. On the sofa with a basket of sewing by my side, I try hard to concentrate on making the hemstitches fine and straight.

Our last conversation is fresh in my memory. It was one of those conversations full of starts and stops and quick deflections, as the children wandered in and out of the upstairs sitting room where I was talking with Henry. Since our walk in the park, Henry visits more frequently and our conversations have become more intimate. I can open the innermost recesses of my being to my dearest friend with no fear that he will misunderstand. We have developed a rhythm of making a rapid turnabout in the theme of an intimate talk whenever Bessie or one of the children pops in, without pausing or changing the tone of voice in which we are conversing.

On his last visit, I finally told Henry about Theodore's confession of infidelity. It was not as difficult to talk about as I had anticipated. Henry expressed no surprise, and he was sympathetic to me without criticizing Theo.

The doorbell sounds. With a feeling of elation, I kiss Henry on one cheek and then the other. For a moment he wraps his arms around me in a hug and then steps lightly aside.

"It is always so good to see you." I welcome him. "Come sit down and have a cool drink."

We sit in the parlor, but Henry declares himself not thirsty. I want to continue yesterday's interrupted conversation about love and fidelity, but don't know how to start. He shifts in his seat, crossing and uncrossing his legs. Then with no introduction, he addresses me. "In our last conversation, my dearest friend, I saw another side of your pure soul, your infinite capacity for forgiveness and love. What sweetness and sacrifice you bring to family life! Instead of blaming Theo you took the blame on yourself, wondering whether it was perhaps some lack of affection and care on your part."

"Some would consider it a weakness on my part," I acknowledge, thinking of my mother, who scolded me for being a fool, letting Theo off so easily.

"Yes," says Henry, "I am sure there are many women, including my wife, who would consider it unforgivable. I believe differently, and I admire you, my dearest friend, because I believe to forgive out of genuine love is not a position of weakness, but of real spiritual strength. Wc are redeemed by forgiveness."

As always, dear Henry has faith in my goodness. Painful memories of intense jealousy and anger against Theo make me doubt whether I deserve such praise. But Henry is right. We must cultivate love, not hate.

"You look sad," says Henry. "What are you thinking?"

"There are many things I don't understand."

"What do you mean?"

"Theo insisted that he never stopped loving me, though sometimes he thought I was indifferent, but while loving me he simultaneously fell in love with someone else. I thought he was just saying that to ease my pain, but now I am not sure. Is it possible to be in love with more than one person at the same time?" I ask Henry.

"I think it is possible." Henry takes my hand and strokes it. "But we won't talk any further of this if it is painful to you, my dear friend."

Henry is paying tribute to my womanly delicacy without understanding my need for an answer. Theo's infidelity is no longer what tortures me. It's my own inner struggle with feelings that can't be suppressed.

I grip both his hands and look directly into his eyes. "Henry, tell me honestly, I must know. It is very important to me."

"Then I will tell you what I really think. Yes, Elizabeth, dearest, I do believe that we can love more than one person. I am sure of it. Our souls are made for love, and the more spiritually developed we are, the more capacity we have for love."

Turning my head away from Henry, I murmur in a scarcely audible voice, "Henry, could I be in love with Theo and also with . . . you?"

The question seems to reverberate in the whole room, and I can hear the sharp intake of Henry's breath.

He reaches out, grasps my shoulder, and turns me toward him, avowing that he has loved me for two long years, passionately, with no hope that his love would ever be returned. He has never spoken of his love because he respected my innocence, and then my bereavement. Henry has never felt so close to anyone in his whole life.

He assures me that our affinity is such that we instinctively think and feel alike. When I start a sentence, he knows already what I will say. The connection between our souls is so deep it goes beyond the ordinary love of man and woman.

Henry kisses me, first on the forehead, my noble brow as he calls it, then full on the mouth, and gently down my neck. My body is trembling.

"The curtains," I gasp, disentangling myself from Henry's embrace and moving to close the drapes that open toward the street. "We must stop," I say softly, pulling the cord of the drapes until they shut. "Our friendship must remain pure. We should love each other but never break our marriage vows."

While saying this, my body is walking back from the window toward Henry with a volition of its own. I grasp his hands and he draws me gently toward the stairway, assuring me our love must be expressed not only in words but also with the whole body and soul.

"Love can never be a sin, my dearest, my loveliest Elizabeth. Our love is pure and can hurt no one. Come with me, my own darling, let me love you!"

At the top of the stairs, he starts in the direction of the main bedroom, but I demur. Henry lets me guide him to the upstairs sitting room, where I close the curtains that face the street. Like one person we move toward the low divan, where I often used to sit while Henry read something of interest to me.

Loving Henry comes naturally. The doubts voiced downstairs have disappeared and I give myself up wholly to the feelings that his lips and fingers arouse. With wonder I trace the smile wrinkles on his beloved face and feel the slight roughness of the shaved skin of his cheek. He murmurs about the depth of my soul being reflected in the darkness of my eyes. Lifting my hair that has fallen from its clasp, he gently caresses the nape of my neck.

Time comes to a standstill. Just moments before, I was acutely conscious of the danger of discovery, but now our surroundings are blurred and only Henry is in focus. Our lovemaking is slow, full of the wonder of discovery. His lips move slowly from my lips, down my throat to my breast, sending waves of pleasure through my whole body. I kiss him and stroke him, wanting his body to melt into mine.

When he withdraws from me, I feel sad that he has not taken his own pleasure. He says that it is safer that way, and we lie holding each other, until the sense of danger returns. We hastily rearrange our clothes and go downstairs.

Time has stood still for us, but not for the clock, which marks twelve noon with its chimes. We confer hastily and decide that it would be best to proceed with the original plan to visit the portrait studio. Henry advises me to put on a light coat because it is a brisk fall day.

He opens the door for me and we carefully make our way down the street maintaining a discreet distance, scarcely daring to look at each other for fear that even a casual passerby will notice we are in love. I shiver slightly in the wind, longing to take Henry's arm but not daring to do so.

April 1897

The windowpane near Elizabeth's bed rattled, and she watched the branches of the great sycamore tossing in the wind. Now fully awake, she remembered seeing Henry often that fall, but intimate meetings were hard to arrange. The necessity for secrecy had weighed heavily upon her conscience. It was not so much guilt about loving Henry, but her inability to confide in Theo that bothered her.

Theo had told her that his love for the woman he met on tour did not lessen his love for his wife. Elizabeth remembered the earnest expression on his face when he swore his love for her was as pure and strong as ever. How much she had wanted to be as honest with him as he had been with her, but in those first months of loving Henry she held back, doubting that Theo would understand.

In spite of these twinges of conscience, and even foreboding for the future, Elizabeth could remember feeling a sense of renewal as Christmas approached. Henry's affection was something she could depend upon, and he also encouraged her to take on more responsibilities for the social work of the church. In addition to taking an active part in church charities and teaching Sunday School, Elizabeth took a leadership role in the Bethel School, teaching poor working women.

When Theo urged her to also take an active part in the meetings of the women's suffrage movement, she hesitated, but then said yes, feeling the need to balance her two loves, helping each with a cause close to his heart. At first it was just representing Theo at meetings when he was traveling on the lecture circuit, but then she remembered that Susan B. Anthony, a frequent visitor at their house, had appealed for her help.

It must have been sometime during that long winter that she had accepted the post of corresponding secretary of the Equal Rights Association of Brooklyn. As her eyes closed, Elizabeth was once more submerged in that world of vivid images, so much more sharply delineated than in the present, and she could see Susan, her graying hair drawn back in a bun.

March 1869

I am feeling pleasantly full after lunch, and very comfortable, seated in a big easy chair in the parlor with Theodore and Susan. Every once in a while, I make a few remarks, but as their conversation becomes more heated, I'm content to listen. Theo wouldn't be interested in what I have to say anyway. He listens only to women like Susan, intellectuals who speak with assurance.

Now that I have been with child for many months, the trials of morning sickness have given way to a sense of well-being. When the first queasiness surfaced, I was dismayed to find myself expecting so soon after Paul's death and unable to think of another baby, but the first movement in my belly changed all that.

Susan is sitting on the sofa, her hands clasped in her lap, listening intently while Theo rattles on. Even for her it has become difficult to get a word in edgewise. As she turns toward Theo, her strong, classical profile is visible, her features as fine as ever, but there is a slight sagging of skin under her chin.

Theo has been talking about the need to broaden the women's movement to infuse new life into the cause. The goal is obtaining not just votes for women but also economic and social freedom. He is particularly eloquent on the subject of the need for change in the divorce laws that chain women to unhappy marriages.

Susan shakes her head slightly and shifts in her chair. When Theo finally pauses, she replies in a low but emphatic tone, telling us about her recent trip to Chicago to speak to women's groups. These women are ready and willing to launch a movement to pass a constitutional amendment to grant women the vote, but in all her meetings it was clearly indicated they don't want the issue of political rights for women to be mixed with avant-garde social issues.

Susan turns to me and asks my opinion, but before I can reply, Theo looks at the clock, whose hour hand is pointing almost to three, and says that he has almost forgotten about his meeting at the office of the *Independent*.

"I will leave you ladies to discuss this important question," he says, smiling, as he gets up. I start to rise to help him into his coat, but he says, looking pointedly at my oversized belly, "Don't get up, my dear."

Before leaving, Theo says to Susan, "I am so glad that you have made my wife into a suffragist," and then turns to me with an approving smile.

"Oh, it was not my doing at all," Susan replies. "Elizabeth has quite a talent for organization."

After Theo departs, Susan says, "Men don't always realize how much organization is involved in managing a family. It's almost as difficult as running a country. I don't understand how you do so much outside the home and still raise such wonderful children."

Although Susan has no children of her own, she understands. I smile at her and offer to make tea. She won't hear of me getting up in my condition. We compromise on going to the kitchen together. It's more intimate here than in the parlor, and there are no heavy drapes to make it gloomy. The sunshine enters through the window. The maid has taken the day off after cleaning the luncheon dishes, and the kitchen feels like my own personal domain. As we sit down at the small table with a red-and-white checkered tablecloth, Susan remarks on how the pots shine.

We talk for a while about housekeeping and all the little difficulties of a woman's life that men don't understand. I pour the boiling water into the teapot and select a quilted tea cozy with blue flowers and red cardinals. Once it has thoroughly brewed, Susan pours us two cups. Only then does she return to the parlor conversation about the suffrage movement, asking my opinion. She doesn't allow me to escape by saying I don't know enough about it.

"Most women are mothers, you know," I tell her.

Susan nods. Her gaze is fixed on the parting of the folds of my dress over my enlarged belly. A warm flush suffuses my face.

"A noble calling," she says, almost inaudibly.

"We want political rights, but we don't want to endanger our homes," I explain.

"Elizabeth, tell me what the vote means to a woman who sees herself first and foremost as a mother?"

"Well, I think we want the vote to be able to make this country better for children."

Susan considers this. "Do you mean that we should talk less about equal rights and more about how the vote would enable women to improve society, provide better education, and help the poor and others who cannot help themselves?"

"Yes," I exclaim, "but I could never have expressed it as well."

"On the contrary," she replies. "You've given me some very good arguments."

Her words make me proud, but when she urges me to take on more responsibilities at the Equal Rights Association convention planned for May, I decline. By that time, I will be too big with child.

Susan expresses her happiness that Theo and I are expecting a baby so soon. "Theo is looking so much better and he seems happier. You both do."

She understands the pain we have suffered because of little Paul's death. I describe Theodore's deep melancholy and how difficult it was for me because he would not even talk about Paul for many months.

"It was Mr. Beecher who helped me in that terrible time. Without his wise counsel I don't know how I could have gone on living," I add.

"Yes," Susan replies, "the sermon he gave at the funeral was very fine."

My eyes mist over at this recollection while we sit in companionable silence.

The Human Heart Is Unruly

April 1897

Florence roused her mother to take the medication left by the doctor. After dutifully swallowing the prescribed dose, Elizabeth said softly, "I was dreaming about Susan Anthony."

Florence looked surprised. "You mean the suffragist leader? But, Mother, you gave up all that business about women's rights years ago!"

"I still believe in women's rights, but I don't think the suffrage movement is the correct path."

"What do you mean?'

"There are other, quieter, less confrontational ways to improve women's lives and build a better society. But I still remember Susan warmly. I didn't always agree with her, but she was a good friend. Her heart was in the right place."

"I'm glad you told me. Grandma Morse was always saying awful things about Susan and Elizabeth Cady Stanton."

Elizabeth sighed. "My mother was a wonderful woman. She loved you and all her grandchildren dearly. But once she formed an opinion, she didn't want to hear the other side."

"I remember she often disagreed with Father," said Flory.

Elizabeth nodded but said nothing. It was true that her mother had hated Theodore's advanced views. How much had Flory observed as a young girl? Better not to further awaken painful memories.

Receiving no reply, Florence announced that her sister, Alice, and her two brothers, Carroll and Ralph, would be coming soon to visit their mother. Elizabeth gazed fondly at her daughter. Florence had intuited her unspoken wish. She had to see her children one more time.

It was a great comfort to be so close to her eldest. Her own mother had loved Elizabeth just as dearly but always treated her as a child in need of guidance. Elizabeth hoped that she herself had given comfort to her daughters when they needed it but also respected their decisions once they were adults. If only her mother had not constantly criticized Theodore. She was such a meddler.

December 1869

My mother, who stayed the night, is walking to and fro with baby Ralph to calm him and give me time to finish breakfast. Although it's piping hot, Theo drinks his coffee quickly. He refuses a second cup, remarking that he has to be going.

Carroll is loudly announcing that he does not want any oatmeal, but he stops in the middle of the sentence when he catches his father's stern glance. Flory admonishes him in a grown-up voice that he had better eat if he wants to grow up as tall as Daddy, and he finally tastes the oatmeal, screwing up his face.

"Elizabeth," says Theo, laying the morning paper aside, "be sure to read what Henry wrote defending his decision to marry Abby Sage McFarland to Albert Richardson."

Before I have time to reply, my mother interjects, "To my mind, Reverend Beecher made a terrible mistake. How could he consent to marry that woman when she was already married?"

Theo frowns and goes to the foyer to put on his coat. When he returns to the dining room to take leave he says, "I think that if you read the story carefully, you will see that Abby obtained a legal divorce in Indiana. It was right and proper for Reverend Beecher to join her to the man she really loved."

"No, no, you're wrong, that divorce is not legal and the marriage is immoral," my mother replies in a loud voice. Startled, little Ralph begins to cry, and she resumes rocking him. Theo rapidly departs, but Mother is not finished.

"I knew Theodore would agree with the reverend. He is always spreading all sorts of dangerous ideas. What surprises me is Mr. Beecher. How can a man of religion support such immorality?"

Carroll is playing with his porridge, trying to put it on Alice's plate, and she is spooning it back, but Florence and Bessie are gazing at my mother with wide-eyed interest.

Mother is in one of her moods. It is quite useless to argue with her when she's like this, but if I keep quiet, the girls will hear only her side.

"You know, Mother, Reverend Beecher took a courageous stand."

"Elizabeth, how can you say that? I brought you up to be a good Christian woman. Don't tell me that you are being influenced by these newfangled ideas."

I explain to her that Abby had lived for many years with an abusive husband before getting a divorce. When she came to New York, she fell in love with a journalist and wanted to marry him. Her former husband, in a fit of jealous rage, shot him.

"Mother, don't you see? The man was on his deathbed. They loved each other. How could a Christian minister refuse to marry them when it was the dying man's last wish?"

Mother hands the baby to Flory while I am speaking and paces to and fro. "My child, you do not understand. Marriage is a Christian sacrament, the basis of civilized society. To make divorce easy is a sin. What God has joined let no man put asunder!"

Mother is panting by the time she finishes this speech. She has become stout in recent years. Her face is flushed and part of her hair in her bun has come undone. Before I can reply, she plows on:

"These men talk about equal rights for women, but really they want to make divorce easy so they can get rid of a wife who is no longer young and marry again. Then what will happen to the children with no father to support them? Answer me that!"

"But, Mother, in this case, it was the wife who wanted to escape from mistreatment. Don't you remember the woman I told you about in my Sunday class?"

"The one with the drunken husband?" she asks.

"You yourself said that she should not stay with him if he beats her."

Mother sits down. She looks a bit deflated but continues to mutter about immorality. I go over to her and start to rearrange her hair.

Bessie, who has been busy reading the article left on the dining table by Theo, suddenly interjects, "Grandma Morse, let me read to you what Reverend Beecher says about the case."

Although Bessie is our ward and not her real granddaughter, Mother likes it when she calls her Grandmother. Bessie reads a section in which Henry explains that at the time he performed the marriage, he believed that the divorce was completely legal in New York. He consented to officiate at the ceremony in response to the wish of a dying man. If he has done any harm, he sincerely asks pardon.

"Well," says Mother, "at least he apologized. That's the way a man of religion should talk." Suddenly, she looks directly at Bessie. "What are you reading such things for? A young lady should not be talking about immoral subjects. Put that paper down and take Carroll to wash his hands."

Bessie obediently guides Carroll and then helps the maid clean the table. Mother turns to me. "Really, Elizabeth, you should not let the girls listen to such things. They are too young and innocent."

I sigh, thinking that it was Mother, not I, who brought the topic up. She gestures to me to follow her into the parlor where we can talk with more privacy.

"You know, Lib, the reverend has been greatly criticized for performing that marriage. He should have talked with members of his congregation before rushing into something like that. It makes Plymouth Church look bad."

I nod but point out that there was really no time for consultation. My mother says she hopes the whole thing will blow over now that the reverend has explained that he acted to grant the wish of a dying man.

"Don't you think a Christian minister should provide an example to his flock by acting according to the higher law of his conscience?" I retort. "If he just follows public opinion, what kind of spiritual leader is he?"

"No man should set himself up as superior to the commonly held notion of what is right and wrong. And that reminds me, Lib," she says, "take care that Theo doesn't begin to write articles defending the reverend."

"Theo has stayed out of the controversy."

"Mark my words, he won't be silent for long. I know my son-in-law. He'll take an extreme position and embarrass us all. Can't you do anything to stop him, Lib?"

"Mother, Theo has deeply held convictions about what is right and wrong. He has taken unpopular positions before in dangerous times."

"Not because he is so courageous," she retorts. "The truth is that shocking people with extreme ideas makes him feel important. That's what it's really all about. If he goes on writing articles for the *Independent* about women's rights, liberalizing divorce, and all that nonsense, no one will buy the paper, and he will lose his job. But what does he care?"

"Mother, please. The *Independent* is doing well since Theo took over as editor. Subscriptions are fine. Don't worry so much."

"Well, he is your husband. But I think he is a very selfish person. He thinks only about himself and never about his wife and family, and I will tell him that to his face if he writes anything about this scandalous marriage, you wait and see."

I glance to see if any of the children are within earshot, listening to this attack against their father. "Mother, please, you know it upsets me when you talk like that about Theo."

"Well, I will say no more." But she adds, "Just one more thing, you had better tell him not to let that scandalous man Mr. Andrews enter this house. The man is preaching gross immorality and free love. I won't have him in the same house as my daughter and grandchildren."

May 1870

Theodore and I have rearranged the furniture to accommodate extra chairs in our parlor for the large group that has come to hear Stephen Pearl Andrews, the same man my mother said shouldn't be allowed to cross the threshold of our house. Andrews pulls back the heavy chair where he is sitting, so that all the guests are in his line of vision, and starts speaking rapidly with precise articulation. His hands are in constant motion, either stroking his full beard or gesturing to make a point. His wide brow is emphasized by a receding hairline.

"This country was founded on the proposition that the least government is the best government. The state should represent only the legitimate interest of the community but not interfere in the private lives of its citizens."

Theo is listening intently, seated next to Elizabeth Cady Stanton on the far side of the room. Andrews glances about the room as though to ascertain he has our complete attention. "The state should not interfere in matters of the heart," he continues. "You cannot legislate who will love whom, nor will a court order change the human heart."

Mr. Andrews's eyes stop at mine. I think of the unruly human heart that is beating in my own breast. How I wish I were somewhere else, far from such troubling talk that makes me feel as though my heart will burst.

The speaker's eyes sweep past me, and he continues. "The state has no legitimate right to interfere in marriage, divorce, separation, or to penalize adultery or sexual relations between members of the same sex, or any other affective relationship. The individual must be free to choose polygamy, monogamy, or any other—"

"But would not such individual sovereignty result in general immorality and the mistreatment of women?" pipes up a voice from the back in a diffident tone. It is a young, dark-haired woman named Laura Bullard. Earlier in the evening, Theo had introduced her to me as a new friend.

Theo cuts in before Mr. Andrews can reply, "I don't think that the state can really dictate to people how they should feel and whom they should love. Any attempt to do so results in deception. Lying is the source of immoral behavior. I'll give you an example. The husband who puts up a front of monogamy but secretly visits a prostitute, thus endangering the health of his wife, is more immoral than an open bigamist. The wife of the bigamist knows the score and can choose to leave."

The young woman who has raised the question does not pursue

it, but Mrs. Stanton calls out, "But you are forgetting the economic inequalities between men and women."

She is a large woman of imposing presence. Her face is round and good-humored, her figure matronly, but her tone is that of a woman accustomed to commanding attention. She pauses. Theo is about to cut in, but she holds up her hand and clears her throat before continuing. "I, too, believe strongly in individual rights, but I am concerned that a woman with several children may not be able to leave the bigamist because she has no means to support herself or her children."

Her words remind me of what Susan has often said about the unfairness of divorce laws for women. I've never felt warmly about Mrs. Stanton, but I'm glad she has spoken up. Someone has to bring men like Mr. Andrews down from their lofty rhetoric to the realities of human life.

He spends the next fifteen minutes trying to counter Mrs. Stanton's argument, but I pay no attention. After he finally falls silent, everyone begins to talk at once, and there are multiple debates instead of one conversation. Theo catches my eye. I endeavor to converse with the group around me and then rise to check on the refreshments to make sure Theo will not find fault with my role as hostess.

When I return, the dark-haired lady has moved closer to Theo, and is listening to him intently, occasionally interrupting with a question. Only a few phrases are audible, but they seem to be discussing whether the doctrines of free love would encourage immoral behavior.

Mr. Andrews's wife comes up to me. She is dressed more soberly than usual, and her eyes look weary. Being married to Mr. Andrews must be difficult. After the usual family inquiries, our talk turns to spiritualism. She mentions a new medium, a very young woman whose spiritual powers enable her to communicate with those who have passed to the other side. She must be telling me all this because she knows I recently lost a child, but I feel no need to attend a session. God in his infinite mercy has granted me, through the power of prayer, a compelling feeling of Paul's presence. It's not something I can share with people I hardly know. Henry is the only person I have ever talked to about this experience of reuniting with my dearest little one.

Some guests assemble around Stephen Pearl Andrews, others gravitate toward Elizabeth Cady Stanton, and another small group has formed around Theo and Laura Bullard. Mrs. Andrews rejoins her husband, and after a moment's hesitation, I join the group around Mrs. Stanton, who is criticizing the acquittal of Daniel McFarland, Abby's first husband, of the murder of her lover.

"He saw his wife as a mere possession and committed murder to assert his property rights," observes Mrs. Stanton. "The court not only acquitted him but gave him custody of the children."

"How can they take custody of the child away from the mother and give it to a man with a history of drinking and violence?" I cry. "Poor Abby!"

The other women agree, and the conversation turns to the organization of a rally to protest the verdict.

The guests do not begin to depart until half past eleven. Theo and I accompany them through the foyer to the front door. It is an unusually warm evening for May, and people say their goodbyes slowly, while everyone continues to chat on the wide porch that spans the front of our house. Laura Bullard comes over to me to ask how little Ralph, my youngest, is doing. She is a handsome woman with pale skin set off by very dark hair and blue eyes, but her manner is simple and shy. Theo talks about me and the children all the time, she says. I can't help being pleased when she compliments me on the house and its decorations and marvels that I am able to be so active in church and suffrage work while maintaining a household and tending four children.

After the last of the guests has departed, Theo and I linger for a few moments on the porch to enjoy the warm spring night. The moon is partially hidden behind a cloud, and we marvel at the brightness of the stars.

When we go upstairs to the bedroom, Theo is in a talkative mood. While I sit at the vanity, brushing out my hair, he flings himself prone onto the bed, pillow under his arms, with his head propped up in one hand.

He wants to know what Mrs. Stanton had to say about the acquittal of Daniel McFarland. After I tell him about the plans for a protest rally, he says, "I always thought that it was an error for our friend Henry to back down and apologize for performing the marriage ceremony. People should have the courage of their convictions."

"It took courage to perform the ceremony, and he did not back down completely."

Theo gives me a sharp look. "As usual, you defend Mr. Beecher."

I hold my breath.

Theodore changes the subject. "You know what I admire most in Stephen? His unflinching advocacy of truth. The root of all immorality is falsehood and hypocrisy."

I turn from the mirror to face Theo. "But don't you think that there are other roots of immorality, such as selfishness?"

"No, if human relationships are based on truth and honesty, the whole society will be healthy because it is built on a firm foundation. The relationship between husband and wife must be based on complete honesty. Otherwise, the marriage is really a material convenience rather than a spiritual union."

I turn back toward the mirror to continue brushing my hair.

"For instance, Lib, dear, you glanced several times in my direction while I was talking to Laura Bullard. As an honest man, I should tell you that I find her a very pretty woman and a cultivated woman of intelligence, but that is all. I think she admires me, we have long talks, go to lunch together, she says she has learned a lot from me, but it is a friendship, nothing more. You see, I am completely honest with you. I hide nothing. I tell you of all my feelings."

I turn around to look at him, wondering if he is protesting too much, but decide to trust my instinct that Laura is a sincere person who would not have offered me her friendship if she had taken Theo as a lover.

"Laura is very nice," I say. "Did you say that she was working on the *Revolution*?"

"Yes, Mrs. Stanton and Miss Anthony will probably have to give up the paper because it is losing too much money. Laura has offered to take over as editor. I am glad you like her."

"She told me she wants to come over and meet the children."

"That's good," replies Theo. "Lib, I feel you are not as honest with me as I am with you. Your friendship with Henry is very close, you are much closer to him than I am to Laura, but you no longer talk about him or his visits."

"There is not much to tell. Henry does not visit as often as before because he is so busy."

"But what do you talk about?" Theo insists. I describe how we talked of church business and the Virgin Mary the last time Henry visited.

I'm telling Theo the truth but not the whole truth. It would be impossible to explain the sudden joy Henry and I felt when we discovered a mutual sympathy with the Catholic vision of the all-merciful Mother of God. Henry and I can talk about almost anything and feel a shock of recognition that we both feel the same way.

Theo demands a fuller account of the nature of my friendship with Henry, and I try to oblige him.

"Darling, don't you see, you and I were so despondent after Paul died that we could not comfort each other. In this hour of need, Henry as a minister was able to console me. Then I was able to reach out to you in your sorrow."

Theo shakes his head. "Yes, but Henry was the one who comforted you when death struck our family. My place has been taken by another man. I do not blame you for my own failure to offer you the solace you needed. You must be in love with Henry. He deserves your love. I do not!"

"I love you as my husband and I love Henry as a friend."

"Lib, I would not blame you if you took Henry as a lover."

"What do you mean?"

"I was unfaithful to you. And I have failed you as a husband in so many ways."

"No, you haven't," I reassure him. "Believe me, Henry is just a friend, like Laura."

Theo shakes his head. "True love is based on trust. I told you everything, Elizabeth. Why won't you be equally honest with me?"

"There is nothing to tell. If my talks with Henry bother you, I'll stop seeing him so often."

"Now you are insulting me," cries Theo. "I am not trying to tell you whom to see or not to see. I don't want to deprive you of your liberty!"

"I just meant that you and the children are the most important of all to me."

After we go to bed, Theo strokes my hair and tells me how much he loves me. I kiss him and tell him I love him, too.

"Then trust me, tell me the truth!" he urges.

I stiffen and mutter that there is nothing to tell, and it's time to sleep. Theo turns away from me.

July 1870

The *clop, clop* of the horse's hooves on the pavement sounds in my ears as my carriage nears home. Sweat is trickling down the back of my neck. My right hand shakes as I pry open the window to get a bit of air. Feeling the soft breeze on my face, I close my eyes and endeavor to order my thoughts.

I had left early for the country to escape from Theo's constant importuning for a confession. He was badgering me constantly. Every day he begged me to confess. Each time it cost me more effort to summon up the energy to make a denial. He said over and over again the only obstacle between us is my lack of honesty. A few days after I arrived in the country, a letter arrived filled with accusations. I hid it and went berry picking with the children, but my eyes kept misting, making it difficult to see the tiny wild strawberries nestled on the hillside, the last of the season. When we got back, I tasted them while serving the children, but the sweet pungency of the fruit on my tongue gave me no pleasure. After a sleepless night, I wrote back saying I would leave the children with my mother in the country and return home for a day to talk things through.

A sharp pain in my abdomen comes and goes. Although I am in a horse-drawn carriage, I have a mental image of being seated in a gleaming railroad car, going at lightning speed down a steep hill. I want to get off as we pass a station, but the train picks up speed, and I have no choice but to go on.

The carriage comes to a stop with a jolt. For a long moment, I sit motionless. My limbs are heavy and my breathing labored. I have come home to tell the truth. What's wrong with me? My fingers are too clumsy to open the carriage door to get down.

Theo opens it, greeting me with a warm kiss. We talk of the

children and their summer activities while the driver is paid off and the meager luggage brought in. The cook brings us tea in the parlor. I ask after Theo's health and chide him for not joining us in the country. He talks about how much he has missed me and the children.

As we finish tea, I run out of stories of family life in the country, and conversation flags. I steal a glance at Theo, but he is looking toward the fireplace with an abstracted air.

He turns to me. "Elizabeth, I am sorry that I made you leave the country and our good friends there, but I am grateful you came. I have been in torment. I need to talk to you. Only you, my darling, can help me out of this slough of despond."

"I know, that is why I am here." I reach over to grasp his hand, but Theo stands up abruptly and begins to pace the room.

"Lib, I am demanding honesty from you, but I should not ask this without being completely honest myself. I have not told you everything."

"There is no need; I trust that you have told me what I need to know."

Theo dismisses my comment impatiently. "There is need. I cannot live unless there is complete and total honesty between us." He informs me that he told me of only one love affair, the only one that was based on intellectual affinity, but there have been other encounters with women on his travels. If our marriage is to be the ideal coupling, we must know everything about each other.

I feel a twinge of physical shock, but to a lesser degree than the first time Theo made a confession. Theo sits down across from me with his head in his hands, while I think about berry picking, prying apart the green leaves, searching for the last of the tiny red fruit.

"Elizabeth," says Theo, lifting his head and looking directly into my eyes, "I am sorry to burden you with all this. Please, my darling, do not hold back. Be as honest with me as I have been with you. Tell me everything in your heart. Then we will be able to forgive each other and go on."

I am silent. Surely, he will not blame me for loving Henry when he has confessed multiple affairs. But I still can't get the words out.

"Perhaps you are worried that I will not keep my word. I have promised you many times that I will not think the less of you for loving someone else, but only for not telling the truth. I will never do any harm to anyone you love. You have my solemn word."

"I love you very much," I reply, "and I also love Henry. You two are both very dear to me." I stop.

"When did the love affair with Henry begin?"

"After Paul . . . our baby left us, I could not bear it. It was Henry who made it possible for me to believe in God's goodness again. He loved Paul very much, and when I talked to him about Paul, I felt very close to him."

"You mean that your pastor took advantage of your grief to persuade you to have sexual relations with him? Is that what you are saying?"

Oh, Theo, you don't want to understand! You are twisting my words. "It was not like that," I tell him. "It was just that my feelings changed when he helped me. We became closer."

"And what arguments did he use to persuade you?"

"Well, he didn't use arguments exactly. We talked about our affinities of opinion and sentiment."

"You seem to be saying that you have a natural affinity with your pastor and not with your husband."

"N-n-n-no," I stammer, "I did not mean that. It is just that you were very distant at that time, and, well, I could not talk to you."

Theo shakes his head.

I compare my situation to the time when he felt that I made no effort to understand his troubles and sought consolation from the woman he loved, the one he had met on lecture tour.

"It is not the same at all," he cries. "She was an innocent young lady, but in this case, we are talking about an experienced older man who has seduced several other women in his congregation." He looks directly at me. "And you fell for his sympathy routine. How could you be so stupid and naive?"

"Theo, please, try to understand, it wasn't like that!"

Theo turns his face away.

"Theo, you wanted me to tell the truth. Please look at me. I did not want to lie to you anymore."

Theo turns to face me. "You are a pious woman, a much better Christian than I am. Does it not bother you that you are committing a sin?"

"Sometimes I feel I am committing a sin, particularly now, because I know I am hurting you, but . . ."

"But?"

"If you really love someone, with a pure love, then any manifestation of that love is pure."

"Is that what Henry says? Is that how he justifies breaking a commandment?"

"He says I am a pure and chaste woman."

"And what do you think? Do you think you are pure and chaste while you are in his arms?"

"Oh, Theo . . ." I cannot go on.

Theo's lip is trembling. He takes my two hands in his. "I am very upset, Elizabeth, terribly upset. I thought you had more judgment. But don't misunderstand me. I am glad you told me the truth."

I get up and kneel beside his chair, putting my arms around his waist and my head in his lap. "Darling, I love you. I am sorry I hurt you. Forgive me. Do you want me to stop seeing Henry?"

Theo lifts me gently and wipes away the tears that I had not even noticed. He reassures me that he forgives me although there is nothing to forgive and says that he has no intention of telling me what to feel or whom to see, since I am his wife, not his possession. He then rises from his chair and says that he needs to go out for a while.

Left alone, I wander into the kitchen to talk to the cook. She asks me what to serve for dinner, and I suggest beef stew, Theodore's favorite.

"Don't forget to put in lots of potatoes," I remind her, "but not too many peas. Mr. Tilton doesn't like too many vegetables in his stew."

I return to the drawing room and sit down to the piano, but after a few notes, I get up again, unable to play.

When Theo returns, he is silent and withdrawn. I try to converse during supper, but he answers me in monosyllables and avoids my eyes. When I ask him whether he likes the food, he does not reply.

The evening wears on. I rise to retire to bed. Theo says that he must finish reading something and bids me good night. I lie down and close my eyes, but sleep does not come.

After about an hour, I hear footsteps. When he enters the bedroom, I stir slightly and call his name. "Theo?"

"Yes, it's me," he replies, and lies down without touching me.

I long to break the silence but do not know what to say. "Theo, please, I want you to forgive me."

Before I can say anything further, Theo grabs me and pulls me toward him. His kisses make me gasp and struggle for breath. He fumbles roughly with my nightclothes. I try to help, but I am pinned under his weight. I hear a screeching noise as he tears my gown. "Sorry," he mutters. His voice is guttural, different.

Our coupling is frenzied. When my head hits the brass rods at the head of the bed I cry out that he is hurting me. Theo stops, protects my head with his arm, and then slides me, our bodies still entwined, toward the middle of the bed. The smell of his body in my nostrils is unfamiliar. He asks whether I am all right. Now his voice sounds more like Theo. While he rubs my head with his fingers, my body relaxes slowly. He kisses me again, more gently this time, and beseeches me to love him a little, to tell him I need him as much as he needs me. I tell him I *do* love him and kiss him back. He pulls me close again and tells me I am his own darling. When it is all over, he moans and calls out my name.

I hold him tightly for a long time. My breathing gradually returns to normal, but Theo is trembling and I realize he is weeping.

He sits up suddenly, and cries, "Elizabeth, how could you do this to me? I cannot rid my mind of the picture of you in Henry's arms. He was my best friend. How could you both betray me?"

I grasp his arm. "Please, Theo, forgive me . . ."

He shakes me off, and rises to his feet. "Is he a better lover than I? Is that it? Do you enjoy it more with him?"

"Theo, don't."

"Forgive me, Elizabeth, I did not mean it."

Theo sits beside me and holds me. I return his embrace, and we both weep.

Late July 1870

Little Carroll enters the upstairs parlor where I am sitting doing some mending. He is holding two jars with perforated lids where he keeps the grasshopper and other insects he collected while we were in the country. I tried to persuade my dear little boy not to bring them to Brooklyn. These small creatures are better off in the country, where God intended them to be.

Carroll is looking with concern at one of the jars. His brow wrinkling in a frown, he says that the praying mantis has not moved all morning. "Do you think he is sick, Mommy?"

I look carefully inside the jar, recalling that Henry once told me a praying mantis stays very still for a long time after eating.

"I don't know, my son, but no creature of God likes to be kept prisoner. Shall we go to the park in the afternoon and let him go?"

The praying mantis is Carroll's favorite, but he finally says yes.

The clatter of hooves on the pavement announces the approach of horses down below in the street. Could it be Henry? I peer out the window, half concealing myself behind the heavy drapes. Theodore goes down the steps and engages in an animated conversation with whomever is in the carriage. He looks up and calls my name. I draw back from the window and then approach once more to call down, "Coming, dear."

When I reach the front door, Henry and Theo are conversing on the porch about the division between the two camps of leaders of the movement for women's suffrage and how best to reunite them so that the cause is not weakened.

"Look who has stopped by," Theo exclaims. "Your friend has got himself a very fine pair of grays indeed! He wants to take you riding in the carriage, Elizabeth."

A warm flush suffuses my face. I manage to say something about having too many things to do.

Henry looks disappointed.

Theo says, "Oh, surely you cannot be all that busy. You have been complaining of insomnia; a ride will do you good. I would go myself, but I think I should be getting along to the office."

Wondering whether Theo really wants me to go, I fetch my hat and gloves. Theo hands me into the carriage and then waves goodbye. As the carriage draws away, his tall figure standing on the porch recedes from view.

I turn to Henry. It has been a long time since we last met, and so much has changed. He smiles at me warmly and asks about my stay in the country. I recount our little adventures and how the children responded to the wonders of nature.

"My dear friend," he asks, "is something wrong? You seem worried about something."

"It's just that Theo seems to suspect something."

Henry considers this. "Oh, I see, now I understand why you were reluctant to come out riding. But Theo was as usual. I am sure there is nothing to worry about."

I explain that Theo keeps hinting that I am not telling the truth about my friendship with Henry, and I try to convey the importance that Theo attaches to honesty in marriage.

"You told me before how much Theo's demand for honesty affects you," Henry says. "I know that you want to be completely honest, that concealment affronts the purity of your soul. But believe me, Elizabeth, I am older than you and Theo, and I have seen more. Life cannot be reduced to a single principle like truthfulness."

I swallow hard.

"Of course, I cannot tell you what is right for you, my dear, but think carefully. Do not put yourself in danger," Henry continues. He reaches over to caress my cheek, the touch of his hand as light as that day in the park when he traced my tears with his fingers.

Henry brings the horses to a stop at the next crossing. We both glance around. No one is approaching. I lean over and kiss him on the mouth. We draw apart discreetly. Henry tells me in an almost inaudible tone that he has been dreaming of me and missing me. He is so glad that I am back. I gently squeeze his hand.

When Henry drops me off, Theo has already left for work. In fulfillment of my promise to Carroll, I go with the children and Bessie to the park in the afternoon. We choose a dense thicket to let the praying mantis go. I explain to Carroll that the peculiar-looking insect will be hidden from predators and able to readjust to his surroundings. Afterward, sitting on a bench while the children romp, I think about Theo's generous gesture.

I close my eyes to say a prayer of thanks and then open them to look upward through a nearby maple tree's canopy of leaves toward the vast expanse of the sky. Some leaves are light green, almost chartreuse, but whenever an upper leaf casts a shadow on a lower one, the bright sunlight is filtered and I can see darker, cooler shades of green.

Dear God, the leaves are beautiful against the sky, the children are playing, and the praying mantis is free. Everything is going to be all right.

When we return, Theo is already home. Although he says very little to me, he laughs and jokes with the children. Later in the evening, he does not join me in the bedroom but stays up reading in the second-floor sitting room. After a few minutes, I enter the room and take up the novel I have been reading. When Theo looks up, I blurt out that I want to thank him for being so kind when Henry came to ask me to go out riding.

"Elizabeth, you misunderstand me. I do not want you to go with Henry, but I do not stand in your way. It would be against my principles to do so."

"I thought . . . you urged me to go."

"What did you and Henry talk about?"

"The children's summer activities, mostly."

"I suppose he took advantage of the situation?"

"Took advantage?"

"Don't be dense, Lib. Did he kiss you?"

"Yes."

"How?"

"On the cheek." I feel a hot flush.

"You expect me to believe that? You are a liar."

I say nothing.

"Did he touch you?"

I am still silent.

"Answer me. Did he touch you?" Theo is almost shouting now.

"No, no. Theo, please."

"You know I blamed him for seducing you, for using his smooth religious oratory to seduce you, but you are equally to blame. You carelessly display your legs, your bosom, hoping to attract male attention. You project a sensuous desire that attracts men against their will."

The book in my hand falls to the floor with a thud.

"But, Theo, you always complain that I don't know how to dress, that I am too plain, too short, that I know nothing of fashion. You know I have never tried to attract men."

"You don't have to dress fashionably to project sensuous desire."

"But, Theo, even if I wanted to, I would not know how to be what you say I am, a sensuous woman," I reply, repeating the word reluctantly. "Stop it! You know I am not like that. When Laura Bullard walks into a room, men look at her. But no one looks at me. Why are you doing this to me?"

"Don't deny it. You are a sensuous woman. You come on to me and ask for it. No decent woman would act that way."

"Theo, you are my husband, I love you."

"And Henry is your lover. Do you come on to him, too?"

I cover my face with my hands. Theo starts to apologize, blaming the demon of jealousy, pleading for my forgiveness. He explains that he wanted to be fair, to let me choose as a free individual whether to ride with Henry or not, but he cannot bear to think of me alone with him.

"Theo, listen to me, my love for Henry is not based on lust or sensuous desire. Our love is based on—"

"Were you going to say mutual esteem?" asks Theo. He is looking fixedly at me, his lips parted in a half-smile.

"Yes, mutual esteem. Henry does not think I am stupid."

"I have never said or thought you were stupid, Elizabeth. Don't invent things."

"No, maybe you don't say it, but you think I am stupid compared to your brilliant friends. Don't deny what you know is true. I am not enough for you. It embarrasses you that I am only five feet tall. Henry believes that I am a worthwhile person just as I am."

Theo is silent. I notice that his lip is trembling, but I cannot stop. "Henry believes in me, values me. He listens to my opinions. My feelings are important to him. He—"

Theo gets up and abruptly leaves the room.

Early August 1870

The clattering of footsteps on the stairway announces that someone is ascending with great haste. Mother bursts into the upstairs parlor, where I am cutting out paper dolls with the children. With hair disheveled and her face splotched red, she screams, "Do you know what that husband of yours is doing? He's spreading rumors all over Brooklyn about you. He—"

"Mother! Not in front of the children! Are you crazy talking this way?"

Alice and Flory stare at me. Little Carroll, on the other hand, pays no attention. He is having trouble cutting out his own paper figures. Initially, the girls had not included him in their doll-making project, but I intervened and suggested that he could make animal cutouts.

Grabbing Mother by the arm, I guide her toward the door, saying that we will talk this over calmly downstairs where we will not bother the children.

Carroll begins to wail that he will never be able to cut out his grizzly bear figures. "Mommy, you said you would help me! You promised!" He looks at me reproachfully, eyes filling with tears.

We enter the library, downstairs, and I close the folding doors.

"Mother, you cannot talk that way in front of the children."

Mother pays no attention. She marches over to Theodore's desk and picks up a faded photograph of him standing with Susan B. Anthony and Elizabeth Cady Stanton. "You hypocrite!" she cries, gazing at Theo's likeness. "All that talk about women's rights and free love! You lecher!" The glass cover rattles against the frame. I lunge for it, but she is too quick for me. Holding it just out of my reach, she cries, "I know his type, pretending to be a great social reformer to justify his own lusts."

"Give it to me." Her fingers loosen their grip and I replace the photograph on the desk, face down. Her face is mottled and she is breathing hard. "Mother, calm down." I lead her by the hand, sit her down in an easy chair, and gently sweep back the strands of hair that have fallen into her face. "What is upsetting you? What did Theo do?" I ask.

"He is the adulterer, but he is accusing you, my child!"

"What are you talking about?"

Mother's words come out in a confusing jumble, but it seems that she was visiting our dear friend, Mrs. Mattie Bradshaw, and Mattie asked her, "What has come over Theodore? Is there some problem between him and Reverend Beecher? He keeps talking about how the reverend is not really such a saint as people believe." According to Mother's version of the story, Theo had told Mattie, "If you really want to know the truth about Beecher, go ask Elizabeth."

"Oh my God! He didn't say that!" I hold the edge of the desk to steady myself before sinking into the easy chair next to my mother. "How could he?"

Mother tells me that she isn't in the least surprised. From the beginning she knew that Theo was the wrong husband for me. He always had those strange ideas, and then he lost his religious faith. "Why didn't you throw him out after he told you about his affairs with other women?"

"Mother, don't talk that way! Theo was in one of his despairing moods then and he thought I did not love him. God wants us to forgive."

"And how does he repay you for your love and forgiveness? By spreading rumors, to make *you* look like the guilty one."

"Mother, he is not the only one who . . ." I cover my face with my hands and turn away.

"My child, what are you saying? Elizabeth, look at me!"

"I tried to tell you before."

"No! No! Don't tell me there is something between you and Reverend Beecher! Elizabeth, for God's sake, tell me it isn't true!"

"It is true."

"But why? I brought you up to be a God-fearing Christian woman! It can't be! My pure little girl who never knew the meaning of sin."

"Mother, believe me. My love for Henry is pure. When I had lost my way after losing Paul, Henry brought me back to God!"

My mother draws herself up tall in the chair and screams at me, "What does that have to do with it? You . . ." She stops midsentence, hunches her shoulders, and collapses into herself like a hermit crab folding into its shell. Sobs rack her small frame. "My innocent child, what have they done to you?"

"Don't cry, Mother, don't cry. Everything will be all right."

"My child, don't tell me you have been taken in with all that talk about free love! God save us!"

"Mother, please."

My mother sits upright in her chair and blows her nose forcefully. "*No!* You listen to me! Those so-called reformers talk about equality, but free love is not for women, it is for men to gratify themselves. The whole world has gone crazy. How could a respected preacher seduce a woman in his congregation?"

"Mother, stop it right now! Don't ever talk about Henry like that!"

"Elizabeth, my daughter, how could you be such a fool? You don't understand what men are. But I understand their vile tricks."

I shrink back. "I won't listen. Henry did not—"

"I wasn't talking about Henry. I meant Theo. Of course, men are all alike."

"What about Theo?"

"He talked to you about free love and encouraged your friendship with the reverend in order to be sure that you would not object to his affairs. I wondered why he was always insisting that you invite the reverend to dinner. It was a nuisance to have his mother-in-law around, but the reverend was always welcome. Now I understand."

"It wasn't like that!"

"My dear child, when men get what they want, they throw the woman to the wolves!"

"Stop it! No one is throwing me to the wolves."

"Then what is your husband doing? Tell me that."

"He's not himself. He's going through a difficult time."

"Oh, so he's in one of his moods again, is he? It's always been all right if he yells at his wife because he's despondent. Now he needs to have other women, because the poor man is despondent. It is all an act."

"Mother, please. I have not been a perfect wife either."

"Theo drove you into Reverend Beecher's arms. Now he is spreading rumors about you. He will not stop until he ruins you."

I put my hands over my ears. "Stop! Stop!" I scream. My mother closes her mouth in a firm line.

"Mother, listen to me."

"I'm listening."

"I want to save my marriage. I don't want a divorce. I could lose my children. I must break off with Henry." My voice is choked.

"You poor child. At least Henry is kind to you."

"I have to give him up. It's the only way. Then Theo will be able to recover from heartache."

"What heartache? That blackguard has no heart."

"Theo is in a morbid state right now, but believe me, he loves the children, and he loves me. We have to give him time."

My mother snorts and shakes her head. "And what will Theodore give up? Tell me that! Who is this Laura Bullard he is always running around with, supposedly helping her with that silly suffrage paper? You should both go back to your marriage vows."

"Laura is a friend of the family. She adores the children."

"To throw you off track."

"Laura has nothing to do with this. If you want to save me and the children from ruin, you must listen to me. I will talk to Theo."

"Lot of good that will do."

"Mother, are you going to help me?"

"Of course."

"We must stop the rumors. If anyone asks if there is anything wrong between Henry and Theo, tell them everything is just fine."

"If you say so."

"That's not enough. If you love me, don't say anything against Theo. Everything is fine between Theo and me. Everything is fine between Theo and Henry. Mother, do you understand?"

She nods.

"Give me your solemn promise."

Mother bows her head and replies in a low voice, "Yes, I promise."

I hear a slight rustle as though someone is in the next room listening, but when I open the folding doors, no one is there.

Mid-August 1870

Flory bursts into the room and cries, "Guess who is here! It's Mr. Beecher. Are you coming downstairs, or shall I bring him up here?"

"Bring him up here. Tell him that I am still unwell," I reply.

I can hear his footsteps on the stairs. He strides into the up-stairs sitting room, gives me a light kiss on the cheek, and sits on the adjoining sofa. Glancing at the open door, he leans forward and takes my two hands in his.

"Elizabeth, your letter alarmed me. I came down to the city as soon as I could. My dearest friend, are you still unwell?"

"I am feeling a bit better. The fever has gone down, but I still have some chest congestion," I reply. "Oh, my dear Henry, it is not only my health. I am sorry to make you interrupt your well-earned vacation in Peekskill, but I need to speak to you."

"Tell me, dearest, what is it that troubles you?"

I glance at the door. Henry stands up, looks down the hallway, and then closes it soundlessly.

"It's Theodore," I say in a low voice. "He suspects something."

"What do you mean? Elizabeth, you are such an honest person, are you sure that it is not your own guilt about keeping something secret from Theo that is making you imagine that he knows?"

"No. Theo is acting very strangely, making accusations. I'm afraid."

Henry looks directly into my eyes. "Tell me the truth, you haven't told him about us?"

I drop my eyes and break into a cold sweat. Should I tell Henry? Won't he see my telling Theo the truth as betrayal? And what if he tries to talk to Theo? They could come to blows. Theo could denounce us and take my children from me.

"No, I didn't tell him."

"Elizabeth, something is very wrong. Please tell me what is happening."

"I have been praying to God for guidance every day," I say, "because my marriage is in trouble and I am worried about my family life." I then describe Theodore's suspicions, his moodiness, and some aspects, but not all, of his increasingly erratic behavior. I don't mention what my mother said about Theo spreading rumors.

"I feel my first duty is to Theo and to my children," I tell Henry.

"Elizabeth, you mean we cannot continue loving each other?"

"Not in the same way," I explain. "Oh, Henry, I could never stop loving you."

"Our love is not doing any harm to anyone. Theo has suspicions, you say, but he does not know. He often sinks into melancholic moods and recovers after a month or two." Henry sinks back into his chair, his shoulders bowed.

"Henry, are you all right?"

"Yes, just a bit tired after the journey from Peekskill. I am no longer a young man." He sighs. "I see nothing but a vast emptiness in the future. You are the only person that I can really talk to."

I bow my head. Henry has told me many times that his wife is a good and loyal woman, but there is no sympathy between them. Both her intellect and her feelings are rigid and unbending. The gospel of love he preaches has no meaning for her. He turns toward me and makes a direct appeal. "Before we became close friends, I was thinking of giving up the work of the Lord, because I felt a dryness in my soul, but you have given me inspiration and made it possible for me to bring the word to others. Do not desert me, Elizabeth. I cannot bear it."

"I will never desert you."

After a moment's silence, Henry replies, "You are so much a part of me that I know what you will say before you utter a word. Do you remember one evening long ago, when I visited you and Theo in the country, we heard what sounded like the hoot of an owl? We both shuddered, thinking of all the furry little creatures holding still, trying to overcome the impulse to run, because they know any movement will result in instant death."

His words conjure up a clear image of a tiny mouse trying to repress the twitch of its body as the fearful hoots reverberate across the sky. "Henry, I'm afraid."

"We must part. Is that it, my dearest?"

My eyes fill with tears. "Henry, you remember long ago that we swore that our love would always be pure and that it would never take away from our love for our families?"

"Yes. Now you feel that your family is threatened. I must let you go even if it breaks my heart."

We are both silent. It's not only my family that is threatened, but his career and reputation. Henry's expression is somber, and I notice the slight sagging of his cheeks.

"Henry, let us pray, together."

"Yes, let us pray." Henry wipes away the tears and gestures for me to kneel beside him. We bow our heads.

"Lord, have mercy on us. Give us the strength to overcome our physical desires and purify our love. Without your divine guidance, we are caught in sin and suffering. Lead us to the light. Forgive us our limitations. Show us the path toward sacrifice, give us the fortitude to overcome selfishness, and embark on the voyage toward divine love."

"Amen."

Flory calls from downstairs, "Mother, the cook wants to know if you will have tea upstairs or down in the parlor."

I hastily open the door and call back, "We're coming down."

Henry is still kneeling in prayer. When he looks up, I kiss him on the forehead and give him my hand to help him up. He declines to take tea, telling Flory that he has several errands to run in the city before returning to Peekskill. At the door, he kisses me goodbye on the cheek, his eyes moist with tears. Then he walks away, his shoulders bent over, not looking back.

September 1870

Susan has been telling me that she is worried about the divisions in the suffrage movement. She says that some of the leaders won't listen to her call for a moderate platform that will appeal to larger numbers of women.

"Women like me, you mean, who put their children first." I smile at her and excuse myself to help the cook serve the children's dinner in the dining room.

When I rejoin Susan in the front parlor, she puts down the book she has been leafing through. "I wonder what has happened to Theodore and Elizabeth, I mean Mrs. Stanton. They were supposed to pick us up before six o'clock. We'll be late for supper at Laura Bullard's house."

I glance at the clock. It's almost seven. Something is not right. The plan was for all of us—Theo, Elizabeth Cady Stanton, Susan, and I—to go together to Laura's house. Later Susan would return with Theo and me and stay the night at our house.

"I can't imagine what is keeping them," I tell Susan. "I confess to feeling very hungry myself after watching the children eat. Ralph is such a good eater, but only if the meat and vegetables are cut up fine. The cook still doesn't know how to prepare things for him."

"All your children are so healthy."

"There is plenty of food. Maybe we should wait another hour or so and then go ahead and eat ourselves," I suggest as I sit down next to her in one of the big easy chairs.

"I cannot believe that they would just forget about us," Susan replies.

"Maybe they got very involved in some conversation about the editorial policy of the *Revolution* and forgot about the time."

"It seems very odd that they should go ahead with important policy discussions without me," she replies, and then quickly adds, "and *you*, Elizabeth."

"Oh, I am used to that. Theo never gives much importance to my opinion, but they certainly should have come back for you."

"Elizabeth, is there something wrong between you and Theo? I don't want to pry, but he seems very moody and preoccupied."

"Yes, things are not going well." I lower my head.

Susan is silent.

"He is always talking about free love," I begin tentatively.

"Yes, he seems obsessed with that topic," says Susan. "He is always talking with Elizabeth Stanton about divorce reform and the need for personal freedom. You know that I think women's rights must be protected in divorce cases, but the suffrage cause should not get involved with all sorts of newfangled social theories."

"It's not just politics," I say in a low voice. "I'm talking about my life and Theo's."

Susan looks into my eyes. "Of course, I have heard rumors, but I gave no credence to them. Theodore is devoted to you and the children."

"Yes, but that does not mean that he does not find that he has more in common with another lady. He believes in soul affinity," I stammer. "I believe in it, too." The heat of a sudden blush suffuses my face as I think of Henry.

Susan assures me that she understands what I am talking about. She also thinks that it is possible that certain souls have a special attraction for each other but believes that we have responsibilities that should override such feelings. She admits that she is old-fashioned about the marriage bond. "But, of course, I do not condemn others who may feel differently."

"Do you think it is a sin to break the marriage vow?"

"I don't think we should talk about sin. It is just that all this business of free love is likely to bring on heartbreak, most particularly for women. Society allows men more leeway."

I take a deep breath and tell her, "I know Theo practices free love. He has confessed his love affairs to me, and I also have . . ."

"You poor child." Susan reaches for my hand. "I heard rumors, but I had no idea. How could Theodore do such a thing to you? Elizabeth, you have been a perfect wife. Does he not understand how lucky he is?"

Susan's warm sympathy and support overwhelm me and the

tears flow. I tell her about Theo's various loves, but I cannot make myself tell the truth about Henry. I want to tell her. The truth is welling up inside me, but my lips won't form the words. True love can never be wrong. My love for Henry is pure, as is his love for me. But how do I explain this to my dear friend Susan? She's a social reformer, but can I be sure she will understand?

I serve supper to the two of us and then put the children to bed. As the evening wears on, Susan becomes more indignant. "Theodore's conduct is inexcusable!" she tells me. I'm not sure whether she is talking about his infidelity or his failure to fetch us for the supper meeting at Laura's house. I share my suspicions about Theo and Laura Bullard and then hasten to add that I am not certain.

"Laura is a good woman and she is very fond of the children," I tell Susan.

At that moment we hear the musical sound of the door chimes. Theodore comes in, in a gay mood, and greets the two of us, smiling.

For a moment we stare at him in silence, and then Susan says sternly, "We have been waiting for hours for you to pick us up."

"Was I supposed to pick you up? I thought Elizabeth wanted to stay home. I am so sorry there was a misunderstanding."

"Theodore," replies Susan, "there was no misunderstanding. Elizabeth said she could not go early in the afternoon because of her home responsibilities, but she expressly agreed to come later for supper at Mrs. Bullard's home. You said you would pick us up at six o'clock. Those were your precise words."

Theo looks embarrassed and mutters something about how he must have forgotten.

Susan, unwilling to let the matter drop, explains why she is so upset about this so-called misunderstanding. Ever since she took a strong stand that the Fifteenth Amendment should include votes for women as well as for the former slaves, Theodore and Mrs.

Stanton seem to think that her views are too extreme and she may be a liability to the movement. "If that is the case, the two of you should come out openly and tell me so! It is not right to forget to pick me up and then discuss editorial policy of the *Revolution* without me."

Theo protests in a humble tone that Susan is mistaken. It was strictly a social evening with hardly any mention of the *Revolution*. His words confirm my suspicions.

"He would have come back for you, Susan. He did not want *me* at the supper."

The two of them stare at me. I turn to Susan. "He thinks that I am not intelligent enough to be in such enlightened company. I will say something stupid, and he will be ashamed of me. He does not think I am the equal of Laura and Mrs. Stanton."

"Elizabeth, you are upset; you don't know what you are saying. I am so sorry, and I apologize to both you fine ladies." While saying this, Theo looks at me fixedly.

Ignoring him, I continue to address Susan. "He is just saying that. He looks for soul affinity with other ladies finer than I."

"Elizabeth, stop, stop it right now!" Theo says in a warning tone.

"No!"

Theo turns to Susan. "What has she been saying to you? Tell me; I should have the right to answer if she has been saying things about me."

I interject before Susan has a chance to reply, "You have no right to ask what we have been talking about unless you tell us what you and Laura and Mrs. Stanton were talking about. Tell me, what have you been telling them about me?"

"I have told them nothing but the truth," Theo replies.

Susan looks puzzled, but to me Theo's meaning is clear. He must have told them something about Henry and me.

"Very well, if you want truth-telling, I have been talking to Susan about your theory of free love, how you—"

Susan interrupts before I can go further. "My friends, I don't think I should be present at this argument. It is between husband and wife. The hour is late. It would be best if I go upstairs to retire for the night." She rises from her chair.

"No, please stay," I reply.

Susan sits down again and tells Theo, "Elizabeth was talking about all these theories of free love, which sound very attractive. But I was telling her that a good marriage is a very precious thing. The two of you should guard the wonderful family you have at all costs."

Theo replies as though he had not heard what Susan said. "I suppose she has been telling you that I am an unfaithful husband?"

"Well," replies Susan, "are you?"

"Maybe I am, but what about her? Do you know that she has taken Reverend Beecher as her lover?"

Susan draws in her breath sharply. I look down at the floor.

"No," she cries, "impossible! I do not believe it! How could you say such a thing about Elizabeth! My dear Theodore, you must be mistaken. Who has planted such suspicions in your mind?"

Theo and I rise simultaneously and begin shouting at once.

"She confessed, ask her yourself!"

"He's the one that started all this business of free love!"

"She chose my best friend to get revenge, don't you see?"

"Ask him how many lovers he's had!"

Theo has taken a few steps toward me, gesturing with his fists.

"Stop it! Both of you!" yells Susan.

Theodore collapses into his chair and covers his face with both hands. I sit back down next to Susan and weep. After several unsuccessful attempts to mediate, Susan once again announces her intention to retire. When she is halfway up the stairs, she turns and asks me to accompany her to the guest room. She says that we all need a good night's sleep and that everything will be much better in the morning.

I stand up. Theo takes a step forward to block my access to the stairs and calls after Susan, "Don't tell us what to do. How dare you tell Elizabeth where to sleep! She will sleep with me in our bedroom where she belongs."

Without making a reply, Susan turns around and continues her ascent. Theo takes my hand and says that we should sit down and discuss the matter calmly without interference from any third party. I sit in the chair that he guides me to, trying to control the trembling of my body and the sobs that rack me.

Theo offers to get me some drinking water from the pitcher we keep in the dining room. As he leaves the room I bolt for the stairs, but trip on the top step, and Theo catches up with me. He puts two hands on my waist and helps me right myself, but I pull away.

"Elizabeth, what are you doing? What is wrong with you? Come down so we can talk."

"I don't want to talk. I need to rest."

Theo grabs my arm.

"Let go! Don't touch me!" I scream, clinging to the banister.

Susan opens the door of the guest room. "Elizabeth, are you all right?"

Theo turns toward Susan and drops my arm. I rush into the guest room, almost knocking Susan over in my haste. She swiftly turns the latch.

"Open that door. Let me in!" Theo says this in an even tone, without raising his voice.

My fear is that he will break down the door. "I had better go to him," I whisper to Susan. "Otherwise, he will blame you."

She gestures me to be silent and says through the door, "Your wife needs to rest, Theodore. You need to rest, too. Trust me, everything will be better in the morning."

"What do you mean? How dare you come between my wife and me? You interfering old maid. Open the door at once. This is my house!" Theo yells, pounding on the door.

"Theodore, go away. Stop acting like a child. I will not open the door. You know it is quite useless to threaten me. Get some sleep!"

The pounding begins again, stops, and then we hear footsteps retreating. There is complete silence except for the faint sound of crickets.

Susan puts her arms around me. When my sobs have quieted, I relate the whole story, beginning with Theo's first confession. I describe the shared preferences and perspectives that drew Henry and me close together in a special harmony. Susan listens sympathetically, but her questions and comments show that she doesn't really understand the nature of the love that binds me to Henry. Like Theo, she thinks that the reverend has taken advantage of my innocence.

In response to Susan's gentle prodding, I attempt to define my feelings for Theo. Although I always feel small and insignificant when I am with him, I do love him, I protest with tears in my eyes, and I want to save the marriage and our family. A few weeks after confessing to Theo, I realized that he would never become reconciled to my friendship with Henry. It was like cutting out my own heart, but I broke off the love affair. I expected Theo to recover, as I did after he confessed that he loved another woman, but things are not getting better.

"I don't know what to do next."

"You know, Elizabeth, dear, time is a great healer. You and Theodore love one another. You have both made mistakes, but we all make mistakes. Your children need both parents. Why don't you take a breather? Go and visit a friend in another state for a few weeks and give Theo some time to pull himself together."

"I am afraid to leave him. He is so distraught he could do harm to himself."

"A short separation would ease the pressure on his mind."

"Sarah Putnam is in Ohio. She is always urging me to come visit her."

"Perfect."

I sit still, thinking over Susan's advice. The silence is absolute. Even the crickets are quiet.

"I think I should go to Theo."

"Elizabeth, don't. Let him think things over and calm down."

"Let me go to him," I plead. "I don't want him to blame all this on you."

"Don't worry about me. Theodore is used to my stubbornness. It is your safety I worry about."

After drowsing off, I awaken with a start and find Susan sleeping soundly at my side. Very quietly, I get up and go to the door. The latch creaks, but she sleeps undisturbed. When I tiptoe into my own bedroom, Theo is breathing evenly. My fears that he could harm himself are unfounded. I climb in beside him and feel the warmth of his body. He does not awaken. I lie next to him for a long time and then return to the guest room.

October 1870

Sarah Putnam opens her pale blue eyes wide in disbelief. "Elizabeth, how could he say such things? What has happened to Theodore? How could he accuse you, a modest and pious woman, of adultery? And with such a saintly man as Reverend Beecher? Has he lost his mind?"

"He has been very despondent," I reply, turning my head to be sure the door of the upstairs parlor where we are sitting in her house in Ohio is shut. It was a mistake to mention Theo's accusations.

"Oh, Elizabeth, my poor dear, when I received your letter saying there is trouble on the home front, I never imagined it could be something like this. You have always been a devoted wife, ministering to all Theo's needs, nursing him through his difficult moods. What could put such an idea into his head?"

To tell Sarah what really happened is impossible. Even Susan does not understand my love for Henry. If I tell Sarah, she will conclude that I am immoral, an impure woman. Or she'll blame Henry, see me as the victim of a conniving minister who seduces members of his congregation. And what if she confides in mutual friends? Dear God! Henry will lose his ministry, my marriage will be destroyed, and my children will be taken from me.

But some explanation of Theo's accusations must be given.

"It all began after Paul died," I tell Sarah. "Theo was paralyzed with grief and so was I. Reverend Beecher helped me recover faith in the goodness and mercy of God. I began to rely on Mr. Beecher's friendship, and Theo questioned why he visited so often."

"But surely he should understand your need for succor from your pastor at the time of the death of your child." Sarah frowns and shakes her gray curls as though trying to decipher a puzzle. "It is all those friends he cultivates, suffragists and champions of free love. That's the trouble! He is adopting their way of life himself," she says, looking at me significantly, for I have already mentioned Theo's infidelities, "and so he imagines that everyone is living according to the same immoral code."

I shift in my chair uncomfortably, conscious that Sarah is making judgments based on half-truths from my own lips.

"Theo's friends are not bad people," I say. "They believe in honesty and sincerity in human relations, that a marriage without love is not a true marriage but only a sham."

Sarah waves aside my attempt to defend the unorthodox opinions of Theo's circle. "I am ready to believe that they are sincere and well-meaning," she says, "but their doctrines are a dangerous threat to the basic institutions of civilized society, marriage, and the family. But let us not talk in generalities. What are you going to do, Elizabeth?"

"I came here to give Theo time to recover his balance and realize what harm he is doing to the children, to me, and to himself. Oh, Sarah, I think I am expecting, but I cannot go home, unless Theo promises to stop these accusations."

Sarah urges me to stay for as long as needed. "He'll come to his senses soon enough," she assures me. "He won't be able to live without you for more than a few weeks."

There is a knock on the door. It's Bessie, who has been staying with Sarah for several months to help out with her elderly mother-in-law. She is holding little Carroll by the hand.

"He was looking for you, ma'am."

Cad runs into the room and hugs me and then Sarah.

"Well, here's my big boy!" exclaims Sarah. With a friendly smile, she invites him to accompany her to the kitchen for some milk and cookies, and he follows her. We have been here only a few hours, but he already adores Sarah. She tells me to get some rest. She will put Carroll to bed. She takes him by the hand and goes downstairs.

Bessie starts to follow them and then hesitates at the doorway. "Can I get you something?"

"Come sit beside me." I smile invitingly. Bessie bounds back and sits next to me on the divan where I am resting. Looking very grown up, she must be several inches taller than I am, quite the young lady. Her hair is fashionably curled, but she wants me to comb it out the way I used to do at home.

After I have given her hair a thorough brushing, she abruptly puts her arms around me and holds me tight. "Oh, ma'am, I missed you so much. And the children, too! How I want to see Flory and Alice!"

I hug her back and notice with surprise that there are tears in her eyes.

"Ma'am, I love you very much," she says between sobs, and then turns away from me, embarrassed. I stroke her hair and tell her that I love her, too.

"Mrs. Putnam has been very good to me, but I want to go home with you," she tells me.

"You know, Bessie, I am not sure that I will be able to go home very soon," I reply. "Mr. Tilton and I are having problems, very serious problems."

There is a pause, and then Bessie says in her direct and forthright manner, "I could not help hearing what you and Sarah—Mrs. Putnam, I mean—were talking about."

"Bessie! That's eavesdropping!"

"I don't believe a word of it. Don't worry! No one will ever believe such lies about you."

"Bessie, I am innocent of wrongdoing. Mr. Tilton has been in very low spirits. His mood is bad. He has many problems in his job. But I am sure that with God's help he will come to his senses soon, and I can go home. Are you sure you want to go with me? Maybe it would be best for you to stay here with Mrs. Putnam for a couple more months."

"Ma'am, I want to go with you to help you. Please. Alice wrote and said she wants me to come home."

"Yes, I will take you with me," I reassure her, but Bessie is still frowning.

She blurts out, "Ma'am, I wanted to tell you something before, but I was afraid to."

"What, Bessie?"

"It's about Mr. Tilton." Bessie moves away from me to the far end of the divan. She does not meet my eyes but stares at a distant point on the floor.

"Tell me."

"It was when you went away for summer vacation with the children, but I stayed in the city." Bessie goes on to describe how Mr. Tilton has always been like a father to her. She has always been very grateful that he guided her reading so that she would not be a stupid and uneducated person. "He was always good to me, and never scolded me as much as you, ma'am, when I was naughty," she says, stealing a glance at my face.

"I know," I say smiling, "he often told me to be patient with you when you were little."

"That is why I don't know what to think," Bessie frowns in puzzlement, "because one night when you weren't there, he came to my room to kiss me good night, and then touched my hair and said that I had turned into a beautiful young lady and he was proud of me."

"What's wrong with that?" I query. "You don't think he should kiss you good night now that you are a grown-up young woman?"

"No, it wasn't that. But afterward he asked me if I should like to be married and put his hand on my neck. I said, 'Don't do that!' and then he told me that I am too shy and proper, and that ladies and gentlemen in the best society do that all the time. There is nothing wrong with it. He said that he would like to show me how a gentleman loves a lady. I should learn about that just like I learned to read good books and play the piano."

My fingers grip the side pillow. Bessie is like a daughter in the family. Do I mean so little to Theo that he must look for another woman right under our own roof?

"Did he do anything else?" I ask.

"No. I told him that I didn't think Mrs. Tilton would like that, and then I took his hand off my neck," says Bessie. "He went away, but afterward I didn't know what to think. Maybe he just wanted to say that he would explain to me in words about men and women when the time came, if he thought I needed to know . . . like before getting married or something." Bessie looks at me doubtfully. "You don't think he meant any harm, do you, ma'am?"

"You know, Bessie, Mr. Tilton is very fond of you and has always looked out for your best interests," I begin.

Bessie nods. It's obvious she expects me to defend him. All of a sudden, I find myself saying something quite differen t.

"A young lady like you has to be very careful. A man may act like a father at one moment and want something very different at the next moment. You don't know anything about the relations between husband and wife? How babies are made?"

Bessie shakes her head. "No, ma'am."

"Well, one day before you get married, I will explain it to you. You have to be careful not to let any man take away your virtue."

"Was Mr. Tilton trying to take away my virtue?"

"I hope not, but . . ."

"But what?"

"He has seduced other young women."

Bessie stares at me.

Enough said to warn her, but I can't refrain from saying a few words about Theo's affairs, details that a young girl doesn't need to know.

Bessie's shoulders slump, and she clutches her head with her two hands.

"Don't worry," I tell her, putting my arm around her shoulders, "I will take care of you. Just be sure you tell me if anything like that ever happens again."

"Yes, ma'am, I will."

Our conversation is cut short by the entrance of Sarah, who announces that Carroll has finally fallen asleep. Bessie says good night and then kisses me impulsively before leaving.

"I think she has been lonely without you," Sarah says. "She is always talking about you, Elizabeth. She loves you like a mother."

I wish that I could take back what I told Bessie about Theo. Maybe he meant no harm. But if all he wanted was to educate Bessie about the relations between men and women, why didn't he ask me to talk to her?

November 1870

"Ma'am, there is Mr. Tilton with the carriage," cries Bessie. "He doesn't see us."

We are standing with our baggage in the train station. "Here, let me hold Carroll while you go after him," I reply.

Soon Bessie and Theodore come running up to us. Theo grabs Carroll and me in a giant embrace. "How is my best girl?" he says, kissing me. "You both look healthy," he says to Carroll and me. "It must be Sarah's excellent food!" Carroll clings to Theo. "Well, Cad, my little man, you are almost a world traveler. How did you like the train ride? Did you have a sleeping berth?"

It is a great relief to get out of the cold November wind and into the carriage. I'm weary, for I hardly slept on the train, but my spirits lift as the carriage turns into our street and the houses of our neighbors come into view. Our own tall and sturdy house, with square lines and a wide veranda stretching all across the front, comes into view. The poplars, which were just saplings when we first came, almost reach to the second story now.

When we alight, the girls come running out of the house to greet us. I admonish them to hurry back inside before they catch their death of a cold, but they protest that it isn't even below freezing, and so far this fall it hasn't even snowed in Brooklyn. Once inside, they crowd around me with questions about our stay in Ohio.

Flory and Alice snuggle up to me while we talk, one on each side. Then they both dash off to talk to Bessie. I suddenly realize that my baby Ralph is nowhere in sight. Theo assures me that he is just fine and so fat that I will hardly recognize him. The new housekeeper, Mrs. Ellen Dennis, is excellent with little ones.

Mrs. Dennis is feeding Ralph some porridge in the dining room. She is a tall woman, her face dominated by a large nose, and her hair worn simply in a bun. After greeting her, I rush over to give Ralph a kiss. He stops eating, beams, and gurgles at me. I hold out my arms to pick him up.

"Oh, Mrs. Tilton, can you wait a moment? We don't want to interrupt baby's breakfast, do we now? There, Ralphie, that's a good boy. Have another spoonful."

"Here, I can feed him."

"Oh no, Mrs. Tilton, you must be tired after your trip. Why don't you sit down in the back parlor? It will just be a couple more moments and I will bring him to you."

I enter the back parlor and notice it looks different. The sofa is no longer facing the window, and one of the easy chairs has been removed. The leafless poplar in the backyard, its branches swaying in the wind, looks forlorn. When Mrs. Dennis brings Ralph to me, I eagerly take him in my arms, but he is shy of me and emits a few fretful cries.

"Don't worry, ma'am. You have been gone for a long time, but he will be used to you again in no time."

Without a glance at Mrs. Dennis, I begin to play peek-a-boo with Ralph, finally getting a smile out of him.

After we have all breakfasted, Theo urges me to take a nap. He follows me upstairs, pulls me close, and says how happy he was to receive my last letter confirming that I am indeed expecting.

"Let our new baby be a fresh start," I tell him, hugging him close. "We will forget everything that has happened in the past and go forward."

He says that he is sure the approaching New Year will bring us good fortune. There have been some problems with Mr. Bowen, the proprietor of the *Independent*, but he is sorting everything out. On the home front, he is confident that I will be very pleased with the services of Mrs. Dennis. "Don't worry about anything, dear. Try to get some rest."

After Theo leaves, I fall into a deep, dreamless sleep. Bessie, tiptoeing into the room, awakens me. Her eyes are red and swollen. Drowsily, I inquire, "Is there something wrong?"

Bessie flings herself onto the bed beside me, sobbing loudly about an encounter with Mrs. Dennis. It all began when Alice insisted on making cookies. Happy to oblige, Bessie was supervising the mixing of the dough, when the housekeeper appeared and demanded to know what she thought she was doing. "She acted like I was a servant!" Bessie cries. "She ordered me out of the kitchen like trash."

She goes on to describe how Alice cried and begged to be allowed to finish the first batch, but Mrs. Dennis said there had to be some discipline in this house. When Bessie defied her, Mr. Tilton intervened to insist that the new housekeeper should be obeyed. "Ma'am, I reminded him that I have been taking care of the children since Carroll was born, and I know which activities are permitted to them. Mr. Tilton just told me to be quiet and not bother him. He always used to tell me how good I am with the children, but now he acts like I am not needed anymore."

I tell Bessie that things will sort themselves out, but she wails, "Ma'am, you don't understand—that woman wants to replace you as mistress."

When I come down for dinner, Mrs. Dennis is seated at the foot of the table where I usually sit, next to Ralph's chair. Bessie, her countenance glum, asks the housekeeper whether she is aware that the seat she is occupying is Mrs. Tilton's. Mrs. Dennis replies that it is more convenient for her to be near the kitchen so she can supervise the help.

I am about to say something when Theo remarks, "Yes, that makes sense, don't you think so, dear?"

I move to the seat on the other side of Ralph and take up my knife and fork to chop his meat more finely.

Mrs. Dennis looks at me. "Oh, ma'am, Ralphie is a big boy now. He can handle big chunks. Can't you, sweetie pie?"

"He is only seventeen months old. I don't want him to choke."

"My dear," interjects Theodore, "you have to let him grow up. Mothers always like their children to stay babies forever. He made great progress while you were away. Let's not go backward now."

I stop cutting Ralph's meat and slice my own, but my appetite is gone, and the tears well up in my eyes.

Theo says sweetly, "Why aren't you eating, dear? This meat is delicious. Mrs. Dennis has found a new butcher who provides excellent cuts."

I rise quickly and go into the adjoining back parlor and then start up the stairs. Hearing my name mentioned, I linger for a moment, listening to the conversation at the dinner table. Theo is asking Bessie whether there is anything wrong with Mrs. Tilton. "She is acting so strangely. Did anything happen in Ohio or on the train to upset her?"

"Oh no, sir," replies Bessie, "she is fine, but any lady will get upset if people don't give her respect as mistress of the house."

"Bessie, what are you saying? No one is being disrespectful. On the contrary, everything is being arranged so that Mrs. Tilton can have the rest she needs in her condition."

"When I was this young lady's age," interjects Mrs. Dennis, "young people did not talk disrespectfully to the father of the house."

"She is the one being disrespectful!" cries Bessie. "What does she know about the customs of this family? Nothing, but she is telling everyone what to do!"

"Bessie, I forbid you to talk that way. You should be setting an example for the children instead of acting like a spoiled brat yourself." Theo's statement is followed by silence. Hearing nothing further, I go upstairs and lie down.

After a few minutes, Theo enters the bedroom and says that he hopes that I have calmed down sufficiently to listen to what he has to say. It is very difficult to get good help these days, and now that our family is so large, we need a housekeeper to supervise. He points out that I have never been a good household manager. "My dear, I don't know why you are hostile to Mrs. Dennis, who is an excellent manager and ready to take the burden off your shoulders."

"What are you saying? I am not hostile. Who is mistress? I may not be the perfect household manager in your eyes, but no one has ever questioned the way I raise my own children."

"Don't be irrational, Elizabeth. None of us is perfect. We can always listen to suggestions."

"What does she know? How dare she tell me how to feed my baby? And you supported her in front of the children."

A few moments later, Bessie bursts into the bedroom without knocking, crying, "Oh, ma'am, that woman won't let me give Carroll his milk. He always has milk after supper, but she says it is not good for him to have milk so late." She stops short when she sees Theo seated in the rocker near the window.

"Sit down, Bessie, I want to talk to you, too."

Bessie sits down at the foot of the bed next to my feet, her back straight as a rod, her expression somber. Theo ignores me and turns his attention to our ward.

"Bessie," he says in a softer tone, "you know that Mrs. Tilton is not a good household manager. While she was away resting in Ohio, I was left with three children and a nonfunctioning household. I found an excellent woman and now Mrs. Tilton wants to throw her out."

"But, sir, Mrs. Dennis was disrespectful to Mrs. Tilton, and she wants to get rid of me."

"Bessie, no one is trying to get rid of you," Theo says in a reassuring tone, "and if they do, I won't let them. I want you to be patient and tell Mrs. Tilton to be patient, too. She is very upset now and cannot think clearly. She is overworked with such a big family and so are you. I have always wanted what is best for all. You are a mature young lady now and I know I can count on you to help out. All I want is what is best for the family and best for you." Theo never looks at me while he makes this appeal. Bessie's body relaxes. Theo smiles at her.

I begin to tremble, acutely aware of the smallness and weakness of my body. Theo is not going to get away with playing the caring husband and father. Leaning forward, I enunciate each word slowly. "Theodore, you say you want what is best for the family and what is best for Bessie. Then why did you attempt to ruin her when I was in the country? Tell me, were you doing what was best for her then?"

Bessie draws her breath in sharply. Theo starts and looks at me wide-eyed. I shrink back, but he turns toward Bessie and continues to address her in the same reasonable tone of voice.

"Bessie, did you hear that? Unbelievable! Your mistress must be demented to say something like that. I have always been like a father to you. Tell her, my dear child, that she is imagining things. I would never harm a hair of your head."

Bessie looks at me and then at Theo. She has the hunted look of a small animal waiting for the hawk to strike, but she straightens her back and says in a low but steady voice, "Sir, you talked to me about spiritual affinities, and touched me and said you would teach me about—"

"Stop, you're lying, you ungrateful wench! Elizabeth, don't listen to her, don't believe a word she says. I never said anything like that. It is all a pack of lies!"

I am silent.

"Oh, you have nothing to say. You believe her, then?" Getting no reply, Theo rises from the chair, approaches the bed, and takes me by the shoulders. "Tell me, do you believe her?"

I turn away my head.

"Ah, now I understand the lay of the land. Bessie must have told you that I talked to her about relations between men and women, in strictly theoretical terms, mind you. And then you, my dear wife, put it into her head that I was insulting her and ruining her virtue. Is that how it was? You are trying to turn her against me." He shakes me to and fro.

"Don't hurt her, sir. Please don't hurt her!" yells Bessie.

Theodore releases me. I clutch my neck.

"Stop playacting, Elizabeth. I did not hurt you." And then he turns to Bessie. "My dear child, I forgive you. I know that you don't want to accuse me of something that is not true. Tell me, has she been telling you all sorts of lies about me and other women? Making up stories about me?"

"No, sir, Mrs. Tilton never made up stories about you."

"I know you want to protect her, but I promise I would never hurt her. Tell me the truth, Bessie. What did she say about me?"

"Nothing, nothing." Bessie is crying.

"Be that as it may," Theo says very softly, "I have something to tell you about her. You think she is a pure and chaste woman, a model Christian, don't you?"

"Yes."

He approaches me again and turns my head roughly so that I am directly facing Bessie. "Look at her! Do you know that this good Christian woman confessed to me that she has committed adultery with Reverend Beecher? Do you know what *adultery* means?"

"No! No! It is all lies!" Bessie screams. "Leave her alone! You are lying! Don't you dare touch her!"

Theo raises a fist in front of my face. Bessie lunges to protect me, and he pushes her aside with a violent blow. She falls hard, hitting her head against the foot of the wooden chest of drawers. "Oh, my God! Theo, what have you done?" I exclaim.

We both rush over. Theo helps Bessie rise and sit on the bed. She is trembling violently. He protests that he did not mean to hit her. He was waving his arm to make a point, and she just happened to move that way. It was an accident.

"It's all right, sir. I'm not much hurt."

He sits down beside her and begs her forgiveness, explaining that he has been under great strain lately. His work at the *Independent* has been going badly, and his wife's betrayal is torturing his soul. If Bessie will only forgive him, he will be able to recover and go forward. Bessie maintains a sullen silence.

I go into the next room. Bessie comes in to tell me that Mr. Tilton has gone out and puts her arms around me.

"I can't stay here," I tell her. "I have to go to my mother's house."

"Ma'am, please take me with you."

Mid-December 1870

A small dark room on the first floor of my mother's house that used to be a spare bedroom now serves as a sitting room. The bright and airy parlor of my young days has long since been converted into the best room, let to boarders. The present sitting room has a single side window, which faces the neighboring house with only a narrow, treeless alley between. The stuffed furniture is too large for the small space, and bric-a-brac decorations on every available surface contribute to the atmosphere of clutter. The heavy drapes on the window sag and the white gauzelike lacy inner curtains are yellowed with age.

The spacious rooms and large windows of my own home were the features that most attracted Theo when he decided on the purchase. When I first saw the house, I was also charmed by the simple, square lines of the architecture. After we moved in, Theo insisted that the cluttered look of my mother's home should be avoided. He said that it would be better to have a few original paintings by artists of real quality rather than plaster the walls with sentimental reproductions. In spite of some initial discord about the style of decoration, together we created a home that we can be proud of.

My reflections are interrupted by the entrance of my mother into the sitting room. Although I did up her hair early this morning, it already looks disheveled. Her eyes are very bright and her cheeks flushed.

"Something must be done, my dear child. This cannot go on."

Mother has not mentioned the word *divorce*, which she always denounced, but she has been urging me to get a formal separation. "You need good advice and help from someone with influence and standing in the community," she tells me. "I have sent Bessie with an urgent message for Mr. Beecher. It is his duty to help you."

"Mother, no! How could you send Bessie on such an errand without consulting me? How long ago did she leave?"

"She has been gone for an hour."

"Mother, how could you do this to me? What did you tell her to say to Mr. Beecher? Oh my God, you must have instructed her to tell him about Theo's accusations against me. Mother, how could you? I specifically told you that I do not want him to know."

My mother is about to reply when Bessie comes bounding into the room.

"Bessie, what have you done?"

"I talked with Reverend Beecher just as Grandma Morse instructed me," Bessie says. Then she catches my expression. "Oh, ma'am, you didn't want me to tell him?"

"What's done is done. It's not your fault," I tell Bessie while glaring at my mother. "Just tell me everything you said. Please, Bessie, do not hold anything back. I need to know."

According to Bessie, she obtained a private audience with Mr. Beecher and informed him in detail about Mr. Tilton's abusive behavior since our return from Ohio. She spoke of Mr. Tilton's rages and the imposition of a strange housekeeper who bosses everyone around and cooperates with him to deprive me of my rightful place as mistress of the household. When I pressure her to tell whether she revealed anything about Mr. Tilton's accusations against me, she swears that she never said a word. After a pause, she admits, "But I did tell the reverend all about how Mr. Tilton attempted to ruin me, and how he struck me." She informs us that Mr. Beecher appeared concerned, exclaimed that he had no idea that there was any such trouble in the Tilton household, and finally said that either he or his wife would come to see us.

"Bessie, have you told anyone else about Mr. Tilton's advances?"

"Yes, I told Mrs. Bradshaw and Mrs. Ovington and—"

"Oh my God, Bessie, why did you do that? There are enough rumors going around."

"But, ma'am," says Bessie, "we have to defend you. People will believe that the separation is your fault."

"Yes," cries my mother, "that knave of a husband of yours is busy circulating rumors. Why shouldn't we?"

"But Mother, don't you understand? Rumors do harm. It will become a never-ending cycle of accusations."

Bessie shakes her head, leans forward in her chair, and cries, "What Mr. Tilton says about you, ma'am, is a lie, and he is a rumor-monger because he is circulating untruths. I am not circulating rumors, because I am telling the truth about him!" She looks from my mother to me, seeking confirmation.

My mother says nothing. I avoid their eyes and gaze at the floor. Bessie begins to cry. I finally get up, put my arms around her, and tell her I know she means well.

The following day my mother calls up to me that Reverend Beecher and Mrs. Beecher have arrived. I stop folding the children's laundry, straighten my clothes, and descend the narrow, dark staircase. As I enter the downstairs sitting room, Eunice rises, embraces me, and guides me to a seat next to Henry.

"You poor dear," she exclaims, "we have been so concerned about you and the children. Don't worry. Everything will be all right."

I have seen Mrs. Beecher but seldom in the last few years and only to exchange greetings at church. She is about the same age as my mother, dresses soberly but with care, and speaks in a forthright but kindly manner. On first impression, she doesn't seem as cold and critical as both Theo and Henry had led me to expect.

While listening to the reassuring words of his wife, I am acutely conscious of Henry's presence at my side. We are sitting so close that I can smell the characteristic odor that emanates from his body mixed with the scent of his hairdressing. A physical longing for him causes a wave of heat to flush my face with an involuntary blush.

Mrs. Beecher is asking me questions about Theodore's mistreatment. I reply in monosyllables. Mother proceeds to fill in the details. She talks of Theodore as a bad-tempered man whose moods have gotten worse over the years to the point of threatening his wife with physical violence. Then she complains that he lost his Christian faith and associates with all sorts of objectionable people with radical social ideas who should not be invited to a decent Christian household.

"He's an immoral man," she tells Henry and his wife. "Let me tell you—"

"Mother, please. I don't want to talk about it."

Henry interjects, "I'm not worried about Theodore's religious views. He has always been a seeker after his own truth. Most of his friends are decent people, even if they do have some wild ideas."

My mother raises her eyebrows.

"What does worry me," Henry adds, "is the way Theodore takes out his despairing moods on his family."

"He abandoned his wife and children and left them destitute!"

"But, Mother, he did not abandon us. I left him. I haven't asked him for money."

Henry says quickly that the situation is complicated. He does not think that I should take any precipitate action without due consideration of the consequences.

Later Mother invites Mrs. Beecher upstairs, saying she wants to show her the new furnishings. They seem to be on excellent terms. As the sound of footfalls ascending the staircase ceases, Henry turns to me and says in a low voice, "Elizabeth, tell me what this is all about. Why didn't you tell me before?"

Tears fill my eyes, but I do not give way to the impulse to weep. In a shaking voice I reply, "I thought it would get better. Theo has been through despondencies before."

"Your mother thinks that you should separate from Theo." Henry smiles slightly. "He's incorrigible, according to her."

"She has always exaggerated his faults. I feel uncomfortable here," I gesture toward the surroundings, "but I don't think I can go home yet. The children want to go home."

Henry takes my hand. "Elizabeth, tell me truly, do your troubles with Theo have anything to do with me?"

I hesitate. How do I explain why I confessed to Theo? At the time it seemed like the right thing to do. Telling the truth would strengthen our marriage. But Henry will blame me for betraying our secret. And if he tries to talk to Theo, who knows what could happen? They could even come to blows.

We hear footfalls descending the stairs. Henry quickly drops my hand, and I say in a whisper: "No, my friend, it has nothing to do with you."

Mrs. Beecher and Mother enter the room. Henry says that we should pray together. We all kneel and he asks God to give us guidance to do what is right and best for my troubled family. As they are leaving, Henry promises that they will get back to us tomorrow.

The next morning, the doorbell rings early. I hear the voice of Eunice Beecher returning my mother's greetings, and she enters the small sitting room alone. She politely explains that the reverend has been detained by visitors. In appreciation of the urgency of my plight, she decided to come alone. Mother plies her with offers of refreshment and then withdraws.

Mrs. Beecher begins with an expression of sympathy for my stoic endurance of so much suffering. I am silent, offering neither affirmation nor denial.

"Listen, Elizabeth, under ordinary circumstances I am against divorce, but there are some things no woman should put up with."

I don't answer.

"Physical abuse is one. Another is infidelity, especially if repeated, as in this case."

I look at the floor.

"I consider you like a niece. That's why I'm telling you this. If the reverend did anything like that to me, I would divorce him with no qualms whatsoever, let me tell you."

Her voice is no longer kindly. Mrs. Beecher is looking me straight in the eye, a challenging look, disapproving of my indecision. Now I understand how Henry has suffered having to live with her smug righteousness. She thinks her marriage is perfect compared to mine. If only I could tell her that her husband has been as unfaithful as mine.

"I'm not sure. I have to think about the children. You know, Theodore has always been a good father. He didn't used to be like this."

"You don't have to ask for a divorce right away. Just petition for legal separation and support."

"I think I should try one more time to save my family."

I don't tell her about the bouts of morning sickness I have been experiencing. She's not the sort of woman you can confide in.

Eunice shakes her head. "Elizabeth, do not expose yourself to more hurt! If a man has been unfaithful more than once, there is little chance that he will mend his ways."

"But don't you believe that to love means to forgive? God forgives all and asks us to try to follow in his footsteps," I exclaim.

"Some things are unforgivable," replies Mrs. Beecher, "but I will say no more. If you need legal advice or any other aid, you can count on us and the Plymouth Church community."

She rises from her chair. Without a word, I show her to the door.

The following day, while my mother is out, the bell rings. Could it be Henry? I want to speak to him about my marriage. His advice might be different if his wife is not in the room. But, no, it would be too dangerous for him to visit me without Eunice. Reluctantly, I go to open the door. It's Theo.

He seizes my hand. I shrink back. He says he will go away if I don't want to talk to him, but to please give him a chance. We sit down in the parlor. He begs me to return home, vowing to overcome his morbid state of mind if only I come back to him.

For a brief moment, he glances downward at my hands folded over the curve of my belly. Then, his eyes fixed on mine, he says, "My own darling, we have both made mistakes in the past, but we will make a fresh start."

I hesitate.

"And don't worry about Mrs. Dennis," he assures me. "I talked with her, and you will find that from now on she will treat you with the respect you deserve, or we will find a new housekeeper."

Theo is finally thinking about how I feel. The tears are rolling down my cheeks.

He rises from his chair and gets on his knees. In this position his head is level with mine, just as it was when he proposed marriage. We were so young then, and so much in love.

"Please, Elizabeth. I cannot live without you."

I consent to go home.

Miscarriage and Recovery

Late December 1870

"I never saw any of my patients lose so much blood in a miscarriage," says a woman's voice.

Everything is whirling past me in a blur, but then my eyes focus and I realize that it is Mrs. Mitchell speaking, the same nurse who attended me during the birth of Paul.

"Yes, she was unconscious when I was called, and she has been hemorrhaging profusely for two days," replies the doctor, "but the bleeding is slowing."

"Thanks be to the Lord," exclaims the nurse. "She has four children who would have been left motherless. Oh, my dear," she says turning to me, "you are awake."

I try to smile. The pain is almost gone. The nurse bends to change the soaked cloth, and the blood flow feels warm against my inner thighs.

"I believe that the danger is over," the doctor says kindly, "but she needs a long period of bed rest with no disturbance and plenty of fluids. She will continue to bleed for several more days, but call me immediately if the flow increases or she passes large clots."

After the doctor leaves, I rouse myself to tell Mrs. Mitchell how glad I am that she has come to attend me. She puts her finger to her lips to tell me that there is no need to talk just now. As I slowly come to a realization of what has happened, the relief in the absence of pain that I felt when I first awakened gives way to grief. It is Christmas, time of joyful renewal, but I have lost my baby. It was this child who was to give Theo and me a new start. I struggle to lift my head from the pillow and begin to lament my misfortune out loud.

Mrs. Mitchell strokes my head soothingly, but her voice is firm when she admonishes me not to question the will of God. It is true that I have lost my unborn baby, but my own life has been spared. I must not let myself get agitated. I need rest to restore my health so that my children will have a mother. Mrs. Mitchell sits with me for a bit and then quietly leaves, closing the folding doors, which open to the upstairs parlor, behind her.

I doze off and later I awaken to the sound of Theo's voice. He is talking to his good friend Frank Moulton in the adjoining sitting room. Frank is asking after my health. Very thoughtful of him, but he should keep his voice down. All I want is to go back to sleep, but I am not capable of getting up from bed to suggest they talk elsewhere.

Once informed that the doctor believes that I am out of danger, Frank moves on to another topic. He remarks that it is too bad that Theo can no longer continue as editor of the *Independent*, but perhaps as a contributor he will have more freedom and be able to do some other writing.

Theo says yes, he welcomes more freedom to express his views. And his income shouldn't be too much affected, because Bowen still wants him to continue as editor of his secular paper, the *Brooklyn Union*.

After a short pause Theo goes on, "But I'm worried, really worried. There are people trying to turn Mr. Bowen against me."

My eyes open, and I listen with full attention.

"Why do you think so?" inquires Frank.

"Today, I went in to talk to Bowen and he informed me that there are rumors making the rounds about my private life."

"Anything specific?"

"He mentioned rumors that I am about to elope to Europe with

Laura Bullard, but I laughed in his face and said that she is a close friend of my wife's and nothing could be further from the truth. He also referred to a woman I supposedly met on my speaking tours in the West. I denied any impropriety."

"People should never cite rumors unless they are willing to give details so the subject of the rumor can defend himself," Frank says disapprovingly. "I wonder what Bowen is getting at."

"I don't know, but he also advised me that I should take a more moderate political line in the *Brooklyn Union* and give more news of Plymouth Church, since many subscribers are members."

"It's supposed to be a secular paper," replies Frank. "It seems somewhat out of line to pressure you in that way."

"Bowen is a religious man . . . perhaps not always honest, but very religious."

Frank chuckles. "The two do not always go together. Indeed, I have known people guilty of the most grievous sins who adopt a cloak of piety to cover their misdeeds."

"Bowen went so far as to chide me for not attending Plymouth Church, although he sees my wife and children there regularly."

"What did you say to that?" asks Moulton.

After a short silence, Theo answers in an unnaturally high voice, "I told him that I would never set foot in Plymouth Church again because the pastor is an impostor."

I raise my head from the pillow.

"Careful, Theo, Mr. Beecher is highly respected in this community," admonishes Frank in a quiet tone. "Neither your wife nor mine would be happy to hear such comments."

"My wife knows very well what he is . . . he attempted to seduce her. I used to think he was a great man, an earnest defender of all that is right . . . but I was mistaken. He uses his position as a minister of God to play upon the religious sentiments of women."

Upon hearing this, I stifle a cry of protest. My husband is breaking all his promises to me.

"Theo," rejoins Frank, "what are you saying? I know that you have often said humorously that Mr. Beecher preaches to his mistresses every Sunday, but surely you are imagining things. He would never show such lack of respect to Elizabeth or to you."

In an excited tone, Theo assures him that it is true. Frank warns him to lower his voice and expresses the hope that Theo did not mention this suspicion to Bowen, who is a financial pillar of Plymouth Church.

"Indeed, I did, for Bowen once told me years ago that there was a similar incident with his own wife. He believes that Beecher succeeded in seducing her." Theo goes on to say that Bowen was sympathetic and urged Theo to expose Beecher for what he really is. The words he used, according to Theo, were: "Brooklyn should be rid of this blight." Theo tells Frank that Bowen suggested he write a letter demanding Henry's resignation. Together they drafted a note saying that Henry should quit the pulpit and leave Brooklyn forthwith.

"Who signed the note?" asks Frank in a worried tone.

"I did."

"And Mr. Bowen?"

"No, he said he could not sign but he would back me up. I gave him the note to give to Henry."

"Oh my God, Theodore," Moulton remonstrates, "he is using you. He got you to sign a letter attacking the reputation of the greatest preacher in the country. Either he is trying to use you to settle an old score with Beecher, or else he is attempting to break up your friendship with the reverend so that Beecher will not object when Bowen fires you from the *Brooklyn Union*. What proof do you have that he urged you to send the letter? What if Bowen, instead of backing you up, sides with Beecher? You will lose everything."

There is a long pause. I strain to hear more. Finally, Theo says in a worried voice, "Frank, do you really think so? Surely Bowen would not sink so low."

Frank says that he will have to think the situation through. He has an appointment in half an hour, but he will try to pass by tomorrow.

"Please come as soon as you can, I will be waiting for you," says Theo. "I have been so despondent in recent weeks. My judgment is not good."

Receding footfalls indicate Theo is escorting his friend out. My whole body is trembling. I call out for Theo over and over again. Flory looks in and says she will run downstairs to fetch her father. When Theo enters the room, he seems confused and mutters something about how he thought I was in the back bedroom. I strain to sit up, but then I fall back.

"Elizabeth, are you all right? You look very pale. Don't try to sit up. Shall I call the doctor?"

"No, don't call the doctor! I want to die. Do you hear me? I want to die!"

Theo stares at me.

"Don't pretend that you care whether I die or not. You have betrayed me. You swore that you would never reveal anything if I was honest with you and you would never harm Henry, but you are trying to destroy both him and me. Hypocrite! Liar!"

I have finally managed to sit up, and as I do so there is a rush of warm blood between my thighs.

"Elizabeth, lie down; you are very ill. Now tell me what this is all about."

"You know what it is all about. I heard you talking with Frank. Oh, Theo, you swore you loved me and we forgave each other, and I came back home, but your heart is filled with hatred. You will destroy Henry and his mission, all the good work that he has done. And the reason for your campaign of hatred will come out. The whole world will know. I will be ruined and the children will be ruined. Oh, why didn't I die? I want to die!"

Theo stammers that he may have made a mistake, but I should trust him. He will find a way to be sure that no harm comes to me. I must not worry. He will go now and fetch the nurse. As he hastily leaves the room, I sink back exhausted, feeling dizzy and nauseated.

The nurse is alarmed by my pallor and exclaims that my hands and feet feel icy cold. She fetches another quilt. I lie still, looking out the window. The wave of vertigo and nausea recedes. There is a layer of snow on the ground and the sky is still gray. The window rattles, and swirls of powdery snow are borne aloft by the wind. I cannot get warm.

In spite of the cold, exhaustion overcomes me, and I sleep the night through, only dimly conscious that the nurse has been sleeping beside me and checking on me from time to time. When I open my eyes, it is morning. The nurse asks me whether I am hungry. To my surprise the prospect of food is welcome. Yesterday I wanted to die, but today my wayward body has decided to live. With the nurse's help, I sit up and eat several spoonsful of porridge and drink some warm milk. She says that the return of appetite is a sure sign that I am on the road to recovery.

Upon my request, the nurse permits the children to visit me one at a time for not more than five minutes. Alice stays the longest, chattering about who has come by to call with Christmas greetings, and how everyone is alarmed about my poor health. The nurse finally shoos her out, saying that I have to guard my strength.

Left alone, I say a silent prayer and sleep. When the natural light is already dimming because of the early onset of winter sunset,

I hear Theo's quick step on the stair. He bursts into the room, says something about being relieved that I am recovering, and then without waiting for a reply he cries out, "God help me! I am a ruined man!"

"What is it? Tell me. Come, sit here beside me."

Theo sits down on the bed and seizes my hand in his. He is very pale.

"My God, Theo, what has happened?"

Theo is so upset that he has some difficulty in explaining. He exclaims that he has been a fool and that the conversations with Frank brought him to consciousness that Bowen was using him as an instrument to achieve his own ends and probably misrepresented everything to Henry. At about one o'clock when Mr. Bowen entered the office, Theo told him that he had decided to speak directly to Henry about the note. Mr. Bowen looked very peculiar and demanded to know what exactly he had in mind.

When Theo replied that he wanted to make his own position clear without intermediaries, Mr. Bowen became incensed and said with a sneer, "So you think Beecher is a friend of yours, and you will explain everything and put the blame on me? Let me make one thing perfectly clear. If you say one word to Mr. Beecher about what I told you in confidence about my wife, I will cancel all your contracts and make sure that your career in journalism is over. Don't fool yourself into thinking it will be easy to persuade the reverend that the note was my idea rather than yours. Let me tell you, Mr. Beecher does not have a high opinion of your character. He gave me an earful about your personal misconduct. Your wife is fed up with your affairs and she is considering a divorce, isn't she? Mrs. Beecher told an even more interesting story about your moral character. Apparently, it is your custom to debauch innocent servant girls!"

"No! No! No! Theo, this cannot be true!" I exclaim.

"You see, I am surrounded by enemies, and the chief of my enemies is my own mother-in-law! Oh, Elizabeth, how could you tell Bessie that I meant her harm? You have turned her against me, and your mother is spreading the false story all over Brooklyn."

I stare at him. My stomach contracts and I wonder whether I am again hemorrhaging. "Theo, Bessie was the one who came to me to tell me she was upset. I just told her to be careful."

"Careful of a man who has always loved her as a father, who has encouraged her education so that she can raise her station in life? Oh, Elizabeth, how could you have so little faith in me? Do you want to destroy me?"

I cringe.

Theo goes on in a softer voice, "I'm sorry. Forgive me! I cannot really believe that you would want to destroy me. It must be all your mother's idea. Yes, she turned your mind against me, the poisonous witch, and then started cooperating with Eunice Beecher to ruin me. Henry, who used to be my closest friend, has joined the coven."

My mind is racing. Theo, as usual, thinks that it is everyone's fault but his own. He was the one who took the first hostile step by writing to Henry to demand he resign from the pulpit. Our livelihood is in danger if Henry continues to side with Bowen. If the conflict between Theo and Henry continues, Theo might make an open accusation of adultery, ruining my reputation and Henry's career as well. The children will suffer. Oh, my God, give me strength to say the right thing.

"Theo," I venture, "you know I don't really believe that Henry is your enemy. When I was at Mother's place, she called him over to talk about legal separation. Mr. Beecher defended you when Mother was denouncing your radical friends and he even defended your religious views. He advised caution. It was Mrs. Beecher who pushed me to get a legal separation, not Henry."

"I didn't know that."

"It is not Henry but Mr. Bowen who is trying to make you look bad so he can break the contracts he signed with you."

Theo sits down, cradles his head in his hands, and laments that it is too late and there is nothing to be done now. I urge him to think more positively. Henry has been his friend for a decade and still harbors a real affection for him. We must invite Henry over immediately and explain to him that the note was Bowen's idea.

"You see, Theo," I explain, "Henry has no idea that I made a confession to you. He therefore cannot possibly understand why you would write such a hostile note."

"Elizabeth, what are you saying? I thought he knew. For God's sake, why didn't you tell me that?"

"You never asked. I thought telling him would only make things worse." After a pause, I continue, "Listen, we must invite Henry over. I will tell him that you were reacting to my confession so that he understands your desperate state of mind, and you can assure him that you have cooled down and thought things over, and for your wife's sake you withdraw the note and forswear any intention to do him harm. Then perhaps he can intercede with Bowen to save your job at the *Brooklyn Union*."

Theo stares at me.

"Theo, it is the only way to save your job, my reputation, and our family. Please, we must do something quickly."

"No!" Theo rises and begins pacing the room once more. "What you say makes sense, but I cannot do it. I cannot welcome him into my house and sit down together with him and my wife. No! It cannot be. Not while I still have some pride left!"

I sink back on the pillows and close my eyes.

"Elizabeth, are you listening?"

I open my eyes.

"I have thought of another way to accomplish the same thing without the awkwardness of a three-way meeting," he exclaims. "You must write a note to Henry saying that you confessed so that he will understand my state of mind. I will take the note and explain everything to Henry and assure him he need have no fear on my account."

As I look away, the objects in the room begin to spin.

"Well," says Theo, "what do you say? Aren't you willing to do that much for me?"

"Yes, of course. It is just that it does not seem a good idea to put something like that in writing. Talking it over would be best."

"It is unfair to put me in such a position. Forced to be in the same room as my wife and her lover! How can you be so insensitive? Do my feelings mean nothing to you?"

"Of course, they mean everything to me," I stammer, "but—"

"Elizabeth, for God's sake, you owe me something. You are responsible for putting that stupid idea that I was attempting to seduce her into Bessie's head. You felt guilty about Henry, so you had to accuse me of something. And your mother has ruined my reputation. You are participating in a conspiracy against your own husband. If I am fired from the *Brooklyn Union*, we will starve, lose the house. There will be no money for the children's education. Is that what you want? You have played a principal role in my downfall, and you lie there and tell me that you will not put a few words on paper . . . true words, mind you. I am not asking you to lie to save my job and save your own children!"

"Theo, for the love of God, I have not conspired against you—you cannot believe that of me. I have made mistakes, but not that."

I begin to weep. My shoulders shake convulsively. The warmth between my thighs must mean that the bleeding has started again. Feeling light-headed, I gasp for air.

Theo pulls me toward him and tells me to breathe deeply. Gradually the trembling stops. He gently strokes my head. "Of course, dear, it was not deliberate on your part; you were a pawn in the foul game of your mother and Mrs. Beecher, but the end result is the same. I am facing ruin."

According to Theo, I am responsible for all his misfortunes. His drive to take revenge against Henry, even at the expense of endangering my reputation, apparently has nothing to do with the crisis we face. But what am I to do now? I know I will never be able to persuade Theo to do as I suggested. Something must be done or we all face ruin.

I ask him to bring me pen and paper and to promise that he will be careful that the note does not fall into the wrong hands. He offers to write a draft for me, but in spite of my weakness, I insist that he help me to a sitting position, and with a desperate resolve to order my thoughts, I grasp the pen. The trembling starts again. Theo reaches for the pen, but I hold it close to my breast. He pushes the paper toward me. I start to write in a shaking hand.

Dear Mr. Beecher,

It is with a heavy heart that I write this letter. Since you knew nothing of my confession to my husband, you could not have understood why Theodore wrote the note delivered to you on the day after Christmas. I am very grieved that I have been the cause of enmity between the two people I esteem most highly in the world. Theodore has assured me that for my sake he will take no steps against you. It is the prayer of the undersigned that you and Theodore will bury your differences and unite to prevent an unscrupulous third party from ruining you both.

Yours, Elizabeth

Theo reads it and insists that I should be specific about what I confessed.

"No, I can't." I shake my head vigorously, and the objects in the room begin to spin once again. I close my eyes and sink back down on the pillow.

From what seems like far away, Theodore's voice invades my consciousness. "But the letter has no meaning. You have to name it."

"No. Never. I'm bleeding again. Let me die."

The nurse enters and chides Theo for not letting me rest, thus putting me at risk of a relapse that could be fatal. He takes the letter and departs.

The Following Day

Early in the morning Bessie comes to my room. After asking how I feel, she complains that the nurse is very strict about keeping the sick room quiet and hardly ever lets her enter.

"Where is Mrs. Mitchell now?" I inquire.

"Oh, she had a personal errand, said she would go early, and get back quickly. She told me to look in on you."

"Is Mr. Tilton still at home?"

"No. He went to work very early. Looked a bit worried," says Bessie, always the keen observer. "Is everything all right with Mr. Tilton's job?"

"I hope so. He talked with me last night, and I think everything will work out."

Bessie then asks whether I would like her to read to me. As she goes downstairs to fetch a book, I think about the letter and wonder how Henry will react when he sees it.

Upon her return, Bessie informs me that people are talking about a possible snowstorm. The clouds are threatening and the wind is picking up. I listen attentively while she reads a novel to me, grateful to be able to concentrate on something besides the letter. Just as the heroine is trying to decide whether to accept a marriage proposal from a highly eligible bachelor whose amorous feelings she does not share, Mrs. Mitchell enters the room, announces that it is my lunchtime, and shoos Bessie away. Afterward, I nap for a long time. When I awaken, the room is dim, as though it were already dusk, but I hear the clock in the adjacent room strike three. Feeling restless, I want to try to stand up and get out of bed but dare not go against the categorical instructions of both doctor and nurse. By the time the clock strikes five, it is quite dark.

When the nurse brings me my dinner, Theo has still not returned home. It is snowing hard and the wind is whistling eerily as it batters the house. The nurse says that no one should be on the streets in such a night as this.

The clock strikes nine. Why is Theo so late? Something must be terribly wrong. I start to doze off when the nurse enters to tell me that Reverend Beecher is downstairs and requests a word with me.

"Bring him up. Maybe he has news from Mr. Tilton."

She helps me put on a robe, straightens my hair, and adjusts the pillows so that I can receive the reverend in a semi-sitting position.

Henry comes into the room with his overcoat still on and bits of snow clinging to his scarf.

"Oh, Henry, it is wonderful to see you. But what a dangerous night to come out in!"

"Elizabeth, you look better. Mrs. Beecher tells me that your mother said you are out of danger."

"Yes, I have been very ill, but praise be to the Lord I hope to fully recover."

Henry gives one of those smiles that crinkle up his eyes, reminding me of our happiness together in the old days. His expression quickly turns somber. He removes his overcoat, pulls up a chair close to my bed, and says in a low voice, "Elizabeth, Theodore read me a note purported to be written by you."

"Yes, I gave it to him to effect a reconciliation between—"

"Reconciliation? Elizabeth, have you lost your senses? You put me in a very dangerous situation. Theodore will use that note to ruin me. Don't you understand that? You have struck me dead, ended my usefulness. Everything I have worked for, my ministry, the new religion of love, the good work that the church is doing among the poor and unfortunate, everything is in danger. How could you do this to me?"

"Don't say such things! How could you think I would ever do anything to harm you?"

"Elizabeth, you have been very ill. Did Theo force you to sign the letter against your will?"

I struggle to sit fully upright. Fighting to control the sobbing that is making it difficult to speak, I try to explain how the letter came about, beginning with how Theo was manipulated by Bowen.

"I think I am beginning to understand," replies Henry. "But why put in writing that you made a confession? Don't you realize that Theo can give that letter to the Council of Congregational Ministers and demand an investigation?"

"But Theo would never do that. He knows he was mistaken and he wants reconciliation."

"That is what he says now, and you believe him. But can we count on him? You yourself told me of his erratic behavior. He says he wants reconciliation now, but the moment jealousy and anger rear their ugly heads, he will take that letter and use it to ruin me and you, too, in the process. Oh, Elizabeth, you are too good, too naive."

I sit in mute misery.

Henry is not finished. "I can't believe you confessed. If you really loved me, you would never have told him."

The vertigo starts again. I lower my head and close my eyes until the spinning stops.

He looks at me. "Are you feeling all right?"

I nod. What's the point of telling him that the attack of vertigo has passed, but not the pain in my heart?

"No, no, I do love you," I protest, between sobs. I must get control of myself, make Henry understand. "Theo had trusted me with his confession of other loves," I explain. "He wanted me to be equally frank so that our marriage would be based on absolute honesty. We would then forgive each other, our intimacy would be all the stronger."

"But it didn't happen that way, did it?"

"No, Theo began to accuse me of trying to attract men by some sort of sensuous seduction. I don't know what, exactly. His accusations became more and more violent."

"Elizabeth, why didn't you tell me you confessed to Theo? I asked you at least twice, and you looked me directly in the eye and lied. Is that being honest with a loved one? Or is your honesty reserved only for Theo?"

His words sting like a bandage ripped off an open wound. I protest that I wanted to protect Henry from needless worry in the hope that Theo would pull out of his morbid state. "I wanted to do what was right by both you and Theo, but it seems that I have made only mistake after mistake."

Henry is lost in thought for a long time. He finally says that he sees that I meant no harm when I wrote the letter. Unfortunately, good intentions are not enough. My mistakes have put his reputation, his career, and his livelihood in jeopardy. If Theo decides to use the letter, the Council of Ministers will be summoned, the whole story will come out, and our personal lives will become the subject of common gossip.

"Yes, I know, no one would understand the nature of our love."

"They would make it ugly and cheap," says Henry in a bitter tone. "Everyone loves to call a minister a low-down, immoral scoundrel!"

After a pause, I urge, "Let us call Theo at once and talk all three, frankly, openly. We have all made mistakes, harbored uncharitable thoughts, but if we can express what is in our hearts, if each of us can forgive the others, then there will be no reason to fear. I am sure Theo can be persuaded that exposure means ruin for all three of us and for other innocents as well."

"Elizabeth, I cannot be so trusting. Theo has a good heart, but he is also unpredictable and impulsive. I need something concrete to protect me."

There is a moment of silence. This is a side of Henry I have never seen before. His childlike simplicity of heart always impressed me, but now he appears to be a man versed in the ways of the world, carefully weighing alternative strategies.

He looks me in the eye. "You must write another letter revoking the confession."

"But how can I do that? Who would believe such a recantation a day later?"

"It's simple," replies Henry. "You have been deathly ill. Your mother said you were unconscious for more than twenty-four hours. Your husband took advantage of your weakened physical condition and forced you to write the letter while you were in no condition to resist."

"He pressed me, but he did not force me," I object.

"No matter," Henry assures me, "we will find the correct wording."

Oh God, I am sinking into quicksand. I wrote one letter against my better judgment, and now Henry wants me to write another.

"The letter might anger Theo," I point out.

Henry counters my objections, but I remain silent in answer to all his arguments. Then he kneels beside my bed, takes my hands in his, and beseeches me with tears in his eyes. "If you care for me at all, Elizabeth, you cannot refuse to protect me. If that first letter stands, I have no reason to live any longer. Please, my dearest friend, stretch out your hand and save me from impending doom."

I cannot refuse such an appeal. We work on a draft, using the same writing materials Theo left on the bureau yesterday. I suggest that this letter should simply recall the statements made in the first letter. Henry insists that he needs something more specific.

"Elizabeth, I hate to use the awful word, but you have to make a direct denial of adultery or your letter will not help me."

"My dear friend, please listen to me." I search for words that will convince him. "A direct denial would only confirm what the word *confession* referred to. Please think it over carefully."

Henry frowns and then looks down, cradling his head in his hands. Dear God, make him understand. I cannot sign what he wants. Theodore urged me to be more specific about what I was confessing. I refused. I will not give in to Henry now.

He finally lifts his head. "I see what you mean, Elizabeth. But I still think—"

"No. Never. Not that word!"

Henry looks at me for a long moment. I stare back.

He sighs. "Perhaps you do have a valid point. We must phrase the letter carefully."

Henry suggests various alternatives. I nod agreement to the one that seems least incriminating. Then I pick up the pen and write.

December 30, 1870

Wearied with importunity and weakened by sickness I gave a letter inculpating my friend Henry Ward Beecher under assurances that that would remove all difficulties between me and my husband. That letter I now revoke. I was persuaded to it—almost forced—when I was in a weakened state of mind. I regret it, and recall all its statements.

E. R. Tilton

I desire to say explicitly Mr. Beecher has never offered any improper solicitations, but has always treated me in a manner becoming a Christian and a gentleman.

Elizabeth R. Tilton

Henry reads over the letter, pronounces it satisfactory, and quickly takes his leave. The nurse returns, extinguishes the light, and urges me to get a good night's rest. In spite of my troubled mind, I yield to the welcome oblivion of sleep almost instantly.

Later That Same Evening

I am awakened from deep sleep by an insistent whisper. I cannot make out the words. The voice becomes louder. It is Theodore asking how the interview went. The nurse, who is sleeping by my side, awakens and remonstrates with him, saying that I need to rest. He commands her to leave the room so that he can speak with Mrs. Tilton, and then pulls up an armchair next to my bedside.

It takes me a moment to get my bearings. How does Theo know

about Henry's visit? Theo explains that he met Henry at Frank Moulton's house earlier in the evening. In accordance with Moulton's advice, he assured Henry that he was withdrawing the note demanding the preacher's resignation from the pulpit. The note had been Bowen's idea, and Theo claimed he had gone along with it in a moment of anger. He then proceeded to read my confession letter out loud. Henry turned pale and stammered in a dazed voice, "Oh, my God, Theo, this is a bad dream. I am in Dante's inferno." In response to Henry's appeal, made in the piteous accents of a dying man's last request, Theo granted him permission to visit me.

I blanch at this vivid picture of Henry's distress.

"And what did Reverend Beecher say when he called on you?" inquires Theo.

"He was distraught."

"I know. But what did he say?" repeats Theo.

"Henry told me that the letter I wrote would end his usefulness. He feared being dragged in front of a Council of Ministers. I told him that the intention of my letter was to make him understand why you had written the note demanding his withdrawal from the pulpit, but he felt that my note was like the sword of Damocles over his head."

"And well he should," Theo rejoins. "After alienating my wife's affections and then joining my enemies to deprive me of my livelihood, it is about time that he felt the heat of his own misdeeds!"

"Theo, Henry is your close friend, you fought together for many a good cause, he helped you in your career. I made him understand that Bowen pushed you to write that letter demanding he resign his ministry. I am sure he will help us. Surely, you do not intend to use my note against him?"

"No, of course not. I only wanted to bring him to his senses, make him aware that he cannot mistreat me with impunity."

"Theo, I have broken off with Henry. But he is still a friend. I could not bear to see him destroyed any more than I could bear seeing you ruined."

"You are very concerned with his welfare."

"I am. Theo, he told me that he needs protection against public scandal. I had to reassure him that we mean him no harm, for his sake and for ours."

"What do you mean, Elizabeth? Reassure him? How?" Theo rises to his feet in alarm.

I can't find my voice. Please, God, give me strength to tell him about the letter I wrote at Henry's bequest. All my concealments in the past have led only to further grief.

"Elizabeth, what have you done? For God's sake, tell me."

When I describe the letter, Theo trembles, stands speechless, incoherent with fury, then chokes on his words. Only once before, the time he struck Bessie, did I fear that he would hurt me. He accuses me of never having loved him, of still loving Henry, of betrayal, of conspiring with everyone against him. When I try to defend myself, he yells even louder. I keep quiet. Eventually, his anger spent, he sinks back down into the chair and weeps.

I tell him that he is mistaken, I do love him, and I want the best for him and our family. But no good will come of doing grievous harm to another person who, in spite of his faults, has been a good friend. I remind him of his promise to never seek vengeance against Henry.

"When I made that promise to you last summer," responds Theo in a quiet voice, "I meant that I would never seek public exposure of his misdeeds. I had no intention of resigning my right to challenge my wife's seducer in private, man to man!"

"But that's what my letter was intended to do, relieve him of any anxiety about public exposure."

"So, you agree that I have the right to accuse him as long as it is not done in a public forum?"

I hesitate. Is Theo using his way with words to bait a trap for me? But when Theo repeats the question, I see no option but to tell him, "Yes, of course you have every right to express your feelings in private."

"Well then, if that is the case, you should have no objection to putting in writing that the only reason you wrote that letter was to enable Beecher to defend himself in a public forum, but you never intended to defend him against an accusation made by your husband."

I protest that my delicate health does not permit me to write yet another letter. With tears in his eyes, Theo begs me to do just this one thing for him. I tell him that weariness is affecting my judgment and I would prefer to wait until morning. Theo says he is asking me to do a very small thing for him.

"Elizabeth, answer me."

"Please, I need to rest."

Theodore grips the arms of the chair and leans forward, his face inches from mine. "Listen carefully. I cannot allow Henry to first seduce my wife and then outsmart me by getting a declaration from her that he acted as a proper Christian. Never! Either you clarify the situation in writing or I will take your letter to the Council of Ministers. Then we will see how much the retraction helps him!"

There is no escape for me. I ask whether Theo will give me his pledge that if I write the letter, he will do everything possible to avoid public exposure, and he assures me that I have his word. He then brings me the writing materials, which Henry had replaced on the bureau, and I write:

December 30, 1870, Midnight

My Dear Husband: —I desire to leave with you, before going to sleep, a statement that Mr. Henry Ward Beecher called upon me this evening, asked me if I would defend him against any accusation in a Council of Ministers, and I replied solemnly that I would in case the accuser was any other person than my husband. He (H.W.B.) dictated a letter, which I copied as my own, to be used by him as against any other accuser except my husband. This letter was designed to vindicate Mr. Beecher against all other persons save only yourself. I was ready to give him this letter because he said with pain that my letter in your hands addressed to him, dated December 29, "had struck him dead, and ended his usefulness."

You and I both are pledged to do our best to avoid publicity. God grant a speedy end to all further anxieties.

Affectionately, Elizabeth

Theo takes the letter and exits the room without a backward glance.

April 1897

Regaining partial consciousness, Elizabeth was briefly aware that daylight was streaming into the bedroom window, but her eyelids were leaden. She heard a male voice speaking softly and struggled to make out the words. Then the darkness closed in, engulfing her once more in a voyage back to that cold, snowy night. She recalled fearing that things had gone too far to effect a reconciliation between Henry and Theo. Only the worst could be expected.

But in spite of the withering of hope that blighted her spirits, she remembered her body becoming stronger. On New Year's Day she had been able to stand up briefly and receive a few friends who were making the rounds with greetings. The nurse let the children stay with her. Alice and Carroll took to playing board games in her room, while little Ralph watched solemnly, occasionally trying to touch the pieces.

Elizabeth had hardly seen Theodore at all for about a week after the horrible night of the letters, but then he suddenly appeared in her bedroom in a cheery mood. He told her that Henry had apologized and expressed the desire to help him recover his journalism career. He wants to compensate for all the injury he has done me, explained Theo. He went on to say that he had almost forgotten what a wonderful friend Henry had been for so many years, but now he was once again feeling the strength of that special bond between them. It's a true reawakening of our friendship, Theo assured her.

"I'm so glad."

A male voice, similar to Theodore's but slightly deeper, said, "Did Mother say something?"

Elizabeth opened her eyes and the objects in the room came into focus. It was Ralph, her youngest, no longer a toddler but a grown man.

"I didn't hear anything," said a female voice. Alice rose from her chair and looked down at her mother intently. "Her eyes are moving. I think she can see us. Mother, can you hear me? Speak to me!"

Elizabeth tried but no sound came. She moved her hand slightly on the side that was not paralyzed. Alice pulled down the covers and seized her mother's hand in her own, leaning forward to speak directly in her mother's ear. "Press my hand if you can hear me!" Elizabeth concentrated with all the mental force she possessed.

"God be praised!" exclaimed Alice! "It is not too late. She knows that we are here. Ralph, hold her hand!"

Ralph quickly rose from his chair and walked to his mother's bedside. Elizabeth noticed that he was almost as tall as Theodore, but broader in the shoulders, less lanky. She was glad that he had become an editor like his father. As he bent over to press and then kiss her hand, his strong profile and elevated brow confused her for a moment into thinking it was indeed Theodore.

Alice poured some water from the jug on the bureau and directed her brother to lift her mother to a sitting position. Leaning against her son, Elizabeth drank a few drops from the glass that her daughter held for her.

Alice was lamenting that Carroll had left only half an hour ago. Ralph thought it might be worthwhile to go after his brother and try to intercept him before he reached the train station. Elizabeth willed herself to stay awake in case Cad could be found, but as Ralph leaned over her to take leave, his features were transformed into those of his father. Elizabeth again struggled to remain conscious, but the image of Theo was a magnet exerting a powerful pull toward the past, and she found herself in her own home listening intently to what he was saying to Henry.

January 1871

"Do you remember that trip to the South we made just as the war ended?" asks Theo.

"Indeed, I do," replies Henry. "It is one of my most precious memories."

I smile at them both. I love hearing about the days when they were comrades in arms in the abolitionist movement, standing firm for no compromise with the South, chiding Lincoln for his slowness in freeing the slaves during the war. Theo gestures to me to sit on the sofa and gets up to give me a pillow to make me more comfortable. They then return to their animated conversation, almost as though I were not present.

"The speech you gave for the flag-raising ceremony at Fort Sumter was truly inspiring," says Theo. "And afterward, when you spoke to the colored church in Charleston, what an outpouring of emotion! I have never seen anything like it. And I shall never forget how intently the colored children listened when I talked to them at Sunday School. What a day of rejoicing it was!"

Henry nods and smiles.

"Sometimes I think that those were the best days of my life," says Theo. "I had a clear sense of what was right and wrong, a sense of deep conviction that the ideals we fought for were worthwhile." He shakes his head. As the war ended, he recalls being convinced that this great nation was on the threshold of a new day of reform, but his expectations were never realized.

"I understand how you feel," says Henry. "In times of war, or national emergency, it is easy to understand the right path. In times of peace, men lack that sense of the urgency of change and they become complacent. The politics of compromise prevails."

Theo does not immediately reply. "You are right," he tells Henry, "but I do not feel entirely comfortable in this new practical world in which making money seems to be the great business of men's lives. I am often invaded by melancholy." Theo turns to me and asks, "What do you think, Elizabeth? Did I suffer much from despondencies during the war?"

"Hardly ever," I reply. "And when you did become despondent, the mood was of short duration. If we had not been boarding with my mother, perhaps you would not have suffered those moods at all in those days," I add.

Theo shoots me a grateful glance. "How well you understand me." He smiles at me, and then addressing Henry, says, "I am indeed a lucky man to have a wife who comprehends me."

"You must treasure her."

Theo smiles, but then his expression turns serious. He says that the last few years have been very difficult for him. He is aware that his loss of faith in orthodox Christian doctrine has caused great discomfort to his dear wife, nodding to me, but if he had continued to attend weekly services, he would have been untrue to himself.

I glance at Theo because I had not realized that he was at all concerned with my feelings in this matter. Henry responds to Theo's remarks in a kindly tone. He says that it is natural for a man to question his faith and beliefs as he moves from young adulthood to full maturity. He himself went through a period of doubts that tortured his soul. He could reconcile with Christianity only when he discarded the harsh Calvinism of his youth and embraced the doctrine of love and forgiveness.

"I remember that you once wrote a letter urging me to find my own path," replies Theo. "I still treasure that letter."

"And I still believe that no man can be sure that his own path to God is the correct one, or deny to his fellows the right to follow their consciences toward their own vision of truth," responds Henry heartily. "I doubt that our friend Frank Moulton believes in a personal God, in fact I am sure he does not, but I have never seen a more ethical man, a man who puts his friends' interests above his own. Surely, God would not close the kingdom of heaven to such a man!"

Theo agrees wholeheartedly, but I am not so sure. I wonder

whether Theo himself still believes in God. He says he is a believer but openly expresses doubts whether the scripture can be taken literally. For him, God is Truth, but to me God cannot be reduced to an abstraction. The fire is dying down, and the room is becoming chilly. I shiver. Theo fetches me a blanket.

After resuming his seat, Theo begins to talk very rapidly, emphasizing his words with abrupt gestures. He occasionally glances at me, but mostly he addresses Henry. Theo declares that the last six months have been the most trying period in his life. In earlier years, Mr. Bowen always supported an editorial stand based on principle, but in recent months he has been consumed with the fear that controversy will offend the public.

"It got to the point where I felt that he was trying to muzzle my opinions, and that I will not allow. I made the *Independent* great by taking a stand on principle during the war, and I will not change now."

Henry says gently that the public temper is now more conservative. "It is a matter of maintaining a balance, of being progressive, but not too radical, so that you can take the public with you."

"I know that I am not a good judge of the public temper. I have always called the shots as I see them: right is right and wrong is wrong. You, on the other hand, have always had an unerring instinct for what will please."

I hold my breath. How is Henry going to take this? To my relief, he replies with a disarming smile, "As I grow older it is true that I am less prone to take risks, but I am not sure whether it is wisdom or lack of nerve."

In a reassuring tone, Henry praises Theo for his editorial leadership at the *Independent* and expresses regret that Bowen has not been willing to give him time to work out a new editorial policy. "The trouble with Bowen is that he is too nervous about dollars and cents. He becomes panicked by a slight dip in subscriptions. The most reprehensible thing that Bowen did was to resort to spreading rumors about you, Theo, rather than talking things through. But I, too, must confess that I believed some of the things he said about you. I even repeated some rumors that had reached me." Henry slumps in his chair and sighs audibly. "At my age I should have known better."

"You were not the only one drawn in by Mr. Bowen's ugly game," says Theo.

"You know, Theo, I have done my best to undo whatever harm has been done. I wrote a letter to Bowen saying that I had been informed by a reliable source that the rumors concerning you and a certain lady are completely untrue."

"You need not talk in terms of such-and-such a lady. Elizabeth knows full well that the accusation was about Laura Bullard, don't you, dear? It is of course completely untrue. Indeed, they are extremely fond of each other, like sisters."

I nod my assent, although all three of us know that my friendship with Laura does not necessarily mean she is not my husband's lover.

Theo informs Henry that he still has hopes that Bowen will see reason and restore him to his position as editor of the secular paper the *Brooklyn Union*. Henry advises Theo not to despair, even if this is not possible. "You are a journalist of uncommon talent and national reputation. Surely, with the backing of friends, you can start a new paper."

"That's right," I exclaim. "You still have your talent, your greatest asset. This setback is bound to be temporary. You must have faith in yourself, dearest!"

"Yes," Theo half rises in his chair in his excitement and clasps Henry by the hand, "I had not thought of that. I am still young. I must have faith in my own abilities. And, another thing! Bowen owes me money for breaking the contract without giving six months' notice. Frank thinks he can be induced to pay up."

Theo turns, and still holding Henry with one hand, he extends the other toward me. I rise slightly to meet him, we all join hands, and he says in a joyous tone, "Thanks to the two of you, and to my dear friend Frank, I have been delivered from the valley of despond. Everything was dark for me. I saw conspiracy against me, but now I am emerging into the light. You are giving me hope in my darkest hour. Oh, my friends, I feel your love and it is liberating my soul!"

"May God be praised," rejoins Henry, his lip trembling. "Oh, Theo, my dear friend, I know I have done you harm, caused you great suffering, but believe me it was unintentional."

"I believe you, and you must believe me. I was in darkness, and I thought I wanted to harm you, but I really never stopped loving you and never stopped loving Elizabeth."

"God be praised. I, for one, do not feel worthy of your forgiveness. I am older, almost of an age to be a father to you and Elizabeth, but I did not show the wisdom of years. I let my feelings overflow without thought of consequences." Henry pauses, glances at me, and then addresses Theo again with a tremor in his voice. "Please, believe me, it was not Elizabeth's fault. Your wife loves you."

I sit still, unable to raise my eyes or utter a word. Theo puts his arm around Henry's shoulders. "Don't worry. Everything will be all right. You know, Elizabeth also tried to take all blame on herself."

Henry sits back down and sobs quietly. Theo puts his arm on his shoulder and hands him his handkerchief.

"Thank you," replies Henry in a broken voice.

Theo tells us both that after I confessed, he believed that death would be preferable to living with betrayal. "But now," he says with tears in his eyes, "I am beginning to see that I needed that jolt to face my own failings as a husband. I raised my voice against Elizabeth, but inside I was blaming myself. I cannot deny the hurt is still inside me like a dull ache that never completely goes away, but now that I see that you both still love me, I think I can live with it, even rise above it."

Theo turns to me. "Dearest, I can only hope that the shock will make me a better man and that with your help we will go forward together to create a more perfect union."

"Oh, Theo, I want nothing more than that."

"May God bless you both," says Henry.

Theo is gazing at me with a beatific expression, but suddenly his eyes lose their luster. "There is still one thing that tortures me," he declares, looking first at me and then at Henry.

"What is it, darling?" I query.

"Oh my God, how do I say this?" Theo cries out. He has risen from his chair and the light entering from the front window accentuates the pallor of his face. "I cannot be sure that Ralph is my own son. I cannot bear it!"

Theo breaks down. I rush over and put my arms around him, but he will not be comforted. Extricating himself from my embrace, he turns to Henry and tells him in a toneless voice that he needs confirmation of the date of the start of our physical relations. Henry, looking confused and distressed, says something about never having been very good at fixing dates.

Thoroughly alarmed by the dangerous turn of the conversation, I run upstairs into my bedroom to fetch my diary. When I reach the bedroom, panting, my hands fumble about in the drawer of the bureau, but it's not there. Oh my God, what is going on downstairs? Willing myself to calm down, I remember having hidden the diary under some papers.

When I return, the two men are sitting motionless like statues.

Theo is bent over with head in hands, and Henry is looking at the fire with a stunned expression. I quickly open the diary, and remind Henry that on October tenth he had offered to take me to see the work of a famous portrait painter, duly noted in my diary.

"Yes, that was the date," says Henry. "It had to be early fall, because I remember wearing an overcoat walking to see the studio."

Theo perks up slightly, and I hastily point out to him that Ralph was born in mid-June, a full-term baby weighing over eight pounds, so he had to have been conceived before October tenth. "And besides, darling, of all our children, he is the one that looks most like you."

"Yes," Henry chimes in. "My dear Theo, that child will be the spitting image of you when he grows up. A chip off the old block! No doubt about it."

Theo suddenly grins. "You are right. Everyone remarks on how much he looks like me." He beams at Henry and then at me. "Let us drink a toast!" he cries, and goes to the larder to fetch a bottle of port. We drink to love and friendship. Theo kisses Henry, and then gestures to me to do the same. Afterward he draws me to him and kisses me long and hard.

Why Won't People Just Leave Us Alone?

March 1871

On my way to the dressmaker to have a gown altered for Florence, it's hard to avoid the slush on street and sidewalk. The sun, high in a clear blue sky, has melted all but a few patches of snow. After being cooped up so long in the house, suffering from a long illness and the bitter cold, it feels good to be outside.

After skirting a puddle that leaves mud stains on my shoes and stockings, I see Henry on the other side of the street, walking with a slight stoop, lost in thought. He looks up, smiles, and crosses over.

"Elizabeth, how wonderful to see you!"

A quick glance up and down the street reassures me that we are not being observed. Henry relieves me of the brown parcel I am carrying and offers to accompany me as far as the dressmaker's street.

"The last time we met, you were extremely pale and thin," he says, "but now your cheeks are rosy, and your eyes, my dear friend, do not look so sad."

As we are about to cross the avenue, several carriages passing in rapid succession block our way. While we wait, a squirrel descends from a maple tree looking for a handout. I take out some bread that I carry with me to feed the birds and kneel down. The squirrel grabs a piece from my hand and scampers back up the tree.

"What a brave little fellow, but so thin," exclaims Henry. "The creatures get desperate at the tail end of winter."

"It's been a long, hard winter."

"More of the spirit than of the flesh," Henry exclaims.

"There is no snow that chills to the bone more than loss of faith in human nature."

"But, Elizabeth, spring is coming, don't you feel it?"

I smile up at him. "Oh, yes, the birds will return from the south; the flowers will bloom once again."

"The worst of our troubles are over, I think," Henry says.

"Yes, my heart is singing. I feel a rebirth of faith in God and mankind."

"You know, Elizabeth, I was convinced Theo had set on a course of vengeance that would ruin and disgrace us all. Through the grace of God, and the kind offices of Frank, he has seen the light."

"Theo has a big heart."

"Yes, he does," Henry agrees. "It was my failure to reach out to him in his pain or to understand what you were suffering that brought on the crisis."

"It wasn't your fault, my friend. It was my mistake to betray our secret to Theo."

"Perhaps your confession was an error of judgment, but your motives were pure. You wanted to tell the truth and save your marriage."

"Even if you forgive me, dear Henry, I will never forgive myself for not telling you that I confessed. I told myself that it was to spare you from pain and anxiety, but in my heart, I was afraid that you would accuse me of betrayal."

He sighs. "My dear friend, I understand. Don't blame yourself! That night I was frightened. I saw my whole life crumbling, so I blamed you."

"Do you forgive me?" I look into his eyes. His face is close enough to mine to see the sandy stubble on his cheek. I want to reach out my hand to trace his jawline with my finger.

"I forgive you, if you forgive me," he replies with a smile.

We resume our walk in silence.

After progressing about half a block, Henry asks, "How is Theo doing? I see him frequently at Frank's place and he is cordial, but he often looks sad. He is really like his old self only when he talks about his new newspaper. He has great plans for the *Golden Age*. How does he seem to you?"

"Theo is fine," I reassure Henry. "He is very busy. Starting a newspaper is just the sort of challenge he loves. We are both grateful to you and Frank for helping him."

"It was the least I could do."

"But, you know, although cheerful, he seems distant."

"How do you mean?" A note of anxiety enters into Henry's voice.

"He rarely stays at home. He takes many of his meals at Frank's house. And when he is at home, he does not confide in me." I explain that Theo has financial worries because it will take time for the new paper to yield an income, but he doesn't discuss his problems with me, only with Frank.

"You must feel left out."

"I wish I knew more about all the talks among the three of you at Frank's house."

"Theo has been through a great shock. If we all came to your house to talk about business matters, my presence would make him uncomfortable. We must give him time to recover. Frank and I are trying to get more financial backers for the *Golden Age*. But it is your love and support Theo needs most."

"I am doing my best." My voice chokes, and Henry gives me a sharp glance.

"Elizabeth, don't misunderstand me. I am not saying that you have to stick by Theodore if you are unhappy."

Henry cannot mean what he says. He and I both know that I cannot leave Theo.

"Don't worry," I tell him. "I want to rebuild my family."

"I'm glad. My prayers are with you." Henry looks much relieved.

We have reached the dressmaker's street. Henry gently squeezes my hand as he hands me back the parcel with Flory's gown, and I tell him how much I miss his sermons.

"Sundays are so sad and strange. I hope that dear Frank will tell me soon that it is safe to attend Plymouth Church again."

"We must trust his judgment. He has been a true friend to all of us," Henry replies. "I will pray for your speedy return. Believe me, you are sorely missed."

June 1871

On either side of the open stairway from the street to the landing before Laura Bullard's front door there is a miniature garden filled with blooming flowers. The door is of dark mahogany, finely carved. The doorbell sets off low musical tones that echo deep within the house. I'm praying that Laura is at home.

A middle-aged woman, soberly dressed and dignified in manner, ushers me into the parlor and announces that Mrs. Bullard will be right down. My eyes, recovering from the brilliant sunshine of a hot summer day, slowly become accustomed to the dim interior lighting. The ceilings are high and separated from the wall surfaces by intricately carved moldings. There are two fine tapestries on the wall and an Oriental rug on the polished wooden floor. A painting of waterfalls in deep woods draws my attention.

Laura enters and comes over to affectionately embrace me. "Do you like the painting? The artist is an American, not very well known, but I love his work."

"It is very fine. It speaks to me of the grandeur of nature. I don't know much about art, but this painting speaks to my soul."

"Yes," she agrees. "The human figures are small, and they seem to be contemplating the vastness of God's creation."

We sit down, and I compliment Laura on the beauty of the furnishings. It's easy to understand why Theodore, who values good taste, loves to visit. Laura kindly turns aside my compliments on the elegance of her home. She professes to prefer the coziness of mine, which speaks to her of the joys of family life.

Conversation turns to her mother's illness. Laura has just returned from the family home in Maine, and she speaks with great sorrow of her mother's fortitude in withstanding pain.

Laura had no choice but to come back to Brooklyn for a short time to make sure that there is sufficient revenue to keep the women's suffrage paper *Revolution* afloat. Her plan is to broaden the subject matter of the paper to include women's health concerns to line up advertisements for new remedies. Theodore always admired Laura's shrewd business sense and said she would make the *Revolution* into a self-sustaining women's paper after taking over from Susan and Mrs. Stanton.

"I have to get the next issue ready, but I can't concentrate," Laura says.

"Your heart is in Maine?"

"I want to be at my mother's side, but she urged me to go. She is so patient, so little concerned with herself. But her eyes seemed to tell me to stay. I must go back soon."

Laura's eyes are filled with tears. I abandon the easy chair to join her on the sofa, embracing her and then putting her head on my shoulder.

"Don't feel guilty. No one has ever been a more caring daughter. If only I could go and help your mother while you are here in Brooklyn."

"Elizabeth, you are a true friend. I knew that you were a special person the first time I met you. I loved the way you dress so simply and the deep, sweet expression of your eyes."

While holding her close, drinking in the warmth of her body and the scent of her hair, I too remember taking an instant liking to Laura the evening that Stephen Pearl Andrews talked of free love in my home.

"I miss you terribly when you are out of town," I tell her. "At the end of December when I had a miscarriage and Theo's job was in jeopardy, how I longed to see you!"

"I wish I could have been there. Didn't Mattie visit you?"

"Yes, she comforted me about the loss of my baby, but I could not tell her the truth about everything torturing my soul. Mattie has been a dear friend for many years. But, you know, I can't risk ruining Henry's life and his mission."

"You have to be very careful. Your life is in greater jeopardy than his. Men are not judged as harshly. Be very careful; you could lose everything, even your children."

"To none of my friends have I told the truth about Theo and Henry but you."

"You can trust me completely. But Elizabeth, I'm very worried. Are things getting better with you and Theo?"

"Yes, thanks be to God, we are on the mend. Theo is totally engrossed in his new paper and slowly his despondency is lifting."

"I would never have imagined that he would experience such prolonged heartache. He talks of the right of each individual to follow the dictates of his own heart."

"Our hearts are unruly and often do not respond to the dictates of our heads."

"Elizabeth, I have a confession to make . . . about the waywardness of my own heart."

"Whatever you tell me, I will still love you."

"When I met Theodore, I was fascinated by his intelligence and disappointed that he had a wife and children. But when I met you, Elizabeth, everything changed. As we became friends, I felt a kinship with you, and then with the children. Do you forgive me?"

"There is nothing to forgive. Laura, you are a giving person. You give all of yourself, to your parents, to me, to Theo, to the children who adore you."

Laura leans forward to embrace me. I kiss her warmly, and tell her that God has given her a finer nature.

The housekeeper enters with tea. The cups are of fine porcelain decorated with a delicate bird motif.

"I should have brought Alice with me," I say. "She would have loved this tea set and all the paintings and tapestries."

"Next time," replies Laura.

"It is so good of you to encourage her artwork. She has been painting much more since you took an interest. And Miss Haynes is a treasure. Alice loves her art classes."

"I am so glad. She was highly recommended by an artist friend as a person who not only knows her subject but also has a special way with youngsters."

"How is your novel coming along?" I ask Laura.

"I have been too worried to write a single line. You know, I used to think it was unfair that all the burden of nursing the ill falls on women alone, but now I think that taking care of those we love is most important."

"For women, family always comes first."

"Still, it's important for women to try their hands at other things. Have you thought of sending Alice to an art academy to study when she is older?"

"Yes, Theo was talking about it a few days ago, but I hope that the *Golden Age* turns a profit soon so that we will have the resources to do so."

"Are you worried the *Golden Age* won't succeed?"

I explain my concern that Theo may be going out on a limb with the demand for radical reform of the divorce laws. Laura looks thoughtful and tells me she defines herself as a moderate reformer, a person who by nature avoids extremes. Theo, on the other hand, is at his best when defending a radical position, serving as a gadfly that forces the public to rethink political truisms and accepted social custom.

"Yes," I reply. "It would be wrong of me to expect Theo to alter his fundamental nature just to please the public."

"And if he did, the public might be disappointed with a tame version of the caustic Mr. Tilton. They expect controversy from Theodore."

"I understand. That's not what is bothering me."

Laura waits patiently for me to explain but it's difficult to put into words.

"Well, it's just that Theo no longer keeps company with our church friends. Even Susan Anthony is too old-fashioned for him. He is interested only in people with advanced ideas."

"What people are you talking about?"

"He is always over at Victoria Woodhull's house. Day and night."

Laura looks doubtful and asks whether I am sure. She was not aware that Theo knew Victoria that well. She is surprised to hear that he is editing Mrs. Woodhull's autobiography and helping her draft a new suffrage proposal.

"What do you think of her?" I ask.

Laura looks uncomfortable. She recalls how impressed she was by Mrs. Woodhull's fiery speeches in favor of women's suffrage. She says, "I admire her because she was born into humble circumstances and overcame many obstacles. I have never known want, and Victoria has. But I must admit that I have doubts about her character."

"So do I. What bothers you?"

"Victoria is polite and respectful in front of Susan Anthony, goes on about how Susan is the founding mother of the movement, but behind her back she ridicules her for being an old maid with old-fashioned ideas. Of course, she does have a genuine difference of opinion with Susan about the best way to go about obtaining the vote."

"You are too kind, my friend. I don't think that Mrs. Woodhull cares about suffrage for women or any other cause. She just wants to push Susan aside and take over the leadership. She will trample on anyone who gets in her way."

"I don't know whether I would go that far, but certainly she is very ambitious."

I ask, "Did you read the letter she published in the paper?"

Laura looks at me questioningly. "You mean the letter in the *New York World*?"

"Yes."

"No. I was in Maine in late May, but several people mentioned reading a letter making strange insinuations. I never quite understood. What was her purpose in writing it?"

I explain that Mrs. Woodhull had been criticized in the press for championing free love and for inviting her former husband, Mr. Woodhull, to come and live in the same house as her and her present husband, Colonel Blood. In the letter, she said that Mr. Woodhull was very ill, and that it would have been uncharitable to refuse him shelter. She also said that many prominent men live according to the doctrine of free love but do not acknowledge their true opinions openly.

"You mean that she posed as a heroine who dares to live by her beliefs, while everyone else is just a hypocrite?" asks Laura.

"Exactly. But there was more. At the end of the letter, she said that a public man of eminence is living in . . . concubinage with the wife of another public man of almost equal eminence."

Speaking the ugly word completely unnerves me and I collapse in sobs of misery. Laura holds me close until I quiet down. The references are very vague, she points out, and only a few people could have possibly connected it with Beecher, Theodore, and me. It is quite possible that Mrs. Woodhull wasn't referring to us at all. She chides me, "Don't assume the worst, Elizabeth! Victoria had no way of knowing anything about the troubles between you and Theodore."

I remind her that Mrs. Woodhull was on intimate terms with both Miss Anthony and Mrs. Stanton, and both women had some knowledge of the crisis.

"But if Miss Anthony or Mrs. Stanton mentioned anything, they would have done so in strict confidence. I can't believe that Victoria would be so unprincipled as to publicize something told to her in confidence."

"I have no faith in her principles. I doubt she has any. I don't think Susan would have said anything to her. But Mrs. Stanton was very close to Mrs. Woodhull."

"Does Theodore also think the letter referred to him and Reverend Beecher?" asks Laura.

"Yes, and so does Frank Moulton."

"Then why is Theodore seeing Mrs. Woodhull?" wonders Laura.

"I am not really sure. No one consults me about anything. But Frank and Theo think that the best way to keep her quiet is to do her favors."

"But how can he do favors for someone who has just attacked his reputation and yours in print? What is Theodore thinking?"

Laura is lost in thought for a moment, and then she turns to me and says with uncharacteristic vehemence, "We all know that Victoria is beautiful and she can turn on her charm at will. She has but to smile and men surround her like bees around nectar."

"Laura, he is bewitched by her. He talks about her as a true woman of courage who is being pilloried for her advanced ideas. Of course, I am too stupid to even understand the exalted level of her thinking. Can you speak to him? Explain to him that she is dangerous?"

"I don't know, Elizabeth. Theo did say he would come to the *Revolution* office next week. I could tell him some of the stories I've heard about Mrs. Woodhull."

"That would put him on his guard."

Laura sighs. "I doubt Theodore would pay heed. He will brush aside my comments as feminine jealousy."

July 1871

"Where's Dad?" asks Carroll, chewing his chicken. "He never comes home for supper anymore."

"Don't talk with your mouth full. Your father just started a new newspaper, so he has to work late."

"You had better eat with us, Mother," advises Florence. "Father did not come until very late last night, and he must have left early in the morning." She looks at me inquiringly.

"But I'm here early tonight." Theo comes striding into the dining room, dispenses kisses all round, and announces that the fried chicken looks delicious. He declares that he is famished. When I return from the kitchen to serve him, Theo is entertaining the children with tales of strange people he met on his last trip to the West.

Later, when we are alone in the front parlor, I venture, "Dearest, I was very worried when you didn't come home last night. You could have sent me word."

"Sorry, I was too busy and then it got too late." Theo goes back to his newspaper.

"Listen to me!"

He looks up.

I try to get my voice under control. "You are hardly ever home. Is the company of your family that irksome?"

Theo lays down the newspaper. "Here we go again! Well, if you must know, your constant complaining is driving me to despair. The home should be a man's harbor to leave the storms of the world behind, but in my case—"

"In your case," I retort, "the world outside the home is your harbor."

"There is very little joy at home. A man has to find it where he may."

"And where did you find it last night?"

"Find what? What are you talking about?"

"Never mind."

"I do mind. You are talking nonsense. After a busy day at the office, I rushed over to Mrs. Woodhull's place to finish that letter to a congressman suggesting how to mount a new demand for suffrage. It was so late by the time we finished that it seemed better to get some sleep there. Colonel Blood had the guest bed made up for me."

"You could have come by in the morning to let me know."

"I was on my way home, but I remembered that Laura will be leaving for Maine soon, and I stopped by the *Revolution* to see her."

"How is she? I don't think her mother can last much longer."

"She's leaving for Maine tomorrow. She invited me for lunch. Her cook is marvelous."

"Oh, Theo, why didn't you send for me? You knew I wanted to see her again before she left for Maine."

"No, I don't remember your saying anything about it," he replies. "In any case I had business matters to discuss with Laura."

"You mean my presence would have stopped you."

"Of course not. I just didn't think of calling for you."

That's the way it always is, Theo keeping me away from his special friends, but why didn't Laura suggest he call for me?

Theo has gone back to his newspaper. Without a word, I close my book and go upstairs to prepare for bed.

After changing into nightclothes, I sit down at the vanity and let out my hair. The face of the woman in the mirror has tiny lines beginning around the eyes that stare at me wearily. A knot forms in my throat and my chest feels tight.

The door opens and Theo enters. In the last few weeks he has been sleeping in the spare room, so I am not expecting him. He stretches out on the bed.

"Lib, I forgot to tell you that Laura said that she was very comforted by your visit. You are the only person who has helped her endure the pain of her mother's illness. She gave me an earful about how wonderful my wife is. Of course, I agreed."

I'm careful not to turn around so as not to reveal the tears in my eyes. I had been thinking that neither of them cared a whit for me.

"I only wish I could be of more help. Laura is such a dear friend."

"Come here." When I turn to face him, Theo is smiling. "There is something else I want to talk to you about." He reaches over and gently pulls me over to the bed.

"What is it?"

"Laura's opinion of Victoria is not all that different from yours. Did you two ladies discuss Mrs. Woodhull? Come, tell me honestly."

"Laura said that she had heard about the letter published in the *New York World*. She thought it was a very mean-spirited thing to do."

"Victoria herself said that it was a mistake." Theo sighs. "She apologized to me for that letter. The letter was not directed toward you and me. She wanted to get back at Henry."

"Henry?"

"His sister is leading an underhanded campaign to discredit Mrs. Woodhull, never mentioning her by name, but portraying her as a ridiculous figure to undermine her position in the suffrage movement."

"Ridiculous in what way?"

"According to the Beecher clan, she is a wild-eyed woman, always tapping tables to speak with spirits and preaching the immoral doctrines of free love. In this country it is impossible to offer serious ideas for social change without being vilified by an army of counterfeit reformers who have never come up with an original idea in their entire lives."

"Which sister are you talking about?"

"I am not sure. Catharine Beecher or Harriet—Mrs. Stowe, I mean."

"And why blame Henry?"

"You don't understand. Henry brought this on himself by publishing his sister's attack in his paper. And besides, Reverend Beecher believes in free love, too, yet he is a party to an attack on Victoria for immorality. She hates such hypocrisy. She was so angry that she published the letter impulsively without thinking what harm it could do to others. She is genuinely sorry."

I shake my head.

Theo looks at me fixedly. "Elizabeth, she is a sincere person, a bit impulsive at times, but her heart is in the right place. Believe me."

"I don't believe that she did not realize that the letter would cause harm. She didn't care!"

"You are very harsh in your judgment. I have noticed that the more beautiful a woman is, the quicker other women are to condemn her."

"It has nothing to do with looks. How can you accuse me of being that mean-spirited? To me Laura is even more beautiful because her heart is also beautiful, but I don't condemn *her*!"

"I take it back. It is true that you have a generous soul, more so than most women. But, why do you dislike Victoria so?"

I lean forward and touch Theo's arm. "I have a bad feeling about her. Mrs. Woodhull is unpredictable. I know in my heart that she is dangerous. Please, stop seeing her. I beg you."

He moves back to rest his shoulders against the headboard. "Are you trying to pick my friends for me?"

"No. I have never tried to restrict your friendships. It is just that—"

"Then why start now? I won't have it! You may be happy with the Plymouth Church community, but to me they are a limited bunch of people. They talk of the religion of love but they are unable to act upon it. They resist any attempt to build a more just society."

"Theo, there are many good people, like our friends Mattie and Andrew Bradshaw and Maria and Edward Ovington."

"I don't disagree, but they are the exceptions. I am tired of all this self-righteous religious posturing by people who say one thing and live another. Mrs. Woodhull is like a breath of fresh air. She is worth a thousand ministers who preach about changing the world but do nothing."

Theo is trying to provoke me into a defense of Henry, but no, I won't take the bait.

"You think I am being unfair?" prods Theo relentlessly.

My silence only provokes him to say more.

"I once saw Henry as you do, but now my eyes are open to his true nature. He postures as a great reformer, but as he grows older he compromises with the worst elements. It all began when he abandoned the emancipated slave to the tender mercy of the white Southerner. But whatever I think of him, I have never told you not to see him."

"It's true you never told me to cut off with Henry," I acknowledge. "I came to that decision by myself because you and the children are most important to me. At that time I didn't fully understand that my love for Henry was wrong. Now I do."

"What do you mean?" asks Theo.

"Do you remember recommending the novel by Charles Reade, *Griffith Gaunt*?"

"No. It must have been a long time ago."

"Several years ago, but I never got round to reading it until last month. The heroine, Catharine, becomes deeply attached to a priest, a man of high ethical standards and refined nature, but she eventually realizes that this attachment is wrong. You see, I believed that my love for Henry was pure, and that loving him would make me love you and everyone else more, but it only caused you pain. I did not understand how much I was hurting you. I want to tell you that I am deeply sorry."

Theo starts to say something about forgetting the past, it's all over now, but his voice chokes.

I tell him that the doctrine of free love is fundamentally flawed. "It is easy to say that the heart should be free, but in life there are many ties that bind. And besides, free love can work only if everyone is a generous soul like Laura."

"Why only Laura? There are many people of higher natures that could form a freer, better society," protests Theo.

"And there are many others who think only of their own selfish desires and try to climb up by putting others down."

"I suppose you are referring to Victoria?"

"No one in particular. All of mankind is mired in sin and selfishness."

"You put it very philosophically, my dear," replies Theo with a smile, "but it all sums up to allowing me to see Laura because you like her, but not Victoria because you disapprove of her."

My likes and dislikes should matter to my husband if we are truly soulmates, but it's useless to argue about it. "That is not what I am trying to say, darling!" I grasp his two hands in mine. "Please listen to me!"

"Go ahead."

I look Theo directly in the eyes. "What I really want with all my heart is to go back to the way we were before all this happened, so much in love, just the two of us."

He pulls me to him and says huskily, "That is what I want, too! You do not know how much." He cups my face in his hands. "When did I last tell you that you have beautiful dark eyes?"

I smile up at him. "You said the same thing the first time you kissed me, long ago, when we were courting."

"I remember." Theo's tone of gallantry gives way to a more somber expression. "Sometimes, your eyes are like deep wells that I cannot fathom. You seem far away from me. Once, in a dream, I could see you inside a castle looking out at me through a second-story window. The entrance gate was closed and I could not remember the secret words to open it. I could hear a voice calling to you and you left the window. Then I woke up."

"You gave up too soon." I smile at him. "If you had kept dreaming, you would have seen that I left the window to descend the dark winding staircase and run out to open the gate for you."

Theo laughs, pulls me to him, and says that we both read too many novels.

I tell him almost in a whisper that I love the way his eyes twinkle when he laughs, and then kiss him softly, just brushing his lips with mine. Theo strokes me gently and I close my eyes, yielding to pleasure, feeling my innards turn soft and liquid. He guides me to stroke him in turn, telling me that I am his loveliest darling, the only one who knows how to make him happy.

An image of another Theo floats into mind. He is staring at me with hard eyes, accusing me of being a sensuous, wanton woman who comes on to men. My body stiffens.

"Elizabeth, what is it?"

"Nothing, darling."

When he enters me, his thrusting gives me outward pleasure, but the inner recesses of my body are numb. When it's over, he disentangles his body from mine.

"Did I hurt you?"

"No! Not at all!"

"You're sure? Nothing's wrong?"

"Nothing, darling."

Theo turns his back to me as he changes into nightclothes in the dim candlelight. "Oh damnation," he says while struggling to put on a sleeve, swinging his arm awkwardly. I step toward him to help and then fall back so his flailing arm will not strike me. I wonder whether either of us will ever find the magic words to open the locked gate.

In the morning, I accompany Theo to the door as he leaves for work. He starts to give me a peck on the cheek, but I pull him toward me for a proper kiss on the mouth. He looks away when telling me not to wait up for him because he has to go back to the Woodhull place tonight to finish the letters to members of Congress.

On the steps he turns and calls out, "You understand, don't you? Befriending her is our best protection."

"Yes. I know. It's all right."

But in my heart I know it's all wrong.

November 1871

The doorbell chimes. Frank Moulton is waiting on the steps. He speaks softly with his customary politeness. "Good morning. Is Theodore home?"

"Yes. Come in. Is there anything wrong?"

"No. I need to talk to him."

Wondering why he is here so early in the morning, I usher Frank to the upstairs sitting room and call to my husband, who is still dressing. Theo strides in and gives his friend a hearty embrace. Frank's head just reaches Theodore's shoulder. His stance is firm and his gray eyes take in everything around him.

"Would you gentlemen like some tea or coffee?"

Theo shakes his head, but Frank smiles at me and says that a cup of tea would be most welcome. Once I start descending the stairs, the door is closed behind me.

I tell the cook to prepare two cups. If Frank wants tea, my husband will be happy to join him. The cook offers to take up the tray, but I insist on carrying it myself. Once upstairs, I walk slowly down the hall, pausing in front of the closed door. Balancing the tray with my left hand, I reach out to touch the knob with my right, but my fingers stop short of twisting it open. Theo has no right to exclude me from a discussion of problems that intimately concern me.

Theo is talking. "But why are you so worried?"

Frank replies, "I fear you are going too far in defense of Mrs. Woodhull."

"But you yourself said that it would be advisable for me to introduce her speech at Steinway Hall."

So it was Frank who advised Theo to introduce Mrs. Woodhull, and he listened to his friend and not to me. And then Theo insisted I go to hear her.

Frank sighs audibly. "At the time it seemed the right thing to do. She asked Henry to introduce her, but he told me frankly that his church people would be very unhappy if he appeared to be defending the woman."

"And then he gave some fake excuse to Victoria, who was counting on him, so I had to help out." Theo's voice rises to a shout. "Henry is a coward."

"Perhaps. He is also a keen judge of the public temper."

"I know what you are saying, my friend," replies Theo, "but remember that in my introduction I did not vouch for her views, just her right to express them."

He doesn't mention that his introduction was so flattering it sounded like Mrs. Woodhull was the greatest reformer in the country.

"I was following our strategy of befriending her," continues Theo, "but I also believe wholeheartedly that she has the right to be heard. It would be a shame if no man active in public life in all of New York could be found to introduce her, because she is an open advocate of honesty between men and women."

Frank points out that Theo not only introduced Mrs. Woodhull at Steinway Hall, but he also published a laudatory biography of her that excited much comment. Theo has allowed himself to become too closely associated with a woman whose public image has deteriorated. Even the suffrage ladies like Miss Anthony and Mrs. Stanton are concerned that her flamboyant lifestyle may discredit the quest for votes for women.

"I cannot abandon Victoria because others are turning their backs on her," Theo responds. "It would be against all my principles. She is an admirable woman who lives honestly according to her beliefs."

"Living according to your own beliefs is not an easy task," Frank says. "It requires judgment and tact as well as defiance. I believe in freedom of conscience as much as any man, but I am cautious about expressing my views in certain circles for I would not want my family to be victimized."

"You mean your religious views?"

"Or lack of them. I freely admit to you I do not believe in a personal God. I order my life by a creed of ethical humanism, but I don't discuss it with everyone. Society is all too quick to condemn the nonconformist. One must choose the time and place, and back causes that the public is ready for. Once a man gets ridiculed, his public usefulness as a reformer is over."

"Not always. Many abolitionists who were pelted with eggs for defending their beliefs now are honored and occupy high positions."

Frank acknowledges that this is true but insists that the abolitionists preached radical ideas but generally maintained a dignified mien that did not violate social decorum.

"Theo, to my mind there is something too showy and theatrical about Mrs. Woodhull. Emma took an immediate dislike to her. She told me that she is not a woman to be trusted."

The tea tray feels heavy in my arms and I lean against the wall for support. Thank God that Frank's wife sees through Mrs. Woodhull. It's the men who are taken in.

"Elizabeth says the same thing," replies Theo.

"My wife is a good judge of people," comments Frank. "Henry is also worried."

"About what?"

Frank explains that Henry spoke of a rising wave of criticism against Theo among the faithful of Plymouth Church. Those who think that Theo's views are too removed from Christian teachings and disapprove of his close connection with Mrs. Woodhull are calling for his resignation.

"Does Henry think I should resign? He has always posed as the most liberal of Christians who welcomes all to his church."

"No. He has been defending you. The problem is that important church members are questioning his stance as being too liberal."

"Henry should deal with his own problems. Why should I resign? My wife and children go regularly. Let them kick me out if they want to."

"You don't think it would be wiser to quietly withdraw your membership rather than risk becoming the butt of controversy?"

"Elizabeth would be terribly upset. The church community is very important to her."

"Well, in that case, it would be wise to publish some articles clarifying your views on marriage and religion."

"That's the solution," says Theo. "My views have been much misrepresented. I am not nearly as radical as some people believe."

I step forward to knock on the door, but stand stock still when I hear Frank say, "The sooner the better!"

"What's the rush?"

"One of the financial backers of the *Golden Age* told me he was withdrawing his support. Others may follow suit."

"I see." The bravado has gone out of Theo's voice. "I will write something up right away."

Silence. I knock on the door and serve the tea. Theo complains that it is cold. My cheeks feel hot, and I mutter something about speaking to the cook. Frank says that he does not like tea scalding hot and helps himself to a biscuit.

Late November 1871

Emma opens the front door for me and ushers me into the downstairs parlor of the Moulton home. Although it is before noon, she is stylishly dressed and her wavy dark brown hair is carefully coiffed. Her smile is warm as she mentions that she saw me at church last Sunday with the girls.

"Your daughters are so big now, almost young ladies."

"Yes, my eldest, Florence, is fourteen."

"I thought you had another one even older," replies Emma.

"You must mean Bessie, our ward. She has been with us since she was about eight years old. For almost a year now she has been away at boarding school. I miss her very much. She was wonderful with the children, and now I have no help. Theodore strongly believes that young women should have a good education."

"Oh, that must be why Reverend Beecher talked with Frank about a special education fund."

"A special fund?"

"Yes, if I remember correctly." Rising from her chair, Emma says I must have come to see Frank and leaves the room to see whether he is dressed.

After Emma goes upstairs, I ponder what she let slip. Does this mean that Henry is paying for Bessie's education? I knew Theo wanted Bessie out of the house, but we didn't have the money to pay for boarding school. Is Henry paying for anything else? How did Theo get enough money to start the *Golden Age*?

To dispel these troublesome thoughts, I walk over to a large mahogany bookcase that occupies one parlor wall and examine the titles. The room is elegantly furnished. The couch and chairs are covered with a beautiful fabric, almost as fine as tapestry, with lacy arm covers. An old-fashioned desk with tiny cubbyholes completes the furnishings.

Frank enters the room with a purposeful gait, gestures for me to be seated, and takes a chair opposite. After greeting me he comes to the point at once.

"Emma said you called to see me. Is anything wrong?"

"Yes."

I take out a clipping from the *Golden Age* and ask Frank to read a poem written by Theodore called "Sir Marmaduke's Musings." His brow furrows as he reads several stanzas aloud.

I won a noble fame,
But, with a sudden frown,
The people snatched my crown,
And in the mire trod down
My lofty name.

I gained what men called friends.
But now their love is hate,
And I have learned too late
How mated minds unmate,
And friendship ends.

I clasped a woman's breast,
As if her heart I knew,
Or fancied, would be true,

Who proved—alas, she too—
False like the rest.

Frank puts down the paper. "Under the circumstances, it seems indelicate."

"Theodore insists that it is a poem, like any other, that has nothing to do with his own life. He accuses me of being an alarmist, of imagining things, of being scared of my own shadow. But everyone will think it refers to me." After pausing to take in a breath, I blurt out between sobs, "Theo promised me we would forget the past. Make a fresh start! But we will never be able to save our family this way. People are talking. I am ashamed to go to church."

Frank waits for me to regain control before telling me in a kind but firm voice, "I understand how you feel, Elizabeth. But we must remember that Theodore had a terrible shock, the greatest shock that a husband can experience. It was a mistake on his part to publish this poem, but from a man's point of view, I must tell you that it is an understandable mistake. He is like an injured wolf that cannot help but lick his wounds even if it makes them worse."

Oh God, Frank believes I am the only one at fault. He knows nothing of Theodore's infidelities and judges me an immoral woman.

Frank asks me whether I understand what he is saying. I nod. He assures me that he will talk to Theodore right away and make him understand that publishing a poem of this nature amounts to putting his family and his own reputation in danger. He then points out that I also have a part to play.

"You know, Elizabeth, family harmony is always the responsibility of the woman. Men are always too absorbed in making a living, and representing the family in the wider public world, to be aware of the fine adjustments and accommodations that must be made among the members of the family unit. We rely on your feminine intuition to create this inner harmony. You must succor Theodore, give him the love and support that he needs to rebuild a happy home."

"Believe me, I am trying. But it is very hard. Theodore is scarcely ever at home. The children miss him. But if I say something, he accuses me of nagging or trying to restrict his movements."

"I see."

"The *Golden Age* is still not making money, but he won't talk to me about money problems. He gives me a weekly allowance, but it is not enough. Last week, I tried to talk to him about ways to reduce expenses, but he got angry and said that the only problem is my lack of managerial ability. I suggested maybe we should let some rooms to boarders, but he wouldn't listen. The next day I let the cook go. He hasn't even noticed."

Frank looks thoughtful. He says that I am wise to take steps to reduce expenses, but he has hopes that Mr. Bowen can be persuaded to pay what he owes Theo as a penalty for breaking his contracts as editor of the *Independent* and the *Brooklyn Union* without notice. This would give Theo time to gain acceptance for the *Golden Age*. I remember Theo saying something about compensation due to him after Bowen fired him, but don't dare to ask Frank how much we can expect. Instead, I thank him for helping me understand Theo's business problems.

"Don't worry too much," Frank replies. "I am sure the *Golden Age* will eventually be a success. The most important thing for you to do is to provide Theo with support at home. I was thinking that it would be a good idea for you to go with Theo when he goes on lecture tour this year."

"I would like to go if my mother agrees to look after the children. Theo doesn't like her, but there is no one else."

"Talk to her then. I will talk to Theo. Touring together will show the world that you are a united couple."

April 1897

Elizabeth thought she heard a voice calling her name far in the distance. The image of Frank faded from her mind, but the pull of the voice was not powerful enough to catapult her into full consciousness. Having yielded to the undertow, she was floating effortlessly in the cool and shady depths of a current from the past and no longer had the desire or the will to pull her body up with the powerful strokes needed to break through to the surface.

She had followed Frank's advice to accompany Theodore on his winter tour. The first week was like a vacation for them both. Later, Theo reverted to his moods and complained bitterly that Henry had not done enough to persuade Mr. Bowen to pay the money owed for firing Theo without the required six-month notice.

Once they returned home, Elizabeth remembered an atmosphere of intense negotiations. She was not a participant. It was all among the men. She had to piece together what was going on from the brief comments of Theo and what she overheard from time to time. After frequent conferences with Frank, Henry, and other friends, Theo announced that the legal tussle with Bowen had been settled. He had signed a tripartite pact with Beecher and Bowen. What did that mean? No one explained it to her. But in response to her persistent questions, Theo finally said that each of the three apologized for spreading rumors against the others in the past and promised to refrain from attacking one another's reputations in the future. In addition, Mr. Bowen had signed a check making a reasonable payment for breaking Theo's contracts.

The agreement must have been signed in the spring. Theodore had talked about how his own sense of inner renewal reflected nature's bounty. Now that he was released from financial worries, he would be able to dedicate himself totally to making the *Golden Age* a success.

Elizabeth, too, had felt confident that their troubles were over. Theo brought her back the note she had written to Henry about her confession, and she burned it. She asked about the other two letters written the following night and other incriminating notes and papers. Theo swore that they would all be destroyed. Meanwhile, the demand for Theo's resignation from Plymouth Church had subsided. After Victoria Woodhull launched an attack on Susan Anthony and Elizabeth Cady Stanton, Theo finally broke off his friendship with her.

But it was Mrs. Woodhull who had the last word.

November 1872

Elizabeth, are you alone? I have to talk to you!" Mattie Bradshaw is standing on the porch with an anxious look on her face.

"Mattie, what's wrong? Why are you standing there in the cold? Come in."

"Is Theodore at home?"

"No, he's still in New Hampshire. Tell me what this is all about."

Mattie barely responds to my warm hug. I take her coat and usher her to the upstairs sitting room. She is a diminutive person, very thin and short of stature. Her small form huddles in one corner of the sofa and her eyes wander restlessly over the room. She refuses my offer of tea.

"Mattie, is something bothering you?"

"It is so horrible!" she blurts out. "Andrew did not want me to come and talk to you. He said you would ask for advice if you needed it. But I couldn't stay home knowing you are in such trouble. And if you still don't know, I thought it would be better if you heard it from me rather than someone else."

"Know what? Mattie, what are you talking about?"

"You don't know about the article in *Woodhull & Claflin's Weekly*?

"No. I haven't heard anything." I feel a heave in my stomach and I lean back against the chair. "Mattie, for the love of God, tell me!" My voice sounds high-pitched in my own ears.

"Mrs. Woodhull has written horrible things about you and Reverend Beecher. I can't believe that anyone could have a mind so twisted."

"What did she say? Tell me!"

Mattie tries to tell me the story, but it comes out all garbled. She hesitates, blushes, stumbles over words like *enceinte*, and keeps apologizing for repeating vile gossip.

"It is all lies!" she cries. "Reverend Beecher is the most saintly man I know. He has given all his flock guidance, and now that shameless woman accuses him of this. And my dear friend, how could she accuse you? You are such a good Christian woman, so devoted to your husband and children. You are the last person on earth who would do such a thing."

If only she would stop beating around the bush.

"Mattie," I shriek, "what exactly did she say about me? *For the love of God, tell me!*"

Mattie hands me the clipping. I read the first paragraph, and then the words blur and go dark. I close my eyes, lean forward, and breathe deeply until the words come back into focus.

Dear God, give me strength to bear the unbearable.

Mrs. Woodhull says Theodore discovered my love for Henry, and believing that I was *enceinte* with Henry's child, he abused me so much that I lost the child I was carrying. What a twisted account of what really happened! The article says that the adultery was carried on right in front of the children, who then complained to their father. But the children knew nothing. She makes us appear depraved. Oh, Henry, how right you were when you said that they would make our love ugly!

Mrs. Woodhull claims she sympathized with my distress and persuaded Theodore that he should look upon the whole affair as a problem of social institutions rather than the fault of any individual and uphold his own rhetoric about the freedom of the individual rather than playing the part of a tyrant in his own home. As usual, she is the heroine of the story. According to her, the Reverend Beecher practices radical social ideas in his private life, but he dares not advocate them in public, because he is a moral coward. Her purpose in publicizing the story of his adultery is to ensure that hypocrisy does not go unpunished.

But the real hypocrite is Mrs. Woodhull. Everything she does is for revenge, but we are to believe that she is a crusader for truth. Oh, Theo, I told you about her!

I bow my head.

Dear God, are you punishing me? *No! No!* Do not be of so little faith! Blame not an evil woman's revenge on God! God is good! God is merciful! God sees into my heart and knows that my love was pure. Victoria Woodhull cannot take that away.

Mattie comes and puts her arms round me. I cry and cry, while she tells me not to worry, no one will believe such complete nonsense.

When I calm down, Mattie says, "Elizabeth, I don't think that you are the main target. Andrew thinks that Mrs. Woodhull wants to get at Mr. Beecher. He is such a wonderful man, who has devoted all his life to helping people. What does she have against him? Of course, evil people don't need a reason to spread their venom. Just the fact that he is a great and good man is enough to arouse the envy of people like her. But we noticed something of personal spite in her tone."

"Yes," I reply, "I remember Theodore telling me that Mr. Beecher refused to introduce her at Steinway Hall and she has hated him ever since. You know I was always against Theodore's friendship with her."

"Yes. Andrew and I never understood how he could write a biography of her."

"Theo wouldn't listen to me. It wasn't until she attacked Miss Anthony and Mrs. Stanton that he finally realized what she really is. She probably wants revenge against Theodore because he wouldn't support her campaign for president."

"President?" snorts Mattie. "I hope this country will never sink so low. When is Theodore coming home? He must do something at once."

"He's supposed to come tomorrow."

"Andrew was surprised that no one made a statement yet. But, of course, we did not know Theodore is out of town."

"Oh God, I hope he comes tonight."

"You know, I don't want to be indiscreet or to hurt you more, my dear." Mattie glances at me and hesitates.

"Go ahead. Tell me. After this blow, I can bear everything."

"Mrs. Woodhull says she got information from the suffrage ladies, but Andrew pointed out that—"

"What?"

"In the article Mrs. Woodhull says she also talked to Theodore."

"She's lying. The whole thing is a pack of lies from start to finish!"

"Of course," replies Mattie. "Come to our house as soon as Theo gets here. I am very worried. Andrew has some ideas about how

Theodore should handle this. It is very important to publish something that puts an end to this story for your sake and to protect the reverend and our beloved Plymouth Church."

The Following Day

The curtains and blinds in my bedroom are closed. The light makes my head ache even more violently. Twenty-four hours have passed since Mattie told me. Theo has not arrived and there has been no word from him. I lie very still, praying for the pain to go away. The vertigo overwhelms me when I attempt to rise. If Theo doesn't come soon, I must write a letter of denial myself, but what should it say?

I pull myself up to a sitting position. A wave of nausea causes me to retch and reach for the chamber pot. Dear God, do not abandon me! I must save Henry from ruin, save my children!

The nausea and dizziness recede, but the throbbing pain continues.

"Flory! Flory!"

"What is it, Mother? Are you all right? Should I fetch the doctor?" Flory sits on the bed and holds my hand.

"Are the boys all right? Are you and Alice watching them? Oh, I wish Bessie were here."

"Mother, don't worry. We are taking care of them. I am not a little girl anymore. You just rest. Everything will be fine."

Oh, Flory, if only you knew. Nothing will ever be fine again.

"Mother, it sounds like someone is opening the door. Maybe Father has come."

"Go and see, dear."

Theo comes striding into the room.

"What's wrong? Are you sick?" He opens the blinds. The light makes me groan in pain.

"I am sick in body and in soul. You have done this to me. You and your soulmate, Mrs. Woodhull!"

Flory is cowering at the door, her eyes fixed on my face, but I'm beyond caring. It's Theo who tells her gruffly to go check on her brothers.

"I don't understand. What did Victoria do? You know I broke off with her. I haven't seen her for months. What did she do?"

"Theo, you fool! You never listen. I told you she was evil! I wish that God had really created hell, so she could suffer the everlasting torment she deserves."

"But what has she done? Stop screaming! Tell me, what has she done?" Theo grasps my wrist.

"Let go! Don't touch me! The whole town is talking about it, and you don't know! Go ask her! Isn't she your great friend? Didn't you tell me how wonderful she is? Go ask *her*!"

"Elizabeth, for the love of God, tell me what is going on. Has Victoria published another letter?"

"A letter?" My laugh is mirthless. "There is not enough space in a letter to damn us all. She wrote a whole article this time, filled with lies and filth."

"Oh my God, this cannot be true. Where is it? Darling, I must see what she wrote!"

Theo leaves the room to get the article from the study. Nausea grips me and I throw up again into the chamber pot. The pain in my head has become unbearable. I lie motionless with my eyes closed, trying to form the words of a prayer, but other thoughts intrude. Everything she says is twisted, but Mrs. Woodhull knows a lot.

Where did she get her information? She says that she talked to Mrs. Stanton. I never talked to any of the suffrage ladies but Susan. She doesn't mention Susan. Probably Theo talked to Mrs. Stanton. Yes, I remember. They must have talked that night he didn't take me and Susan to the dinner at Laura Bullard's house with Mrs. Stanton. But that is not all. Mrs. Woodhull says that Theo talked to her about his misery. How could he betray me to her?

Theo's footsteps sound on the stairs. He enters the bedroom, kneels down beside me, and takes my hand. "Elizabeth, I know what you must be thinking. That vile woman says that I talked to her. Darling, you must believe me. I would never discuss you with a woman like her. I never said anything about you and Henry to her. I swear to you by all that I hold sacred!"

In all our life together, Theo has never before told me a lie about something important.

"I don't know, Theo. I don't understand anything. I just know we are all ruined."

"It's my fault! Why didn't I listen to you when you told me that you had a bad feeling about her? I should have trusted your woman's intuition, my own darling. What a fool I have been! If it were only I who must suffer for my mistakes, but I cannot forgive myself for causing you such misery. Of course, Henry can fend for himself, but my darling, trust me, I will protect you."

"His reputation and career will be ruined, too. What is to be gained by destroying him?"

"I just meant that as a man of the world, he should be able to protect himself. My first duty is to protect my wife and family. I will meet with Henry to decide on a common strategy."

"We must deny the story. Take a strong stand!"

"Don't worry, darling. I will do everything necessary to protect you and the children. Trust me."

"Mattie was the one who told me."

"What was her attitude?"

"She assured me that no one who knows me would believe anything like that. But she said that Andrew thought that a strong denial should be made right away."

"I trust Frank's judgment more than Andrew's. I will go over to his house right now. Now, you rest easy. Should I call the doctor?"

"Forget the doctor. What is important is making a quick denial of everything that woman said."

"Trust me, darling. Believe in your husband."

December 1872

I put on my coat hurriedly. My fingers are clumsy and it is difficult to do up the buttons.

"Mother, where are you going so early?" asks Flory.

"I have to find your father. I am going to his office. It is very important."

"Aren't you going to take a hat? It's bitterly cold outside."

My daughter hands me a hat and winds a scarf around my neck. Outside a strong wind stings my face, but I do not slow my pace. When I reach the office of the *Golden Age*, Theo is not there. There are papers strewn on the chairs in the minuscule front room. The typesetter shows me into the back room, a small cubbyhole, which serves as Theo's office. From my pocket I pull out a clipping from the morning paper and reread Theodore's letter addressed to "a complaining friend" explaining his position with regard to the charges made by Victoria Woodhull.

No. 174 Livingston Street

Brooklyn, December 27, 1872

My complaining friend: Thanks for your good letter of bad advice. You say, "How easy to give the lie to the wicked story and thus end it forever!" But stop and consider. The story is a whole library of statements—a hundred or more—and it would be strange if some of them were not correct, though I doubt any of them are.

Oh, Theo, you said that I could count on you to protect your own! Are you protecting me? *No!* You don't denounce Mrs. Woodhull's story as a pack of lies! On the contrary, you imply that parts of it are true!

So extensive a libel requires, if answered at all, a special denial of its several parts; and, furthermore, it requires, in this particular case, not only a denial of things misstated, but a truthful explanation of the things that remain unstated and in mystery. In other words, the false story, if met at all, should be confronted and confounded by the true one.

But you cannot tell the true story without destroying me, destroying Henry, making our children suffer!

Now, my friend, you urge me to speak; but when the truth is a sword, God's mercy sometimes commends it be sheathed. If you think I do not burn to defend my wife and little ones, you know not the fiery spirit within me. But my wife's heart is more a fountain of charity, and quenches all resentments. She says: "Let there be no suffering save to ourselves alone," and forbids a vindication to the injury of others. From the beginning she has stood with her hand on my lips, saying, "Hush!" So when you prompt me to speak for her you countervail her more Christian mandate of silence . . .

What do you mean by saying that I am the one who wants silence? You know that I want a full denial of the story!

Theo enters. "What is it?" he asks. "Is something wrong at home?"

"Everything is wrong. You betrayed me!"

"What are you talking about?"

"The letter you published in the *Brooklyn Eagle*."

"But the letter defends you. It praises your Christian spirit. Why are you so upset?"

"Don't pretend that you are my defender. You know how to fool people with words, but you don't fool me."

Theodore lowers his voice to a whisper. "Elizabeth, for God's sake, don't be hysterical! Look at this from my point of view as well as your own. I know you want me to make a full denial of the Woodhull story, but why should I lie in print? I didn't seduce Henry's wife. He seduced mine. Why should I lie to protect him?"

"You swore that you would keep my secret and protect *me*."

"I am protecting you. The letter shows that you and I are of one mind. Therefore, the public will assume that the charges are false. The letter implies that you are innocent."

"It implies no such thing. It hints that there is some dark dreadful secret. Don't pretend, Theo! You want revenge."

"No other husband in this city would have been as generous as I in similar circumstances."

"Generous! You have been pounding me with blow after blow. You started the thing with free love, but now you are throwing me to the wolves."

"That is not true."

"The truth is that you are willing to sacrifice me to get revenge against Henry. No wonder you kept company with Mrs. Woodhull. You are birds of a feather."

Theo grabs my arm in a painful grip. "Elizabeth, you don't mean that. Say you don't mean that!"

"Let go of me!"

The typesetter coughs in the next room. Theo drops my arm.

I seize the *Brooklyn Eagle*, which is lying on Theo's desk, and rip the page with the letter to shreds.

"Keep your letter and leave me alone!" I cast the shreds at him.

"Elizabeth, stop! Why is it my responsibility to publish a denial? I am not the accused. Henry is. Why doesn't he deny it publicly?"

"Since neither of you will protect me, I will write my own letter."

"Elizabeth, wait! For God's sake, listen to me."

The typesetter looks up as I pass by on my way outside and then bends over his work again. The cold wind feels good on my flushed face as I enter the street. My pace slows as I near home. There is tightness around my temples. It's a relief to get out of the bright sunshine and close the blinds in my bedroom.

After several hours, Alice tiptoes in. "Mother, are you asleep?"

"No. I don't feel well."

"Father and Mr. Moulton are in the study. They want to talk to you."

I get up, feeling a wave of dizziness. After a moment the room steadies and I straighten my hair and dress.

When I enter the upstairs sitting room, Theo stands up and offers me a chair. Without looking at him, I sit down and direct my words to Frank.

"I have decided to make a public denial of Mrs. Woodhull's charges."

"That's just what we were talking about before you came in," says Theo. "I think Frank can explain to you why there are problems with making a sweeping public denial. You should know Frank agrees with you that my letter was less than adequate."

"The tone was not right," comments Frank.

"I will leave you two to discuss the problem without me," says Theo. "Frank is not directly involved, so he can see things more objectively. When you and I talk," he glances at me, "we get emotional."

As if I had no right to become emotional after reading that cowardly letter.

"I can't go on like this," I tell Frank. "Theo has betrayed me!"

"The letter is weak and indecisive but it is not a betrayal. Theodore would not have stayed with you if he did not love you very much."

"I don't know anything anymore."

"Elizabeth, you must be strong. Just when things were on the mend, Mrs. Woodhull has created a very difficult and dangerous situation. A false step in this delicate situation, and all three of you will be ruined."

"An open public denial would not be a false step. Our friends expect it. Mattie and her husband told us to do it weeks ago."

"There are pros and cons that must be weighed carefully."

"It doesn't seem all that complicated to me," I reply.

"It is. When Mrs. Woodhull first published the charges, we talked about who should make a denial and how it should be worded. Theodore thought it was incumbent on Mr. Beecher to make the denial, because he was the one accused of the offense. The reverend went ahead and prepared a draft."

"Why was it never published?"

Frank glances at the door, which is closed, and lowers his voice. "This is a rather delicate matter. But I think I should tell you the truth."

"Please do."

"When the conflict began, Mr. Beecher wrote a note of contrition begging for Theodore's forgiveness. Now, the reverend feels that he cannot publish a denial of Mrs. Woodhull's story unless Theodore gives him full assurance that he will back it up."

Oh God, now I understand why Henry never did anything.

"You mean the reverend could be accused of lying?"

"Exactly. Under these circumstances I advised silence. Mrs. Woodhull already has a bad reputation. What she wrote is so full of wild statements that most people will conclude for themselves that it is a sensational invention by a person who craves the limelight. Why dignify such filth by a response?"

"But after Theodore published that cowardly letter, I must publish a denial. I have to think of my children."

"I am not telling you not to do it. All I say is think it over carefully. Remember, Elizabeth, you are a lady. You cannot sink to the level of Mrs. Woodhull. If you answer her, she will answer back. Perhaps invent more tales about orgies carried on in front of your children."

My stomach heaves. "I see what you mean."

"Perhaps there is a better solution. Why don't you write a private letter of denial and give it to me. Such a letter will permit me to say publicly that Mrs. Tilton denies the charges."

"Yes. I will write it today." The tears are flowing down my cheeks.

"Send it over with Theodore in the evening. And take heart!" Frank pats me on the shoulder reassuringly. "No one believes a word of Mrs. Woodhull's stories."

But will a statement from Frank, based on a letter of mine that is not made public, be enough? Frank is so sure his strategy will work, but I'm afraid.

October 1873

"We have to go over to Frank's house," Theo tells me. "We're late."

"But I haven't given the children their supper."

"Trust me. This is more important."

Frank answers the door and guides us down the hall to the Moulton family sitting room, which is dominated by a large mahogany bookcase. The quality of the leather bindings suggests rare first editions. If only this were just an ordinary social call and I could ask Frank about his library. Emma would come down and we could talk about the children's education while the men discussed Grant's presidency.

But this is a different type of visit. Frank informs us that the Reverend Beecher is on his way. The three of us sit quietly without saying a word. I can guess why Frank has called this meeting. He was so certain that the strategy of silence that he and Theo had adopted, and imposed on me, would work. But it didn't. Silence was not enough. The Plymouth Church people were deeply disturbed by the Woodhull charges against their pastor and expected public denials from all those named in the scandal. When months passed and no denials were forthcoming, Mr. William West, a deacon of the church, made a formal charge that Theodore was slandering the reverend, and demanded a full investigation by a church committee. Why didn't you listen to me, Frank? Together we might have persuaded Theo to write a letter of outright denial.

Henry arrives, greets us all warmly, and takes a seat.

Frank clears his throat. "I have called all of you together to discuss a very serious situation—a new threat that is going to require all our ingenuity and goodwill to surmount," says Frank. He looks first toward Theo on his left and then at me, seated by Theo's side. Then he turns to his right toward the reverend, but Henry is slumped in his chair staring at the floor.

My thoughts are interrupted by the sound of Theo's voice. "It seems to me," he observes in a loud voice, leaning forward in his chair, "the problem of Mr. West and his charges is an internal problem of Plymouth Church." He looks directly at Henry. "You are the leader of the church. All the faithful look up to you. Meet with Mr. West and persuade him to drop the charges against me."

Henry lifts his eyes and smiles wanly. His face is lined and tired. "I wish that it were so simple," he says. "Theodore, my friend, you overestimate my influence. I attempted to dissuade Mr. West from taking any action at the beginning of the summer, but he insisted that he was honor bound to protect the church from scandal. If I say anything more, they will accuse me of using the office of pastor to obstruct justice."

Theo shrugs.

"We need a different strategy," interjects Frank. "The only way out of this mess is for you," he says, addressing Theo, "to withdraw from the church."

"I have already told many people that I am no longer a member." Turning to Henry, Theo exclaims, "I have not set foot in Reverend Beecher's church for four years. But that doesn't seem to stop them."

Frank points out that Theodore must put in writing that he is no longer a member. Then the church committee will have no jurisdiction over him. They won't be able to call him up to question him about statements he made about Reverend Beecher.

"I don't understand," I interject in a low voice. "What does Mr. West claim Theodore has been saying?"

Frank explains. "Mr. West has charged Theodore with spreading scandalous stories about Reverend Beecher, which cast discredit on the church."

"But with the exception of the letter he published, Theo has said nothing about Mrs. Woodhull's charges," I protest, looking at Theo. "You've followed the policy of silence, right?"

Theo stares at the floor.

I turn toward Frank, who explains, "Recently, Theodore has said nothing. But Mr. West is alleging that as early as August 1870 Theodore mentioned *it* to several witnesses who are willing to testify."

"Mentioned *what*?"

"For God's sake, Elizabeth, I said that Henry seduced my wife, that's what!" cries Theo.

"Who did you tell?" I shriek. Theo turns his head away.

"The most damaging allegation is that he told Mrs. Martha Bradshaw," explains Frank.

"No! For the love of God, Theo, tell me you did not tell Mattie!"

"I don't remember. I was half out of my mind."

A lump rises in my throat. I look over at Henry. His face is buried in his hands. Theo is staring out the window. Frank is looking down at the floor.

I feel so alone. Please, God, help me.

Finally, Frank says in a toneless voice that what is done is done. We have to move forward and not let the situation get out of control. Theo should immediately send a note clarifying that he is no longer a member of the church. Then he advises me to persuade Mattie not to testify.

As we walk toward home, Theo complains bitterly he has been made to appear to be a liar and a low-down scandalmonger. He should have been more careful as to what he said, but he never told an untruth about Henry. Now, to prevent an investigation, he has to resign from the church. Everyone will think that he does not dare face the investigation because he lied. "None of this is my fault, but my reputation will be ruined while the precious Reverend Beecher is hailed as a long-suffering saint." He talks continuously without looking at me or pausing for an answer.

What does he mean none of this was his fault? No one from Plymouth Church would be questioning Theo if only he had come out with a straightforward denial of Woodhull's story, but it's no use talking to him when he is in this state of mind.

As we near home, Theo proposes that we walk on together to visit Mattie right away.

"Wouldn't it be better for me to talk to her alone?"

"No. It's important that she sees that we are united as a couple."

Theo walks very rapidly on the way to Mattie's house, making it difficult for me to match my gait to his large strides. It is unseasonably warm for October, an Indian summer day. The sky is blue and children are playing and calling to one another in the street. I arrive at Mattie's house panting and dripping with sweat.

Mattie opens the door and stares at the two of us. Her dark curly hair streaked with gray frames her face, which looks unusually pale.

"Do come in."

After seating us in the parlor, Mattie takes up her knitting, and then replaces it on the side table, folding her hands in front of her.

Theo clears his throat. "We wanted to talk to you about the West charges."

"Perhaps I should send for Andrew." Mattie rises from her chair.

"No! That will not be necessary. It won't take long to say what we need to say," replies Theo. Mattie sinks back down.

Looking her in the eye, Theo comes directly to the point. "There has been lots of scandalous talk since Mrs. Woodhull published that article."

"Yes," replies Mattie, looking down at the floor.

"Elizabeth and I," says Theo, "are convinced that the best way to deal with such rubbish is to take no notice." I nod. "You see there has been some trouble between the reverend's family and mine," continues Theo, "but he apologized and we all want to forget about it. This church investigation will only bring up old wounds and go into private matters that concern only us."

"But I want to put a stop to the rumors. The scandal is hurting Reverend Beecher and Elizabeth!" Mattie cries.

"Elizabeth herself doesn't want an investigation," Theo says in a loud voice. And then more gently, "Do you, my dear?"

"No."

"And Reverend Beecher doesn't want an investigation," adds Theo.

"Are you sure?" queries Mattie. "Did he say that?"

"Yes, but you don't have to take our word for it," replies Theo. "Why don't you ask the reverend himself?"

"I will," Mattie replies softly.

"If he confirms that he does not want an investigation, will you tell Mr. West you will not testify?" asks Theo.

"I don't know. I have to talk to Andrew. He feels that we must protect the reverend." Mattie's voice shakes. Against her pallor, the redness of her nose and eyes stands out, but she lifts her chin and meets Theo's gaze squarely.

Theo stands up abruptly, muttering something about keeping an appointment at his office. While taking leave, he looks at me. I accompany him to the door.

"You have to convince her," he whispers.

When I return to the parlor, Mattie is blinking back tears.

"Please don't testify against me, Mattie."

Mattie sobs loudly. "I don't want to, Elizabeth. Believe me."

"I know, my friend."

Once Mattie has calmed down, I take her two hands in mine. "Did Theo tell you something about me and the reverend? Tell me. I need to know."

"Yes, yes," Mattie blurts out. "What is wrong with him? Has he gone crazy?"

"What did he say?"

"The first time he talked to me he said Reverend Beecher is not as saintly as he appears. If you want to know more, he said, talk to Elizabeth. The next time I saw him he told me that the reverend was an evil man who had seduced you. I didn't tell anyone, not even Andrew, until Andrew told me that Theo had said almost the same thing to him. I don't believe a word of Theo's accusations. Something must be wrong with him!"

"Theo went through a prolonged period of deep despair after baby Paul died."

"God rest his sweet soul!"

"I was very despondent, too. It was Reverend Beecher who helped me. Theo resented us becoming such close friends."

Mattie is looking at me as though expecting me to explain further. "Theo did not fully understand how I needed spiritual help from Mr. Beecher. It was a pure friendship based on the spiritual help he gave me."

I want to tell her that everything between Henry and me was pure because we loved each other deeply. But, of course, she wouldn't understand.

Mattie nods. "Now I think I understand. Sometimes husbands see things differently. Jealousy is part of human nature."

"Yes. Theo would have gotten over it, but at that time, he was going through a crisis with Mr. Bowen. Henry did something that made it worse. He didn't mean to hurt Theo, but things happened.

That is why I don't want an investigation. Theo will begin to say things about the reverend, and to defend himself, the reverend will have to say things about Theo. You know how men are. They never want to back down or admit they were wrong. Then the committee will call me to ask what I remember, forcing me to take sides between my husband and the reverend."

"I see."

"I love them both, in different ways, of course."

"Don't worry! I'll tell Mr. West I won't testify. Andrew will want me to talk to the reverend first."

"I am sure that Reverend Beecher will say the same thing."

"Then I promise I won't testify."

We hug. Our conversation turns to plans for the church to offer more classes for working women. She says that there will be a meeting at our friend Maria Ovington's house soon.

The next few days are very tense at home. Theo is extremely moody. He spends most of the time pacing in his study. He writes a letter to the church committee saying he ceased attending Plymouth Church about four years ago and no longer regards himself as a member. We are both relieved to hear the news that the committee will recommend to the congregation that his name be removed from the church rolls with no further action, but Theo remains troubled and despondent. He is sure that people are criticizing him for dropping his membership so as not to have to appear to answer the charge that he slandered the pastor.

On Friday morning, Theo announces that he intends to go to the evening services to make his position clear. He doesn't want me to accompany him. After he leaves, the time passes very slowly. I try to work on a wool sweater I am knitting for Carroll. What if Mr. West criticizes Theo in front of everyone and Theo lashes back? What if he points to Henry and says this man is the liar who pretends one thing and lives another? Noticing that I have not counted the drop stitches correctly, I give up trying to knit and start pacing the floor.

When Theo returns, he says that everything went well and he is very tired. He goes to the guest room and closes the door. I notice his light is still on and walk up to the closed door but do not knock.

The next day there is a meeting of church women at Maria's house. She welcomes me with a big hug at the door. Mattie is already there conversing with Maria's husband, Edward. Next to the Ovingtons, she looks very petite. They are both big-boned, a bit round in the middle, and full of good cheer. Maria's prematurely white hair sets off her clear blue eyes in a round face full of good humor. Edward gets up to welcome me. He calls me the ministering angel of Plymouth Church and teasingly inquires whether I have brought him any of my special chicken soup.

"There are definite advantages to a long illness," he tells Mattie. "When I was bedridden several years ago Maria was always cooking all sorts of delicacies to stimulate my appetite and Elizabeth brought over all her healing recipes. For almost a year I was treated like a king! Now that I am fully recovered it seems they have forgotten me," he adds with a smile.

"Don't be such a tease!" admonishes his wife. "Elizabeth brought some delicious cookies just the other week and you ate much more than is good for you."

"They were very palatable, I must admit," he replies. "And now I will leave you ladies to your meeting. My further presence will only hinder your charitable good works."

I sink into a soft chair and eat the biscuits and jam Maria brings me. Her house is not elegant like Laura Bullard's. The oversized chairs seem large for the room and there is clutter everywhere, but it is cozy. I feel safe here.

Mattie asks, "Should I call our little meeting to order?"

Maria says, "Before we begin, maybe Elizabeth would like to know what happened at the Friday services."

"Yes. Please tell me."

"Both Mr. Tilton and Reverend Beecher were magnificent!" exclaims Maria. "Theodore asked for permission to speak. He then stood up and said there were erroneous reports circulated that he had slandered the pastor of Plymouth Church. Although he had not attended services for many years, he was present tonight to answer that charge in front of the reverend and all his friends. If the reverend had any complaint to make of his conduct, he was ready to answer as an honorable man. The reverend rose and said in a kindly tone that he had no complaint against Mr. Tilton. He thanked Mr. Tilton for all his past contributions to the church and hoped their friendship would endure in the future."

"Mr. West and his group must have felt ashamed for stirring up trouble between old friends," says Mattie.

"Yes," replies Maria, "the reverend and Mr. Tilton gave them a lesson in Christian charity and forgiveness."

"Glory be to God!" I cry, tears streaming down my cheeks.

"Are you all right?" Both of my friends stare at me with concern.

"Yes! God has answered my prayers! All will be well! I am so grateful!"

Mattie comes over to the sofa where I sit and puts her arms round me.

"Thanks for helping us when we needed it most," I tell her. "God has protected us from those who would do us harm."

Mattie shakes her head slightly. "Andrew doesn't think the danger is over. He still thinks that Theodore should make a strong statement denying the Woodhull story."

"I am sorry to have to agree," says Maria. "It is the only way to put the case to rest forever."

March 1874

"I'm so glad you've come," exclaims Emma as she opens the door for me, "I was just about to go to your house." She takes my coat and ushers me into the parlor.

Emma and I have become close. Since Laura Bullard left for Europe to recover her spirits after her mother's death, Emma is the only woman friend with whom I can talk frankly. Mattie and Maria are still good friends, but they are puzzled that Theo has never made another statement. I cannot tell them the truth, so I have to make lame excuses. With Emma it's different.

Once we are seated, Emma leans forward and tells me, "I finally talked to Reverend Beecher yesterday afternoon."

"Did he come here?"

"Yes. Frank wasn't home, so I had a chance to talk to him alone."

"I hope you didn't tell him everything we talked about last time."

"Why? I thought you wanted him to know that you are thinking of leaving Theodore and going to your mother's house," replies Emma.

"Last week I was very discouraged and it was difficult to think things through. Theodore was acting so strangely. He kept talking about my sin."

"You poor dear! As if he hasn't sinned himself."

Unlike her husband, Emma understands that what happened is not so simple. Henry wrote me that she is a fine person worthy of our trust, and now I see that he is right. Seated on the chair opposite, the black velvet ribbing in her ivory dress setting off the contrast between her dark hair and pale skin, Emma reminds me of Laura. Emma is not so handsome of face, but she has the same natural touch of elegance and the same generosity and fairness in her judgments of people.

"Both Theo and I must be willing to forgive and forget," I tell her.

"Right. Either he should make a genuine effort to renew the marriage or ask for a separation. One way or the other."

"What did Henry say when you told him I was thinking of leaving Theo?" I inquire.

"He is very worried," replies Emma. "He knows Theodore is not an easy man to live with. But he says that you must have faith. When Theo is suffering from melancholia he is unreasonable, but when he comes out of it he can be the most generous of men."

"I pray to God to give me strength to endure Theo's moods. I know he has a noble heart."

At this moment Frank comes in with their son, who is about twelve. He rushes over to give his mother a hug and kiss. He is already taller than she, but his demonstrative affection for his mother is like that of a small child. Frank greets me cordially and then his wife. He tells us that he would like nothing better than to stay and converse with us, but unfortunately he has to go back to the office for another interminable meeting, in which the elders of the firm will resist new ways of doing things that would improve efficiency.

"I wish I could take you with me, dear." He smiles at Emma. "You have more common sense than any of them."

There was a time when Theo paid me such compliments. After Frank leaves and the boy goes upstairs, I tell Emma in a choking voice, "Tell Henry not to worry. I have taken a vow to create a happy home for Theodore and the children."

Emma grasps my hand. "I know it is not easy. You have suffered terribly since that Woodhull woman launched her slanders. I told Frank and Theodore not to trust her."

"So did I, but Theo wouldn't listen to me. He was bewitched by her."

"He was not the only one," Emma replies. "Henry is afraid that you will break under the strain of what you have gone through. He asked me whether you have any household help these days."

"We can no longer afford it. But my girls help."

"The reverend asked me to give you something for the children. He wanted me to buy something for them, but since I did not know exactly what they need, I thought I would just give you . . ." Emma does not meet my eyes as she hands me an envelope. A hot flush spreads over my cheeks. I have no choice but to take it. Flory and Alice are young ladies now and they have no decent clothes.

"Henry is always talking about what a wonderful mother you are and how exceptionally talented the children are. Is Flory still taking piano lessons?" asks Emma.

I still can't meet Emma's eyes, but I reply, "Yes, she wants to be a pianist. Does your son play?"

"Yes. His teacher says he is doing well. I'm surprised because Frank and I have no musical talent."

"It's the same with drawing and us. Theo is a talented writer and poet but he has no inclinations toward the visual arts. But Alice and Ralph are very talented at drawing."

"And you?"

"I play the piano and I like arts and crafts, but I have no special talent."

"You are too modest," replies Emma. After a moment, she says, "Henry will be relieved to hear you are not thinking of going to your mother's house. He told me things are taking a dangerous turn and now is not the time for a separation."

"What do you mean?"

"The reverend did not explain. He talked about new clouds on the horizon. Frank told me he is worried about the Advisory Council of Congregational Churches."

"Yes, Theodore mentioned that the council is calling for an investigation. According to them, it was improper for Plymouth Church to drop him from the membership rolls without investigating the charge of slander against him." I add that Theo did not seem too worried. He dismissed the whole thing as shenanigans among rival ministers. "Much ado about nothing!" was his comment.

"Frank doesn't see it that way," says Emma. "He agrees with Theodore that Henry's rivals are using this issue to embarrass him, but he thinks they could be dangerous."

"I can't believe that Christian ministers would be so low as to call a meeting to embarrass a fellow minister."

"They may be ministers, but they are also subject to the passions of ordinary men," Emma replies.

"Oh dear, when Theo went to the Friday night services and the reverend said he had nothing to accuse him of, I thought life was going to return to normal."

"I feel so sorry for you—all three of you have suffered more than enough."

"The danger to Henry's reputation is what tortures me the most. Sometimes I wake up in a cold sweat thinking that his life's work is ruined."

Emma nods her head. "The reverend is also very worried. Each time he survives one crisis, some other problem pops up. He feels tired and sick at heart."

If only I could talk to Henry, comfort him.

Emma continues, "You know there is quite a bit of feeling against Theodore among the Plymouth Church people. They feel he should speak up and defend the reverend."

"I know. My friends Mattie and Maria told me that Theo must make a public denial of the Woodhull charges. They are very concerned about the damage to the church."

"Just yesterday, people at church were saying Mr. Tilton is behaving very strangely. Why doesn't he stand up like a man and defend his wife and children? Why is he letting a good man's reputation sink?"

"I tried to get Theo to make a denial."

"I know," Emma replies.

"What else did people say?" I inquire.

"They think that it is impossible that a man of Mr. Beecher's reputation could have done something so low. If anything had really happened, Mr. Tilton would not be living with his wife. They suspect that it is just some scheme between Theodore and Mr. Beecher's enemies."

"That's not fair," I protest, suppressing my own doubts about my husband's motives.

"I agree it's not fair to Theodore," responds Emma. "But fair or not, that's the way the church people see it. Frank is worried that some scheme could be afoot to pressure Theodore to take a definite position. Flush him out!"

"Why can't people just leave us alone?"

"Oh, Elizabeth, how I wish they would, but I'm afraid they won't."

Things Fall Apart

April 1897

Elizabeth became aware that someone was bathing her forehead with something cool, but the terrible, pounding headache did not go away. It was like the migraines she suffered that awful spring when the scandal hit the newspapers. Emma had been right, she thought. People did not leave us alone. The press hounded us.

She hadn't wanted to read the newspapers, but Theo always brought them home. One day, when her migraine was so bad that she had to lie down, he had sent the newspaper up to the bedroom with one of the children.

"Mother, did you say something?"

Elizabeth's eyes were beginning to focus, but she wasn't sure where she was. There was something on the side table that looked like a newspaper. Had Flory brought it for her to read?

"Please take it away. I don't want it."

"Mother, what's wrong? I'm just trying to bathe your forehead with this cool towel."

"*No*, the newspaper. Take it away, please, please take it away. I don't want to read those awful things."

"Mother, I canceled the local paper years ago. That's not a newspaper on the table. It's Father's book of poems, open to the one about the seashore that you like so much. You remember, the book Aunt Annie brought you. Rest easy. Here are the pills for your headache."

Elizabeth dutifully swallowed the pills. She wanted to explain that she had confused the past with the present, apologize to her dear daughter, but the words wouldn't come. She gave up and concentrated on the past, trying hard to remember exactly what had come out in the newspapers that precipitated the final crisis. It was important to understand how things had begun to fall apart.

At first the details were fuzzy, but the sequence of events gradually became clear. The Advisory Council of Congregational Churches had met that spring and criticized Plymouth Church for allowing Theodore to withdraw from membership without an investigation of the charges he allegedly made against Reverend Beecher. A few days later, Frank came over to show Theo an article in the *New York Herald* suggesting that the members of the council had ulterior motives. Their real object, according to the *Herald*, was to rake over the embers of the Woodhull scandal and embarrass a fellow minister.

Elizabeth remembered how Theo and Frank gloated that the manipulations of those supposedly pious men of God on the council had been found out. But they rejoiced too soon!

Dr. Leonard Bacon, the chairman of the council, stung by the suggestion in the press that he was going after Beecher, stated publicly that he believed in the reverend's integrity. Beecher's only mistake was in being too magnanimous with the real villain, Mr. Theodore Tilton, the vile spreader of malicious rumors.

The day that Leonard Bacon's speech was published in the news, Elizabeth recalled hearing a sound like a wounded animal coming from the parlor. When she ran into the room, Theo was trembling and weeping, his arms flailing like a person berserk. He grabbed the newspaper lying on the table, threw it at her, and yelled, "Look what you have done to me! Read it! My good name is gone forever. Bacon has publicly branded me a vile slanderer, a knave, worse than a dog because I tried to save a lying clergyman who does not deserve to be protected."

She had tried to reason with him, but it was no use. They hardly spoke for a week.

June 1874

"I have to go out." Theo opens the front door.

"Will you be home for supper?"

"No. Don't wait up for me."

I go on with my household chores. The hours pass by. When darkness descends, I light a reading lamp and pick up a book, but it's impossible to concentrate. Theo must be at Frank's house.

It's almost midnight. Should I stay up? He probably won't come home tonight. I walk into the bedroom. Just as I'm leaning over the night table to blow out the candle, I hear footsteps. Theo's tall body frames the doorway.

"Elizabeth, I must talk to you."

Straightening up, I beckon him to come in. "It's very late. I was just going to bed."

"Come to the study," he says.

I put on my slippers and follow him down the hall.

Books and papers are scattered everywhere. A sudden summer breeze coming through the open window lifts papers from the desk and floats them onto the floor. The lamp flickers. Theo pays no attention. He searches in the mess and uncovers a newspaper, which he holds tight in his hand.

"What is it?" I ask, extending my hand.

He moves his arm out of my reach. "Sit down. I must tell you what has been happening before you read it."

In the lamplight Theo's face is very pale. He meets my gaze for a moment and then shifts his eyes. His legs are crossed and the top foot is jiggling, occasionally hitting the side of the desk. *Thump, thump.* A cramp in my stomach subsides into a dull ache.

"Tell me."

"I have suspected this for a long time," says Theo, tossing the stray locks of hair back off his face, "but now I am sure. *Your* beloved pastor has decided to strike at me to save his own skin. He has organized all the church stalwarts against me."

"But—"

"Let me finish!" Theo rises from his chair and paces the room. "They pretend to be liberals, your precious pastor and the whole lot at Plymouth Church. All roads lead to God, says Reverend Beecher, even the Catholics and Jews, maybe the Hindus too can be saved. But it is all a sham. A disgraceful hoax!"

"What do you mean?"

"While they talk of the many roads to God, they condemn me for having doubts about the literal inspiration of the scriptures. They accuse me of being a godless man because I say that the divorce laws in New York State are too harsh. What hypocrisy!"

"Shh! Please, Theodore, don't shout! The boarders can hear every word."

"I have done nothing to Reverend Beecher," Theo continues in a whisper so loud it is almost a hiss. "Although he injured me, I turned the other cheek and kept silent so as not to injure him. They say my silence is cowardice. These godly Christians think I should lie to protect their pastor. If I refuse, I am a vile slanderer, a knave, a dog."

"It is true you never said anything against Henry in a public forum, but you did talk to Mattie and her husband."

"Don't interrupt. I am not finished," cries Theo, glaring at me. In a softer tone, he adds, "I have to tell you what is in my heart. Listen, I know it is hard for you to believe this, but I am convinced that Henry is behind the attack that Leonard Bacon made upon me."

"How can that be? Frank doesn't think Bacon is a friend to Henry. On the contrary—"

Theo stops pacing. "What do you mean?"

"Emma told me Frank thinks that all those ministers in the council are envious of Henry's renown as a preacher and would like nothing better than to humble him. What they wanted to do was force discussion of the Woodhull charges to tarnish Henry's reputation."

"Maybe that was true at the beginning. But now Henry is working with them to destroy me. Bacon says that I refused to answer the charge of slander. Where does he get that false information? From Henry and his people. Henry knows full well that I went personally to the Friday services and said before everyone that I was willing to answer any charge against me. But he fed false information to the council that I resigned from the church to escape answering the charge of spreading slander. To save his reputation he is willing to sacrifice mine."

"Theo, you know Henry would never do that."

"Henry or one of his followers at Plymouth Church. What does it matter? Elizabeth, you don't understand what is happening. They have launched a campaign against me. I am one man against the most powerful congregation in America. I didn't tell you this before, but the issue published a month ago is the last. The *Golden Age* has failed because they are painting me as a godless radical."

"But Henry has always supported the *Golden Age*. Didn't he help Frank get financial backers?"

"Because he was afraid that I would reveal his secret. Now he has decided to crush me. I can't get backers for another paper with all this slander against me. I am finished. I cannot even maintain my family without renting out the best rooms of my house to boarders. And you still think Henry loves you!"

"As a friend. And he loves you, too, Theo. I am sure we can persuade him to make some statement about Bacon's speech."

"More than two months have gone by and the man of religion has said nothing. If he were a true friend, would he try to destroy your husband's livelihood? What will happen to our children now that they have branded their father a godless knave? Do you and your children matter to him? *No!* The only thing that matters to Henry is Henry!"

"Let's talk to Henry. I can't believe he would do this to us."

"I'm through talking."

Once again, a gust of wind ruffles the papers on the desk. I hear a soft patter of rain and smell the scent of wet earth. Theo goes to the window and stares out at the night.

After returning to his seat, he announces, "I wrote a letter in reply to Bacon's attack. Since neither Bacon nor Beecher has said anything to remove the stain on my character, I decided to send it to the newspapers."

"Is that it?" I ask. Theo hands the newspaper to me and I examine the letter addressed to Dr. Bacon. The date is June 21, 1874. I start reading. On the first page, Theo says that he had been a member of Plymouth Church for many years, during which time he became a close friend of the Reverend Beecher. In 1870, the reverend "committed against me an offense which I forbear to name or characterize."

My stomach contracts. I read on, trying to grasp where Theo is going with this. The letter is very long.

Theo tells me, "There's an important addition at the end." I turn to the last page and see a letter dated January 1, 1871, quoted in Theo's text:

> *Brooklyn, Jan. 1, 1871*
>
> *I ask Theodore Tilton's forgiveness, and humble myself before him as I do before my God. He would have been a better man in my circumstances than I have been. I can ask nothing except that he will remember all the other breasts that would ache. I will not plead for myself. I even wish that I were dead . . .*
>
> *H. W. Beecher*

After quoting from Henry's letter, Theo's text goes on to say:

> *The above brief extract from Mr. Beecher's own testimony will be sufficient, without adducing the remainder of the document, to show that I have just ground to resist the imputation that I am the creature of his magnanimity.*

This must be the note Frank was talking about when he said that Henry was afraid to deny the Woodhull story because he had written a letter of contrition. A wave of heat rises from my chest through my throat, suffusing my face. Driven by the wind, the rain batters the window. I rise, holding on to the side of the chair to steady myself, and wave the newspaper under Theo's nose.

"What is this? A letter to you from Henry written in 1871. You liar! You gave me my letter to burn and then told me that all correspondence would be destroyed. You swore on your word of honor."

"I thought it advisable to keep some evidence. It was a good idea, seeing that now Henry is out to destroy me."

"What? It was part of the agreement. The tripartite pact you signed with Henry and Bowen. All correspondence was to be destroyed."

"Elizabeth, you don't understand. They are out to get me. I have to defend myself. You must stand by me. I am your husband."

"Defend yourself by destroying a dear friend? *No! No!* I cannot stand by you!"

"Listen, my letter to Bacon is not against you, my darling. I held my anger against Henry for all these years just to protect you. The letter says that he committed an offense but does not say what."

"Theo, you have a way with words, but I have learned to look at your intentions. You talk of an offense you refuse to name, but your dear friend Mrs. Woodhull named it, didn't she?"

"The letter was specifically designed to defend *my* reputation without accusing *you*. Believe me, Lib, darling! I rewrote it several times to be sure nothing could be interpreted as a stain on your character."

"Oh my God, Theo, you know an attack on Henry is an attack on me!"

"My darling, I swear I will protect you, but please don't ask me to lie for you." Theo grabs my hand and pulls me toward him, but I push him away as hard as I can.

"You're the liar! You swore the letters were all destroyed. You claim to be a truth lover. You're so pure you can't lie to protect your wife. Then how come it was so easy to lie about the letters? Hypocrite! No one is trying to destroy you. You are out to destroy Henry and me. You will stop at nothing until we are all ruined."

Theo comes toward me. "Please, Elizabeth, listen to me—"

I put out my hands to fend him off. "Get away from me!" I scream. "Give me the letters! Where are they? Where are you hiding them? Liar! Cheat!"

I start to search through the papers on the desk. Not finding anything, I throw the papers in heaps on the floor. "Where are they? Give me my letters!"

"Stop!" cries Theo. "The letters are not here. I left them with Frank for safekeeping."

"You gave my personal letters—letters I wrote to you about my innermost thoughts and intimate feelings—to someone else?"

"He's not going to read them. They're in a box. Sealed." Theo sits down and cradles his head in his hands.

I go to the door and turn back to look at Theo. His face is still hidden. Very softly I say, "Traitor!"

He does not move.

The hallway is dark. I walk slowly, groping the walls with my fingers. The stillness of the night is interrupted by the sound of a door on the next floor being quietly closed.

It's hard to fasten the latch of my bedroom door with my shaking hands.

July 1874

I pick up the sweater, a new one I am knitting for little Ralph, and sit down in the parlor near a window, willing myself not to think about the Bacon letter.

An offense you forbear to name or characterize. How are the readers of your letter characterizing it, Theo?

Count the drop stitches, knit, count again, purl. The knitting needles are heavy in my hands and my thoughts become disjointed.

My hand is clutched to my chest holding a letter proclaiming my innocence, while my feet propel me toward the building that houses the office of the *Brooklyn Eagle*. A bronze sculpture of a golden eagle perches atop the portico, its wings spread as though about to swoop down on hapless prey.

Entering the portico, I come upon a glass door with brass knobs. An old man with a flowing white beard opens the door a crack but shakes his head when I offer him the letter.

"The *Brooklyn Eagle* only accepts letters written by ladies."

I protest that I *am* a lady and push the door. The old man staggers backward.

Once inside, I smooth my hair and try to stop panting. The old man takes the note from me, looks it over, and then calls to a young clerk at the front desk. "Hey, Mulligan, have a look at this."

The younger man reads it and exclaims with a smirk, "Ladies don't write letters like this. Show her the door."

The old man whistles. The eagle perches on his arm and then dives toward me with long talons extended. I drop to the floor and hear the swish of its wings swooping past me, and then the *clop, clop* of horses' hooves. Through the glass doors, a carriage can be seen approaching. I struggle to stand up and run toward it, but my petticoats drag me down. "Help me!"

The sound of my own voice startles me awake.

I jump up from my chair to look out the window, almost tripping over the sweater I was knitting that had fallen to the floor. It's Maria's carriage. I shake my head back and forth to banish the image of the swooping eagle before rushing out to greet her. I return inside briefly to get my gloves and bonnet. The leering faces of the old man and the young clerk come back momentarily in the shadowy interior of my home, but the bright sunlight banishes them. Seated next to my friend in the carriage, I feel safe.

"I hope you are not busy, but it seemed too fine a day to waste indoors." Maria smiles at me. "How are you feeling? Edward was worried because you looked so poorly when you came by."

"I don't feel physically ill, just very tired. I can't sleep at night."

"Do you want to talk about it?"

"It's Theo's letter to Bacon. The one he published in the newspaper. I want to do something, but I don't know what! I can't just stand by and let a good man's reputation be ruined."

"What does your mother think?"

"I can't talk to Mother about this."

Maria nods. "She came by Mattie's house yesterday while I was there. She was very excited. Kept insisting that you should leave Theodore and go to live with her. She said that she would give notice to the boarders so that you and the children would have enough room at her house. But you don't want to do that, do you?"

"I want my children to have a father."

"Of course."

"I love my mother dearly. She would sacrifice anything in the world for me and the children, but it is very difficult for me to live in the same house as her."

"Lib, you are like a sister to me. If ever you need a place to stay, my house is yours."

"Oh no! You have a husband and two children. That would be asking too much!"

"A husband and two children who adore you! Edward and I will never forget you were the one person of all our friends who never deserted us during his long illness."

"Maria, you are a sister to me. Edward is a brother."

"Edward will not permit any criticism of you. After Mrs. Woodhull's vile story was printed, he used to say that if a compassionate angel like you were guilty of such immorality, we might as well give up hope for all mankind!"

I look away.

Maria goes on to say, "Of course neither Edward nor I have ever had any doubts about you or the reverend. But since people are talking constantly, I would like to be able to say I have heard a denial direct from you. Do you mind if I ask you if the reverend ever said or did anything to you that was improper?"

My pulse quickens. *Improper* is the perfect word for how society defines the ties between Henry and me, but it wasn't improper, it was love, and I won't let the word *improper* sully the deepest and truest love that can unite two human beings. I turn and look Maria directly in the eyes. "Never. Absolutely not."

The carriage comes to a stop with a jolt. While conversing, I did not notice we were approaching the park. We descend and walk slowly arm in arm.

"I talked to my brother and my stepfather about Theodore's letter to Reverend Bacon."

"What did they say?"

"My brother counseled me not to write a letter to the newspapers denying that the offense mentioned by Theodore referred to anything improper between me and the reverend. He urged me to maintain a united front as a couple, to think twice before doing anything independently of Theo."

"And your stepfather?" asks Maria.

I recount my meeting with my stepfather, Judge Morse, in detail. Now that he had initiated a separation from my mother, the judge was reluctant to counsel me out of concern he would in some way contradict her advice and thus come between mother and daughter. I assured him that I look to Mother for emotional support, but she knows little of the practical world and thus cannot give me the kind of counsel I expect from him. When I explained my intention of writing a letter for publication in the newspapers, he cautioned me not to act with haste in such a delicate matter.

My stepfather told me he had read Theo's letter in reply to Bacon with attention. If I were to write to the newspapers denying that the unnamed offense referred to anything "improper" between my pastor and me, some people might see my letter as a confirmation of their suspicions. At the very least they would infer that Theodore believes something improper occurred.

Maria suggests we sit down on a bench. A few pigeons come round hoping for a handout, but when an elderly lady on the next bench begins to give them dried corn, they quickly abandon us.

"I see what the judge means," says Maria. "Edward and I thought of advising you to write a letter—not only for the reverend's sake but for your own—and for your children—but I see his point that a letter might do more harm than good."

"I feel terribly guilty about not doing anything," I tell her. "The thought that I am in some way responsible for a stain on Henry's . . . Reverend Beecher's reputation keeps me awake at night. The last time you and I took a drive and stopped to visit Mattie, I felt she had lost confidence in me. She thinks that I do not have the courage to stand up and protect our pastor."

"Why do you say that? Mattie knows you are in a difficult position," replies Maria.

"When we went to see her, she was so silent and withdrawn. She kept looking at me with reproachful eyes."

"She is probably just terribly worried about you. We all are."

"I know. I do not deserve such true friends."

Maria puts her arm round me and says in a low voice, "Lib, listen. Maybe it would help if you could talk to some of the brethren of the church and tell them what you told me. You want everyone to know nothing improper occurred. A letter to the newspaper is not the right way to do it. But you could talk to some leaders of the church, and they could spread the word."

I stare at Maria. "Dear God! Now I remember. Judge Morse told me now is not the time, but be patient, God will open a path. You're right. I must talk to the church brethren."

"But how would Theodore take it?"

"He won't like it. He says the church brethren are out to get him."

"Elizabeth, dear friend, do what your heart tells you. Of course, Edward and I want you to have the opportunity to clear your reputation and the reverend's—but our intention is not to drive a wedge between husband and wife."

"Theodore will never agree. I have to do it on my own. I have waited almost two years to answer Mrs. Woodhull's lies and I mean to do it."

I rise from the bench, frightening two pigeons that have strayed back to us after finishing the elderly lady's provisions. "Can we go back now? Can you tell Reverend Beecher I want to speak to some lay leaders of the church?"

Maria assures me that she and Edward will make the arrangements.

"When you talk to Reverend Beecher, please tell him I had nothing to do with Theodore's letter to Reverend Bacon. He did not consult me or show it to me before publishing it in the newspapers."

Maria nods her assent. The *clack, clack* of the carriage wheels alternates in imperfect syncopation with the *clop, clop* of the horses' hooves.

"Some things cannot be helped!" I blurt out. "Sometimes we just have to do what our hearts tell us is right, what we believe God would want us to do, and just hope that our loved ones understand."

"Are you afraid Theodore will leave you?"

"Yes. And even more afraid to lose my children."

"*No!* Surely there is no danger of that."

"Susan always used to say that the laws of New York State give women very little protection in case of divorce."

"I don't want to criticize Miss Anthony, but don't you think the suffrage ladies sometimes exaggerate injustices to women? Most judges, like your stepfather, are fair-minded men."

"I don't know much about the law, but I am willing to entrust my fate to God. I want to talk to the brethren. Today."

Maria and I get down at her house. Her husband, Edward, is not in, so she asks her eldest son to accompany her and departs in the carriage to look for Reverend Beecher. Several hours pass by. Finally, Maria returns and says that arrangements are being made for me to testify before a special committee of Plymouth Church. The meeting will take place at her house. Everything is happening too quickly.

"I need to talk to my stepfather first."

Maria agrees it would be best for me to get some legal guidance before meeting with the committee. I walk quickly to Judge Morse's residence and find him at home. He looks grave when I mention the nature of my errand but immediately agrees to come with me. He is more stooped than ever and walks slowly.

When we return to the Ovington residence, Maria greets us at the door and ushers us into the parlor. A short gentleman of large features and a powerful build, whom I have never seen before, rises from his seat as we enter the room. My stepfather salutes him warmly and the man responds with a broad grin and a hearty handshake. Judge Morse turns and introduces me to General Benjamin Tracy. Theodore once told me Tracy is a man of considerable influence in the Republican Party.

General Tracy tells us he is advising the investigative committee as to how to proceed in fairness to all parties in the controversy. He then expresses high regard for Judge Morse and says he is glad that Mrs. Tilton will have access to advice of such high caliber. Turning to me, he says with a smile, "Of course, this is not a court of law, but a more informal proceeding. You will be free to say anything you like to the committee, and you do not have to answer each and every question the committee chooses to ask. We want to hear what you have to say. Our object is to find out the truth and, hopefully, put to rest any untrue rumors. We would be very grateful if you would consent to testify."

I nod in silent assent. Judge Morse asks some questions about the procedures of the committee and the safeguards to ensure that his stepdaughter will not be unduly pressured. General Tracy has ready answers for everything. He assures the judge that he will look out for me. I shift in my chair and fold and unfold my hands.

"I would like to speak to Judge Morse alone for a moment."

"Yes, of course," says Tracy.

Edward guides my stepfather and me to the upstairs sitting room and leaves us.

"Are you having second thoughts?" inquires Judge Morse. "You don't have to testify if you don't want to."

"I want to testify to clear Reverend Beecher's name and my own. But I am worried about Theodore. He will see my testimony as a betrayal."

"Why? You have a right to clear your own good name."

"He believes the Plymouth Church people are out to destroy him. They are blaming everything on him, deliberately trying to make him look bad."

"I understand, but his refusal to name the offense is what is creating the trouble. A statement that the reverend is not guilty of any improper conduct toward you from your own lips will clear the air. That is all the Plymouth Church people want to hear. A stain on the reverend is a stain on the reputation of their beloved church and its congregation. Once the reverend is cleared, I don't think they would have any reason to continue to attack Theodore."

Now I see the light. In one stroke I can clear not only Henry but also Theodore. Dear God, you are opening the way for me.

"I will testify not only to Henry's innocence but also to the innocence of my husband," I tell Judge Morse. "The reverend is not immoral and my husband is not a slanderer."

"Do you feel prepared to go before the committee?" he asks me.

"I do."

"One word of caution. You do not have to answer all their questions. Don't forget that."

Judge Morse says he will inform Tracy of my decision to testify, and then return home because he is feeling unwell. We descend the stairs. Once the judge has taken his leave, Maria beckons me to the dining room to share a cup of tea with her.

After a few minutes, General Tracy appears in the doorway and asks politely if he can enter the dining room to speak to me. Maria is about to retire, but he asks her to please stay while he gives me some idea of what type of questions will be asked. After he leaves to convoke the committee, I mount the stairs once more to the second-story sitting room, close the door, and kneel in prayer.

Dear God, I know it is a sin to lie, but it is also a sin to betray a friend or to needlessly ruin a good man. I cannot avoid one sin without committing the other. Guide me! When I was a young girl, the way to goodness was straight and narrow, but now the road meanders and I cannot see my way clearly.

Henry made mistakes, many would accuse him of a deadly sin, but he never set out to harm me or Theodore. His sin, if it was sin, sprang from too much love, not from hate. If I tell the truth, I will destroy him. All the good he has done will be wiped out.

Theodore believes that truth is the basis of morality. But is it? Which is more important, love and compassion or truth? Theo says that truth is the law of God, but dear God, love is the way you have been revealed to me.

Theo is going down the wrong path. He says he wants truth, but what he really desires is vengeance. My whole being revolts against standing with him for such a purpose. Help me save him from himself.

As I pray I feel a light concentrated in my head, flowing through my entire being. My limbs feel strong and supple. I rise and descend the stairs.

Maria shows me into the back parlor. Six men are seated around a table. To the right of the committee, slightly apart, sits General Tracy, and to the left of the committee are Maria and Edward. They show me to an easy chair facing the members of the committee.

Dear God, give me the words to absolve both Henry and Theo.

The chairman of the committee, Mr. Henry Sage, a man active in church affairs, begins by asking how many years I have been a member of Plymouth congregation and how I became acquainted with Reverend Beecher. I describe my first visit to the church when I was but a girl, my marriage to Theodore in the church, how I taught children at the Sunday School and gave classes for working women, and then describe the reverend's frequent visits to our house when he was collaborating with my husband in abolitionist work and on the periodical the *Independent*.

"How often did Reverend Beecher visit your home?"

"He visited frequently, played with the children, and had long conversations with both my husband and me. He was a good friend to the whole family."

"Did you ever have conversations alone with him?"

"Yes."

"And what did you talk about?"

"We talked about his novel *Norwood*. He wanted me to give him advice as to whether the women in his book were talking in character. We also talked about church affairs and sometimes about my husband's religious doubts."

"What did Reverend Beecher say about that?"

"He said it was normal for people of deep religious conviction to go through periods of doubt."

Mr. Sage nods.

"Can I say something?" I ask.

"Of course."

"I believe it is both my right and my duty to deny an untrue slander that has been circulating. I have come here to tell all of you that Mr. Beecher always acted as a gentleman. When I was sorely troubled by the loss of my baby, it was Mr. Beecher who guided me back to faith in God. There was never anything immoral between us in either word or deed, as God is my witness."

Dear God, forgive me if I lie. I know that the members of this committee would consider my love for Henry immoral, but it wasn't immoral to me. Dear God, I trust your judgment will be more merciful than that of any committee of men.

General Tracy smiles at me. Edward and Maria are beaming. One of the gentlemen at the committee table is busy writing all this down.

"Now we come to another aspect of the case before us," says Mr. Sage. "Did your husband ever accuse you of improper relations with Mr. Beecher, or express any suspicions?"

"You don't have to answer that," interjects General Tracy. To the committee he says in a low voice, "I don't think the committee should ask about intimate conversations between husband and wife."

"My husband feels very strongly about maintaining privacy," I respond. "As a result he has been widely misunderstood."

"How has he been misunderstood?" asks a committee member.

"Mr. Tilton believes in certain ethical principles and he lives his life accordingly. The highest principle is truth. If you cannot tell the truth without hurting innocent parties, it is best to say nothing. That is why he has said nothing about the hurt he received from Reverend Beecher. It all happened a long time ago. The two men have reconciled. Why should he start talking about it now just to satisfy the public's morbid curiosity?"

My words sound like Theodore. God must be helping me express his point of view.

Maria is smiling at me.

"You must believe me. It is not my husband who is spreading scandalous stories. He is a good man and he has tried to protect me the best he knows how. He was advised to ignore Mrs. Woodhull's attack, because answering it would just provide her an excuse to write more scandalous stories. He wanted to protect me and give her no further opportunity to spread her poison. He means no harm to Reverend Beecher. Other people are spreading rumors, and he is being unfairly blamed."

"But, Mrs. Tilton, several church members have alleged that Mr. Tilton told them—"

"I don't think we can ask Mrs. Tilton about conversations between her husband and third parties," interjects General Tracy.

I interrupt. "I know Mr. Sage is referring to the West charges. Of course, I have no way of knowing what my husband said to other people when I was not there. But I do know his character better than anyone on earth. I am quite sure that he never said any of those things about Reverend Beecher. The reverend himself does not believe that my husband said such things. He said so when Mr. Tilton went to the evening services."

"I don't think I have any more questions," says Mr. Sage. "The committee thanks you."

"There is just one more thing I want to say."

"Go ahead."

"Two good men, my husband and my pastor, are suffering needlessly because one evil woman invented a pack of lies. Reverend Beecher and Mr. Tilton have both worked tirelessly to make our country truly a land of liberty. They are both men of conscience. Don't let evil people destroy them.

"My children are suffering because of all these terrible rumors. My husband and I were wed in Plymouth Church. Our children were raised in the church. My husband is a good man and a doting father. I beg of you to help me save my family.

"My little son, Carroll, came home from Sunday School and told me one of his playmates taunted him, saying his father is telling bad lies about the minister. I kissed him and dried his tears. I told him there are bad people making up all sorts of stories. Then I reassured him that his father is a good man who loves truth and never tells lies. I did not tell Mr. Tilton. It would have broken his heart. He has tried so hard to be a model for his sons so they will grow up to be men of character and courage. Do something to put a stop to all this! I beg you. You are men of God. There must be a way. The happiness of my family depends on it."

For a moment there is complete silence except for the chirping of crickets. I look to see how the committee members are responding to my words, but most of their heads are bowed. Mr. Sage says, "Thank you, Mrs. Tilton. Your testimony has been very helpful. We are very grateful to you for coming."

Maria rises and comes over to me. She puts her arm around me and guides me to the door. My whole body is trembling. Once we are out in the hall, General Tracy approaches me.

"Mrs. Tilton, pardon me for addressing you so freely, but I must say your testimony was magnificent. Every single member of the committee was touched by what you said. You put things in perspective and made us all realize the harm that rumors do to innocent people. Rest assured that I will do everything possible to bring this investigation to a speedy and happy conclusion for all concerned."

I thank him for his kind words. The trembling of my body subsides.

Thank you, dear God, for giving me the right words to touch hearts. Is it possible that I have saved Henry and my family? Oh God, let it be true!

Maria walks me to the door. "The general is right. Your testimony was magnificent. You did the best you could, Elizabeth." She shakes her head. "Now it depends on others."

Later That Same Evening and the Days That Follow

I take leave of my friend and walk out into the night. I gaze upward at the Milky Way, brilliant in a cloudless sky, as I walk the two blocks between Maria's house and my own. A gentle breeze has arisen, tempering the mugginess of a hot July evening, wafting to my nostrils the sweet scent of flowers. Is it the scent of honeysuckle? I am floating, embraced in the all-forgiving love of God.

After years of silence, I found my voice. I carried the committee.

I open the front door, confident of my newly found power to convince Theodore.

"Where were you?" Theo raises his head from the book he is reading by lamplight in his favorite armchair in the front parlor and stares at me. He is in pajamas.

"At Maria's house."

"So late?" Theo uncrosses his legs and sits upright, his eyes fixed on mine. I drop my eyes and busy myself with removing gloves and bonnet.

"What were you doing there at this time of night? Tell me!"

I take a deep breath. "I met with some leaders of the church."

"You did what? You know perfectly well that the Plymouth Church people are trying to ruin me, and you tell me that you talked with them without even consulting me?"

"Theo, I talked with them to tell them you are not responsible for the rumors."

"Wait a minute. What did you say about Henry? Tell me that."

"I denied everything. Blotted it out!"

"That was the purpose then. To save Henry!"

"Not just Henry! To save us all! To save our family!"

Theo flings the book to the floor and rises from the chair. "Who are these gentlemen of the church? What right do they have to summon my wife and question her?"

"It's an investigative committee appointed by the church."

"You mean appointed by Reverend Beecher. He forms a committee to investigate statements I supposedly made about him and then doesn't inform me the committee exists. They secretly summon my wife without even telling me. Can't you see it is all a conspiracy to destroy me?"

"They didn't summon me, Theo. I wanted to speak to them."

Theo takes a step toward me. His face is flushed and his lower lip is trembling. "You betrayed me! You have joined with my enemies to destroy me!"

I shrink back and he turns abruptly and walks toward the stairs. I call after him, "Theo, I defended you before the committee. Please listen to me. Let me tell you what happened."

"*No!* I don't want to hear another word! I am leaving! What kind of marriage is this? No wife who loves her husband would testify against him."

He rushes up the stairs, and then comes down again, breathing hard. His hair is disheveled and he is fully dressed. "I can't find the suitcase," he yells. "For God's sake, get it for me. Pack some clothes. You can at least do that much for me."

I go upstairs quickly. His pajamas are on the bedroom floor. I find the suitcase in the closet and pack something for him. Carrying the suitcase, I descend the stairs and find him sitting in the parlor with his head in his hands. He rises and takes the suitcase from me.

I move toward the front door, blocking his exit. "Please, don't leave! You are being unjust. At least listen to what I have to say. Then do whatever you please."

"Get out of my way."

"Not until you listen to me. For the sake of the children!"

"I said get out of my way!"

Theo brushes past me murmuring, "Goodbye forever!"

In the morning, the children ask after their father, and I tell them he had to go to work very early. A gentleman who boards with us, Mr. Alfred Martin, looks up from his coffee and says that such enterprise is admirable so early in the morning. Soon the house is almost empty. The three older children go to their classes, and my mother arrives to take little Ralph to spend the day with her. After helping the elderly housekeeper clean up, I drift from room to room, incapable of planning dinner for my family and the boarders. I write down several items on a sheet of notepaper to buy at the market, but the words look blurry through my tears.

Maria stops by. She comments that I look very poorly and attributes it to a sleepless night. She herself had difficulty sleeping because she was so worried about how Theodore would react to the news that I testified before the church committee.

"He was furious! He said I betrayed him! He left me!"

"Really? He said he wasn't coming back?"

"It's over. My family is destroyed."

"But didn't you tell him what your motives were in talking to the committee? All the good things you said about him?"

"He wouldn't let me talk!"

"Maybe he will calm down and come back. You don't deserve this! You have been a devoted wife. But like everyone else, you have the right to defend your reputation. Why can't Theodore understand?" She shakes her head. Before leaving, Maria says she will come to take me riding tomorrow.

Maria, you are a good friend, always trying to take my mind off my troubles. But even you cannot mend what is broken. My marriage is over. How many years is it since I first fell in love with Theo? When he first spoke to me at church, I thought my heart would burst through my ribs. Now I am alone. Dory, my darling Dory, you used to say we were soulmates, fated for each other. Even if you come back, we no longer understand each other. We no longer pray to the same God. We look back at what has happened in the last five years, and we don't have the same history. I see what happened to us in one way and you see it in another. So, even if we try to put the pieces back together, how do we become a whole like we once were?

At suppertime, the children don't ask where their father is. They are used to his irregular comings and goings. But when I go into the kitchen to bring out the dessert, Florence follows me and asks in a low voice, "Mother, have you been crying? Is something wrong between you and Father?" I admit that we had a disagreement but reassure her that all married couples do from time to time.

Later, after making sure the children are in bed, I fall into an uneasy sleep myself. A loud *tap, tap* on the door awakens me. "Who is it?"

"It's me." Theo enters and places the candle he is carrying on the night table. I sit up and rub my eyes. He sits beside me, takes me in his arms, and begins to kiss me on the forehead.

I withdraw from him. "Why did you come back? What do you want?"

Theo kneels in front of me and begs my forgiveness. He says he must have been out of his mind when he left me last night. All the time he was thinking of me, half-crazed thoughts that he had lost me forever.

"Please, take me back," he beseeches. "I treated you abominably. Forgive me."

"Theo, you know I want us to be together. But it's no use if you think I betrayed you."

"I was mistaken!" Theo recounts how after leaving home he stayed with friends and then visited Frank in the morning. "Emma and Frank both scolded me for leaving home. Emma said the least I could have done was listen to what you were trying to tell me. Then Frank said General Tracy had come to visit and told him you did a wonderful job before the committee."

Theo narrates how Frank arranged for him to meet with Tracy in the late afternoon. "Oh, Lib, you cannot know how wonderful I felt when the general told me you had testified for me, not against me. He said you melted hearts and carried the committee not only for the reverend, but for me. I am never so happy as when I hear people praise you."

"The Lord be praised! He will save us all." I cry and clasp Theo to me.

He kisses me over and over again, pulls me onto his lap, weeps, and declares that he has always loved me and always will. After a while, he releases me and asks for a detailed account of exactly what I said to the committee. I reproduce what was said as well as I can. Theo stands up and begins pacing up and down the room.

"Now I know what to do. We will put an end to all this once and forever!" he cries. "Instead of waiting for the committee to act—they may waver and change their minds—we will take the initiative and present a draft agreement for their approval. It should be based on the main points you made before the committee but phrased in a slightly different way. Come with me to the study."

Oh, Theo, we are once again together on the same side.

It must be about one in the morning when Theo begins to dictate a draft to me. I make some suggestions. He reads it over. It's like old times when we worked into the wee hours on Theo's speeches for the abolitionist movement.

The basic gist of the draft is that Reverend Beecher committed an offense against Mr. Theodore Tilton for which he apologized. It would serve no useful purpose to inquire further into the nature of the offense, since it would involve other persons who had so far escaped gossip and require explanations of interest to no one except the parties directly concerned. Theo tells me to write down that Mrs. Tilton's testimony confirmed her innocence and purity of character and rejected the allegations that her husband had spread libelous stories against her. The document ends by saying the committee members talked with the principals in the case and examined the pertinent documents. They found no evidence of any immoral behavior on the part of any of the three parties and, on the contrary, affirm that all parties have acquitted themselves with moral integrity under difficult circumstances.

In the morning, Theo wakes up early and rushes over to Frank's house with the draft. I quickly write a note to Maria about my reconciliation with Theodore and his restored confidence in me. Now that my heart is light, I write, I would rather stay home, so let's postpone the riding trip for tomorrow. Carroll, always eager for any excuse to visit the Ovington children, is happy to deliver the note.

The following day, Theo goes out early but returns to look for some papers just as Maria passes by to take me out riding to Coney Island. I offer to stay home in case he needs me, but he urges me to go and get some fresh air.

I look for a wide-brimmed bonnet to protect me from the sun. When we get there, we do not go bathing but sit in chaise lounges and enjoy the cooling sea breezes. Chalky white clouds float leisurely across the sky, sometimes shading us from the sun. Our conversation is casual, touching on the children's progress in school and the problems of a recently widowed member of the Plymouth Church congregation. Afterward, we have lunch at a restaurant near the sea that Maria assures me is suitable for ladies.

On the way back, Maria says abruptly, "You know, Lib, I wanted you to have a relaxing day away from all pressures, but there is something you should know."

I smile at her. "Now that Theo is with me trying to solve this problem, nothing can bother me."

"It's about Theodore."

"Tell me."

"He came by our house yesterday to talk to Edward about the church investigation."

"What did he say?"

"He kept saying the reverend forced him into this thing against his will. He never wanted an investigation. But if Reverend Beecher wants to fight it out, so be it."

"But Theodore is working with General Tracy to reach a compromise."

"He did not talk that way when he visited us. Theodore told us he believes the committee was called to whitewash the reverend. We pointed out to him that the members are all good and honest men with a commitment to finding the truth, but he was not persuaded. I told him that if evidence were produced showing the reverend to be guilty, I would not support him and I am sure the committee members wouldn't either. But I believe him to be innocent, because Elizabeth assured me he never said or did anything improper."

I turn the brim of my sunbonnet round and round in my fingers.

"What alarmed me most was what he said about your testimony to the committee," adds Maria.

I wipe drops of sweat from my brow.

"Elizabeth, Theo said you are a real trump. You want to save everyone. But what you said was all fiction, well-intentioned lies."

"Oh, my God! *No!* He didn't say that!"

"I told Theodore I was there and you certainly didn't look or sound to me like a person telling lies, but he just shook his head."

Dear God, I thought you had shown me the road, but I was mistaken. I am lost in the wilderness.

"Maria, what am I going to do now?"

"Lib, I'm worried. Do you think something is wrong with Theodore? He kept pacing up and down, and his voice was so strange. He seemed unbalanced, full of hatred for the reverend. He really seems convinced something happened between the two of you. He actually used the word, you know, you committed . . . I can't say it. Sometimes men become insanely jealous for no reason. Is he having some sort of breakdown? Has he been accusing you? Making threats? Do you want to stay at my house tonight?"

"No. I will be all right. I have to talk to Theo."

When I return home, Theo is in the study, looking through heaps of papers as though trying to find some missing document. He tells me he may have to appear before the committee.

"But isn't General Tracy putting a stop to the investigation?"

Theo stops shifting through the papers on the desk and turns to me. "I don't know about Tracy. Maybe he's trustworthy. Maybe he's not. But the other members of the committee just want to whitewash the reverend. They don't care what happens to me. Or to you either."

"But didn't the general promise he would try to get the committee to adopt your draft? What happened?"

"I don't know. Maybe Henry is not willing to admit he committed any sort of offense, even an unnamed one. Maybe it's the committee that doesn't want him to admit anything. The church defends its own!" Theo resumes searching through the papers.

"Theo, we have to talk."

"I don't have time now. Later!" He does not look up.

I go upstairs to change. When I come back down, Theo is gone.

The hours pass by. After giving the boarders and the children their dinner, I enter the study. What was Theo looking for so feverishly? I don't believe he is trying to solve this problem. He must have been looking for something that would incriminate Henry and me. I rifle through heaps of papers, but they all seem to be business papers related to other matters.

Flory pops in to tell me someone is at the door. It is a messenger with a note for me.

Dear Elizabeth, I have been informed that Mr. Tilton is meeting with the committee tonight. I only hope our worst fears do not become reality. Remember, you are always welcome in our home. Your loving friend, Maria.

I tell the messenger to wait for the reply.

Beloved friend: Do not fear for me. I will stay tonight and come to you in the morning. We will both trust and wait on the Lord. Affectionately, your own sister, Elizabeth.

Theo comes home very late. When I greet him at the door, he does not tell me where he has been. I follow him to the bedroom when he goes up to change his clothes. "Theo, have you thought about what you are going to tell the committee if you are called?"

"I talked with them tonight," he says, not looking at me directly. He sighs and sits down on the bed. "It was just a preliminary discussion. I'm too tired to talk about it now."

I may never be able to face my own children again, and you don't want to talk about it. I mean nothing to you.

"Theodore, it is very important to me. I must know your intentions."

"If you must know, I do not intend to take the blame for the sins of another. I am tired of being the sacrificial goat." He stands up and shakes his fist. "If Henry wants to fight this out, he will find me ready."

If you fight Henry, you fight me!

Theo turns to me and asks, "Why should I lie to cover someone else's sins?" He shakes his head. "Sometimes I wonder why I stood by and did nothing while Victoria went to jail for several months for telling the truth. They tried to use the obscenity laws to convict her, but the real issue was that she dared to tell the truth."

I stare at him.

You think she told the truth? She twisted and perverted everything. Ruined all our lives out of spite!

He leaves the room, muttering something about how he has to work late in the study. I sit down on the bed in the same spot as where he was, feeling the warmth left by his body.

It's over. I showed you the path to save me without dishonor to yourself, but you chose not to take it.

The dress shirt that Theo has just taken off is draped over the chair next to the bed. I reach over to draw it toward me and bury my face in it, drinking in the familiar odor. Memories of our courtship come to mind, followed by a clear image of Theo holding our eldest child, Flory, in his arms for the first time, looking down at her with wonder, cradling her very gently as though she could break. I thrust the shirt away from me, and my mouth opens wide in a grimace that threatens to sunder my skull. My breast heaves and I hear howls emerging from my throat through my tautly drawn lips, but for a long time no tears come.

I cry until I am too exhausted to cry anymore. In the morning, I awaken early from a fitful sleep. Theo is not by my side. I dress quickly and put some clothes in the suitcase I packed for him a few nights ago. Then I enter the spare bedroom where Theo is sleeping. He rolls over and asks, "What is it?"

"I'm leaving you, Theo."

He rubs his eyes. "What are you talking about? Why are you wearing gloves?"

"I'm going to the Ovingtons'. Maria told me you accused me right to her face. It's over. I'm saying goodbye."

It's only a few minutes' walk to Maria's house. She shows me to the guest room on the second floor. I apologize for coming over so early before the household is fully awake. After she leaves me to attend to the morning routine of breakfast for the family, I sit down on the bed, the suitcase by my side. Maria comes dashing in, out of breath. "Theodore is here. Should I let him know you're here?"

"Yes. It's all right. I told him I was coming here."

"Well, then, I will act like everything is normal and invite him to breakfast."

Some minutes later, Maria calls me to come down for breakfast. Theo is seated at the table discussing politics with Edward. He stands and pulls out a chair for me. I sit down next to him without a word. About midway through breakfast, Theo turns to Maria.

"I think Elizabeth is under some misapprehension regarding her conversation with you yesterday. She told me she is leaving me."

Maria replies, "Mr. Tilton, don't you remember telling Edward and me that your conversation with us should be kept confidential, except for Elizabeth? I trust I reported it to her faithfully."

Theo pauses for a moment before saying, "Reverend Beecher should kiss the hem of Elizabeth's dress for saving him in front of the committee."

I move back so quickly that my coffee spills. The cup teeters but does not tip over when I rise to go upstairs. Edward beseeches Theodore to stop, because he is destroying his own family and the reverend, who is a good man. While I sit trembling on the bed in the guest room, Theo calls my name.

Maria comes up and says Theo wants to speak to me. "Of course you don't have to go if you would rather not."

"I will go down," I reply.

Maria precedes me. Theo is waiting for us below. As we reach the last step he puts one hand on my shoulder and the other on Maria's. His eyes are filled with tears.

"I leave Elizabeth in your care, Mrs. Ovington. Any kindness you show her I regard as a kindness to me."

I turn and go back up the stairs.

Late July 1874

"I was talking to your mother yesterday," says General Tracy. "She is very worried Mr. Tilton will take the children away from you."

"Mother worries too much," I reply. "Theodore brought Ralph, our youngest, to be with me."

"Does he let the older ones come to visit you?"

"Sometimes they stay here and sometimes with him. They go back and forth."

"Well, in that case, I would not advise you to sue for divorce at this time. A divorce suit, or even a suit for separate maintenance, could infuriate Mr. Tilton and make him more hostile."

We are sitting in the back porch of Maria's home, the coolest spot in the house on a hot July day. A huge old maple tree gives shade from the brilliant sunlight. Maria told me last night that the general would come by to help prepare me to give my testimony to the church committee, now that a formal investigation process has been initiated. He began the interview by asking how I was faring and whether the children and I have any financial needs. He assured me that the church community would ensure we suffer no want.

Tracy says, "You know, of course, Mr. Tilton has made a charge of adultery to the church committee?"

I nod. "I did everything I could to stop this. I tried to work with Mr. Tilton on a compromise statement to avoid all this."

"I know. God willed otherwise."

The general informs me Mr. Beecher has requested him to be one of his attorneys. He is working not only with the reverend to prepare him for testimony but also with other persons important to the case. He says that he talked with a number of people close to either Mr. Beecher or Mr. Tilton, including my mother and Mrs.

Beecher. The two ladies both mentioned an incident that occurred between Mr. Tilton and our ward, Miss Bessie Turner. He asks me for further details.

"But, General Tracy, what does this have to do with Mr. Tilton's charges against the reverend?"

"Everything. You see, my dear Mrs. Tilton, your husband has launched charges of immoral behavior. Adultery. A very serious charge indeed! If he convinces the investigative committee of the truth of these charges, you and the reverend are ruined forever. Mr. Beecher will lose his life's work. If Mr. Tilton sues for divorce, you will be in danger of losing your children. It pains me to mention it, but you know that people judge women more harshly than men in these circumstances."

"I know."

"If a man accuses others of immorality, he must be prepared to have his own life examined. Fair is fair. If we can show that Mr. Tilton had liaisons with women . . ."

I cover my face with my hands.

"Pardon me, Mrs. Tilton, the danger you are in compels me to speak of indelicate matters that I would normally never mention to a lady."

"Go on."

"If, as I was saying, we can show that he himself has indulged in immoral behavior to the extent of trying to seduce an innocent ward who was alone in the house with him, completely at his mercy, then the battle is half won. He will lose all credibility."

"But, General, I am not completely sure what his intentions were. When Bessie told me, she was not sure either."

"Mrs. Tilton, you are too good, too charitable. A grown man does not caress the neck of a young woman with good intentions. I am a man. I know."

I nod. What does General Tracy want from me?

"Mrs. Tilton, it is very important that Bessie Turner testify. Everyone says she is devoted to you. Could you talk to her?"

"I don't know. She is very young. It would be awful for her to have to say things like that about Mr. Tilton. She always thought of him as a father."

"But Mrs. Morse told me Bessie took your side when Mr. Tilton first began to make accusations against you. Surely you can persuade her to testify."

"I will talk to her, but I can't promise anything."

The conversation then turns to my own testimony. General Tracy asks me in detail about Theodore's first accusations before I went to Ohio to stay with Sarah. He wants to know why I left my husband to stay with my mother and my reasons for returning. I also tell him about what happened after I miscarried at Christmastime. He is particularly concerned about the three letters I wrote—two for Theodore and one for Mr. Beecher—after my husband lost his job as editor of the *Independent*.

"What happened to those three letters?" he asks, knitting his eyebrows.

"After he signed the tripartite agreement with Mr. Beecher and Mr. Bowen, Mr. Tilton brought the first letter back to me and I burned it."

"Do you remember what that letter said?"

I feel the heat of a blush spreading over my face. "The first letter said I had—"

"No, Mrs. Tilton, on second thought, I think it's best you don't tell me what was in that letter. The important thing is that it was destroyed. To your knowledge there is no copy of the letter, so no one can prove what it did or did not say?"

"I never heard about any copy."

"Well, if your memories of the letter are embarrassing, there is no need to summon them up. You were very ill, you had been unconscious several days before. How could you remember what the letter said?"

"It's true, I can't remember it very clearly. I know Mr. Tilton wanted me to write to help solve a business problem he was having."

"And the other two letters—where are they?"

"I don't know. Mr. Tilton said he would destroy them, but I don't think he did."

"What did the other letters say?"

"The second one, which I gave to Mr. Beecher, said he always behaved toward me as a gentleman should."

"Good."

"The third one, which Theodore insisted I write, said Mr. Beecher asked me to save him from an investigation by the Council of Ministers."

"Oh dear, that doesn't sound good. Mrs. Tilton, was it your idea to write those letters?"

"No! Mr. Tilton insisted that I write the first one and the third one. Mr. Beecher asked me to—"

"Mr. Tilton pressured you a few days after you had miscarried?"

"Yes."

"It's very important to tell the committee you were pressured to write the first letter and the third one. If the words in the letters were dictated to you by your husband, or suggested to you, don't neglect to mention it. Search your memory carefully. How much pressure did Mr. Tilton put on you? Could it be said he forced you to write the letters?"

"He put pressure on me. I wanted to be a good wife to my husband. He said he needed the first letter to solve a misunderstanding that had made him lose his job. But I am not sure I could honestly say he forced me."

"Of course, I would not want you tell anything but the truth. But think hard about the circumstances in which you wrote the letters. And emphasize how sick you were at that time. Too ill to resist the insistence of your husband! Were you attended by a nurse at that time?"

"Yes, a very good nurse. Without her expert care, I am not sure I would have pulled through. Her name is Mrs. Mitchell."

"We will try to find her."

General Tracy leaves about noon. When I rise to accompany him to the door, my legs are unsteady, as though they would buckle under me. I hold on to the chair to steady myself.

Dear God, what torment is in store for me? The first time I talked to the committee it was to defend Theo as well as Henry, but the second time will be different. In my mind, I see myself in the parlor with Theo and Henry, the day they reconciled, talked of old times, and drank to eternal friendship. What happened? Why did everything go wrong?

In the late afternoon, Henry stops by. Maria shows him into the back parlor and calls me. It is the first time I have seen him in many weeks. Maria is about to leave us alone, but he insists she stay.

Henry looks weary. His jowls are more pronounced and his hair is grayer than I remember, but his smile is still warm. He clasps my hands in his and says how glad he is to see me looking well. He inquires anxiously about the children and expresses relief when I tell him Theodore has not forbidden them to see me.

"I have been thinking of you all the time. How I wish there was something I could do to put your marriage back together again. Believe me, Elizabeth, I tried to get Theodore to see things differently."

"I tried very hard, too."

"Yes, I know. The general said your testimony to the committee was magnificent."

Henry asks whether there is anything he can do to help with the children. "Just let me know," he says. Maria interjects to say that several people have offered to help and she had the impression that Mr. Tilton would be willing to pay boarding school tuition for the two middle ones.

"That's good," replies Henry. "Theodore really has a good heart, but somehow he is obsessed with false accusations and he imagines a conspiracy against him. There is nothing any of us could do to reach him. This is the worst thing that has ever happened to me."

The worst thing that ever happened to you. What about me?

"It is my trust in God that saved me," concludes Henry. "There were days when I wanted to give up, but God urged me to have courage. I did not want this fight, it has been thrust upon me, but if I must fight, I will!"

My throat tightens.

Don't talk this way, Henry! You sound like Theo. But maybe you are right. You have no choice and neither do I. The die is cast.

Maria turns the conversation to other topics. Before taking leave, Henry says that General Tracy told him I have doubts about calling on Bessie to testify. "Why are you worried, Elizabeth? You don't think she can handle it?"

"Not exactly. I am worried about how she will be affected."

"She's over twenty, isn't she? But still, I understand your doubts. It's a shame to put a young person through this kind of experience."

That's why you came, Henry. To persuade me to talk to Bessie.

"Your mother thinks she would be willing to testify," Henry adds with a sigh. "Elizabeth, we are facing hard realities. I can't count on Frank. He will favor Theodore. They've been friends from schooldays. I guess it's to be expected, but it still hurts. I thought he would at least try to remain neutral. He impressed me as a just man." Henry wipes his brow with his handkerchief. "The worst thing about this type of crisis is finding out that someone you were very fond of is not a true friend." He sighs.

"I don't know how Mr. Moulton can support Mr. Tilton!" exclaims Maria. "But it is also hard to imagine anyone remaining neutral in this situation."

I nod. All of our friends will take sides.

Henry turns to me. "Bessie's testimony may be crucial."

"Don't worry, I will talk to her tomorrow."

Bessie, who has been staying with my mother for a few days, gives me a big hug and kiss when I visit her the next day. To my surprise, she is enthusiastic about testifying. She wants to meet with General Tracy right away.

"Don't you worry, ma'am," she cries, "Mr. Tilton will be sorry he ever accused you of anything. I remember everything he did. The way he used to yell at you and say you were not a good housekeeper. He would lock the door and yell at you. I could hear you crying!"

"But, Bessie, you don't have to testify if you don't feel comfortable."

"Don't worry about me, ma'am. You have been more than a mother to me, and I won't let anyone destroy you. I would rather die than let anyone harm you. You know, before I came to you, I had a pretty rough life. After my father died, my mother was so poor she gave me to another family for a while. Then she got remarried and came and got me. My stepfather used to yell at her all the time and hit me with a belt."

"Bessie, you never told me." I wipe away her tears.

Bessie smiles at me. "But I learned one thing. You can't run from a fight. Mr. Tilton never should have struck me. He will find out it was a big mistake."

When the day arrives for Bessie to testify, I tell my lawyer that it will be too painful for me. I would rather not be present. But Bessie comes running to me and insists that I must be there. My presence will give her courage.

Holding her chin high, at first Bessie begins her testimony in an unnaturally high voice. General Tracy smiles reassuringly at her when he takes over the questioning, and she slows down.

How long had you been with the Tiltons when you first noticed infelicities in their life?

I think about a year after they moved to their new house, about 1865.

What did you observe?

Well, I observed that Mr. Tilton was a very selfish man, very hard, very fastidious, very difficult to please.

How was Mrs. Tilton?

Mrs. Tilton was always the same—of a lovely and amiable disposition. I never saw any change in her. She was the most devoted wife and mother that I ever saw in my life, in every sense of the word. The moment Mr. Tilton came home she always knew his footstep and his ring (if he had not a night key with him) and she dropped her work, no matter what she was doing, and was always ready to minister to his comfort and bring his slippers and dressing gown. All the time she was looking out for his comfort and his pleasure.

Bessie steals a quick glance at me. I smile at her through my tears. Bessie holds her head high as she answers the next question from the general.

Were Mrs. Tilton's habits domestic or otherwise?

Remarkably domestic considering—especially considering that she was the wife of a public man. If Mrs. Tilton had been a gay, worldly sort of a woman, fond of going into society and of going out at night and all that sort of thing, there might be some cause for remark, but she is the last person in the world that ought to be accused of the crime which is now charged. I never heard of anything so perfectly outrageous, and it seems particularly so with Mrs. Tilton, because she is such a lovely Christian woman, and such a devoted wife and mother.

Well, state whether or not the difficulty continued to increase from the time you first observed it?

Yes, sir, I think it did. I noticed Mrs. Tilton crying and sobbing. He had a way of closing the door of their bedroom and talking very loud to her. I could hear him scolding at her and then she would cry, and I have heard her say several times "Why, Theodore, I do the best I can, you know that I make every dollar go just as far as I possibly can." She would be remonstrating with him in that way and crying.

I feel tears running down my face. I wipe them away with my hand but they keep on coming.

Bessie assures her questioners that she never saw anything improper occur between me and Mr. Beecher. She talks about how Mr. Tilton became obsessed with jealous suspicions. He hit me when I defended Mrs. Tilton, she says. When I tried to block Mr. Tilton from hitting his wife, he turned on me. He struck me so hard I was knocked clear across the room and hit my head.

Is This War Never to End?

April 1897

Looking back on that summer as she drifted in and out of consciousness, Elizabeth recalled that Bessie's testimony had been a turning point. All of what Bessie said about Theo was true, but she hadn't mentioned any of the good things. Not one word about how he encouraged her education, choosing books for her to read, correcting her grammar in a kindly way, and praising her compositions.

Elizabeth's thoughts skipped to her own appearance before the church committee to testify once again to Henry's innocence and her own. This time there had been no intent to clear Theodore's name. Dear God, it wasn't only Bessie who told one side of the story. Elizabeth herself couldn't remember saying anything good about Theo. The examiner, a stout man with a graying mustache, had begun by questioning her about the problems in the marriage before the accusations of infidelity. His questions were persistent, probing every detail, but his voice was soft and sympathetic. He nodded frequently when she talked about Theo's criticism of her home management and smiled at her when she described being scolded severely in front of the butcher in a public place. Her husband had apologized later, she told the committee, but of course, there was no mention of how genuinely remorseful he had been or their passionate reconciliation two days afterward. That was not what they wanted to hear.

She had also told the church committee that Theo was ashamed of her short stature, and he made her feel stupid, a person of little intellect compared to the suffrage ladies. She never mentioned how frequently he told her that she was more advanced spiritually than he was, expressing admiration for her willingness to make sacrifices for those she loved and her capacity for forgiveness. It was all too complicated to explain to a committee of men.

Lying motionless in the bed, she could once more feel the nervous ache in her stomach that had stayed with her all during the questioning that long summer of 1874. In her testimony, she had again denied any impropriety in her relationship with Henry, but told them that the reverend had made her feel like a worthwhile person. She went on to explain her husband's jealousy as a misunderstanding of her need for friendship and guidance from the reverend after the death of her son. With regard to the letters written while she was sick in bed, she told the committee Theodore had dictated them and she could not remember precisely what the notes said.

She had lied about her intimacy with Henry. *Criminal intimacy*. Those were the words they used. And those words were all wrong. That's not what happened. How could her love for Henry be criminal? But, of course, she knew what the words meant to the men who were questioning her, and she had vehemently denied the charge. She had also lied about not remembering what the notes said. Even as she lay ill in bed, whereas she did not remember every word, the gist of each letter was still clear in her mind. But what choice had Theo given her? It was wrong to lie. But wouldn't it have been wrong to let Theo destroy lives to satisfy his desire for revenge? Why had he driven her to the point that she felt she had no choice but to lie? Why hadn't he forgiven her as she had forgiven him?

While engrossed in these reflections, Elizabeth was dimly aware that someone was trying to rouse her. She wondered who was stroking her hand. A man's voice was saying, "Didn't you see? Just a minute ago, Mother moved her hand."

Then Elizabeth could hear a voice that sounded like her

daughter Flory, but her eyes distinguished only shadowy forms against the light. "Mother, dear. It's Carroll and his wife, come to see you. Press his hand, so he will know you recognize him."

Ah, Carroll, you have come to say goodbye. It's your hand I feel touching mine. Elizabeth tried hard to press the fingers that held her own. Her mouth formed the word *Cad*.

Cad! Little Carroll! When she left Theo, Elizabeth recalled, Carroll was the most visibly upset of all the children.

Late August 1874

A voice calls, "Mommy, Mommy." I approach the window of my room on the second floor of Maria's house, trying to shield myself from view behind the diaphanous white curtain. It is indeed little Carroll standing outside with Theodore on the walkway. Theodore looks upward, scanning from window to window, before going up the front steps hand in hand with the boy.

I rapidly descend the stairs and run toward the door. Edward intercepts me.

"Elizabeth, let me go out. I don't think it's a good idea for you to talk to Theodore."

At this moment Maria enters the parlor, and Edward tells his wife that it would be even better if she attended Theodore. She dashes out and I can hear her hearty greeting. They stay outside talking for quite a while, and then she comes in holding Cad's hand.

"Cad will be staying with us for a few days," she says, smiling. Cad comes over to me shyly and I give him a big hug. He begins to talk in a rush. The neighbors have a new puppy that is brown and white with large floppy ears and likes to lick his face. Then Cad tells me he doesn't like the food the new cook prepares, and neither do the boarders. "The food is so disgusting," he says, wrinkling his nose. "Alice says she never ate such awful stuff. Mommy, you should come home and give the cook some lessons!"

"I wish I could, son."

"Dad says the boarders are too much work for you. You're getting a good rest here, aren't you?"

"Yes, I feel much better."

"You'll be coming home soon, right?"

His big brown eyes look up at me questioningly and I feel a lump in my throat. "I don't think I can."

Cad looks on the point of tears, but at this moment one of the Ovington boys pokes his head in the doorway and calls to him. He runs off to play.

Maria says, "Mr. Tilton told me that he has been crying for you. That's why he thought it best to bring him over for a few days."

I sigh. "But when he's here he misses his father just as much. Of all the children, he is the most attached to Theodore." I recollect how a much smaller Cad clung to his father when Theo came to pick us up at the train station after we returned from the visit to Sarah Putnam.

"I know," Maria replies. "Your separation is very hard on the children. I talked to Mr. Tilton again about sending the two middle ones to boarding school. I told him you and I had visited an excellent school in Connecticut with a liberal curriculum, a good art program for Alice, and excellent sports for Cad. He said it sounded like a good idea."

"I wonder if Alice already spoke to him. She is so excited about taking painting classes at the school."

"Maybe so. He did mention it would be good for Alice."

"You know, Theodore is always thinking about his own problems or some political matter. I wonder whether he has noticed that the children are terribly upset by the gossip."

"He should have thought about the children before," says Maria. "But it's no use talking about that now. Luckily, Ralph is too young to understand much."

"Alice ignores most of it. Florence is old enough to understand that much of what is being said is unfounded rumor. Cad suffers the most."

"Well, I think Mr. Tilton is coming round to the idea of a school outside New York. He said he probably could afford to send two of them."

"I often feel I should talk to him. There are so many things about the children that have to be sorted out. But Edward doesn't seem to think it would be a good idea."

"Edward is worried. You know Theodore talks reasonably and then all of a sudden he says something bitter and angry. He is probably even angrier now because the hearings of the church committee did not go his way."

I nod, thinking she is right, Theo must be incensed by my testimony to the committee. But what did he expect me to say? He told me he forgave me as I had forgiven him, but it was all a lie. He promised to protect me, but that was an even bigger lie. In order to exact his revenge against Henry, he threw me to the wolves. He lied to me. He betrayed me. What right had he to expect truth-telling?

I tell Maria, "He is not the only one who is angry."

"It's taken you a long time to get really angry, Elizabeth. Most women would have left him long ago. You know, I talk to Theodore for your sake, and the children's, but when I think what he has done to his wife and family and the reverend, I would rather never see him again."

"When I left him, there was no other choice," I reply, "but even at that moment I had not yet got to the point of never wanting to see him again."

"And now?"

"Of course I would see him, if it was necessary for the children's welfare, but not for myself."

"Elizabeth, I don't know if I should mention this." Maria hesitated. "I mean, do you know about the letters?"

"Letters? What are you talking about?"

"Mr. Tilton published your correspondence, your letters to him."

"What?"

"In the newspaper, the *Tribune*."

"No! For God's sake, Maria, tell me it isn't true. He couldn't do that. We loved each other. How could he?"

My throat gags, and I struggle for breath. I'm shaking all over, trying to hold back hoarse cries.

Maria grabs me and holds me tight. "You don't deserve this. You're the last person who deserves this," she says softly. "What an unpardonable breach of trust. I'm sorry that I told you. But you don't read the press, and I thought you should know."

She holds me until I stop trembling and the tears flow. "Oh, my God. I put my soul, my whole heart into my letters. And now the whole world knows my most intimate thoughts. How could Theodore do this to me?"

"Elizabeth, I didn't read them. Neither did Edward. It would be like sneaking into your drawers to look at private letters. I kept the paper in case you wanted to see them."

I never want to see them, I tell her, but in the evening, after little Cad has gone to sleep, sharing a bed with Maria's son, I change my mind and ask her to bring me the *Tribune*.

After closing the bedroom door, I spread the newspaper out on the bed and sit motionless beside it, staring at the black print, controlling an impulse to rip it to shreds. I leaf through it. The whole paper is full of letters, Theo's to me and mine to him. I scan the first two paragraphs of a letter on the front page. I'm telling Theo about the doctor giving Maria hopeful news that her husband will recover from his illness, which, thank God, has come true. Then there's news about Flory not feeling well and my sister-in-law Annie deciding to stay with me for a while. And then I read:

> *My beloved, I have been thinking about my love for Mr. B considerably of late, and those thoughts you shall have. I remember Hannah More says: "My heart in its new sympathy for one abounds towards all." Now, I think I have lived a richer, happier life since I have known him. And have you not loved me more ardently since you saw another high nature appreciated me? Certain it is that I never in all my life had such rapture of enthusiasm in my love for you—something akin to the birth of another babe—a new fountain was opened, enriching all—especially toward you, the one being supreme in my soul.*

I stop reading, thrusting the paper from me. I told Theo all that was in my heart, but now he is ripping my heart out from my ribs, enclosing it in his two fists, and crushing it. No one will understand my deep love for two men. The whole world will think I'm crazy or a depraved woman.

I hear footsteps on the stairs. I stifle my sobs, pull the coverlet over me, and blow out the candle. There is a light knock on the door. I keep quiet. The footsteps recede. At breakfast Maria doesn't mention the letters.

The doorbell rings. "That must be General Tracy," comments

Maria as she rises from her chair. "He said he would come by to give you a copy of the findings of the church committee."

As she opens the door, I hear the general asking in his deep voice whether Mrs. Tilton is at home.

Maria ushers both of us into the back parlor and leaves us alone. The general hands me the report of the committee. He will wait to see whether I have any questions. I move to a chair closer to the window for more light.

The long summary is an interpretation of the testimony of the witnesses. The basic gist of the narrative is that Theodore trumped up the charges, with the help of Frank Moulton, to force Reverend Beecher to provide support for his floundering career. I am portrayed as a wife completely under the influence of her husband who gave in to his pressures while physically ill and made some sort of accusation. Later, realizing the harm done to an innocent man, I retracted and denied that anything improper had occurred. My face flushes as I read the less-than-flattering description of my moral character. The general is staring out the window.

Dear God, what can I expect under the circumstances? They have to give some explanation of my contradictory statements.

I finally read the conclusions. The committee absolves Reverend Beecher of all charges of adultery or improper solicitation and reaffirms its belief in his moral integrity and Christian character.

I hand the papers back to Tracy. "I am very relieved this is all over, and the committee has found Reverend Beecher innocent."

The general frowns slightly. "Mrs. Tilton, we should not rejoice so soon. I don't think it's over. It may be just beginning."

"What do you mean?"

"I wouldn't be surprised if Mr. Tilton takes the case to the courts."

I open my eyes wide. "What would be the charge?"

"I don't think he will charge you directly. In any case, adultery is not a criminal offense in New York. Perhaps he will go to civil court, charge Reverend Beecher with alienation of your affections, and demand damages. He needs money."

"Oh no!" I hold up my two hands and turn my face away. "General Tracy, I don't think my children can take any more of this."

"Well, maybe he will think of the children, but I doubt it. Mr. Tilton is a very angry man. You know that he published your private correspondence in the newspaper?"

For a moment I am too close to tears to speak. "Yes. Maria told me. How could he do such a thing?"

"I think he had two reasons for publishing the letters. One was to show that you often received Mr. Beecher in your home when he was on tour, but frankly I don't think he will gain much. The letters are frank and open about the visits. Why would a wife with a guilty conscience tell her husband openly about another man's visits?"

"What was the other reason?" I ask. "To shame me?"

"Perhaps, but I think he had yet another motive. He must have been stung by Bessie's testimony about how he scolded and threatened his wife, and criticized you in front of the children and the servants, and threatened you with his fists. The letters show there was affection in the marriage. If the case goes to civil court, he means to show he is a man of good character."

"Well, we did always write to each other with loving words. How could he broadcast our words to the whole world?"

"Undoubtedly, it was an act of poor taste—something a true gentleman would not sink to. But I don't think he will accomplish his object. One of our lawyers is reading the letters carefully—pardon me, but we have no choice—and he tells me there are some expressions of regret and penitence on the part of Mr. Tilton, which could be used to show that it was he, not his wife, who was guilty of adultery."

As he rises from his chair, a broad grin makes the general's strong features look almost boyish. I feel a jab of pain in my lower abdomen.

Oh, Theo, is this war never to end?

April 1897

It was far from over, thought Elizabeth as she lay motionless, unaware of her surroundings, her mind turned inward.

After a few weeks, Maria had come to her room to tell her that General Tracy was waiting downstairs to talk with her. She recalled descending the stairs slowly with a strong sense of foreboding. The general's face was grave when he informed her that Mr. Tilton had gone ahead and filed suit against Reverend Beecher for criminal intimacy or adultery. She had uttered an involuntary cry.

Startled by a hoarse sound from her own throat, Elizabeth opened her eyes.

Why was Theo doing this to her? And why did he have to destroy Henry? Was it money he was looking for, as the general had said? No, no, Theo was not like that. It wasn't money. It was his reputation, his honor. But what about hers?

The room was dark but a dim light was filtering in through the window as though dawn were breaking. Elizabeth wondered whether she was in the second-floor bedroom at Maria Ovington's house, but the window should have been on the other wall and the shape was wrong. Where am I? Do I have to get up early to dress for the trial?

She started to struggle, trying to get up from the bed. Her legs were motionless, and she was unable to lift her head more than an inch or two off the pillow. Her one good hand shook back and forth, attempting with increasing desperation to grasp the coverlet to push it aside. A gurgling sound was coming from her lips.

"Mother, Mother, what's wrong? Stop, stop! Are you in pain? Should I call the doctor?"

Elizabeth tried hard to focus. It was her daughter Flory.

"Help me! Help me get up," she muttered, trying to get her hand loose from her daughter's firm grip. "I have to go to court. Where are my clothes?"

"Mother, that's all finished. You don't have to go anywhere. You were having a bad dream. I'm here. You're safe now."

Elizabeth sank back on the pillow and let her daughter gently stroke her hair. The trial was long ago, she told herself. It had started after New Year's and gone on for months and months. But Flory's right. It's over. I'm safe now. No more prying eyes.

Most of the trial was a painful blur, but one day came back to her in vivid detail.

February 1875

"I'm so sorry I could not come with you yesterday," says Maria as she climbs into the carriage and takes her seat beside me. "How are you holding up?"

"I hate going to court. There are always lines of people milling about outside trying to get into the courthouse."

Maria sighs. "Yes, I know. It's hard to get tickets."

"Every day, the moment I get down from the carriage, people starting calling out my name, and the press hounds me. Inside the courthouse it's always packed. All those curious eyes following my every move! It's so difficult to keep my head up and smile day after day. I don't like to be thinking so much about whether my clothes are appropriate. It seems so idle and vain. Like an actress in a play."

"I know how you feel, but General Tracy did say that the impression that you make on the jury is important."

She glances at my hat and then looks away.

"Do you think this hat goes with my dress?" I ask.

"It's fine." Maria looks at me. "But I have one that would be more suitable. I'll go fetch it." She tells the driver to wait.

Maria hands me the hat. "Much better! More elegant," she comments. "Did anything important happen in court yesterday?"

"Not really. The lawyers were arguing about some technical points. It was something about under what circumstance a wife or a husband can testify against the other. When Mrs. Shearman saw I was sitting alone, she came right over. I used to see her at church, but I never knew her very well."

"How long were you sitting alone?" inquires Maria.

"Just a few minutes. Mattie was with me, but she had to go home because she wasn't feeling well."

"You know, it's important that the jury and the public see you accompanied by friends, people who believe in your innocence."

"Mrs. Shearman came right over when Mattie left."

"Her husband is on the reverend's legal team, isn't he?"

"Yes, she knows quite a bit. She explained some of the legal issues they were talking about. But it didn't help me understand how the courts work. The job of lawyers seems to be to twist everything in favor of their client. Theodore's lawyers take a letter written by Mr. Beecher and interpret it in a horrible way. They call witnesses and don't let them talk. You can't tell us about that, they say, it's not permissible evidence."

"It's hard to understand the rules," replies Maria, "but a good lawyer who does not operate by the rules can never win justice for an innocent client."

I nod and pull open the window flap of the carriage to see outside. We are about halfway to the courthouse. Last week's snowfall has turned to dirty slush. Gray buildings are etched against a gray sky. A man walking on the sidewalk holds his hat on his head with one hand and hunches his shoulders against the wind. I turn back toward Maria. "Going to court every day weighs on my spirits. I feel so useless. All my church friends have been wonderful helping with the children's needs, but I shouldn't accept charity forever."

"It isn't charity, Elizabeth! These are your friends. When other brothers and sisters of the church were in need, you helped them. You came to my house every day when Edward was ill. Now we are helping you. That's not charity."

"I am very grateful for your friendship and all the others who have extended a helping hand. But I want to find work. Be useful!"

"What were you thinking of?"

"Well, I could join with Mother and open a larger boardinghouse, or I could teach."

"Yes, you taught Bible classes for children and for adults. I'll talk to Edward and the other church brethren about it. But you shouldn't start looking for a place until this court case is over."

I nod. She means nobody would give a teaching position to a woman accused of adultery. If the court case goes against Henry, not only will he lose his ministry, but no one will give me a place.

The carriage comes to a halt outside the courtroom. There are droves of people lining the steps, hoping to get in. My back stiffens. Reporters are already surrounding the carriage.

Maria grips my hand before we alight. "Chin up," she says. Sleet is falling, but as soon as it hits our coats it melts. We make our way into the courtroom and find our seats with a group of church friends.

Theodore, his head bent, is conferring with his lawyers. Henry is not in his usual seat, but his wife is there, sitting erect, her hair now completely white, staring straight ahead. Henry joins her, bends over, and says a few words. She nods her head in reply and they both rise. I look the other way.

"Mrs. Tilton, how good to see you!" I turn toward Henry's voice. He and his wife are right behind me. "My wife was just saying she wanted to come over and ask you how the children are doing," says Henry in greeting.

Mrs. Beecher is silent but she stretches out her hand. I press it quickly, feeling my face flush. "How kind of you! They are all very well. Two of them are studying at the Gunnery School in Connecticut. I just got a letter from the director saying that Alice shows remarkable artistic talent."

"I am very glad to hear that," replies Mrs. Beecher, and then she falls silent. She is holding her shoulders erect, looking directly at me, her unsmiling lips set in a firm line. I cannot think of anything further to say. Henry launches into a funny story about the children in the Bible class at Plymouth Church. It has something to do with how children can sometimes come up with surprising interpretations of the stories in the Bible. I don't understand the punch line, but I laugh on cue and Mrs. Beecher manages a mirthless smile. A crowd has formed around us.

"I think it's time to take our leave," remarks Henry with a low bow. He then bears his wife away on his arm.

Henry must have brought his wife over to talk to me on the suggestion of his lawyers. Judge Neilson calls the court to order and the lawyers proceed with their arguments. Another day of boring legal wrangles. Reverend Beecher's lawyers are trying to establish that Theodore should not be allowed to testify, because, in effect, he would be testifying against his wife, which the law does not allow. Opposing counsel argues that the legal action is directed not against the wife, against whom no penalties would apply, but against the seducer.

My mind begins to wander as the lawyers cite precedents from Rhode Island and New York. Many people from Plymouth Church are in the audience. Theodore's counsel raises his voice, addressing the jury in an emotional tone. I snap to attention and listen carefully to his words:

> *Imagine, sir, a happy and honored and a cultured home. The wife, a frail and delicate woman, eminently devotional and pious in all her impulses, and devoted to the husband of her early choice and the father of her children. She had a pastor, learned and eminent, gifted beyond his fellows, one who stood at the very head of his honored and sacred profession. Ah, sir, he had those qualities of mind and heart; he had that persuasive power of eloquence, that insidious and silver tongue which would lure an angel from its paradise. He was her accepted and chosen teacher and guide. She looked up to him with a veneration second only to that with which she regarded her God.*
>
> *He exerted upon her all his arts, his specious wisdom, his prayerful devotion. Consider how submissive she was to his teachings, and imagine with what a specious and insidious tongue he propounded to her the theory which he advanced, that fornication was but a natural expression of love. He taught her to believe in pious adultery. By slow, but by steady steps, he led her along upon frail paths to the precipice from which she fell.*

> *The honorable counsel of this gifted seducer argues that his client should be allowed to take the stand, but the injured husband should be forced to remain silent. I cannot imagine a greater injustice!*

Thunderous applause sounds from the galleries. Oh God, do I have to sit here and listen to this! Henry did not use arts of seduction. We felt a natural affinity, a genuine love.

Theodore is staring directly at me. The lawyer is speaking your words, Theo. That is what you have always believed, but it is not true.

The judge calls for silence in a loud voice.

Maria puts her hand on my arm. "Steady, Lib, steady." All eyes in the courtroom are on me. I make an effort to sit still and focus my eyes on the chair in front of me.

The lawyer continues:

> *The defendant in this action is a man of great renown and vast prosperity. He is surrounded by powerful friends with unlimited resources. The charge brought against him has not laid him low. On the contrary, he goes from triumph to triumph protected by powerful interests and friends in high places. His victims face a less rosy future. The family of a humble man has been destroyed: the husband rejected by society because of false accusations of slander made by powerful friends of the seducer, and the wife dishonored. While the seducer prospers and basks in the adulation of the multitudes, his victims, both husband and wife, are crushed.*

The lawyer is right when he says my family is crushed.

Oh God, whose fault is it? Henry's alone? Surely Theo's stubbornness and failure to forgive also had something to do with it.

And what of me? None of us is completely free of guilt. Why should Henry alone take the blame?

Once again, there is the sound of applause from the galleries, but people sitting around me on the main floor, many of them from Plymouth Church, sit stone-faced and silent. Henry's eyes are cast down, but Mrs. Beecher stares straight ahead with her head held high.

The judge decides in favor of allowing Theodore to testify. The afternoon wears on as other technical questions are taken up. My eyes follow the clock. The judge finally declares the court recessed until Monday, when Mr. Tilton will take the stand.

I wait quietly for Maria, who has gone over to talk to Mr. Beecher's lawyers. Upon her return she tells me to go to one of the consultation chambers for a meeting. She will wait for me so we can return together in the waiting carriage.

I find Henry conversing with Mr. William Evarts, the senior counsel, and General Tracy. Evarts, a small man of chiseled features whose formal manner contrasts with the hearty good humor of Tracy, is talking in a gentle, reassuring tone to Henry, who sits on a low chair with his head in his hands, his eyes on the floor. The two lawyers are seated together on a dingy tweed sofa. A split in the armrest reveals the shredded inner lining. The only light in the dim room comes from a single grimy window, streaked with sleet that has turned to rain.

Tracy rises and pulls up a chair for me. Once I am seated, Mr. Evarts turns toward me.

"Mrs. Tilton, I was just telling the reverend that it is natural for our side to feel despondent at this stage of the trial. The plaintiff, in this case Mr. Tilton, has the privilege of going first. When he presents his witnesses, most of them are going to strengthen his case. His lawyers are skilled—they made an excellent opening statement. But we should not be disheartened. You will notice that they do not have that many witnesses to call. They are depending almost entirely on Mr. Tilton's testimony and that of his intimate friend Mr. Frank Moulton. We intend to show that these two men tell the same story because they have always acted in concert to take advantage of Mr. Beecher's goodness of heart and get him to bankroll Mr. Tilton's journalistic ventures. I am a bit more worried about Mrs. Emma Moulton's testimony."

I cry out, "Oh no!"

"Mrs. Tilton?"

"Emma didn't testify at the church hearings. She always had a very high opinion of Reverend Beecher. Is Mr. Tilton's counsel presenting her as his witness?"

"Yes, but don't worry. Perhaps putting her on the stand is a sign of desperation on the other side. In any case, I think we can show she has a vested interest in supporting her husband's statements."

"Sir, will I have to testify?"

Mr. Evarts explains that I cannot testify unless the other side waives its objections. He doubts the opposing counsel would let me testify, because they know already from my church testimony that I will strongly deny any wrongdoing on the part of Mr. Beecher. Even though they would relish the idea of having the opportunity for cross-examination, he doubts they would risk the impact that a straightforward denial from the wife would have on the jury. Even if they waive their objections, he thinks the reverend's case will be strong enough, so my testimony will not be necessary.

"But then I will not have any opportunity to defend myself!"

Tracy suggests that probably the best strategy would be for me to issue a public statement of my innocence. Mr. Evarts agrees but cautions that the timing of such a statement must be carefully considered.

Tracy addresses me. "Mrs. Tilton, the best way for you to help establish your innocence and the reverend's innocence is to help us locate witnesses to strengthen our case. Have you been able to locate the nurse? I believe her surname is Mitchell?"

"Yes. I saw her last week. She's willing to testify."

"Good. I will need to talk to her first to see whether her testimony concurs with our position that you were too weak to resist your husband's importuning when you wrote those letters."

"Now, let us look at the problem immediately at hand," says Evarts. "We did not succeed in blocking Mr. Tilton's testimony, and he will take the stand on Monday. He will tell his story, but we intend a rigorous cross-examination that will begin to sway the jury toward our side. We will question him carefully about Bessie Turner's allegations of immoral advances. Of course, later she will appear as a key witness for our side. One of the reasons I asked Mrs. Tilton to be present at this meeting is to point out that we must not allow the other side to cast doubts on Bessie's testimony. In the next week," he says, turning to me, "I want you to pay careful attention to whatever objections Mr. Tilton makes to Bessie's previous testimony at the church hearings. Later, you have to see whether the dates she said you were in the country, and she was alone in the house with him, are correct. You can rest assured that the other side will try to pick holes in her testimony. Do you think you can work with her?"

"Yes."

"Good. That's settled."

Henry removes his head from his hands and sits up straight in his chair. "It's time for us to go on the offensive. We must use the cross-examination to delve into Tilton's unorthodox ideas about free love and how much he has strayed from standard Christian doctrine."

The gleam in Henry's eyes is unfamiliar to me.

Didn't you yourself tell me to be tolerant of Theo's religious quest when I expressed how much it upset me? Henry, you have changed so much I hardly recognize you.

Henry picks up some newspapers from the small table in front of him. "I have some clippings from the *Independent* and the *Golden Age*, which demonstrate how far Tilton deviated from accepted views of morality. Elizabeth . . . Mrs. Tilton," he says, turning toward me, "take a look at these articles; perhaps you can remember the approximate dates of others he wrote." He hands the clippings to me and tells Tracy, "Tilton often dictated to his wife."

I look through them and mention another article written after he became friendly with Victoria Woodhull in the summer of 1871. It was titled "The Coming Social Upheaval" or something similar.

"That's what we want," says Evarts. He tries to jog my memory to pinpoint the span of possible dates. "We will put someone to locate it."

Tracy directs his next remark to Henry. "My dear friend, it all comes down to character. We will show that your character is beyond reproach, while Tilton is a man who did not hold fast to proven moral values. But that is only one side of the coin. Character and action go hand in hand. We also intend to show that Mr. Tilton practiced what he preached, namely free love. He was guilty of the immoral conduct he imputes to others."

"Tilton has blackened my name before the world," replies Henry, "and that of this innocent lady. He should not go scot-free. But do we have credible witnesses?"

"During the cross-examination we also mean to question Mr. Tilton about reports that a young woman was seen in his hotel room while he was lecturing in Winsted, Connecticut. I think we will be able to produce the man who observed them."

I recollect that Theo told me it was the daughter of a family we both knew, prominent abolitionists. Theodore insisted that it was all completely innocent. Since he told me about other affairs openly, it seems unlikely that he would have lied. "Mr. Evarts, I don't really think anything immoral happened. If you introduce the subject, the girl's reputation could suffer."

"Oh no, we will be careful to keep her identity secret."

Henry looks at me. "Elizabeth, I know how you feel. But we can't afford *not* to use whatever evidence we have. The other side is using everything they can against us."

Late February 1875

"I'm shocked Emma is going to testify against the reverend," says Mattie, leaning toward me, in a whisper.

"I know. She told me many times that Reverend Beecher is a man of pure heart, one of the best."

We are sitting in the court waiting for the proceedings to begin. They are calling Emma to the stand. I feel that gnawing pain in my stomach that comes and goes. General Tracy said it was particularly important for me, and also Henry and his wife, to be present. The jury must not think we are afraid of what Emma may say. I look cautiously over at Henry. He is conferring with Mr. Evarts, but Eunice is nowhere to be seen. Perhaps Henry doesn't want her to hear Emma's testimony.

Emma looks around the courtroom uncertainly. I shrink back into my chair. As she takes the oath, I watch her face intently. Emma, what are you going to say? Her head is down and her voice is very low as she answers questions regarding her place of residence and the date of her marriage to Mr. Moulton. The judge calls for quiet and requests Emma to speak up. She lifts her head, straightens her shoulders, and raises her voice. A soft-spoken lawyer on Theodore's team is questioning her regarding Plymouth Church and Reverend Beecher.

Mrs. Moulton, what connection, if any, have you had with Plymouth Church?

I have been connected with Plymouth Church since 1858.

As a communicant?

Yes, sir.

How long have you known Mr. Henry Ward Beecher?

I have only known him personally since 1871.

Under what circumstances did he make your acquaintance?

He came to the house to see Mr. Moulton in reference to this case sometime in January.

Now, from that time on, Mrs. Moulton, state whether Mr. Beecher visited at your house, and how often as nearly as you can recollect.

Sometimes twice a day, two or three times a week, sometimes every day in the week, when he has been in town.

And at what hours of the day?

At all hours—before Mr. Moulton was up in the morning, after he had retired at night, before the Friday night prayer meeting, after his Sunday evening service, after his morning service on Sunday, and at all hours of the day. I have known him to come to the house as late as eleven o'clock at night.

Tittering can be heard, particularly from the galleries. Mattie whispers that it is only natural for a man who has been falsely accused to be very worried. I nod, thinking that it was not so long ago that Henry came to my house, sometimes talking to Theo, sometimes to me, sometimes playing with the children. The judge calls for order. The lawyer resumes the questioning.

With whom did Mr. Beecher confer?

With Mr. Moulton.

Was that so in all cases, or did he sometimes confer with you?

Sometimes with me.

When did you have the first conversation with Mr. Beecher in regard to any difficulty that he spoke of?

I don't remember exactly, but it was in the spring of 1871, I think, late in the spring.

Please state, Mrs. Moulton, what he said to you upon the first occasion when his troubles were the subject of conversation.

He was waiting in the parlor for Mr. Moulton and I went into the room. He took my hand and said, "Do you know anything of the great sorrow of my life?" and I said, "Yes." He said, "Then Frank has told you the facts, has he?" I said, "Yes." He said, "I am very glad that he has. I am very glad that here is one woman in this world to whom I can go and talk of my troubles without reserve. There is no one else I can talk to, unburden my troubles. In my church I have to wear a cheerful smile. At home it is the same." As nearly as I can remember that was all our conversation at that time.

I look at Emma closely as she says these words in a matter-of-fact voice. Henry, why were you not more careful? You and Frank were always telling me to be careful what I said.

> *Do you recall having any further conversations with him about his difficulties?*
>
> > *Yes. He would ask me if Mr. Moulton was still hopeful that the story might be kept quiet. He would ask me also the condition of Mr. Tilton's mind towards him—if he was friendly, or if he was angry or annoyed, or—*

One of Henry's lawyers objects that the witness cannot talk of what Mr. Beecher generally said, she must describe a particular conversation. Maria whispers to me that none of this proves guilt.

The lawyers continue to wrangle for several minutes. Emma resumes testifying. I come sharply to attention when I hear the phrase *letter of contrition*. I glance quickly at Theo, who is staring impassively straight ahead. Theo's lawyer continues his questioning.

> *Mrs. Moulton, do you remember what Mr. Beecher said and what you said about the letter? Try to give us the words to the best of your recollection.*
>
> > *Yes, I do. Mr. Beecher said, "Did Frank tell you Mr. Tilton is threatening to publish my letter of contrition?" I said, "What letter of contrition?" He said, "The letter of apology I wrote for Frank to show to Theo when this whole difficulty started." I said, "But surely Mr. Tilton wouldn't publish a private letter." He said, "Of course, it would be a breach of confidence. But I don't have very much faith in Theodore anymore. He has been faithless—he is a faithless man. He seems to lose sight of the fact that in striking at me he strikes at*

his wife. If that letter of apology is published, it is useless trying to live it down."

Was there anything further said about the letter?

Not right away. Mr. Beecher said he was feeling very poorly and lay down on the lounge. I brought him a blanket. He began to cry and said he didn't want to live anymore. I kissed him on the forehead. I think I told him that he is basically a good man. After a while, I said I thought he should confess. I think I told him it would be better to confess than to wait for a public accusation, but I don't remember exactly.

What was his reply?

He said, "No, I cannot do that, for the sake of the woman who has given me her love, for her children, for my family, for my influence throughout the whole world, that I can never do. I will die before I will confess it."

I hear Mattie's quick intake of breath. Otherwise, the courtroom is completely still. She takes my hand. I am looking at the floor, but I feel hundreds of curious eyes on me. It's no use trying to keep my head up. Emma's testimony continues. She says that sometimes she carried messages from Henry to me. I blink back the tears and pray to God for the strength not to break down in open court.

Finally, a short recess is declared. I stay in my seat, praying that no one will approach me. Henry is huddled with his lawyers. Mr. Evarts, who has not taken charge of questioning for several days, comes forward when the judge calls the court to order, to handle the cross-examination. He questions Emma about the kissing incident.

Mrs. Moulton, you said that you comforted Mr. Beecher when he began to weep. You kissed him on the forehead. Do you remember saying to him at that time, "If ever there was a good man, you are one."

Not in those words. You see, ever since I knew what he did, it destroyed my faith in human nature. I think I said that I thought there was still a great deal of good in Mr. Beecher.

Have you altered your mind on that particular?

I haven't any faith in Mr. Beecher.

When did you lose it?

My faith in him as a moral teacher was destroyed when I knew what he did in his life.

What are you saying, Emma? You always told me that you believed that Henry had made a mistake, but you still believed he was a good man and a great religious leader.

But, Mrs. Moulton, you just said that you still thought he had good in him. That remnant of faith in him, when did you lose it?

Afterward, when I saw the way he has treated my husband who always tried to help him. Mr. Beecher told the church committee that Mr. Moulton was lying, when he knew perfectly well that every word my husband spoke was the truth.

It is only then that I understand why Emma consented to testify against Henry. When the court is finally adjourned, I tell Mattie I have to go home right away. She tells me to remain seated for a second while she checks to see if Maria, who couldn't make it to court today, has sent her carriage for the two of us. "Don't talk to anyone," Mattie warns. She comes back quickly and informs me that the carriage is waiting. We stay seated for a few minutes to give time for the crowds to disperse and then walk rapidly outside. As we climb into the carriage, someone shouts a question at me. Mattie quickly closes the door and orders the driver to depart.

"What an awful day!" Mattie exclaims. "I have never heard such a pack of lies in all my life. And I actually thought she was a nice, pious woman. How could she invent all those awful things? And she was your friend, too, wasn't she?"

"Yes. But she is very loyal to her husband."

"That's no excuse for making up lies to ruin a good man. I love my husband, too, but I wouldn't make up all sorts of stories just to make him look good."

"People do all sorts of things to save someone they love."

"What are you saying? She is a vicious woman—she deserves to roast in hell for those vile lies, God forgive me."

I start to sob. Mattie puts her arm round me.

"Elizabeth, forgive me. I am so upset, I'm forgetting about your feelings. There, there, I won't say any more."

We drive the rest of the way in silence. I try to sort out my own feelings about Emma. There were moments in the courtroom when I hated her. But by what right do I hate you, Emma? I lied to protect someone I love and you told the truth to protect someone you love.

Maria comes out to greet us. Mattie tells her that we have had an awful day in court. Maria invites her to stay and have tea with us. As we enter the house, I excuse myself, to go rest.

"Oh, Elizabeth," calls Mattie as I begin to ascend the stairs, "I forgot to tell you that General Tracy said he would call on you tonight. About eight o'clock. I saw him while I was looking for the carriage."

"Thanks."

"See you tomorrow."

Once inside my room, I close the door and lie wide-eyed on the bed staring at the ceiling, wondering what will become of me if the case is lost. When Maria calls me for supper, I plead a headache.

"If the general comes by, should I tell him you're ill?"

"No. I think I should see him."

When I come down a few minutes after the clock strikes eight, General Tracy is already in the parlor talking in animated tones with Maria and Edward, describing Emma's testimony. He rises and extends his hand, while Edward pulls up a chair for me.

"I still don't understand," says Maria. "What could be Emma's motive for telling such elaborate lies?"

"To protect her husband," I reply.

"Mrs. Tilton has hit the nail on the head," exclaims Tracy.

"Protect him against what?" queries Maria. "Mr. Moulton is not being accused of anything."

"Not in a court of law," responds the general, "but in the court of public opinion, yes."

"What do you mean?"

"Just this. Moulton was mediating between Mr. Tilton and the reverend, carrying messages back and forth. But what was the substance of all this mediation? The reverend came up with a large sum of money to help Mr. Tilton with his new journal. This money was given to Tilton through Moulton. First, Mr. Tilton slanders the reverend. Then Moulton gets the reverend to pay money. A neat swindle!"

"I see," says Maria.

The general shakes his head. "Mrs. Moulton has every motive to protect her husband."

"She loves him very much," I interject.

"Of course," continues Tracy, "they are man and wife and we assume she loves him. But, Mrs. Tilton, there is more to it than love.

His good name is her good name. His prosperity is her prosperity. His future prospects are hers."

"Very good point," says Edward.

"Which reminds me of the main point, the reason I came by," continues the general, looking directly at me. "I want to tell you not to become disheartened. Mrs. Moulton was their last major witness. Now it's our turn."

"It sounds like she did a great deal of damage. I imagine she must have made a favorable impression on the jury. She has a refined way of speaking," says Maria.

"Yes, but we will attack her testimony. Mr. Evarts and I have already jotted down a few points for his final summation. Firstly, she herself gave us her motive for lying. She said on the stand that she turned against Mr. Beecher because of his differences with her husband. Furthermore, Mrs. Moulton said she was a close friend to Mr. Beecher until the summer of 1874 when the reverend and her husband parted ways. But how could a lady, and she very much appears to be a lady, consent to be an intimate friend of a man she knew to be an adulterer? Inconceivable! She must have believed in his innocence until it became necessary to consider him guilty to protect her husband's reputation." The general smiles benignly. "So, you see the case is not lost. It's our turn now to present witnesses. Many of Mrs. Tilton's friends are willing to testify to Mr. Tilton's bad temper and his irreligious views. The nurse, what's her name?"

"Mrs. Mitchell."

"Yes, Mrs. Mitchell will testify to Mr. Tilton's harsh treatment the night he made Mrs. Tilton write the letters. Bessie Turner will testify again. Then there are the businessmen who know of the money fed to Mr. Tilton's journal. And we have a whole list of witnesses that saw Mr. Tilton in compromising circumstances with Mrs. Woodhull. The tide will begin to turn."

Spring 1875

I'm sitting next to Maria, waiting for the next witness, a Mrs. Giles, to be called. I have no idea who she is. "Have you heard of her?" I ask my friend.

"No, but she must be another witness who can testify to Mr. Tilton's immorality. Remember the general said the tide will turn once the reverend's witnesses are called."

I look down. There have been lots of witnesses giving Theo a bad name. I've had enough. I don't want to hear more. There was that young man, president of the local Young Men's Christian Association, who said he had been appointed to escort Theo to a lecture hall. He claimed that when he arrived at Theo's hotel, he found him without his jacket with a lady who looked disheveled. The lady told him she had been reading Milton's *Paradise Lost* to Theodore. The courtroom had erupted in laughter.

Several witnesses have testified to seeing Theo in compromising circumstances with Victoria Woodhull, the two of them riding together or bathing in Coney Island, or at parties conversing together about the coming social revolution and how to expose the Reverend Beecher's hypocrisy.

The new witness is being sworn in. Mrs. Giles is a Negro woman, of medium height and complexion, attired in a navy blue dress and hat. Probably about forty years old. The lawyer is going through the usual routine, asking where she lives, her occupation.

Mrs. Giles, how long have you lived upon Long Island?

Well, sir, I was brought up on Long Island.

Raised on Long Island?

Yes, sir.

Mrs. Giles, have you ever worked in the family of Victoria Woodhull in New York City?

Yes. sir.

In what capacity?

As cook.

As a cook?

Yes, sir.

Is that your ordinary business?

Yes, sir.

Your ordinary employment?

Yes, sir.

Did you cook all the while? Were you engaged as cook all the while, Mrs. Giles?

No, sir. I was engaged as cook for six months steady in the kitchen, and then they had some difficulty in the family, and after that I came to do general housework.

Please state, Mrs. Giles, on what day you first saw Mr. Tilton coming to Mrs. Woodhull's house while you were engaged there as cook and housekeeper.

The first time I saw Mr. Tilton there was the third day of July.

July—what year?

1871.

The third of July?

Yes, sir.

Henry's lawyer keeps repeating questions. She said she was brought up in Long Island and he asked whether she was raised there. Now she's saying Theo slept in the front parlor when staying overnight, and he still wants to know whether it was the front or the back parlor.

Why does the lawyer keep repeating as though she were a child or simple-minded? She's giving him precise answers in good English. Henry's lawyer was insistent when he questioned Emma, but he treated her like a lady. Oh dear. If they had put me on the stand, would Theo's lawyers have treated me like a lady? I shake my head to dispel such thoughts. Better to pay attention to what's being said.

Mrs. Giles says that Theo was working on a biography for Mrs. Woodhull, but the lawyer doesn't ask about that—all the questions are about the type of bed or sofa, who brought the bedding and sheets, and who slept where. Which floor did Mrs. Woodhull sleep on? And her husband? When Theo visited, where did he sleep? In the parlor? On the second floor? Third floor?

How I wish I didn't have to listen to this. If only I could get up and go home. A woman seated several rows in front of us turns her head, her eyes seeking mine. I look away. Maria clasps my hand. The lawyer isn't finished with Mrs. Giles.

Now, how often did Mr. Tilton continue to come there, Mrs. Giles?

Well, he used to come there three or four times a week—he would be to dinner and to breakfast.

You mean he stayed all night?

Generally, when he came, he would stay all night.

Did you ever go to Mrs. Woodhull's room to serve refreshments at night?

Yes, sir, quite a few times.

When Mr. Tilton was there at night?

Yes, sir.

How late at night were these calls when you brought refreshments?

Well, eleven, twelve, and one.

Do you recollect of their going out to dine and returning late?

Yes, sir, I remember their going to ride out to Central Park.

Do you remember their going to Mrs. Woodhull's room after returning?

Yes, and carrying up broiled chicken and wine, and cake and champagne.

How were they dressed when you went up to serve refreshments?

Well, when I went the fourth of July night, Mrs. Woodhull was in her night garment and Mr. Tilton had his coat off and vest off, and was in his stocking feet.

The courtroom bursts with laughter. The judge raps for order but the laughter continues. I glance at Henry. He's laughing heartily. Theo is staring ahead, his blue eyes blinking rapidly. He pushes his long curly sandy-colored hair back with his hand, and twists his mouth into a smile.

How well I know that smile. It is Theo's way of saying, I know the joke is on me, but I'm trying hard to be a good sport.

August 1875

"How are you feeling?" Maria asks me with a look of concern.

"Now that the trial is over, I'm getting better. Every minute was awful. And thanks so much, dear friend, for explaining to me that a hung jury means that the defendant was not convicted."

"I remember you were in tears."

"I was confused. I thought we had lost."

The doorbell rings.

"It must be Mattie," says Maria. "Elizabeth, can you let her in? She will be going to the evening services with us."

I hurry to the door. Mattie greets me affectionately and I usher her into the parlor. While taking her seat, she asks Maria whether Reverend Beecher himself will be conducting the evening services this week.

"Yes," replies Maria, "I heard from Mrs. Shearman that he returned from the country the day before yesterday. He looks ten years younger, she said."

Mattie expresses her joy on hearing such welcome news. "I was afraid that he would not get through the ordeal of the trial," she comments. "He looked so ill and weary during the last month. I did not think he would survive. Thank the Lord it is all over!"

"How I wish the jury had handed down a definite verdict," Maria says. "I was sure they were going to find him innocent. The summation of the case by Mr. Evarts was magnificent. I was so disappointed when the foreman informed the judge that the jury was hopelessly deadlocked."

Mattie says that she was also disappointed at first. "But we must remember that our judicial system presumes a man innocent until proven guilty. A hung jury is a victory. But the reverend should never have gone through such an ordeal. Why is it always the best people who suffer the most? You know, before the trial, I was not angry with Mr. Tilton. I thought he was suffering from some terrible unbalance of mind—that he was not himself. But during the trial, he was completely coherent. I could not understand how he could pronounce such hurtful lies with such complete self-possession."

I pick up my teacup and then put it down, realizing that it is already empty.

Oh, Mattie, Theo didn't seem calm and self-possessed to me. Henry's lawyers did everything they could to embarrass him.

"Lib, would you like more tea?" asks Maria. "I will get a cup for Mattie."

"Thank you. I forgot I had already finished mine."

When Maria returns, she serves us both. The tea is still warm.

After taking a sip, Mattie says thoughtfully, "It is still a mystery to me. I knew Mr. Tilton for years and he seemed to be a good man. What changed him? How could he do such a thing?"

"He was a very desperate man in the last two months before I left him," I reply. Maria and Mattie are both looking at me intently. "After the Reverend Bacon attacked him—called him a knave and a dog—he was distraught. He kept talking about a conspiracy of church people against him. I sometimes ask the Lord whether I should have tried harder to reach him."

"But, Lib," replies Maria, "you did everything you could. The testimony you gave to the church committee provided him with a way out—a way to withdraw the charges without dishonor. It was his choice."

"He felt cornered. He told me that General Tracy was willing, but the rest of the church committee did not want to compromise."

"I am sure that is not true!" cries Mattie. "The committee would have done anything to avoid a public trial, except consent to let him continue to spread slanders against the reverend. Mr. Tilton was lying to gain your sympathy."

I nod to put an end to the conversation. In my heart I know it was impossible to tell who was lying and who was telling the truth in those final days. It was already open warfare, and all anyone thought about was winning. When I reach to put my teacup back on the table, my hand trembles.

"Well, all's well that ends well," says Maria. "Let's talk about more cheerful subjects. I am sure these memories are very painful for Elizabeth."

Later that evening, we walk together to church. People are taking advantage of the balmy summer night to linger outside talking to friends before the services begin. Mr. and Mrs. Shearman greet us. I notice Mrs. Beecher talking animatedly with a group of elderly ladies. We go over to greet her and she nods politely. I extend my hand, but she appears not to notice and enters into a long discussion with Maria about a mutual friend who is bedridden.

Mattie glances at the two of them deep in conversation and suggests to me that we should find seats before they are all taken. After we enter the church, the finery the ladies are wearing draws my attention. I myself have chosen a simple dress, relieved that it is no longer necessary to dress up as a fashionable lady day after day to go to court. But why are people so dressed up here? What does all this lace and finery have to do with God?

Henry comes in and begins to address the congregation in a booming voice. My mind goes back to those days long ago when each sermon was a revelation. I recall the time when he talked of the maternal aspect of God and it seemed to me that a spark was entering my head and lighting up my soul. Henry's voice is still deep and sonorous, but at times it cracks and wavers. The timbre and cadence are different. I try to concentrate on what he is saying. The sermon is about how the conscience should serve as a barometer to guide the soul at the time of making a difficult decision. Oh, Henry, did your conscience serve as an ethical guide when you exhorted the lawyers to go after Theodore, expose every radical line he ever wrote, every luncheon he ever had with a woman other than his wife?

The first time I came to Plymouth Church as a young girl, the architecture awed me. The high ceiling seemed to be a symbol of the presence of the Almighty. But now the church appears smaller and more congested. I look around slowly at the altar, at the figure of Henry gesturing dramatically to make a point, and then at the congregation, some listening with rapt attention and others shifting restlessly in their chairs. My mouth is dry. For a moment, I gaze at the lights on the ceiling above and then I close my eyes.

God, where are you?

As Henry finishes speaking, Mattie touches me lightly on the arm. Her cheeks are flushed and her eyes are glowing. "The reverend is himself again," she exclaims. "I have never heard a more inspiring sermon. Let's go and congratulate him!"

I rise with her, but after taking a few steps I spot Sarah Putnam among the congregation. "I have to say goodbye to Sarah before she leaves for Ohio," I tell Mattie. "You go ahead and speak to the reverend."

My Truth,
My Very Own Truth

April 1897

Elizabeth remembered that she had talked to Sarah for quite a long time. Afterward, she looked for Maria and Mattie, but neither of them had waited for her. She walked back to Maria's house alone.

A voice interrupted her thoughts.

"I don't think she recognizes me."

Elizabeth opened her eyes and saw a tall figure. Her vision was too blurry to make out his features, but there was no mistaking the voice of her dear son Carroll.

"But darling, yesterday your mother pressed your hand." A female voice was speaking, perhaps Carroll's wife.

"I can't be sure," said Carroll. "Each day Mother seems further and further away."

"My poor darling," said the female voice. "I know how painful this is for you. Flory said yesterday that she was thinking of letting your mother's friends know. They will want to see her."

"Shh, maybe Mother can hear us."

How thoughtful of dear Carroll, but Elizabeth wanted to protest that there was no need to shield her from reality. She knew she was dying. It would be good to see friends one last time.

Which friends? Some had preceded her on the journey to the next world. And then there were others who were no longer close. Her dear friends at Plymouth Church, Mattie, Maria, Sarah, the women who had offered solace and support when she lost two of her children, who had been her refuge in the difficult moments of her marriage—none of them were close to her anymore. Of the three, she missed Maria the most. Such a kind-hearted person and so careful to take a balanced view. Maria and her husband had opened their home to Elizabeth when she had no choice but to leave her husband. At the same time Maria had been careful not to antagonize Theo, speaking to him in a friendly manner so that he would come to some agreement with Elizabeth about the children's education. But she hadn't spoken to her dear friend Maria for many, many years.

Oh, Theo, your decision to go to trial ended not only our marriage; it put an end to many things. But life went on, and God did not desert me.

May 1876

I ring the doorbell at my mother's place.

"Oh, Elizabeth, I am so glad you've come. I have a visitor I'd like you to meet."

"But, Mother, I am not dressed for a social call. I came to help you with the weekly cleaning."

"It can wait. And don't worry about your dress. Mrs. Wentworth believes in living simply."

She escorts me into the parlor and introduces me. As my eyes adjust to the dim light, I notice that Frances Wentworth is indeed attired in a plain gray dress. She is sitting in one of Mother's overstuffed easy chairs with slightly frayed lacy arm covers. Her white collar and the white cuffs of her sleeves have a simple elegance. Her hair, streaked with white, is drawn back in a bun. She greets me with a warm smile. Her voice is low for a woman and melodious.

"We were talking about all those ridiculous ideas about women voting," says my mother. "I was just telling Frances that you used to know Miss Susan Anthony and Mrs. Elizabeth Cady Stanton very well."

"Yes. They visited our house very frequently. My husband was a strong supporter of suffrage for women," I explain.

"Of course, Elizabeth never believed in all that nonsense," Mother interjects hastily. "She shares my view that the suffragists are doing more harm than good. Women don't need the vote. We have other ways of making our influence felt."

There is a short silence, and then Frances turns to me. "I don't agree with their views either, but I have always wondered about the suffragists as people. What was your impression?"

"The only one I knew well is Miss Anthony. She sincerely believes women should have more rights. She always said that women would use their rights to protect children and the poor."

"What's in the heart is the most important," Frances says softly, her dark eyes looking directly into mine. "I, too, have always had the impression that Miss Anthony is sincere."

"Sincere, perhaps, but misguided," snorts my mother as she leaves the room to look after the refreshments.

"Perhaps your mother is right. It is misguided to think that you can change the world by your own efforts. Like playing at being God!"

I start slightly. The same thought has often occurred to me. "We can try to be the instruments of God, but we cannot know his purpose."

"How well you understand!" Frances smiles at me, and her eyes crinkle at the edges, reminding me of someone else. "Your mother was telling me that you devote many hours to helping working women," she says. "To my mind, helping individual people in the spirit of Christ is more important than trying to pass new laws."

"Yes, I agree." I lean forward in my chair to tell Frances how much the work with poor women at Plymouth Church's Bethel School has meant to me. The words come gushing out as though I had been confined in solitary for a week. There are so many things to tell Frances. "Now, I am teaching elementary school full-time and helping my mother with the boardinghouse. I feel bad because I no longer have as much time for the Bethel School."

"Yes, of course. The Lord sometimes presents us with difficult choices. After my husband died, God rest his soul, I worked as a nurse for many years, but when my mother and aunt became old and infirm, I decided that my first duty was to attend them."

I sigh. "To tell the truth I would hate to give up the Bethel School. I still teach once a month. I am very fond of the women and I think they return my affection. Their lives are hard, but they try to give the best to their children. I still try to visit many of them in their homes and help them in any way I can."

My mother enters and sets down the tea. She says that she will have to deal with a problem with a boarder and apologizes for leaving us on our own.

"Don't worry," says Frances, "Elizabeth and I are discovering that we have much in common." As my mother leaves the room, Frances turns back to me. "We are really very much alike. I would like to devote my life to nursing the poor, if and when my personal circumstances permit. One of the brethren at my church group is a doctor who gives free services to the poor two days a week. I help him when I can."

"Does your church run a dispensary for the poor?"

"Not exactly." Frances shakes her head. "You see, we don't believe in institutional giving but in individuals giving from the heart. And we are not really a church, at least not in the usual sense."

"What do you mean?"

"We call ourselves the Plymouth Brethren. It's just a coincidence that Plymouth Church has the same name."

"Tell me about the Brethren."

"We meet in small groups to pray and read the Bible. We want to return to the original teachings of Jesus."

I feel a tingle at the nape of my neck and I look Frances in the eyes, trying to fathom what sort of person she is.

"We meet in a simple hall or in the home of one of the believers. We have no ministers. Our only ceremony is the weekly passing of the bread and the wine in memory of our Lord."

As she speaks, I try to picture the simple meeting hall of the Brethren, but the memory of all the ladies in fancy attire at Plymouth Church intervenes.

"You have a penetrating eye," Frances exclaims. "A moment ago, I felt you were looking into my soul. I hope it was not found wanting. Your mother told me that you are a woman of deep Christian faith."

A flush suffuses my cheeks and I drop my eyes. "I used to be."

"Why the past tense?"

"I used to feel the presence of God in my church and when I prayed. But I now feel dry and cold as though God were far away from me." My voice wavers.

Frances reaches out and touches my hand. "We all go through dry spells when God seems far away. Have you talked to your minister?"

I glance up quickly, but her face is impassive. Is it possible that she does not know of the scandal? "I don't think it would help," I reply. "For many years I was inspired by Mr. Beecher's sermons, but now I feel that he is repeating the same thing by rote. The Spirit does not dwell in his words, or maybe it does and the fault is mine, because I cannot hear it."

"I listened to Mr. Beecher preach at Plymouth Church long ago and it was an excellent sermon, but it is not possible for any one individual to be inspired every week." My mother enters the room and resumes her seat. Frances nods to her and continues, "In our simple services, whoever feels the inspiration of the Spirit leads us."

Mother shakes her head. "How can that be? There has to be leadership and discipline in a church as well as in society, or everything will be confusion."

Frances replies, "I know it may appear strange, but it works very well."

"Indeed, Mother," I interject, "if no one speaks unless inspired by the Spirit, there is more likely to be silence than confusion. And silence is good for the soul! What's the use of talking of God when you do not feel God in your heart?"

"The weekly sermon at Plymouth Church is good enough for me," retorts my mother.

"You don't have to leave your own church to attend our services," Frances says to me. "Would you like to come with me next week?"

"Very much."

After Frances departs, my mother asks, "You liked her, didn't you? I knew you would."

"Yes. Talking to her was like breathing fresh air."

"She is a deeply religious woman, but she does have some strange ideas. I wish you hadn't promised to go with her to the services of the Brethren. I don't think our circle of friends at Plymouth Church would like it."

What are you talking about? Am I to be bound by their likes and dislikes? Aloud I retort, "I just want to go and see for myself. The sermons given at Plymouth Church no longer inspire me."

My mother shakes her head but makes no comment.

I blurt out, "Mother, I have been thinking about your idea that we could join together to open a larger boardinghouse in a better neighborhood."

Mother looks at me sharply. "What's going on, Elizabeth? You're not getting along with Mr. and Mrs. Ovington? You're not comfortable living in their house?"

"No. That's not it. They have been very kind and helpful. I am grateful for all they have done for me. I just don't want to be beholden to them any longer. And the children should have their own home."

March 1878

"Are you coming to the service with me today?" asks my mother.

Why does she keep asking me? I have not gone to service at Plymouth Church for three months. "No, Mother. I can't. The Brethren are coming here for the Sabbath morning service."

"Do you mind if I take Carroll and Ralph with me?"

"Carroll said he wanted to see how the Brethren do the service," I reply, but Mother's disappointed face makes me change my mind. "Maybe they should go with you," I tell her. "It's a nice day and an outing would be very good for them."

Mother beams at me. I tell her she looks very good in her new blue dress and then call the boys and help them get into their coats. Mother mentions she is expecting a gentleman to come to see the vacant room on the second floor, but she tells me not to worry, because the appointment is for late afternoon.

After she leaves with the boys, I enter the back parlor on the first floor. It is a corner room with two large windows. I pull back the curtains and the early morning sunlight streams in. The wooden floor, which Mother and I worked on for many days when we first rented the house, gleams with a high shine. The room is very simply furnished with straight-backed wooden chairs arranged in the shape of a horseshoe with the open end facing a long high table. Everything must be made ready for the morning service. On the table, I place small earthenware plates for the bread and a simple glass decanter for the wine. I fetch an additional chair from the adjoining room to put behind the table for whomever is elected to preside over the breaking of the bread. All is in order, and I stop for a moment to breathe in the peaceful atmosphere of the room.

The doorbell rings. It is Frances with the bread. I fetch wine from the cellar and all preparations are complete. She admires the way I have arranged the back parlor for the meeting. "It's perfect, Elizabeth."

Mr. Samuel Porter and his wife, Caroline, arrive. They remind me of Edward and Maria, a devoted couple, both plump and invariably cheerful. Mr. Porter is a retired doctor who now devotes himself entirely to the Brethren and dispensing medicine to the poor. He stands with me at the door to greet the new arrivals. He knows everyone and has a kind word for each.

The next to arrive is Mr. James Dunn, a young man, perhaps thirty-five, with reddish-brown hair and a beard. I noticed him at the first service of the Brethren that I attended with Frances almost two years ago. He concentrated with all his might on the sermon and then went into a trance for many minutes. For the first time he is accompanied by his wife, a tall, dark-haired woman. He introduces her.

"Maureen," he says, addressing his wife, "this is Mrs. Tilton!"

"James talks a great deal about you," she says with a smile. "He says you are closer to God than anyone he knows!"

"I wish that were true!" I reply. "Welcome. He has talked about you so much that I feel I already know you well."

The rest of our little circle of about twenty believers arrives quickly and we all take our seats. When everyone is settled, Mr. Porter gestures toward the rear window and remarks that the morning light streaming in is a symbol of the presence of the Almighty sanctifying this simple meeting place. I feel glad that I insisted that Mother allow me to use this room for the meeting.

Mr. Porter asks one of the Brethren to read aloud from the book of Job. The familiar words take on a new meaning for me. I too have suffered the cruel blows of fate. I have borne six children and two have been taken away from me. As little Paul lay suffering on his last day on this earth, all my attempts to soothe him were to no avail. I have loved two men with all my heart, but each is now a stranger to me. I lied to cover for them both and labored in vain to preserve the worldly reputations that both valued so much. How proud I was when I walked from Maria's house to my own, confident that I had convinced the church committee that both men were innocent. I believed that a lie could solve everything. But God would not let the lie stand. Did he condemn me as a sinner? No! He knew my intentions were good. But he would not let me get away with so easy a solution. He wanted me to walk a more difficult path leading to the truth. God had some greater purpose. He tested me with the suffering of the trial in order to bring me closer to him.

I rouse myself with a start. The reading from the book of Job is over. The earnest young man, James Dunn, has risen from his chair as though he wants to speak. In a kindly tone, Mr. Porter asks him to tell us what is in his heart, to allow the Spirit to address us through him.

James looks anxiously around him. His lower lip trembles, but he steadies himself enough to blurt out that he has been suffering from a deep sense of despair and unworthiness. "I pass my days in dread of the Second Coming of Christ!" he cries. "I am unworthy. I do not deserve to be saved."

I look at his anguished face.

"I know that God will save all who believe in him!" explains James. "But I still feel unworthy of his mercy. I have not learned to curb my temper. I cause all manner of suffering to those around me, including my dear wife. I have a little girl, a very sweet child, but sometimes I yell at her and punish her too severely. My heart is not pure. I long for recognition and riches. I know there will be no sign before the Second Coming. If God comes tomorrow, I am not ready. How can God call me to heaven, if I have not lived so as to fulfill his will on earth? Every day I pray for the Coming to be postponed, and then I am ashamed of my own cowardice!"

I listen and understand. James, your agonies are my agonies. In my dreams of the Second Coming, God raises my dearly beloved little Mattie and Paul from their graves and calls us all to him. But as I am floating toward God, reaching out my hands to touch Mattie and Paul so we three can make the journey together, something drags me back down. God, I too am unworthy! I now know I chose the easy but crooked path of telling falsehoods to save myself and those I loved, rather than the arduous road of the truth. I cannot meet you with a lie on my conscience.

As James sits down, his wife reaches for his hand. Mr. Porter reassures him that faith in God's mercy will save him and suggests that he should preside over the breaking of the bread.

While James directs the simple but beautiful ceremony commemorating our Lord, I think to myself that it would be wrong of me to tell the truth out of fear of damnation. The faithful must have no fear of God! I want to tell the truth because I love God and I have faith that he will never condemn me, never let me go! As I think these words, the light seems to be entering my head. The sense of illumination has never been as strong as at this moment.

When I come to myself, my head is in the lap of the lady sitting next to me and Frances is rubbing my temples and asking, "Elizabeth, what is it? Are you all right?"

"Yes. It is just that what brothers Dunn and Porter said made me feel the presence of the Spirit. I forgot where I was for just a moment." I realize that I must have lost consciousness for a moment and fallen.

"Well, it is lucky that Mrs. Cole caught you before you fell to the floor."

"Glory be to God! Let us all give thanks," declares Mr. Porter.

The momentary physical weakness has passed and I sit up straight in my chair. James leads us all in a hymn. I hear my own voice singing strong and clear.

The meeting is over. People linger for a while, talking in low voices. Mr. Porter and Mrs. Anna Cole are asking anxiously whether I am fully recovered. I assure them I feel like a person renewed.

Frances and I see everyone off at the door. Afterward, she tells me to sit quietly in the front parlor while she instructs the cook to prepare us some tea. A sense of well-being permeates my limbs. I have an impulse to run and shout, but it seems easier to just lie back and let the stuffed chair cradle my body. In the soft morning light, even the heavy curtains that I once told Mother look hideous now seem beautiful.

When Frances returns, she observes that she is very happy with the spiritual progress that James is making. She is overjoyed that he has finally persuaded his wife to join and feels that he has the potential to become a leader of the Brethren. "You know, Elizabeth, he was telling me how much he is inspired by you."

I smile happily.

As Frances pours out the tea, I tell her, "I have come to a decision."

"About what?"

"About telling the truth."

She looks at me. "What do you mean?"

"The Second Coming of Christ. I am not ready."

"None of us is fully ready, Elizabeth, nor will we ever be."

"No! You do not understand. I, Elizabeth Tilton, am truly not ready. I told a lie, a well-intentioned lie, but a lie nevertheless. What my husband said was true. I did commit adultery!"

Frances puts her teacup back down on the saucer with a loud clang. The tea spills onto the saucer and the table. Frances stares at me. "No! Elizabeth, it can't be."

"Don't look at me that way."

Frances drops her eyes and carefully wipes up the spilled tea with her napkin. "I'm sorry. I don't know what to say. Many people thought the reverend was guilty, but I never thought so. After getting to know you, I was even more certain he wasn't guilty."

"Now that you know the truth, you won't want me as a friend." My eyes are moist.

"Elizabeth, please. I have lived long enough to know the human heart is unruly and can lead us into treacherous waters."

"Into sin. Isn't that what you mean?"

"It's not for me to judge. I have done some things in my life that I would give anything to undo."

"I broke a commandment. That's what you're thinking."

"Yes. But you repent. God forgives those who sincerely repent."

"I repent the lies and deceit."

Frances picks up the spoon and stirs the tea remaining in her cup.

"I know the world considers it a sin," I tell her. "But at the time it did not seem like sin at all!"

"What are you saying?"

"It all started because Reverend Beecher comforted me when

my child died. I was in deep despair, doubting the goodness of God. He was the one who helped me heal and restored my faith."

I go on to tell Frances the whole story. She listens intently, occasionally asking questions. When I fall silent, she tells me that she doesn't quite understand why I felt I had to lie in front of the church investigative committee.

I try to explain that I could not bear for all the good work Henry had done in his life to be destroyed. "You see, if loving too much is a sin, we were all three guilty. Why should Henry be the one to pay the price?"

"You must also have been worried about your children."

"Yes. I thought all our lives would be ruined. I blamed Theodore for sacrificing the children and me to get revenge. I felt that since he chose the path of revenge, he deserved whatever he got."

"Do you still feel that way?"

"I'm not sure. At the trial, the reverend's lawyers made it look like everything was a blackmail scheme between Theodore and Frank Moulton to get money out of the reverend. It wasn't that way at all."

Frances nods.

"Sometimes I lie awake at night thinking about it. My soul is restless. I can no longer live with the lie."

"What are you thinking of doing?" inquires Frances.

"I have to draw up a declaration and present it to the *Brooklyn Eagle*," I tell Frances.

"Oh no! Not the press!"

"The untruths were spread far and wide in the press. It's the only way to correct them."

"Are you sure?"

"When I denied the charge, I thought I was doing the right thing, protecting my children. I thought God did not want me to betray other people I loved, but now I know that I was taking the easy path. I must tell the truth."

Frances lifts her eyes to meet mine, reaches out, and takes my hand. "I understand this is tormenting you, my dear friend. Elizabeth, I want you to do what you believe is right. I promise to support you. But don't act on impulse! Have you thought this through? What will happen to your children if you confess to a lie?"

"I will have to trust in the Lord to protect them."

"Your two girls might be very much affected. They are already young ladies, and society can be very cruel."

"Alice and Florence are both abroad. Mr. Tilton sent them both to Europe to study for several months."

"Is he well-off financially?"

"No, I don't think so. He is a self-made man. He hasn't had a steady job since the trial. But he sold the house."

"The two girls are certainly safer far away from our American newsmen. But what about the boys?"

"We must trust God will take care of them."

"You still have many friends at Plymouth Church! You still go to the service there sometimes, don't you?"

"I feel terrible about Maria Ovington. She and her husband were very good to me. And Mattie was my best friend for years and years. But about the others, I am not sure. Sometimes, it seems to me they wanted me to lie to protect their church. What worries me is not what the Plymouth Church people think. It's what Bessie will think."

"The servant girl who testified?"

"She wasn't a servant. She was our ward. We took her in when she was eight years old. Her own mother couldn't take care of her. Oh God, she believed in my innocence, did everything she could to protect me. What will she think when I tell her that I am guilty?"

Frances furrows her brow and queries, "Didn't you say Bessie lived with you in the same house? Wouldn't she have seen something, suspected something?"

"She never said so. She testified to my innocence."

"But was it because she believed in your innocence? Or because she loved you and wanted to protect you?"

"My dearest Bessie. I never thought of that."

April 1897

Florence hurried from her mother's side to answer the doorbell. It was James Dunn and his wife Maureen.

"How is she?" they asked simultaneously.

"We are trying to keep our hopes up, but the doctor is not optimistic. He thinks she has had another stroke. We have not been able to rouse her for two days."

"We didn't know she was gravely ill," said James. "We were away visiting Maureen's family. Can we see her?"

"Yes, come in. Here, give me your coats."

"Does Alice know?" asked Maureen.

"Yes, she was here earlier. My brothers came, too, and they are coming again this afternoon. I wrote a letter to my father two weeks ago."

"Where is he?" asked James.

"He has been living in Paris for many years now," replied Florence. "My aunt Annie sent a telegram yesterday."

James nodded and asked no more. The conversation brought to Maureen's mind the publication of Elizabeth's confession about twenty years previously. At that time, she remembered her husband had been deeply shocked. Hoping to calm him down, Maureen had taken the initiative to ask Frances for some sort of explanation. Frances had told them both that no one can see into the heart of another person, but it seemed to her that it was Elizabeth's nature to love intensely, which could be both a blessing and a curse. The important thing was that she had made peace with her own conscience.

Florence beckoned her visitors to follow her upstairs. While climbing the narrow staircase, Maureen recalled having asked Frances how Elizabeth was faring when the death of Reverend Beecher received extensive coverage in the newspapers about ten years earlier. Frances had replied that it would be best to leave her alone and not mention anything. Mrs. Morse, Elizabeth's mother, had indicated that the press was hounding them, but that her daughter steadfastly refused to say a word.

Before leaving the couple alone with Elizabeth, who was lying motionless on the bed, Florence reminded them that people sometimes appear to be unconscious when they can really hear and understand.

After Florence left, Maureen took Elizabeth's hand in her own. "Mrs. Tilton, can you hear me? We bring prayers from all the Brethren for your recovery."

"Don't leave us!" James's voice choked. "You have been a mother and a spiritual guide to us all."

The sick woman gave no sign of recognition. Maureen and James knelt and prayed. As they rose to their feet, they noticed Elizabeth's breathing, which had been regular and even, had become labored and rasping. James reached for her hand and prayed out loud that she would not leave them. As the rasping became more pronounced, he called out loudly for help. A nurse hurried in. She explained to them that the patient's breathing often became blocked by phlegm and she would have to use a tube to aspirate. Maureen took James by the hand and said gently, "We should go now."

They quickly descended the stairs and advised Florence of her mother's condition. Before leaving, they obtained her consent to hold a candlelight vigil that evening for their dying friend.

As the nurse inserted the tube, Elizabeth recoiled slightly, but she did not awaken. Her mind continued to roam in the past. She was going over the words of the letter she wrote in April 1878. She remembered the visit to a solicitor for legal advice. He had attempted to dissuade her at first, but he eventually approved of the draft she had prepared, which was addressed to him to be forwarded to the press.

> *. . . after long months of mental anguish, I told, as you know, a few friends, whom I had bitterly deceived, that the charge brought by my husband, of adultery between myself and the Rev. Henry Ward Beecher, was true, and that the lie I had lived so well the last four years had become intolerable to me. That statement I now solemnly reaffirm, and leave the truth with God, to whom also I commit myself, my children, and all who must suffer. I know full well the explanations that will be sought by many for this acknowledgement: desire to return to my husband, insanity, malice—everything save the true and only one—my quickened conscience, and the sense of what is due to the cause of truth and justice.*

The nurse noted that Elizabeth was moving her lips as though speaking. She called to her by name, but the patient did not stir.

Elizabeth's memories of what had happened in the days and months after her letter was published were blurred and confused. The image of Maria Ovington's distraught face came back to her for a moment, instantly displaced by Mattie Bradshaw's disapproving glare when they met by chance on the street, which then gave way to a vision of reporters swarming around the house and threatening to block the entrance unless she made some comment. She felt once again a jab of pain in her stomach as she opened the letter from Plymouth Church, asking whether the press had mistakenly reported her confession of adultery, and realized in a flash that she, like Emma Moulton, would be accused of slander for affirming that Henry Ward Beecher had committed adultery. She could see her own hand trembling when she took up a pen and struggled to insert it into a small ink bottle on her desk to write a reply, reaffirming her guilt. Elizabeth could hear her mother's hysterical cries when told that the congregation of Plymouth Church had voted in favor of her daughter's excommunication. In this jumble of images juxtaposed one over the other, the one memory that stood out clearly was the arrival of an unexpected visitor at the boardinghouse.

September 1878

I am inspecting the second-floor corner room facing the street to see what must be done to put it in shape before renting it out again. Who would have thought that such a gentlemanly man would move out without notice and leave the room such a mess? This is our best room, with an attractive view of the large elm tree on the other side of the street. I note that there are cup rings visible on both the bureau and the table. Oh dear, not only will the room have to be repainted, but the furniture will have to be sanded down and refinished. I try to think of the man we hired last time for fine woodwork. It occurs to me that it is just as well that my mother took the weekend off to visit with friends in New Jersey.

She gets so upset by these things. It would be best to get everything fixed up before her return.

There is a knock on the open door. It's Susie O'Connell, the new girl who doubles as a cleaning lady and maid for the boarders. "Ma'am," she cries. "Come quick! There's a gentleman caller downstairs!"

"But who is it? A boarder? One of the Brethren?"

"No. I know all the boarders. I don't think it's one of the Brethren either. I didn't see this gentleman come in last Sunday."

"Didn't you ask his name?"

"Ma'am, I'm so sorry. I forgot. I was so embarrassed. I did not hear any knock and suddenly he entered while I was scrubbing the parlor floor on my hands and knees."

"What does he look like?"

"Oh, ma'am, he's a distinguished-looking gentleman. Tall and lanky. Long curly hair, sandy-colored mixed with a touch of gray. Strong features. Right handsome I would say. And so polite! Asked leave to take a book down from the shelf to read while he waited."

I gasp.

"Ma'am, are you all right?"

"I'm not feeling very well."

"Here, sit down for a bit on this chair. Pardon my saying so, ma'am, but you look like you've seen a ghost."

"Did you notice the color of his eyes?"

"Blue, ma'am. Clear blue."

"Listen, Susie, you must tell the gentleman downstairs that Mrs. Tilton is indisposed and cannot see him."

"Are you sure, ma'am? He is such a nice gentleman and he brought a lovely bouquet of flowers."

"I can't see him. Go now and tell him."

"Yes, ma'am." Susie straightens her dress and pats her hair down before descending the stairs.

As soon as the sound of her footfalls dies out, I hurry toward the window. It is a windy day and the leaves from the elm are swirling. After a moment, Theodore comes out on the street. I feel a tingling down the back of my neck as I watch his familiar gait, his tall figure, his hair tousled by the wind.

Oh, Theodore, I knew you would come. Maria told me you said that one day I would tell the truth.

He stops and turns around to look back at the house for a long moment. I start, suppress an impulse to step back, and then press my face to the window to have a better view of his. He turns and walks slowly away.

After he has disappeared, I retreat from the window. My legs feel unsteady and I sit down on the unmade bed.

Oh, Theo, the statement I made is my truth, mine alone. You would never understand. I finally told the truth for the love of God, not for any man.

Susie comes rushing in. "Look, ma'am, what a lovely bouquet for you!"

I hold the flowers she hands to me and smell their fragrance. Theo, you have not forgotten that I like wildflowers best. Along with yellow roses, there are daisies and black-eyed Susans.

"Shall I put them in a vase in your room or in the front parlor, ma'am?"

"My daughters will be coming home from Europe the day after tomorrow. They will have the west room on the ground floor. Put the flowers in their room. Be sure to change the water frequently. Tell them their father brought the flowers as a welcome-home present."

Susie's eyes open wide. "Yes, ma'am."

I hand the flowers back to her.

"Are you sure you're all right, ma'am?"

"Yes, I'll just lie down for a while."

Flowers in hand, Susie turns on her heel and then looks back to admonish me to take a good rest before softly closing the door.

I get up and walk toward the window. The street is completely deserted. Not even a stray cat or a pigeon. The glass feels icy cold to my fingers. Dry leaves are still swirling in the wind. Tears run down my cheeks, leaving droplets on the windowsill.

April 1897

Maureen and James returned at sunset with about fifteen other well-wishers. While they all assembled in the downstairs parlor, James told Florence, "Your mother is dearly beloved by all the Brethren. It is hard to explain what she means to us. Her closeness to God inspired us all. She worked tirelessly to help Dr. Porter's ministrations to the poor after Frances died, but she never desired any credit or recognition. She was always the first to offer help when anyone was in need."

Florence nodded in assent. "She was the same with her family and her friends."

James replied, "I have been talking about her kindness to all, but I would like to acknowledge my personal debt. Many times, when I was overcome by doubt and despair, it was Elizabeth who gave me the strength to go on."

Maureen gestured toward the small group. "Many more people wanted to come, but we tried to keep the group small so as not to disturb Mrs. Tilton."

"Thank you all for coming. My mother and I are honored. Shall we light the candles?"

Florence joined the group as they filed upstairs with candles lit to hold a vigil by the dying woman's bedside. As the twilight shaded into darkness, the candles became points of light surrounding the woman whose life was ending.

Elizabeth was not aware of her surroundings. She did not hear the singing of hymns or see the candles, but the flickering lights surrounding her bed awakened a response in the inner layers of her consciousness. Each point of light expanded and became brighter and brighter until they all merged in a burst of brilliant sunlight.

She was lying on her back in an open meadow, gazing at billowing white clouds promenading lazily across the brilliant blue sky. The smell of recently cut grass mingled with the fragrance of wildflowers and the humming of bumblebees. She was thinking that she should put the picnic things away in the basket, but she was too full and drowsy to move. A single swallow dived and swooped for unwary insects.

Henry and Theo were lying on either side of her. The two men were trying to decide whether the cloud directly overhead looked more like a horse or a flying wheelbarrow. She could feel Theo's shoulder against hers on one side, and Henry's arm lightly touching her on the other. Linked together, they lay perfectly still. The sweet song of a thrush came from the woods on the top of the hill.

Henry sat up and said he still could not believe the war was over. "Just two months ago we were in the midst of the most horrible carnage, but in this lovely spot close to the Hudson with a view of the majestic Catskills, it is hard to believe that brother was killing brother for four long and horrible years."

"We are beginning a new era of hope and freedom," said Theo as he too sat up.

Henry shouted out loud, "The slave is free! This country will finally become the land of liberty it was meant to be."

"We will create a new and better society. Women will no longer be restricted to the home. With their softer natures, their finer moral sense, they will lead us in building a better society. And men and women will be honest and straightforward with each other," cried Theo, waving his straw hat.

Tossing her sunbonnet up high in the air, Elizabeth cried, "And children will be spared the rod! They will be taught only with love."

"My friends," Henry said with a smile, "we have no jug of wine. How will we drink to this brave new world?"

Elizabeth could see herself rising to her feet to reply. "We will be like the bees and the hummingbirds and partake of the nectar of God!" She marveled at the woman who was hiking up her skirts and running toward the morning glory vines growing up over the bushes on the edge of the woods. Elizabeth could feel the wind tousling her long dark hair, which had come loose, and at the same time she could see herself in the eyes of the two men who watched enthralled as she ran with her hair streaming behind her. She brought back three purple-blue flowers and gave one each to Theo and Henry. "These are our cups, and the nectar is our wine. Drink up!" she said, laughing.

"To a better world!" cried Henry. "May we never lose our dedication to the cause of liberty and reform!"

"And to our friendship," shouted Theo. "Let our love for each other endure forever!"

"To us!" cried Elizabeth as she brought the morning glory cup to her lips.

Then she leaned her head far back and gazed at the brilliant blue of the sky above. Her companions faded from sight and the buzzing bees were still. The sunlit day dissolved into brighter and brighter white light, until light and life were no more.

Author's Note

While teaching a seminar on the history of women in the United States at the University of Puerto Rico, I became intrigued by the trial of Reverend Henry Ward Beecher, the most famous Protestant minister of his day, for "criminal conversation" with Elizabeth Tilton, a member of his congregation and the wife of his intimate friend and protégé Theodore Tilton. I remember telling my students that this trial caused as much sensation in 1875 as the impeachment of President Bill Clinton in 1998 for alleged breaches of the law connected with the attempted cover-up of sexual intimacies with Monica Lewinsky. The women involved, Elizabeth and Monica, were both reluctant to testify against their alleged seducers. Powerful political factions that hoped to gain from the public embarrassment of these prominent men pushed their private lives into the public limelight. The consequences were even more devastating for the women alleged to be their lovers than for the reverend or the president.

About a year after discussing the case with my students, I began to explore the historical sources in earnest. Elizabeth Tilton was of particular interest to me. Unlike her husband and her lover, she was not a leader in the public sphere, and yet she became a central figure in one of the greatest controversies of the time. She was a puzzle to her contemporaries, who followed the reports of the church investigation in 1874 and the civil trial of 1875 with avid interest. In many ways, she seemed to be a conventional if not exemplary woman, a woman who defined herself as wife and mother, and yet this same woman was accused of holding beliefs and engaging in conduct that challenged the core values of Victorian society. Why was Elizabeth drawn to the gospel of love and the doctrine of free love? Once the scandal broke, how did she deal with the moral dilemma of being forced to take a position against one or the other of the two men she loved as well as with the fear of losing her position in society, her marriage, and her children? In view of the consequences of her experiment with free love, did she return to a more conventional morality? Was she a passive victim of the double standard of her time, or did she find opportunities for personal growth amid the chaos of the scandal?

I remember a student remarking to me that there seemed to be more depth of feeling between Elizabeth and Henry than between Bill and Monica. After immersing myself in the historical sources, I became convinced that there were deep emotional bonds among all three of the principals in the Beecher-Tilton scandal, making the affair a true triangle. Personal ties were strengthened by their involvement, in varying degrees, with the reform movements to promote the rights of women and former slaves as well as with the reinterpretation of the Calvinist religious heritage. The letters that were exchanged among the three protagonists, as well as the testimony of the two men at the trial and of Elizabeth in the church investigation, provide evidence of the love and esteem as well as the hurt and resentment that each experienced.

My first attempt to come to grips with the fascinating story of Elizabeth, Theodore, and Henry was the preparation of a brief historical study of the impact of the gospel of love on the position of women in the Reconstruction era, as seen in the case of Elizabeth. It was challenging to envision the scandal and its repercussions from the point of view of the woman, the only protagonist who lacked a public platform, whose motivations and feelings were the most difficult to untangle. I soon decided that her life merited a deeper exploration, which would only be possible in a work of historical fiction. Moreover, the complexity of conflicting emotions experienced by all three participants in the triangle, as well as the shifting ground of multiple power struggles, would be better served in a novel than an academic article.

The novel covers the period from 1866, when Elizabeth, then in her early thirties, first developed romantic feelings for Henry, until her death in 1897. There are many primary sources for the period from 1866 through to the trial in 1875, but more material is available for Henry and Theodore than for Elizabeth. Whereas both her husband and her lover testified at length at the trial in 1875, she was not put on the stand. Nevertheless, her testimony at the church investigation in 1874, her letters published by Theodore without her permission, and the testimony of her friends facilitated my attempt to reconstruct her feelings and motivations. Her later life, the period after the 1875 trial, was more difficult to envision. Although several historical sources are available, including obituaries and her letter of confession published in 1878, writing the story of this latter part of her life required greater creative effort.

Secondary sources written by historians were very helpful. I would particularly like to mention the work of Richard Wightman Fox (*Trials of Intimacy: Love and Loss in the Beecher-Tilton Scandal*) and Altina Laura Waller (*Reverend Beecher and Mrs. Tilton: Sex and Class in Victorian America*). Fox gives an excellent accounting of the complex emotional relationships among the three main characters and includes copies of their correspondence. Moreover, he paints Elizabeth as a woman who used the opportunities open to her for personal growth and was able to exert influence over her intimates, rather than envisioning her as a passive victim. Waller provides valuable insights into the power politics and financial struggles that exacerbated emotional tensions and undermined all attempts to reach a compromise that would have salvaged reputations.

The primary sources that an author addressing the Beecher-Tilton scandal must rely upon—the letters and the testimony in both the church investigation and the trial—do not consistently tell the same story. The public testimony of the protagonists often provides conflicting narrations of what happened in what order, as well as conflicting interpretations of the motivations of those involved. The authors of historical studies also have different views regarding which sources are most reliable and how to interpret the meaning of what Fox calls "early stories" and "public retellings." As a writer of historical fiction, I had to make similar judgment calls.

In the course of writing *Unruly Human Hearts*, I thought about the ways in which Elizabeth's story is relevant to concerns about individual freedom and social ethics, not only during the Reconstruction era when expectations that the inalienable right to life, liberty, and the pursuit of happiness would apply to all human beings were dashed, but also in more recent times. The emergence of creeds of sexual liberation in the 1960s raised questions with regard to whether free love (or open marriage) is liberating for women. Many women were still economically dependent on men, which made it difficult for them to insist that men grant their partners the same sexual freedom they claimed for themselves. In an earlier epoch, Elizabeth had to contend not only with financial dependency but also with a more puritanical moral code that frowned on female sexual expression.

The MeToo movement that emerged in the early twenty-first century points to the problems implicit in a sexual relationship in which one partner enjoys the advantage of power and position. Elizabeth insisted that her tie with Beecher was based on true love, but her husband saw it as a pastor taking advantage of a deeply loyal member of his flock. On the other hand, Theodore seemed completely oblivious of the power dynamic in his marriage to Elizabeth.

Practitioners of polyamory today may face some of the same issues that plagued the Tilton marriage, because it is easier to affirm the ethical obligation to be completely truthful about other love relationships than to respond lovingly to a concrete revelation of a partner's romantic feelings for a third person. Hopefully, women involved in open marriages today are less likely to undergo the same degree of heartbreak as Elizabeth experienced, because the power dynamics in intimate relationships are not as skewed in favor of the male partner as they were in the nineteenth century.

My novel explores the lives of all three main characters in detail up to the end of the trial, and then concentrates on Elizabeth's efforts to build a new life apart from Theodore and Henry. Some readers may want to know more about the lives of the two men after 1875. Although Henry Ward Beecher's reputation was tarnished by the adultery charges, his parishioners loyally supported their beloved pastor, who remained an influential public figure until his death in 1887. He continued to take liberal stances on many issues, such as defending universal suffrage and trying to reconcile Christians to Darwin's theory of evolution. Theodore Tilton, unlike Henry, gradually faded from public view. After the trial, he did some public lecturing in the United States on social and political issues, but he was not able to rebuild his career as a journalist. During this period, Theodore began spending summers in France, perhaps to have some respite from the public controversy about his personal integrity, which had been severely questioned by Beecher's lawyers. In 1883, he made a permanent move to Paris, where he lived until his death in 1907. He continued to write poetry and play chess. A collection of his poems dedicated to Elizabeth was published in 1897, the same year that she died.

For those readers who would like to continue exploring the lives of the characters and the social movements of their times, there is a wealth of historical literature to explore. Here are a few suggestions:

Applegate, Debby. *The Most Famous Man in America: The Biography of Henry Ward Beecher.*

Barry, Kathleen. *Susan B. Anthony: A Biography.*

Fox, Richard Wightman. *Trials of Intimacy: Love and Loss in the Beecher-Tilton Scandal.*

Gabriel, Mary. *Notorious Victoria: The Uncensored Life of Victoria Woodhull—Visionary, Suffragist, and First Woman to Run for President.*

Korobkin, Laura H. *Criminal Conversations: Sentimentality and Nineteenth-Century Legal Stories of Adultery.*

Lystra, Karen. *Searching the Heart: Women, Men and Romantic Love in Nineteenth-Century America.*

Rugoff, Milton. *The Beechers: An American Family in the Nineteenth Century.*

Sears, Hal D. *The Sex Radicals: Free Love in High Victorian America.*

Spurlock, John C. *Free Love: Marriage and Middle-Class Radicalism in America, 1825–1860.*

Waller, Altina L. *Reverend Beecher and Mrs. Tilton: Sex and Class in Victorian America.*

Sources of the Poems, Letters, and Testimony in the Novel

Letters and poems have been quoted verbatim from the sources consulted (with the exception of the so-called confession letter written by Elizabeth Tilton, which was destroyed). The testimony included in the novel (at the hearings of the investigating committee of Plymouth Church and at the Tilton vs. Beecher trial) is based on the records, but the testimony has been modified and shortened for the sake of clarity and dramatic impact.

Epigraph page: First published version of the first stanza of Emily Dickinson's famous poem "I heard a fly buzz when I died" as it appeared in T. W. Higginson and Mabel Loomis Todd, eds. *Poems by Emily Dickinson: Third Series* (Boston: Roberts Brothers, 1896), 184.

pp. 2–3: For Theodore's poem titled "Thou and I," see *The Complete Poetical Works of Theodore Tilton in One Volume: With a Preface on Ballad-Making and Appendix on Old Norse Myths & Fables* (London: T. Fisher Unwin, 1897), 125.

p. 121: The letter addressed to Henry that mentions a confession to her husband is a fictional recreation of Elizabeth's first letter written on the insistence of Theodore in late December 1870. The real letter was destroyed at the request of Elizabeth according to the testimony of Frank Moulton at the church hearings (see Charles F. Marshall, *The True History of the Brooklyn Scandal* [Philadelphia: National Publishing Company, 1874], 52–53) and the testimony of Theodore Tilton at the trial (see *Theodore Tilton vs. Henry Ward Beecher, Action for Crim. Con. Tried in the City Court of Brooklyn*, 3 vols., vol. II [New York: McDivitt, Campbell, and Co., 1875], 398, 521–23).

p. 128: For the second letter, which Elizabeth wrote upon Beecher's insistence on December 30, 1870, asserting that he behaved as a gentleman and a Christian, see Marshall, 317.

p. 132: For Elizabeth's third letter, written on December 30, 1870, to appease Theodore, see Marshall, 318.

pp. 168–69: For Tilton's poem "Sir Marmaduke's Musings," see Richard Wightman Fox, *Trials of Intimacy: Love and Loss in the Beecher-Tilton Scandal* (The University of Chicago Press, 1999), 348.

pp. 180–81: For Theodore's letter dated December 27, 1872, addressed to "My complaining friend" (published in the *Brooklyn Eagle*), see Marshall, 540–41.

p. 207: For Theodore's long letter dated June 1, 1874, answering the Bacon charges, in which he included (in the last pages) a quotation from a previous letter written by Henry Ward Beecher, see Marshall, 42–63.

pp. 241–42: For Bessie's testimony at the hearings conducted by the investigating committee of Plymouth Church, see Marshall, 391–92.

p. 251: For Elizabeth's letter to Theodore about her feelings for Beecher dated December 28, 1866, see Fox, 261–62.

pp. 259–60: The speech made by Theodore's counsel in the novel is primarily based on the argument presented by William Beach to persuade the judge to let Theodore testify at the trial, with some additions from the opening address of Samuel Morris. See Beach's speech, *Theodore Tilton vs. Henry Ward Beecher*, vol. I, 371–72, and Morris's speech, *Theodore Tilton vs. Henry Ward Beecher*, vol. I, 58.

pp. 266–70: Emma Moulton's testimony given in the novel is based on her testimony at the trial. For the original, see *Theodore Tilton vs. Henry Ward Beecher*, vol. I, 720–23, 730–31.

pp. 274–77: Lucy Ann Giles's testimony in the novel is based on her testimony at the trial. For the original, see *Theodore Tilton vs. Henry Ward Beecher*, vol. II, 616–19.

p. 301: For Elizabeth's final confession, see Fox, 39. The letter appeared in many newspapers including the *Brooklyn Daily Eagle* on April 18, 1878.

Acknowledgments

I would like to express profound gratitude to María Soledad Rodríguez, Yolanda Rivera Castillo, and Elena Lawton Torruella, three writers of prose and poetry, who read and reread various versions of this novel with a critical but benevolent eye, praising strong points and patiently pointing out weaknesses of plot, structure, character development, and wording. Their supportive critiques have been invaluable to my development as a writer.

I am also very thankful to Pippa Brush Chapell for her structural editing, which included invaluable suggestions, particularly with regard to pacing and character development. Mikayla Butchart, my copy editor, and Tess Jolly, my proofreader, not only looked at grammar, word choice, and punctuation but also pointed out inconsistencies in the timeline of events that might cause confusion. I would also like to thank Brooke Warner, Lauren Wise, and the other professionals of She Writes Press for their expert guidance.

My family has been very helpful. My sister, Marion Percell, read the entire manuscript carefully and made helpful suggestions regarding punctuation, word choice, and the need for more clarity in certain scenes, including those involving legal proceedings. My husband, Parimal Choudhury, made valuable suggestions and thoughtfully provided me with the necessary time and space to write and rewrite.

Finally, I am grateful to my students and colleagues at the University of Puerto Rico. The interest and enthusiasm displayed by students in my graduate classes at the University of Puerto during discussions of the Beecher-Tilton trial, and its importance for understanding the position of women in the nineteenth century, encouraged me to delve deeper into Elizabeth's story. I would also like to thank María Dolores Luque, former director of the Journal of the Center for Historical Research of the Río Piedras Campus of the University of Puerto Rico, and the members of the editorial board, María de los Ángeles Castro, Gervasio Luis García, and María del Carmen Baerga, for encouraging me to write an article about the social and historical implications of the struggles of Elizabeth Tilton. It was while researching primary and secondary historical sources for that article, that I felt inspired to write *Unruly Human Hearts*.

About the Author

BARBARA SOUTHARD grew up in New York City, holds a PhD in history from the University of Hawaii, and has served as a professor of history, Chairperson of the History Department, and Associate Dean of Graduate Studies at the Río Piedras Campus of the University of Puerto Rico. She is the author of a book on Indian history, *The Women's Movement and Colonial Politics in Bengal, 1921–1936*, and has published numerous articles in history journals. Barbara has also published short stories in literary journals, and she is the author of *The Pinch of the Crab*, a collection of ten stories set in Puerto Rico, exploring social conflicts of island life, mostly from the perspective of women and girls. Differing concepts of gender roles and conflicting political and social ideals are important themes. In *Unruly Human Hearts,* Barbara once again explores personal crises embedded in social conflict from the point of view of the woman involved, but in a different place and a different epoch. Barbara has also been active in raising funds for the Shonali Choudhury Fund of the Community Foundation of Puerto Rico, helping local community organizations working to protect women from domestic violence. She does this work in honor of her daughter, a public health professor who died of a brain tumor.